Castle Bloodshed
Murder Collection

Holly Copella

For Lori Cressman

CONTENTS

ACKNOWLEDGMENTS

Copella Books: First Paperback Edition 2017
Printed by CreateSpace, An Amazon.com Company
Cover Artist: Daniela Owergoor
Dani-owergoor.deviantart.com

PUBLISHER'S NOTE

Castle Bloodshed

Holly Copella

Chapter One

It was a cool November evening. A gentle breeze had picked up steadily in the hours since the sun had set. In the distant harbor, an almost mystical castle could be viewed along the neighboring coastline. Wesley Castle was the medieval palace Duke Alden Wesley had moved stone by stone from England to a small, ten-acre island in an American harbor. The duke liked America and wanted to spend his remaining days on the scenic island in the comfort of his own castle. It was a rather impressive sight for most passersby and almost enchanting to those who lived along the coast.

Duke Alden, a man nearly seventy years of age, lived alone with only his servants to keep him company. His only son had run away from home, while home was still on British soil. He was never heard from again. Duke Alden's wife, the duchess, had been murdered twenty years ago after a tragic incident. She was buried in the family crypt, which had also been moved, and she remained the sole love of the duke's life.

The duke sat in his moderately worn, plush antique chair before the study fireplace. He sipped the last of his brandy and set the glass on a small table. His devoted butler, Harrington, approached and removed the glass. Although Harrington was only in his early thirties, he was as proper as they came. He wasn't a tall man, perhaps five-foot-eight, with short, dark hair and a handsome, clean-shaven face.

"Shall I have the upstairs maid draw your bath, sir?" he asked professionally with a deep English accent and only a hint of a smile.

Duke Alden sighed gently with little reaction. "I suppose you will anyway," he remarked with some disgust. The elderly man glanced at the young butler and leaned back in his chair. "Harrington--?"

"Yes, sir."

"Why haven't you married?"

The butler laughed. "I suppose I haven't met the right lady yet, sir."

"Of course not. You're too busy taking care of some old man," Duke Alden remarked then stared at his butler with a serious look. "You've been like a son to me. Have I told you that?"

"That's kind of you, sir."

The duke looked back at the fireplace. "At least the son I should've had." He sighed deeply. "Perhaps we'll holiday in England this summer. Find you a nice English girl."

Harrington chuckled at the comment. "Yes, sir."

The duke eyed Harrington. "Were the others dismissed for the evening?"

"All but Diane, sir," he replied. "She's preparing your night clothing."

Duke Alden nodded with a weary sigh. "Very good. I'd prefer not being disturbed by them anymore tonight," he remarked then eyed Harrington. "It's not that I don't trust them, it's just, well, I don't trust them."

"We'd discussed dismissing some of them," Harrington announced. "If you're unhappy with their performance--"

Duke Alden looked at the fireplace and scratched his head of thick, white hair. "Their performance isn't the problem. I just don't care for them. They aren't anything like the old staff. Things were swift like clockwork around here back then." He sighed and seemed to drift off a moment. "The only one I even partially like is Jake, and he's been in prison before." Duke Alden then smiled. "Though Diane and Joanne are easy on the eyes."

"If you say so, sir," Harrington replied dryly.

"I do. That'll be all, Harrington," Duke Alden announced.

"About that bath--"

Duke Alden waved him off, seeming bothered with the notion. "Yes, yes, yes. I'm going to take a quick tour of the castle first, so tell her to give me a few minutes."

"As you wish, sir," Harrington replied.

"Go on. Get out of here," Duke Alden announced with agitation and waved him off.

Harrington gave a slight bow. "I'll be up with your nightly pills before you turn in."

"Damned pills."

Harrington took the empty brandy snifter and left the room. Duke Alden stood, seeming somewhat stiff, and walked toward the desk. He stared at the painting of his beloved duchess alongside the bookcase and sighed deeply with a look of despair.

"My darling, duchess. I'm sad these days," he whispered to her portrait. "There's not enough money to support the castle anymore. It's become a tourist site. I fear the fate of our beloved home. The original staff have all retired or passed on. Harrington's the only one I trust." He sighed deeply and seemed to drift off. "I'm so tired. I long for the day when I'm finally able to join you, but each morning I wake." He smiled gently. "I don't mean to bore you. Sleep well, my love."

§

Duke Alden walked along the corridors on two levels, traveling down hallway after hallway, passing countless swords and suits of armor. He stopped to study several expensive paintings then continued through the kitchen. He paused before the door that led to the dungeon. Duke Alden opened the heavy door and walked down the stone steps.

§

The dimly lit dungeon was a maze of corridors, chambers, and cells. It seemed a strange place to find comfort. The cool, damp, musty smell generally kept most of the staff away. Perhaps that's why Duke Alden chose the dungeon on this particular walk. He enjoyed privacy but seldom found it. Harrington was less reluctant to let him from his sight for more than half an hour at a time, and the other servants were bothersome. He touched the antique suits of armor lined along the wall as he passed, now adding a somewhat lively step to his gate.

"Carry on, my fine men," he announced while grinning cheerfully.

The lights flickered and went out. Duke Alden paused in the darkness just before the doorway to the workshop and lit a torch. He attempted to remove it from the wall. It turned to reveal a secret compartment. He stared at the small chest hidden inside the compartment. A smile crossed his face.

"Well, I'll be--"

Duke Alden returned the cover to the compartment, lit another torch, and hurried through the corridor with renewed enthusiasm.

§

*D*uke Alden approached his master chamber with anger and disgust clearly upon his face. Something had changed his mood. He paused before Diane, the upstairs maid, who was standing just outside his master chamber. Diane was an American woman in her late twenties. She had long, blonde hair and a figure that could even catch the duke's eye. But not tonight.

"Diane, please tell Harrington I wish to see him immediately," he remarked in a harsh tone.

"Yes, sir." His tone concerned her, but she didn't question him. "I'll tell him right away."

Duke Alden entered the elegant master chamber and slammed the door, rattling the wrought iron door ring. The excessively large master chamber was filled with antique furniture and expensive artwork. He approached the nightstand, removed his journal, and wrote down the location of the small chest before he'd forget where it was. He then turned toward the thick post, king-sized canopy bed with a suit of armor standing guard on either side of it. He placed the journal in a small panel within the headboard. It was a clever hiding place, which he was certain no one knew about. The chamber door creaked open without Harrington's usual knock announcing himself. Duke Alden turned.

Chapter Two

*H*arrington stood toward the back of the wine cellar and placed several bottles of wine in the empty slots within one of many racks. Diane walked down the stone steps and crossed the ancient wine cellar. She paused when she saw him near the back.

"There you are. I've been looking for you for the past twenty minutes," she announced. "Duke Alden wants to see you in his chamber right away. He seemed upset about something."

Harrington glanced back at Diane with a puzzled look as he replaced the bottle to the crate. "What has him upset?"

"He didn't say."

The butler straightened and left the wine cellar with a much quicker step than usual. He had to pass through the entire castle to reach the master chamber, which was quite a journey. He hurried up the grand staircase to the third floor. As he reached the second floor landing, he heard a strange sound followed by a loud splash. Harrington paused on the landing to look out the stained glass window at the dark moat below, but there was nothing to see. Harrington ran up the remainder of the steps to the third floor and paused just before the duke's chamber. Harrington collected himself, straightened his jacket, and promptly knocked on the door. There was no response.

"Sir, it's Harrington," he announced firmly.

There was still no response. As his custom, Harrington opened the chamber door and entered. Duke Alden lay across the massive bed with a dagger plunged through his mid-section. Harrington's eyes widened with a look of horror. He ran across the room and paused by the bedside. Blood covered the duke's shirt surrounding the elegant, gold dagger. A framed photo of the duchess lay on the bed near his outstretched hand. Harrington immediately checked for a pulse then pulled his hand back after his discovery. He spun toward the nightstand while reaching for the bedside phone. His eyes then strayed to the head of the bed. The suit of armor on the side of the bed closest to him was gone.

§

*H*arrington sat at the kitchen table with his head in his hands and a sedate look on his face. A police officer sat across the table from him and continued to ask questions.

"Did you notice anything missing from the duke's room or anywhere else in the castle?" Officer Stevens asked firmly.

Harrington slowly looked up while running his fingers through his moderately mussed hair, revealing his stressed state. "His gold pocket watch, a gold crescent ring, and a suit of armor."

The officer gave him a strange look and leaned forward on the table. "A suit of armor? Are you sure?"

Harrington groaned and lowered his head into his hands. "I wouldn't make it up," he remarked then looked back at the man in uniform. "There are knights in every room on either side of the headboards. Both were there when Diane turned down his bed a few hours earlier."

The police officer took a deep breath and added it to the list. "We're searching the estate for the killer. It's a large area to cover, so it may take a while." Officer Stevens wrote something in his book but didn't look up. "We're still not ruling out suicide."

Harrington glared at the officer, turning angry for the first time. "He didn't kill himself," he growled then attempted to collect his emotions. "It was made to look that way, but he wouldn't do something like that. The stolen watch and ring should tell you it wasn't suicide."

"We have to investigate all the possibilities, Mr. Harrington." He inhaled deeply and held his breath a moment. "Who was the last person to see him alive?"

"Diane, the upstairs maid," Harrington replied. "She told me he wanted to see me immediately."

"Did he usually send for you so late?" Stevens asked.

Harrington shook his head. "No, I always bring him his nightly pills after he turns in. He knew I'd be there shortly," he replied. "The fact that he'd sent for me at all is unusual. Diane said he seemed upset." Harrington held his breath a moment. "We've had some recent staff problems."

"Oh?" Stevens asked.

"He was displeased with their attitudes," Harrington replied then straightened, attempting a more professional appearance.

"So there's a possibility that he'd confronted someone," Stevens deducted.

"Possibly," Harrington replied. "But the others had retired to their quarters for the evening except Diane and me."

A detective in a shabby suit entered the kitchen and looked at Harrington. The butler immediately looked at him with an eager gaze.

"Have you found anything, inspector?" Harrington asked.

"Yes, we have," Detective Addams replied. "The chain on the back gate to the cemetery had been cut. We'd also found marks from a small motorboat pulled onto shore. It would appear someone broke into the cemetery and found their way into the castle with the intent to steal." He shook his head. "Duke Alden must've surprised them. They panicked, killed him, and attempted to make it look like suicide."

Harrington stared at the officer with some confusion. "This wasn't a robbery," he insisted. "Whoever came here tonight came for the sole purpose to murder the duke."

"For what reason," Addams asked calmly.

"Revenge," Harrington replied without hesitation. "The dagger used to kill the duke was the same one that killed the duchess twenty years ago."

Stevens pointed his pen in the air as if he'd solved the entire case. "That explains it then. The duke killed himself with the same dagger that killed his wife. Case solved."

"We'll need to investigate further," Addams remarked without acknowledging the officer's deduction.

Harrington shot up from his chair with anger in his eyes. "It wasn't suicide, and it wasn't a robbery gone wrong. He was murdered in cold blood!"

Addams stared at Harrington a moment with surprise by his outburst then attempted a smile. "Thank you for your help, Mr. Harrington. We'll be in touch."

Officer Stevens and Detective Addams left the kitchen, leaving Harrington alone and frustrated. Both men paused in the hallway just outside the kitchen and glanced at each other.

"What do you make of that one?" Stevens asked softly.

"Pretty strung out."

"Do you think he killed him?" Stevens questioned.

Detective Addams frowned. "I'd have a tough time proving it," he remarked. "Besides, can you imagine me telling my supervisors that the butler did it?"

Chapter Three

Six months later. The small motorboat passed through the harbor toward the castle on the ten-acre island. Wesley Castle encompassed most of the island, which included the moat and the cemetery on the other side of its walls. Naomi Remus sat in the boat and stared at the castle as they approached. She glanced at the other tourists on their way to explore the English castle on American soil. There were six of them, including herself and her friend, George Westinghouse. George was the only reason Naomi was able to visit the castle. All the tickets had been sold in advance, but George happened to have two since his girlfriend broke up with him just a week prior. Naomi insisted she'd buy it from him, but he wouldn't take her money.

George was a handsome African-American man in his late twenties with a slightly muscular build and stood and impressive six-foot-two. His clean-shaven head gave him a moderately intimidating appearance, but his innocent baby face made him look more like a big teddy bear. He always listened to her problems and only occasionally made judgment. They had been close for the past two years, though there was nothing romantic between them. George openly admitted to being a womanizer while Naomi was the complete opposite of George where that was concerned. She wasn't the type to be womanized. Somewhere in their differences, they found a mutual respect for each other. Naomi was his first real friend of the female persuasion, and George found it suited him.

At twenty-three, Naomi's popularity as a writer was growing. Her latest novel sold a significant number of copies, and she was no longer concerned about working at the office. She rarely dated, and when she did, it usually only lasted a few weeks. Naomi wasn't certain what she was looking for in a relationship, but she knew she wasn't finding it in any of the men she'd met. She sometimes wondered if George would eventually become that man. Naomi stood about five-foot-six and had long, dark hair that now seemed to go its own way as the wind whipped it about. She wasn't a very flashy woman, and her newly found success wasn't going to change her outlook on life. Naomi glanced at the woman who sat to her left.

Lydia Beller was a petite woman with reddish-brown hair that didn't fall out of place, not even in the gusty, harbor wind. Lydia was in her late twenties, and even Naomi had to admit she was an attractive woman, though she found it odd for the woman with a princess complex to be traveling alone. Naturally, George was captivated by Lydia. He introduced himself on the dock, but she made it very clear, with one look, that she wasn't interested in black men. George wasn't offended even if Naomi was, although she doubted George could afford Lydia anyway. George had to work his full-time job as a computer repairman, plus a part-time job as a bartender at a small dive at the docks just to pay all his loans and debts.

In addition to Lydia, there was a man traveling alone as well. He sat in the back of the boat near a young couple. Naomi didn't know any of her fellow tourists, but she suspected she would get to know them once they started the tour. It was a small group, but the tours never took more than six, explaining why the tickets were sold out well in advance. As they approached the island, Mark, the boat guide and operator, continued his narrative about the castle.

"The castle had been taken down stone by stone and shipped across the ocean to this island," Mark informed them. "The move and reconstruction took two years to complete."

George leaned closer to Naomi and whispered, "That must have been one heck of a bill."

"Imagine the mess," she said gently with a teasing smile.

Naomi took several pictures with her newly purchased digital camera. She bought the moderately expensive camera specifically for their trip to the castle. She took a few pictures of their boat guide as well. Mark was a distinguished looking man in his late thirties. His dark hair had some gray peppering the sides. Despite his age creeping up on him, he kept in excellent, physical shape, possibly due to some of his duties as a boat captain. Once they docked, Mark helped the six guests from the boat and led them up the block stone path to the castle's lowered drawbridge. Up close, the castle was both impressive and eerie.

"Everything you see is from the original Wesley Castle layout, except this walkway. The walls are eight feet thick with block stone, and they stand thirty feet high. The area beyond the wall, including the courtyard, is six acres."

They could see the huge drawbridge over a body of water that resembled a moat. There was a wrought iron gate over the only opening to the castle courtyard.

"The iron gate you see, called a portcullis, is about two tons of oak covered with iron. The spikes on the bottom embed into the ground about six inches when it's lowered. Back in the fourteenth century, two men could raise and lower the gate with use of a winch. Today our gate is opened by the push of a button."

Naomi stared at the castle walls as they continued onward. She suddenly felt very small.

"The drawbridge is about six inches thick. It's the only way over the moat and is closed every night. The moat you see beneath you," Mark said as they proceeded across the drawbridge, "is thirty feet deep and twenty feet wide. Back in the days of its origin, the moat had sharp wooden spikes embedded in its floor. Any intruder attempting to swim the moat would be shredded. Unfortunately, our insurance company didn't care for the idea."

They paused on the drawbridge and looked over the rope railing attached to prevent any unexpected swimming. Mark let out a slight laugh.

"Then, of course, there's the moat monster," he announced with another chuckle. "A myth started to prevent intruders from crossing. Some believe it's more than a myth."

The small group followed their tour guide the rest of the way over the drawbridge. Naomi remained on the bridge to take several pictures. She saw something move through the water and gurgle just beneath the surface. Naomi lowered her camera while staring at the water with some surprise and curiosity, but she couldn't see anything. She turned and followed the others, now placing herself at the back of the group. They passed under the fifteen-foot-high opening and entered the castle courtyard.

Naomi was the last to enter and looked with childlike fascination at everything surrounding her. She passed under the portcullis and looked up at the spikes just above her. She wanted to catch every detail in hopes that she would be inspired for her next novel. She was only a few feet into the courtyard when she heard a loud metallic clash. The iron gate suddenly came crashing to the ground just behind her. Naomi jumped and fell face first to the courtyard. She flipped on her backside into a sitting position and stared at the lowered gate amongst the dirt and dust floating through the air. Her heart pounded roughly, reminding her that she was still alive. Mark and George ran to her. The guide placed a hand on her shoulder while she held her chest.

"Are you all right?" Mark asked with a look of concern on his face.

Naomi looked at him with wide eyes and nodded. "I'm okay," she said with a slight gasp, though she couldn't convince herself so easily.

George grimaced slightly and handed Naomi her broken camera. Naomi moaned and accepted it. He helped her to her feet and placed his arm around her.

"She's okay. Everything's under control," Mark announced to the others. "Why don't you look around the courtyard garden and wait for your castle guide." He turned and muttered lowly. "I need to have a talk with our gatekeeper."

Once Mark left the courtyard, George released Naomi and glanced back at the gate. He gently squeezed her shoulder. "You could've been killed."

She glared at him. "Don't remind me."

Mark entered the winch room just alongside the gate. There was a long, wooden wheel with old chain wrapped around it. It was the old winch. Mark approached a button on the wall and pushed it. Nothing happened. He looked toward a small shaft in the floor with an iron ladder descending beyond it. He approached the ladder and looked down the shaft.

"Jake?" Mark called down.

There was no response. Mark frowned and glanced around the room with a confused look. He approached the small workbench and removed a flashlight from the wall holder. He glanced at the countertop and saw a cutting torch lying out. Mark tilted his head with a confused look. He appeared to consider something then set down the flashlight and hurried across the room to the door. He opened the door then jumped with surprise.

"You startled me," Mark announced with a shallow breath. "What are you doing here?"

A sword appeared through the open doorway and pierced Mark through his mid-section. His eyes widened with a look of horror while spitting up blood. As the sword was pulled free, he clutched his bleeding abdomen and collapsed to the ground.

§

*N*aomi and George walked around the courtyard together and checked out their new surroundings. On the inside of the wall, there were stone steps leading up to a small walkway a few feet from the top. The elevated vantage point gave some protection and unobstructed firing position to the king's army. There were three floors to the castle, not including the towers, which were about twenty feet above the third floor. George pointed to the window of the first tower.

"I bet that's one hell of a view of the city at night," he remarked with a gentle smile.

"Not that we'll ever see it at night," she reminded him.

"You certainly know how to ruin a moment," George replied while playfully nudging her.

Naomi considered what George said. Unfortunately, they wouldn't be there at night to actually see for themselves, but she was certain he was right. Just then, one of the double doors to the castle opened, and they saw a man in a butler uniform step out of the castle. Harrington looked toward the cloudy, darkening sky. Naomi looked at the darkening sky as well. They would be in for a fantastic storm tonight. Hopefully, the boat would get them back before it actually started. Naomi then took in an eyeful of Harrington in his expensive, tidy uniform. His mannerisms gave an impression of a rather uptight individual.

Harrington shifted his attention back to the guests. "Good morning and welcome to Wesley Castle," he announced with a deep, English accent. He had an almost pleasant smile on his stern looking face. "If you'd be kind enough to come this way, we'll start the tour."

Naomi and George followed the others toward the doors and entered the large foyer just inside the castle. The polished marble floor gave the castle a very wealthy and distinguished look. The ceilings were twenty feet high, giving the castle a rather spacious appeal. Once everyone was in the large foyer, the butler closed the heavy door. The door made a sound resembling that of a casket closing. Naomi felt a slight chill run down her spine. The butler walked to the front of the six guests and turned to face them. His expression still hadn't changed.

"Allow me to introduce myself," he said with a low, soothing voice. "My name is Harrington. I've been the butler at Wesley Castle for ten years. Despite the age of this castle, you will find everything has been completely restored and, in most cases, is authentic."

Lydia let out a slight laugh and grinned with a 'be real' look on her face. "Are you really the butler or just a tour guide dressed the part?" she asked in a disbelieving tone.

Harrington attempted to remain pleasant, although he didn't seem to be in a particularly good mood. "My family has served this castle for over six generations. I've been Duke Alden's personal butler for a little over ten years, after the death of my predecessor. Please, follow me and feel free to ask any questions you may have during the tour."

Naomi glanced at George as they proceeded to follow the *authentic* butler of Wesley Castle.

"Six generations," Naomi teased. "You don't get more authentic than that."

George let out a slight laugh. "A servant with an attitude. I like him already."

Chapter Four

The tour was rather informative, and Harrington told an interesting story. One of the questions that seemed to spring up was a question on the missing jewels of Wesley Castle. Harrington didn't bother to turn while explaining what they wanted to know.

"The jewels were supposedly stolen by a servant many centuries ago under the reign of King Chasity just prior to the overthrow. Had there actually been any such jewels, they would've been found decades ago." He sounded so mechanical about the lost jewels as if he had been asked that same question a thousand times, which he probably had. Harrington glanced back at the group and attempted a smile while swiftly changing the subject. "The castle is filled with secret passageways nearly leading to all corners. The passageways were used during attacks to outwit an intruder and as a safe haven for royalty."

They went from room to room while listening to the deep, English voice of the butler. Perhaps some were bored with his recaps of history, but Naomi found it particularly interesting and his voice rather captivating. The fact that she found him handsome may have held her interest too. Harrington told about secret passageways and their usefulness centuries ago, though he didn't offer any specifics to their locations. Despite all his stories and detailed accounts, he seemed to be forgetting something.

"Where's the duke?" Ryan finally asked. "I thought we'd be meeting him."

As they walked down the long hallway, Naomi counted the nineteenth suit of armor they'd passed in that hallway alone. The castle seemed to be crawling with them. She wondered just how many there actually were. Naomi was then aware of the question that had been asked. She'd wondered the same thing herself.

Harrington turned and looked at Ryan but showed little emotion. "Duke Alden Wesley was killed in his chamber six months ago. I've been left in charge of keeping the castle operational until the estate is settled," he informed them. "The duke, however, is on the premises. You'll meet him later in the family crypt."

There was something very creepy about the way he phrased that last statement. George then spoke out as well. His interest was now captured.

"Are you telling us the duke was murdered? Who did it?" George asked now curious. "I don't remember seeing that in the paper."

Harrington paused and turned to face the guests. He casually placed his hands in his pockets and tilted his head. "The case remains unsolved. The police believe it was done by a thief," he remarked again almost mechanically as if he was told to say just that but didn't believe it. "The story remained low profile to keep it from the papers. I have no further information regarding his death."

"But who inherits the estate?" Ryan once more pressed the subject.

Harrington took a deep breath then released it. "The duke had a son who ran away from home many years ago. If he's alive, he'll undoubtedly inherit the estate. Duke Alden's will was never recovered."

The butler continued with the tour and talked about the paintings they'd passed. Naomi glanced at the suit of armor that stood two feet away from her. She slowly ran her fingers over the armored chest then reached for the helmet and raised the face shield. It made a terrible squeak. Just then, she saw a skeleton staring back at her. Naomi gasped and let the lid drop with a clank. Her heart pounded with nervous surprise. She then heard a voice from directly behind her. Naomi gasped once more and spun around nervously, backing into the suit of armor. Harrington stood calmly before her, one hand in his pocket, and a tiny smirk on his face. She slowly relaxed from her shock.

"Don't let that frighten you, madam. Some were found intact," he informed her. "A sick belief of immortality prevented generations from removing them."

She stared at the butler a moment and felt a cold chill run up her spine. "It doesn't frighten me," she informed him while casting a glance back at the armor. "I just wasn't expecting it."

The butler smiled lightly with little concern. "Shall we continue with the tour, madam?"

Naomi nodded and was forced to walk ahead of him. Naomi knew she had an overactive imagination, perfectly normal for a mystery horror writer, but she felt very uneasy. Perhaps it was the way the butler explained the skeleton; or the look in his eyes; or maybe even the way he walked behind her, making certain she didn't stray from the group. She wasn't sure, but she felt he was hiding something. Naomi shamed herself for thinking something so outrageous about a man she barely even knew. Perhaps he was a really sweet man. Naomi entered the room where the others were now waiting. She wanted to curse George for not waiting for her.

§

Their lunch that afternoon was included, giving everyone a chance to relax from their day of touring. The tour group was finally introduced to the castle maids, Joanne and Diane. They were equally attractive sisters possibly only a year apart in age. Although Joanne had light brown hair and Diane had blonde hair, the two women were nearly identical in height, build, and even facial features. There was no denying they were related. Both women helped Harrington serve the buffet style meal on a sideboard within the massive dining room. The dining room table had enough room to seat twenty guests. Once they'd finished their elegant lunch buffet, the butler showed them to the lounge where they could help themselves to drinks. Harrington excused himself and wasn't expected back for another hour. They would conclude their tour by seven o'clock. This was the first opportunity for the six to get to know one another better

Naomi got a better fix on the others traveling with them as well. Ryan seemed fairly pleasant and was undeniably handsome, but his good looks and muscular build also came with an inflated ego. The man was completely self-absorbed. In addition to his large ego, he seemed more interested in the value of the castle and the items within it than the history. Every question that came from his mouth had something to do with money. His girlfriend, Donna Little, wasn't interested in anything they'd seen so far. Even now, in the lap of luxury, she seemed almost bored. She didn't seem interested in talking to anyone either. Donna was a fairly attractive woman in her early thirties with blonde, shoulder-length hair. She appeared to be the type who was never really satisfied.

Bradly Stewart was the man traveling by himself. He was the opposite of Donna. He was enthusiastic about everything and seemed fascinated by Lydia's conversation. Something inside Naomi forced her to remain suspicious. He was a lean man possibly in his early forties and tended to talk a lot about things that didn't make any sense. Of course, Naomi seemed to be the only one listening to him anyway. Although they were only supposed to take an hour break, three hours had passed since Harrington left them in the lounge. The lounge door finally opened, and all eyes shifted to the butler, who'd been less than punctual. They'd certainly be off schedule now. He smiled awkwardly.

"I'm sorry to have kept you waiting," Harrington announced and tilted his head with an oddly curious look. "I can't seem to locate your boat guide."

Bradly glanced around the room then back at the butler. "He said he was going to see the gatekeeper. The gate fell down when we'd arrived and nearly crushed Naomi."

Harrington gave Bradly an odd, thoughtful look. "I'd better find him." He attempted a smile. "Please feel free to help yourselves to more drinks." He again left the lounge.

Despite the offer of free drinks, the others were becoming tense. Naomi was glad she wasn't the only one who felt that way.

Chapter Five

Naomi decided to explore for herself while the butler was off on his manhunt. If she was going to get any inspiration for a novel, she would need some time to herself, so she could think and allow her imagination to run wild. Naomi informed George of her departure, which he understood perfectly, and she eagerly went out on her own. She wandered down the large hallway not certain where she was going, but the hall had to take her somewhere. She approached the study, considered whether she should or shouldn't, then entered.

She glanced around the huge, tastefully decorated room. All of the furniture was antique and made from expensive, carved wood. The desk itself was a work of art. It was well preserved and contained many sculpted details along its edges. Naomi was particularly fond of a good desk, being a writer. Perhaps she should have been surprised to see the computer sitting on top of it, but she knew computers were almost essential during this day and age, even in a medieval castle thrust into modern times. On the desk was one of the few castle phones, also an antique. She glanced toward the old bookcases and scanned the book titles. Naomi wondered if there was a book on the castle somewhere. Perhaps something that would tell the things their tour guide hadn't.

Naomi could hear thunder rumbling in the near distance. She approached the window and glanced outside at the grounds in the rear of the castle. She could see the cemetery near the back wall about two hundred yards away. There was a lengthy garden and hedges with marble statues and fountains between the castle wall and the cemetery. A flash of lightning lit up the sky followed by another clash of thunder. She could see someone departing the family crypt, but from that distance, she couldn't make out if it was Harrington or someone else from the staff. She felt a chill run down her spine. Cemeteries were certainly creepy, even at a distance. She turned then left the room and continued down the hallway, hoping to locate a source of inspiration.

Naomi entered the monstrous library filled with shelves and shelves of books, encompassing two floors, and extending to the ceiling. There was a small walkway halfway up the bookcase to the second level. A large ladder on rollers was located on each level and ran along a railing. There were sculpted tables and furnishings around the floor. A massive, stone fireplace highlighted the room perfectly. There was a desk near the fireplace with a long, narrow object of gold standing straight up on the desk. It was at least twelve inches high. Naomi stared a moment then approached the desk.

As she approached, she saw it was an antique dagger embedded in the cover of a book on top of the desk. Naomi looked more closely and realized the dagger was through her picture on the back of one of her books! Naomi was horrified. She nervously backed up a step then turned and hurried to the library door, which was partially open. As she approached, the door slowly shut. Naomi ran for the door and pulled the knob. It wouldn't open! Naomi backed a step away from the door, ran her fingers through her hair, and looked nervously around the room. The suit of armor alongside the fireplace appeared to have its helmet angled in her direction as if watching her. Her eyes widened with concern. When she looked back at the door, it was open a couple of inches. Naomi flung open the door and bolted out.

Naomi hurried through the lower corridor toward the lounge at the opposite end of the castle. There were suits of armor every twenty feet. She glared at each one as she passed. She heard a metallic squeak. As Naomi looked back, every knight's helmet was turned in her direction. Naomi gasped, whirled around, and ran the rest of the way. She heard another squeak, causing her to turn her head while running. When she looked back in the direction she was heading, a silver arm appeared just before her. Naomi ran into the arm and fell to the floor, taking the suit of armor with her. There was a tremendous crash. The knight's sword hit the floor only inches from her head. Naomi struggled to remove the armor that seemed to wrap around her. She screamed and beat the armor with her hands.

The armor was pulled off her, but she continued to punch at the air with bleeding knuckles.

"Miss Remus, what's the meaning of this?" Harrington demanded to know.

Naomi pulled herself into a sitting position and scrambled backward, glaring at Harrington with horror in her eyes. Her head turned toward the discarded armor, now detached, lying in a heap. Naomi sprang to her feet and kicked the armor that lay on the floor. Harrington stared in disbelief. She breathed heavily and backed away from the armor.

Harrington's eyes narrowed while glaring at her. "Do you feel better now?"

Naomi stared at him without a word. He looked down at the dented pile of armor. Naomi looked as well. Harrington frowned and shook his head. Lydia, Ryan, and Bradly stood nearby with surprised expressions.

"What happened?" Lydia asked.

Harrington placed his hands in his pockets and glared at Naomi. "Would you care to explain yourself?"

"Self-defense," she replied simply.

Harrington raised his brows without humor. George approached the small group with Donna trailing behind. He pushed past the others and looked at Naomi's bleeding knuckles and her drained expression.

"What the hell's going on?" George demanded to know. He touched Naomi's arm. "Are you all right?"

"I had a little accident," Naomi replied.

"Accident?" Harrington demanded. "That pile of metal on the floor was once an antique."

"I'll pay for the damages," George announced firmly.

"That would be most appropriate," Harrington replied. He looked at Naomi's bleeding knuckles with little emotion. "I'll get some bandages for those cuts."

Harrington turned and walked down the hallway in his same, calm demeanor.

Naomi grabbed George's arm and tugged on him. "I have to show you what I found in the library!" She pulled him along the hallway.

The others followed.

*N*aomi hurried across the library to the desk by the fireplace. The book and dagger were gone. She searched the entire desk and surrounding area.

"What are you looking for?" George asked.

Naomi turned to face him. "I swear to you, George! There was a book on this table. It was my book with a dagger directly through my picture on the back cover!"

"Why would someone do that?" George asked with a confused stare.

Ryan folded his arms across his chest and smiled cheaply. "Was the book that bad?"

Naomi ignored Ryan and pleaded with George. "I have a bad feeling about this place. I want to leave."

George nodded. "Okay. I'll call the mainland and get us passage back to shore." He removed his cell phone from his pocket and pressed in several numbers. A strange look crossed his face. "Huh. I'm not getting a signal."

The others removed their cell phones as well and seemed equally surprised that they too couldn't get a signal. The castle wasn't that far into the harbor.

George then picked up the castle's landline phone on the desk and tapped in several numbers. He appeared surprised and lowered the phone. "The phone's dead."

"What's going on around here?" Donna asked nervously while eyeing the others.

Ryan placed his arm around Donna and smiled. "Everything's fine, darling. She's just being dramatic. The approaching storm's probably knocked the phones out."

"The phones are out often," Harrington replied simply from across the room.

All six turned with some surprise. Harrington stood in the doorway to the library with his hands in his pockets, and the same callous look upon his face.

"It's nothing to cause worry," Harrington said simply. "If everyone would kindly adjourn to the lounge, you'll find drinks available." Harrington glared at Naomi. "If you'll come with me, Miss Remus, I'll tend to your cuts."

The others approached the butler and left the library. Naomi turned toward George and pleaded with him.

"George, I think this castle is haunted. That knight attacked me," she insisted, knowing how insane she sounded. "I couldn't get it off of me. I swear it's true. I don't believe in ghosts, but I know what I saw."

George stared at her a moment then glanced toward the butler, who waited impatiently in the doorway. George looked back at her and seemed tense.

"I'm not certain I buy into this ghost theory," he said softly, "but I'll check into this dagger in your book." George glanced back at Harrington. "Go with Harrington. Keep him busy a while. I'll talk to the others."

Chapter Six

*H*arrington held Naomi's hand gently in his as he cleaned the scrapes and cuts on her knuckles. She silently observed his wonderful bedside manner, unable to deny how incredibly attractive she found him at that particular moment. Despite his earlier attitude, he was gentle with her injuries, almost making her forget how much of a prick she thought he'd been. He wrapped a thin layer of bandage around her hands to protect her knuckles.

"That should do it," he announced and released her hand while leaning back in his chair. "Perhaps you'll think twice before challenging a knight."

Any feelings of attraction toward the butler immediately faded away along with his touch. "It attacked me," Naomi said firmly.

Harrington appeared confused while staring at her. "Who attacked you?"

"The suit of armor in the hallway," she replied. "It grabbed me and wouldn't let go."

Harrington stared at her with a strange look then stood and sighed. "Madam, dead knights have little use for live maidens."

"I want to leave this island," she said firmly. "I assume you'd be just as grateful to get rid of me as I am to leave."

"That's not possible. I've no way of contacting the mainland," he replied casually. "The phones aren't working due to the storm. You discovered that for yourself."

Naomi glared at him through narrow eyes. "You mean I'm stuck here until tonight?" she demanded. "I realize it's only a few hours, but under the circumstances--"

Harrington clasped his hands behind his back and cocked his head arrogantly. "You're going to be completely irrational no matter what

I say," he announced proudly. "You can either continue the tour or remain here. The choice is yours."

He turned and left the kitchen. Naomi sat at the table a moment and contemplated what he'd just said. The comment seemed odd. Her eyes narrowed as she sprang from her seat and ran from the kitchen. Naomi hurried after Harrington, who maintained his usual pace. She stepped in front of him and forced him to stop.

"Why wouldn't I be rational?" she demanded to know. "What aren't you telling me?"

"The portcullis has snapped its chain," he replied simply.

"Yes," she replied dryly. "I know. I was practically underneath it."

"In order to fix the gate, we need our gatekeeper, Jake." Harrington appeared uneasy and shifted slightly. "I'm unable to find him or your boat guide."

Naomi quickly became irritable. "How many places could they really be?"

Harrington raised a cocky brow. "That would depend on whether or not they want to be found. This castle is a maze of halls, rooms, secret passageways, and pits."

"Are you saying they went somewhere to get drunk?" Naomi demanded to know.

"It's a possibility," he replied simply.

Naomi shook her head with annoyance. Harrington continued down the hall, forcing her to hurry after him.

"I'm sure they're looking for a way to fix the gate as we speak," she insisted. "Mark knew about the problem when we'd arrived."

Harrington calmly walked past her and showed little emotion. "Everyone will probably have to spend the night."

Naomi's eyes widened in horror as she watched him walk away. "I'll swim first!" She hurried after him.

"You won't even make it to the dock. Apart from the portcullis, the only other way out of the castle is through the dungeon. That takes you to the cemetery. The cemetery gate was welded shut six months ago," he informed her simply and continued down the hallway. "You'd have to climb the wall before you'd even reach the harbor to swim to shore. Which, by the way, you'd never be able to swim that far."

*T*he tour finally continued and headed into the family crypt. The cemetery was dark, and the approaching storm added to the already eerie setting. The six entered the family crypt only lit by torches since there wasn't any electric. There were two marble tombs within the crypt. Duke Alden Wesley's name was carved on the lid of the tomb to the right, and Duchess Catherine Wesley's name was carved on the other. According to the birth and death dates engraved on the tomb, the duchess was only forty when she died. Harrington turned to face the six and leaned on the duke's tomb, which surprised the guests.

"As you may already know, both the duke and the duchess were murdered. Duke Alden was killed six months ago, and the duchess twenty years ago," he explained.

"What happened to the duchess?" Lydia asked.

"A servant fell in love with her," he explained. "When she refused his affections, he killed her."

"Was the servant sent to jail?" Bradly asked.

"No," Harrington replied. "He was slain by my predecessor with the sword hanging in the duke's chamber."

Ryan cocked his head to one side and smiled slyly. "Your predecessor must've been related to you if your family's been with the Wesley's for six generations."

"Yes," Harrington announced simply. "He was my father."

Silence fell over the group.

Harrington straightened and smiled in a chillingly calm manner. "Allow me to show you the dungeon torture chamber. I always end the tours there."

§

*T*hey took the cemetery entrance into the dungeon for convenience. Once they entered the torture chamber, they discovered torture devices throughout the eerie room. There was a stretching rack, spiked chair, and old devices used to sever, saw, and maim. Shackles hung from the walls, and a collection of knives was displayed. In the middle of the room was a wooden chopping block with a large ax stuck in it. On the other side of the block was an old basket possibly stained with blood. Harrington removed the ax from the block. All six jumped back with alarm.

"A skilled headsman always kept a sharp ax," Harrington explained. "I'm told beheading is virtually painless providing they actually beheaded the criminal first. Most medieval punishment involved a lot of pain before death. They were very careful to keep the prisoner alive and conscious throughout most of the torture." Harrington drove the ax back into the chopping block and smiled deviously. "Treason was taken very seriously. If a prisoner was found guilty, he was hung, drawn, and quartered. A most unpleasant way to die."

"Yeah, well, I'd prefer to be hung over beheading," Ryan replied with a smirk.

Harrington raised a brow along with a sly smile. "You think so? It's not as merciful as it sounds. Their method of hanging didn't usually kill instantly. It was more of a strangulation. When the prisoner was just about dead, they'd cut him open and remove his insides. He was then cut into quarters, hence drawn and quartered, and his head removed. His head was then mounted on a stick as a warning to others. A moderately sick belief would have us believe the brain still functions for some time after death, allowing the severed head to look upon those watching."

Ryan appeared ill.

Harrington appeared satisfied then clasped his hands behind his back and stood proudly. "If you'll follow me--"

Naomi strayed behind to look at a knife in the case along the wall. One of the daggers appeared similar to the one she'd seen in the library sticking through the cover of her book. Something metal struck the floor. Naomi looked around the room. There were spiked balls, whips, and axes everywhere. She nervously walked toward the door across the room to follow the others. She saw a suit of armor to the left of the door the others had passed through. The spear held by the knight seemed to extend across the doorway, practically blocking her path.

"Not this time."

Naomi removed a sword from the wall and casually approached the knight. The spear moved forward, and she knew she didn't imagine it. She swung at the knight and severed its hand holding the spear. The metal hand flew across the room and bounced off a nearby wall. Naomi coiled back for another blow.

"Didn't think I could defend myself, huh?" she cried out in anger.

Naomi attempted a second swing, but her hand was caught by the left, metal hand. Her arm was bent backward, and she was forced to drop the sword. The handless arm wrapped around her waist, pulling her against its armored chest, and lifted her from the floor. Naomi kicked and screamed while struggling against the armor.

"Let me go! You're not even real!"

She pounded on its tin head, causing a metallic echo. The knight carried her toward the chopping block. Naomi looked over her shoulder at the ax and screamed hysterically. The severed hand inched its way behind the knight.

"George!"

As the knight lowered her to the chopping block, Naomi pulled away and lunged for her discarded sword. She spun around and began hacking at the knight with all her strength. The suit of armor fell to a pile on the floor. Naomi was grabbed around the waist from behind.

"Stop it," Harrington shouted from behind her.

Naomi stopped struggling and gasped for her breath. Harrington released her with a groan and snatched the sword from her hand. She spun to face him.

"Where were you when that thing tried to kill me?" she demanded to know.

"I'm very tempted to toss you into the moat." His eyes were narrow and angry. "You should be ashamed; attacking poor, defenseless inanimate objects!"

"Defenseless? Inanimate?" she spat hotly. "You don't even care that those tin cans are trying to kill me every time your back is turned!"

Harrington stared at her with an amazed look on his face. "They're only metal cases. They can't possibly hurt you." He relaxed and frowned. "Now can you behave yourself, or must I take you by the hand for the remainder of the tour?"

Naomi stared at him in disbelief.

Chapter Seven

Harrington poured drinks for the guests in the lounge. Everyone seemed to be enjoying their tour with Naomi being the only exception. She sat in an antique chair and fidgeted uncomfortably. Frank, the caretaker, and Barney, the cook, entered the lounge and paused in the doorway. The guests gave them curious looks since it was the first anyone had seen them. Barney was a large, stocky man in his mid to late forties. His hair was merely stubble on his head, buzzed close to the scalp. He had several visible tattoos on his lower arms, indicating he probably had others hiding beneath his clothes. Frank was lean and built athletic, as a typical outdoorsman would be. He had a dark tan from working outside most of the day. He wasn't unattractive, but he had harsh features, giving him a cold-hearted appearance. He didn't seem to be the sort of man Naomi would care to befriend. Harrington set the bottle on the small bar and attempted a tiny smile to his guests.

"If you'll excuse me a moment."

He walked across the room and approached the two men within the doorway. As the men talked quietly, the six guests became more uncomfortable.

Bradly shifted in his chair and faced Ryan. "I'd love to know what's going on."

"By the looks on their faces, they couldn't fix the gate," Naomi remarked while frowning.

"You mean we're stuck here all night?" Donna asked as her eyes widened considerably.

Ryan laughed. "Sounds like fun to me."

"As long as they don't charge us extra for the rooms," Bradly teased.

"I hope we won't have to stay all weekend," George said with a sigh. "I have a Sunday brunch date."

Naomi's face dropped at his comment, concern flooding her body. "The entire weekend?" she just about cried out. "I'll be lucky if I make it through the night."

George thoughtfully patted Naomi's hand as if that would calm her nerves. When Frank and Barney left the lounge, Harrington returned to the group with an awkward smile on his face.

"Sorry for the disruption," Harrington announced. "Due to the storm and the absence of your boat guide, it's best if everyone remains here for the night. Our caretaker will attempt to fix the gate in the morning. Until then, we'll see that everyone is made as comfortable as possible."

§

*N*aomi entered her designated guest bedroom behind Harrington. The others had been shown to their rooms first since it was obvious he wanted to keep an eye on her. They discovered that Harrington and both maids had taken up residence on the third floor, due to the duke's health conditions. Jake, the gatekeeper, Frank in maintenance, and Barney, the cook remained in the staff wing just off the kitchen. Naomi looked around her room for the night. The chamber was elegantly decorated with expensive antiques, as were all the bedroom chambers. There was a suit of armor standing guard on either side of the headboard of the hardtop, canopy bed. Harrington casually walked across the room, picked up the first suit of armor, and carried it out of the room, placing it alongside the door. Naomi folded her arms across her chest and watched as he returned for the second. Once the second knight was placed outside the room, he stood in the doorway and offered a sly smirk.

"Sleep well, madam," he announced and closed the heavy, chamber door.

Naomi nervously looked around the room feeling her anxiety rise. "Yeah, sure."

She couldn't deny she'd considered staying with George in his room. Their friendship could survive a harmless sleepover, but she decided to save that trumping card for another time. It was still a gamble sharing a bed with a self-proclaimed womanizer.

§

*D*onna lay on the large bed in a seductive position and marveled at the underside of the canopy while Ryan looked around the room, examining walls and the bookcase.

"Isn't this romantic?" Donna cooed. "We get to make love on satin sheets in a medieval castle."

Ryan ran his hands along the wall near the bookcase then gently tapped on it. He frowned.

Donna smiled seductively. "I could be the fair maiden awaiting her knight in shining armor." She eyed Ryan, realized he wasn't paying attention, and stared at him with surprise. "What are you looking for?"

Ryan didn't look at her but continued his search. "Wouldn't it be amazing if we could find the jewels stolen all those centuries ago?" he announced while engrossed in his search of the room.

Donna flopped back on the bed and laughed. "Be serious, Ryan. You heard what the butler had said," she remarked. "Those jewels were a myth."

He looked at her with a stern expression. "He never said they were a myth." Ryan looked back at the wall with his hands on his hips. "I think they're in this castle somewhere. May as well make the best of the time we're stuck here."

"I agree," Donna replied with a lustful smile and patted the bed. "Come to bed."

"We haven't got time for that, Donna," he replied dryly and practically waved her off.

Donna frowned and suddenly shot up in bed. "Is that why you brought me here?" she snapped. "All that talk about touring history? You knew about those jewels the entire time, didn't you?"

Ryan turned and smiled for the first time. "If we could find those jewels, we'd be rich."

"Once we're married, my father hands over my trust fund. We'll have more than enough money," Donna remarked lowly.

"And live under your father's thumb for the rest of my life?" Ryan demanded. "I think I'd rather make my own fortune." He smiled in a moderately charming manner. "I'm just thinking of your happiness."

Donna's smile returned. "Then come to bed."

Ryan watched as Donna stroked the bed seductively while looking at him. A smile crossed his face. "I'll bet Harrington has a few theories on where those jewels are."

Donna groaned and fell limp on the bed. "You're pathetic."

Ryan turned back to the wall and began tapping on it in several spots. "I need to find one of those secret passageways."

A pillow struck him on the back of the head. He jumped and spun around.

Donna sat up on the tall bed with an angered expression. "Get out!"

"What?"

She stood on the bed and threw another pillow in anger.

Ryan dodged the pillow and stared at her. "You're right. I'll have more success downstairs." He hurried across the room and left.

Donna snorted and flopped on the bed. "Bastard."

Chapter Eight

Naomi tossed under the covers, unable to sleep, and groaned. The thunder and the rain could be heard as it poured outside. She heard some movement in the hallway and assumed someone else was unable to sleep as well. The bedroom door across the hall opened and then closed. Naomi sighed, climbed out of bed, and entered the bathroom. When she turned on the light, she saw Duke Alden, dressed in his finest, royal suit, lying dead in the empty garden tub. Naomi stared only a moment at the dead man with horror before screaming and running from the bathroom. She hurried to the bedroom door and threw it open.

"George," Naomi cried out hysterically as she ran into the third floor hallway. She pounded on the nearby bedroom doors, uncertain which room was given to her friend, but she was determined to find him. "George! Someone!"

The doors began opening to the noise. Harrington, wearing a robe and sweatpants, was the first to approach her. Ironically, he didn't look as if he'd been asleep. Without warning, Naomi grabbed his arm and pulled him to her room.

"I'm not crazy," she announced firmly. "And this time, I have proof."

She pulled Harrington through her room and into the brightly lit bathroom. The others were directly behind them now, softly murmuring to one another. Ryan and Donna appeared to be the only ones missing. Naomi stopped in the bathroom and stared at the empty tub. The duke was gone! She looked around the bathroom with confusion.

Harrington folded his arms across his chest and stared at her impatiently. "What am I supposed to be looking for?"

Naomi spun to face him with a distressed look in her eyes. "There was a dead man in my bathtub. I'm positive it was Duke Alden!"

Harrington's expression dropped, stunned by her words, and then became angry. He held his breath and turned toward the others, attempting a smile.

"I'm terribly sorry for the interruption, ladies and gentlemen. Please, return to your rooms," Harrington announced simply with little emotion.

Everyone left the room looking tired and muttering among themselves. Harrington turned toward Naomi as his expression hardened.

"This time you've gone too far, Miss Remus," he growled. "I can tolerate your bashing the armor, and I can deal with you abusing me, but I won't tolerate any comments concerning my late employer."

"I know what I saw, Harrington," she protested then pointed a finger at him. "And furthermore, I can prove it."

"How?" Harrington asked lowly.

"Open the duke's casket," she replied simply.

Harrington's eyes widened with shock and horror. "You're absolutely insane! Go back to bed!"

He turned and left the bathroom. Naomi followed him into the bedroom and watched as Harrington paused by the small dry bar, pouring scotch into a glass. She paused behind him.

"You know damned well what's going on around here," she lashed out. "Hell, you're probably on first name basis with every spook in this place!"

Harrington turned and extended the glass to her. She accepted it with little thought.

"If this castle was haunted, why would they pick you to torment?" he demanded.

"Who cares why? You're going to see that I'm not crazy," she informed him sternly and drank the contents of the glass in one swallow. "We're going out to the crypt." Naomi spun and hurried from the bedroom.

Harrington bolted after her and called out, "There's no way I'm allowing you to--"

Naomi hurried along the corridor. Harrington jogged behind and just about caught up to her.

"Hold it right there," he shouted forcefully.

Naomi stopped and spun to face him. She glared and folded her arms across her chest. "Something to hide?"

"I'm going with you," he announced lowly with disgust. "Give me a minute to change."

Naomi frowned and cast her back against the hall wall as Harrington entered his room just a few doors down. Naomi stared in the direction of his room and strummed her fingers on her lower arm.

"Like I'm going give them the chance to put him back," she scoffed aloud to herself then hurried along the corridor and toward the steps.

§

The cemetery was dimly lit, and the rain continued to pour down on the tombstones. The heavy outer dungeon door opened to reveal Naomi. She caught her breath from her lengthy sprint through the entire castle and ran along the path through the cemetery in the pouring rain.

Harrington called after her. "I'm warning you; don't touch anything!"

Lightning flashed in the near distance as the storm raged on. Naomi reached the crypt door and paused a moment. She felt her head spinning and had to catch her balance. Perhaps it was from the drink and being excessively tired. Naomi opened the crypt door and entered. She approached the duke's tomb and clung to the side of the marble lid. Her eyes involuntary shut a moment. She shook her head and raked her fingers through her wet hair, struggling to wake herself. Harrington entered the crypt.

"Have you no respect?" he demanded to know.

"Respect for what? An empty tomb?" she asked boldly. "Do you want to open it, or should I?"

Harrington groaned lowly. "Step aside."

Naomi moved away. Harrington paused before the tomb, appearing nervous and shaken by the task at hand. He pushed the marble slab aside and exposed the duke's casket. Harrington fumbled with the casket edge and opened it. Naomi's knees buckled as she clutched the side of the tomb for support. She held her head and swayed slightly while watching as the lid was opened. Both peered into the casket. Their tour guide lay dead, covered in blood, within the duke's casket. Harrington gasped with a horrified look, dropped the lid, and jumped back. Naomi began to sink to the crypt floor as her eyes rolled shut. Harrington lunged forward and caught her before she hit the floor.

Chapter Nine

Voices became louder, and Naomi could finally hear the conversation being held around her. She lay on the sofa and looked around the lounge at the rest of the tourists from her group. Donna sat on the edge of the sofa near her.

"Are you all right?" Donna asked gently.

Naomi slowly nodded then looked at George and Harrington, who stood in the middle of the room glaring at each other in an angry faceoff.

"If you would've believed her," George shouted, "we wouldn't be in this mess in the first place."

"We were trapped the moment the gate dropped," Harrington snapped with irritation. "No one could've known it was on purpose."

Naomi slowly sat up. George noticed she was awake and hurried to her side.

"Are you all right?" he asked gently while taking her hand in his and affectionately patting it.

"I'm fine," she replied.

"It was only a sedative," Harrington remarked firmly. "Did you really think I'd knocked her out?"

George sprang to his feet and spun to face Harrington. "That's what I'd like to find out! Who knows what you'd done before we'd arrived."

"I'd never harm her," Harrington lashed back.

George ignored him and sat on the sofa alongside his friend. "What happened, Naomi?" he asked. "Was Mark already dead when you found him?"

Naomi was surprised by his question and looked at both men. "Is that what all this is about?" she demanded to know. "Yes, he was dead long before we got there."

Lydia leaned forward in her chair. "Why did Harrington knock you out?"

Harrington rolled his eyes and frowned at the accusation.

"He thought I was becoming hysterical." Her eyes narrowed. "I assure you, George, if Harrington wanted me dead, he would've killed me when he had the chance."

"The two of you were still in the crypt when we'd found you," Bradly informed her simply. "How do we know he wasn't planning on throwing you into the casket as well?"

Harrington lunged forward. "I object!"

Naomi glared at Bradly and immediately raised her brows in response. "Harrington was just as surprised as I was to find Mark. He'd be the last person to put a body into the duke's casket," she insisted. "Besides that, he lacks imagination. He couldn't possibly be a murderer."

Harrington gave her a cold stare.

Donna looked from the butler to the others. "What about the gatekeeper?" she suddenly asked. "Where is he? Isn't it logical that he'd be the prime suspect? After all, Mark went to see him shortly after we'd arrived."

Naomi's eyes widened slightly. "How do we know he isn't dead too?"

The room was silent.

Ryan groaned and rolled his eyes. "If Jake was dead, don't you think we'd have found him by now?"

"If Jake was alive, don't you think we'd have found him by now," Naomi interjected firmly.

"Maybe he's in the duchess' casket," George suggested.

"The duke's missing already," Harrington announced while sighing. "I suppose it won't matter if we disturb the duchess."

Barney and Frank entered the lounge soaking wet and out of breath.

"We put Mark's body in the meat locker as you asked," Frank informed him simply.

Harrington nodded then straightened proudly. "Very good," he announced. "We're going back to the crypt."

Barney was surprised. "The crypt? Why?"

"We need to check the duchess' casket," Harrington informed them.

§

*T*he crypt was damp from the earlier storm. The grim reminder of their dead tour guide in the duke's casket now gave the crypt an entirely new feel. Everyone stood around and watched as Frank and Harrington slid the marble slab from the duchess' tomb, exposing the casket. Harrington opened the lid with some effort. There was a cloud of fumes with a foul smell from the casket. Everyone coughed and gasped. The remains of the duchess were sunken and decayed. Her elegant gown remained as beautiful as the day she was buried.

Harrington bowed his head shamefully. "Forgive me, duchess," he whispered.

He closed the casket lid while Frank and Barney returned the slab over the tomb. All eyes were on the butler.

Harrington stood proudly and spoke firmly, "The staff is requested to locate the body of Duke Alden." He looked at the guests. "I suggest the rest of you return to your rooms and get some sleep."

Frank and Barney moaned with displeasure.

"Is there a problem?" Harrington demanded while glaring at them and cocking his head to one side.

"I don't see the point, Harrington," Frank announced simply. "The duke isn't going anywhere. Why can't this wait until morning?"

Harrington's look was cold and callous. "Might I remind you that it's Duke Alden's estate that pays your wages; quite handsomely I might add. Our respect and loyalty shall not end just because he's passed on." His eyes then narrowed. "If you disrespect the duke and duchess, then you've no business being employed at Wesley Castle."

Frank immediately backed down. "I just asked a question, that's all. No need to get huffy."

Both men headed out of the crypt. Naomi watched them as they passed.

"Who died and left you boss?" Frank muttered lowly under his breath.

Ryan gently cleared his throat and looked at Harrington. "If you don't mind, I'd like to help look for your duke. I don't think I could sleep anyway."

Donna eyed Ryan, clearly annoyed, and folded her arms across her chest.

Naomi sighed deeply and placed her hands in her pockets. "I think I've slept enough. I may as well help too."

As they left the crypt, Donna stopped Ryan on the walkway in the cemetery while the others continued on their route back to the dungeon entrance.

"Why were you so quick to help look for the duke?" Donna demanded to know.

"Donna, darling," Ryan announced cheerfully. "I just figured if I'd say I'm going to help them, it'll give me a good excuse to search for the missing jewels."

"If you want to go on some damned treasure hunt, then you go right ahead, but I won't be a part of it," she snapped and walked away.

Chapter Ten

*N*aomi walked alongside Harrington through the third floor hallway. She watched the proper looking butler as he walked with his hands clasped behind his back. Although he appeared docile, she knew his true personality was far more commanding than he'd led on to the others.

"Pairing up with you wasn't exactly what I had in mind," Naomi informed him simply.

He didn't look at her. "I'd prefer to have you close by so I might keep an eye on you."

"Are you always this much fun?" she muttered then looked around. "Where are we going anyway?"

"I want to check the towers," he said.

"You're looking for the duke in the tower?" she asked with some confusion. "Quite a few steps to carry someone just to hide a body, don't you think?"

"We're not going there to look for the duke," he replied.

Naomi stopped in the hallway and glared at him. "Why are we going there then? Do you intend to lock me in there?"

Harrington paused and turned to face her. "Tempting, but I doubt I'd get away with it." He continued down the hallway. "Your boyfriend has a problem with me already. If you'd disappear, he'd have my head."

Naomi hurried to join him. "George has a bit of a temper, I'll admit," she announced while laughing, "but he's certainly not my boyfriend." She eyed him suspiciously. "So why are we going to the tower?"

"I just want to scan the castle grounds from above. I want to make certain we don't have any unannounced visitors," he informed her. "I'll be able to see if there are any boats pulled onto shore."

Harrington paused before a tapestry hanging on the stone wall at the end of the hall. He pulled it back to reveal an old door. Naomi was surprised to see the hidden passageway.

"Interesting way to hide a door," she remarked.

"Keeps the draft out," he replied simply then unlocked the door with a key from his pocket.

Harrington opened the heavy door and entered the old, stone stairwell. They ascended the spiral, block stone steps. There were small windows every couple of yards with a view of the castle grounds. Naomi looked out each window as they passed. Once they reached the top, Harrington unlocked the upper door and opened it to reveal the tower that had been conveniently omitted from the tour. The tower room was large and round, resembling a wizard's laboratory. There were old books, tattered furniture, and strange objects, which were beyond Naomi's comprehension. Everything was covered with dust and cobwebs.

Naomi looked around the room and grinned. "Now this is interesting." She ran her fingers through some dust. "Needs a good doodle dusting though."

She approached the old, wooden window with cobwebs and spiders covering it. She carefully unlatched the old window and pushed it open. The cemetery could be seen across the grounds through the darkness. George had been right; the view was spectacular. Beyond the cemetery, she could see the harbor and the city lights in the distance. Cool, damp air blew through the window chilling her, but she didn't want to close the window and lose the view.

"From a distance, the city actually appears peaceful," she announced while leaning on the windowsill.

Harrington approached and stood behind her with his hands in his pockets. "This window faced the ocean in England. The guards could watch for an invasion from every side. I spent a lot of time in this tower as a boy. I'd stare out the window and watch for pirate ships." He laughed warmly. "Of course, there hadn't been pirates on the ocean for hundreds of years, but that doesn't matter to a young boy."

"Pretty serious environment for a child, I suspect," Naomi replied simply.

"Not at all," he remarked. "Duke Alden was like a grandfather to me. He'd tell me stories about the castle and battles throughout the centuries. I was never forbidden to touch the antiques." He sighed and sank into thought. "I believe he missed his own son. I suppose I filled that void in his life."

A cool breeze chilled Naomi. She gently rubbed her cold arms and looked back at him. "You really cared about him."

Harrington smiled warmly for the first time. "He was an endless narrator. His entire family history was stored in his memory. I know everything about this castle, the Wesley's, and King Chasity."

"Why do you leave the tower out of the tour?" she asked.

Harrington stared out the window and was silent a long moment. "Out of respect for the princess," he replied and stared outside as if in a trance. "Sometimes I hear her cry."

"What happened to the princess?"

He snapped out of his trance and looked at her. "Over four hundred years ago, her father locked her in the tower to protect her when intruders attacked the castle." Harrington again looked out the window. "The invaders killed nearly everyone. A few knights rushed the queen to safety. The king attempted to rescue his daughter, but he was killed before he ever reached her." He was silent a moment. "A young knight found the hiding princess a couple of days after the invasion. He fell in love with her and kept her hidden in the tower. He feared his king might kill her."

Naomi sat on the stone window ledge and watched him. His voice and storytelling manner were captivating.

"For nearly an entire year, the young knight managed to keep the princess hidden from his king. Over time, the princess had fallen in love with the knight as well," Harrington continued. "Meanwhile, the queen had gained the strength of another army. They returned to the castle through the passageway in the dungeon and attacked from within. The princess' knight was slain."

Naomi stared at him with surprise, feeling a sad pang.

"The queen was overjoyed to discover her daughter was alive, but when it was revealed she was pregnant by the young knight, the queen insisted the baby would be killed when it was born. The princess feared for her unborn baby and ran away. She was captured a couple of months later but without her child. Her mother banished her to the tower in fear that she'd run away to be with her baby. The princess stabbed herself and died in this very tower."

Naomi continued to rub her chilled arms, this time from the chilling story. "And the baby?"

Harrington looked at her. "No one ever knows what happened to the baby."

"Someone out there is of royal descent and doesn't even know it," Naomi replied then smiled. "That's fascinating."

"I'm glad I was able to entertain you," Harrington said with a tiny smile. "The princess was the last of the Chasity generation.

The next generation to the throne was the queen's nephew, Gerald Wesley, thus bringing about the duke and duchess."

Naomi smiled warmly while staring into Harrington's eyes.

He hid his smile and looked past her out the window. His smile suddenly faded. "Someone's in the crypt."

Harrington turned and hurried from the room. Naomi spun toward the ledge and looked out the window. There was a faint light from the distant crypt. She slowly stood and looked around the tower room. The room was dingy but almost soothing. She walked past the old table and looked at the medieval tools of a wizard. She approached an old bookshelf and ran her finger along the spines of the books. The books were so old; none had any writing on them. Blood ran down one book's spine. Naomi pulled her hand back with a gasp and a look of surprise. She heard the faint crying of a young woman. Naomi scanned the room but didn't see anyone. The crying stopped along with the gentle breeze.

Naomi looked back at the book on the shelf. The blood was gone as well. She uncertainly removed the book and opened it. It was all handwritten and almost illegible. She then realized it was the princess' diary. Naomi gently turned the old, discolored pages and attempted to read the entries. The writing style was old and whimsy, making it difficult for Naomi to read it. She turned to the last entry in the diary.

The entry read, "My child shall forever carry the name of his father, Timothy Harrington. He is the last of the Harrington's." Naomi lowered the book and stared at the stone wall with a look of disbelief. She heard someone approaching. When Naomi turned toward the door, she saw George enter the tower while attempting to catch his breath.

"Harrington said you were here." He continued to breathe harshly. "Damn, there are a lot of steps to the tower."

Naomi set down the book. "What'd you do? Run them?"

"Bradly thinks we can fix the gate. He nabbed Harrington downstairs," George replied and motioned her to follow.

§

Near the gate was a narrow opening in the stone with a vertical ladder in a shaft. The shaft led up to the crank wheel. Bradly appeared from the shaft and straightened. The others stared at him.

Harrington looked into the shaft, up the ladder then straightened, and looked at Bradly.

"What do you expect me to do?" Harrington asked.

"Frank made a clip for the chain. All we have to do is clip it onto the broken end of the chain, and we can raise the gate manually with the winch."

Ryan pointed up the shaft. "Frank's up there with the broken end of the chain. He's going to feed it down from the catwalk."

Everyone stared at Harrington.

"It could work," Harrington replied then looked at Bradly. "Who's going up there?"

Ryan smiled deviously and patted Harrington on the shoulder. "You are."

Chapter Eleven

Everyone stood outside the small shaft while Harrington climbed the iron rung ladder. Bradly kneeled before the opening and stared up the shaft into the darkness while Diane held Harrington's jacket just outside the shaft.

"How's it going, Harry?" Bradly called up the shaft.

Harrington's voice could be heard shouting back. "One more Harry out of you, and I'm dropping this chain on your head." There was a pause. "I found the wheel. The chain's not here."

Naomi walked closer to the shaft to listen.

"Frank, where's the chain?" Harrington called up the shaft. There was no response. "It must be stuck on the other side. The catch seems to be stuck in the locked position. I need a crowbar. I think I can pry it open."

Naomi looked at the crowbar near her. She picked it up and crawled through the opening into the shaft. Harrington came down the ladder just far enough to take the crowbar.

"Thank you, Miss Remus," he said then returned up the ladder.

Naomi watched a moment as he climbed back up the ladder then crawled from the opening.

Diane glared at her and spoke with hostility, "I know what you're up to, but it won't work. Avery and I have been together a long time, and I won't allow you to come between us."

"Don't get yourself overheated," Naomi snapped. "I'm not interested in Harrington. He's too--straight."

Diane appeared embarrassed and fidgeted. "I'm sorry. I didn't mean to accuse you," she explained timidly. "It's just that I've worked hard to get our relationship where it is today. I'm sure you can appreciate my situation."

There was a loud clank from the shaft. A squeak followed and the wheel scraped. They heard Harrington let out a startled cry that echoed through the shaft. The crowbar and thick chain fell to the floor of the crawl space with a thunderous crash. Blood ran down the shaft and to the floor, swiftly collecting into a large pool at the bottom. Everyone stared with horror at the blood while Diane let out a terrified scream.

"Harry!" Bradly yelled up the shaft.

There was no response. Naomi darted past him, crawled through the opening, and stepped over the small pool of blood. She straightened and looked up the ladder. The shaft was dark, and blood continued to drip down the rungs of the ladder. Naomi climbed the ladder, slipping on the bloody rungs several times. She finally reached Harrington's feet. There was no movement. Naomi moved to the opposite side of the ladder, where the space was much smaller, and climbed the last couple of rungs before him.

"Harrington?" she gasped nervously.

Harrington's head rested against the ladder. His eyes were shut, and blood covered his head and body. At first, he appeared dead. He drew a shaken breath as blood dripped from above them. Naomi uncertainly looked up and saw a man wedged in the opening just above their heads. His head was crushed between the wheel and the wall, making it difficult to identify the man. Naomi's eyes widened, and her mouth fell open.

"Oh, my God," she gasped.

Harrington looked at her as if just noticing her for the first time. "Climb down."

Naomi continued to stare with horror.

"Damn it, look at me," Harrington spoke harshly.

Naomi looked at him out of reflex. "Frank--?"

"No, it's Jake, the gatekeeper," Harrington replied gently. "I need you to carefully climb down to the bottom. Can you do that?"

She mechanically nodded, although it took a few seconds to convince her body to move.

Naomi sat on the large bed in a borrowed bathrobe while hugging her knees to her chest as she stared blankly at the wall across the room. George sat on the bed beside her and gently rubbed her shoulder.

"Are you sure you're all right?" he asked gently.

Naomi inhaled a shaken breath. "I'll be okay."

"Joanne said she'd bring you something to wear," he informed her. "Why don't you get some rest? I'm going to see what I can find out about Jake's death."

When she didn't respond, George forced a smile, rubbed her shoulder, and then left the room. Naomi continued to stare at the wall across the room. There was a faint knock on the door. She stirred uncomfortably.

"Come in."

Harrington entered the room having already showered and changed into a fresh uniform. Naomi looked at him then immediately looked back at the wall. Harrington set some clothes on the bed near her.

"Mr. Westinghouse told me it appeared as if I'd been injured," Harrington said gently. "I appreciate your coming to my rescue, so to speak."

Naomi inhaled a deep, shaken breath. "I can't get that horrible image out of my head. I see his face every time I close my eyes." She drew a shaken breath. "There was so much blood." She then looked at her hands and rubbed them together as if they were dirty. "I had his blood on my hands."

Harrington sat on the bed alongside her. He gently placed his hands over hers and stopped her from rubbing them further. "Let it go."

Naomi stared at him and forced a tiny smile. "I guess I'm not as strong as I pretend to be."

Harrington released her hands and attempted a smile. "My ancestors may have been servants, but we've always been fighters."

"So I've noticed," she announced then tilted her head. "Perhaps a descendant of a knight, once upon a time."

Harrington eyed her and stiffened. "Interesting topic."

"I'd stumbled upon the diary of the princess in the tower," she gently replied. "That young knight you'd mentioned was also a Harrington."

Harrington chuckled with a mocking smile. "And you've concluded that my ancestors were of royal descent?" he remarked. "Do you actually think royalty would stoop to a servant's level?"

"I suppose not," she replied gently.

Harrington removed a ring from his pinkie finger and extended it to her. Naomi accepted it and studied the antique gold shield ring.

"That ring belonged to Princess Elizabeth Chasity, daughter of King Chasity."

Naomi looked at him and smirked. "Why keep it a secret?"

"Do you think I want the world to know I come from a long line of bastards?" he boldly announced. "I'd stumbled upon it by accident myself. I found the diary in the tower and left it there, hoping it would remain hidden."

"I'd think you'd be proud," Naomi replied. "If history had been different, you could have been king."

"Had the princess remained in the castle, my entire family would never have been."

"So how did your family come to serve the castle?" she asked while studying him.

"The princess had left her baby with his grandparents. They took the child with them to England and became servants to the Wesley's. They believed the child belonged in the castle. We've been here ever since," he announced then drew a deep breath and sighed. "It's getting late. You should try to get some sleep."

"Yeah, sure," she replied and rolled her eyes. "I don't think I'll be getting any sleep tonight. Someone managed to get the duke into my room without my knowledge. There's no telling what could happen if I close my eyes."

"You could stay in my old room downstairs, and I could stay right next door if it'd make you feel better," Harrington informed her.

Naomi smiled warmly. "You'd do that?"

"Certainly. It's my job to see that our guests are comfortable," he replied then frowned. "Lord knows I've failed miserably so far."

Chapter Twelve

George approached Naomi's bedroom and knocked gently on the door. When there was no response, he knocked a little harder. Lydia's bedroom door opened, and she looked into the hallway while attempting a smile.

"Were you looking for Naomi?" she asked.

George approached her room. "Yes, have you seen her?"

"I think Harrington moved her to another room. I guess the duke really was in her bathroom," Lydia replied with a nervous smile. "Did you discover anything about the gatekeeper's death?"

"When we removed the body, we'd found he'd been strangled. There were marks around his neck," George replied with some tension.

Lydia's eyes widened with fright. "You're kidding? It wasn't an accident?"

"That's not the worst part," he continued. "The chain didn't break; it was cut. Whoever killed him, threw his body into the shaft over the wheel. I wouldn't doubt Mark witnessed something and it got him killed."

The bedroom door across from Naomi's opened, startling both. Ryan backed into the hallway, appearing somewhat defensive. "Come on, Joanne. I was just kidding," he announced with a boyish grin on his face.

Joanne stepped into the hallway and pointed a warning finger at him. "You just stay the hell away from me, you little pervert! I don't like your kind. Understand?"

Ryan lifted his hands in the air. "Okay, okay. Relax, I'm leaving."

Joanne glared at Lydia and George then returned to her room and slammed the door.

Ryan looked at the two standing in the hallway and forced an embarrassed smile. "Women; they turn you on then turn you down," he remarked then frowned. "I need a drink. Anyone care to join me?"

George sighed. "Gladly."

Lydia shook her head in disgust. "You men all stick together, don't you?"

§

Naomi buttoned one of Harrington's borrowed shirts and looked at herself in the full-length mirror inside the closet door. The shirt reached just below her panty line. Naomi closed the closet and poked around Harrington's old bedroom. She opened the top dresser drawer and examined the neatly folded underwear. No one folded underwear that neatly. She tapped her fingers on the dresser top then groaned.

"Oh, why not," she muttered. "He'll never know if I borrow a pair."

She removed a pair of boxer shorts and slipped into them, using them as regular shorts. A few minutes later, she wandered around the small room and sat on the bed with a bored sigh. Naomi glanced at the nightstand then opened the drawer and, to her surprise, saw a copy of her most recent book. She picked it up and turned it over. There was a dagger hole through the back cover! Naomi sprang to her feet.

"Why you son-of-a-bitch," she cried out.

She clutched the book in her hand and hurried from the room. Naomi stormed down the hallway in the servant's wing, paused before Harrington's current room, and promptly pounded on the door. She wasn't concerned about waking the rest of the staff, since they started drinking after the incident with Jake. Harrington opened the bedroom door, appeared weary, and peered at her. Naomi pushed past him into the room with anger on her face. Harrington watched as she passed him.

"Is that my shirt?" He fell silent noting her mood and closed the door. "Is something wrong?"

Naomi spun around and slammed her book on the dresser top. "I'll say! Explain this!"

Harrington approached the dresser and examined the book and her picture on the back cover. He frowned and looked at her. "I can't," he replied. "Where did you find this?"

"In your nightstand drawer," she growled.

Harrington stared at her a moment in silence. "I honestly don't know how it got there. I don't use that room anymore, except to store extra clothing."

Naomi folded her arms across her chest with a look of distrust. There was a faint knock on the door. Harrington groaned, turned toward the door, and opened it.

Diane stood in the doorway. "Avery, I just had to--" She saw Naomi and her expression immediately dropped.

Naomi rolled her eyes and groaned. "Great"

Diane stared at the shirt Naomi wore, and her mouth fell open with a look of shock. "Is she wearing your shirt?"

"This really isn't a good time, Diane," Harrington replied and attempted to close the door.

She kept the door from shutting. "Harrington--?"

Naomi walked toward the door. "I think I'd better leave."

She darted past Harrington and Diane, entered the hallway, and walked back toward her room next door. She heard Harrington yell with anger.

"Diane!"

Naomi turned her head and realized Diane was charging for her. Diane shoved her against the wall, jarring her, but Naomi instinctively pushed Diane backward. Diane lunged forward and tackled her to the hall floor. Naomi punched the woman on top of her, though her shots weren't clean. Diane attempted to slap Naomi while she screamed profanities. Harrington grabbed Diane's arm and pulled her to her feet. Naomi scrambled to her feet as well and tackled Diane, taking both her and Harrington to the hall floor. They rolled off him and punched each other. Naomi got a clean shot and punched Diane in the mouth. Diane fell against the wall into a sitting position. Harrington sprang to his feet and grabbed Naomi around the waist from behind.

"That's enough!" Harrington shouted.

Diane jumped to her feet and kicked at Naomi while she was held defenseless against Harrington. Naomi broke free, allowing Diane's foot to connect with Harrington's groin, dropping him to his knees. Diane gasped with alarm, covered her mouth, and hurried toward him.

"Harrington! I'm so sorry!"

Harrington glared at her. Diane stopped mid-stride, turned, and hurried back toward the kitchen. Harrington slowly moved into a sitting position and rested his head against the wall behind him. Naomi sank down the wall beside Harrington and glanced at him.

"All the times I've broken up fights between her and Joanne, you'd think I'd have learned my lesson," he remarked.

Naomi attempted a pleasant smile. "At least you took it with dignity."

Harrington glared at her without humor then shut his eyes and snarled under his breath, "Tell me, Miss Remus, do you enjoy wearing men's underwear?"

Naomi blushed and quickly stood. "Goodnight, Harrington."

Chapter Thirteen

*E*arly the following morning, Diane approached Joanne's bedroom on the third floor, paused in the hallway, and knocked gently on the door so she wouldn't wake the guests in the nearby rooms.

"Joanne, time to get up." There was no response. "Joanne, I'm getting tired of being your keeper."

There was still no response. Diane groaned, obviously used to the morning ritual, and opened the door without waiting for an invite. She entered the dark room and saw Joanne lying on her bed with a sheet draped over her naked body. Diane shook her head, approached the window, and opened the curtains, flooding the room with light.

"I'm not going to do all the work by myself, you know," Diane said as she turned toward the bed.

Diane suddenly froze while staring at the nearby bed. Joanne's eyes were open, and blood saturated the sheets surrounding the gaping slit across her throat. Diane screamed and ran from the room.

*T*here was a faint pounding on one of the staff bedroom doors in the hall outside Naomi's room. Naomi woke from the sound and looked around the room now brightened by sunlight flooding through the windows. She realized someone must have been knocking on Harrington's door just down the hall. Naomi jumped out of bed, hurried to the door, and opened it to peek down the hall. George stood in the hallway with Harrington, who wearily raked his fingers through his mussed hair. He muttered something and returned to his room. George saw Naomi and hurried toward her.

"What's happened?" she asked with concern.

"Diane found Joanne murdered in her bedroom," George replied while frowning.

"Oh, my God," she gasped while staring at him. "What are we going to do?"

"Don't get hysterical, Naomi," George announced while attempting to keep her calm. "This seems to be staff related. Let's just hope it ends here. Someone will be missing us today. They should be out here to get us."

"Do you think the gatekeeper was also murdered?" Naomi asked with concern.

He shifted uncomfortably. "Yes, he was murdered as well," George reluctantly replied. "He'd been strangled. Someone cut the chain on purpose."

"But why?"

"To trap us here," George informed her.

Harrington approached from his room now in his uniform. "Is Diane calm?"

"Lydia gave her a tranquilizer," George informed him. "She's resting."

"Good," Harrington replied then drew a deep breath. "Has anyone disturbed the murder scene?"

"No one's been in there besides Diane," George responded. "She didn't touch anything."

"I'm going to have a look around the room," Harrington announced. "If there's any evidence of our killer, I'd like to find it before they can remove it."

"I don't think that's a wise idea, Harrington," George insisted. "This is a matter for the police. We should just close the door and not touch anything."

"I don't intend to touch anything. I'm just going to look around," he remarked simply then turned toward Naomi and gave her a curious look. "You write mysteries. Do you think you can find something useful?"

George became angry. "Don't get her involved in this, Harrington."

Harrington glared at George with limited patience. "She's already involved. We all are." He looked back at Naomi. "Will you help me?"

Naomi groaned and reluctantly nodded. "Give me a minute to change."

§

*H*arrington stood across the bedroom staring at the dead woman lying on the bed before bravely entering the room. Naomi followed then immediately hesitated when she saw the blood soaking through the sheet. There was so much blood. Harrington looked over the dead maid without touching her. George joined them but remained in the doorway.

"I'm telling you," George again insisted while watching the butler. "We should seal off the room until the police arrive. Nothing should be disturbed."

Harrington turned with a sigh. "I agree. I just want to have a quick look around," he replied. "We might find something that'll tell us who the killer is so that we can stop this."

Naomi nervously looked around the room. "There's no sign of a struggle." She looked at the dead woman. "Did she often sleep in the nude?"

Harrington became flustered. "I wouldn't really know. Does it matter?"

"It could be an indication that she hadn't been alone at the time of her death," Naomi said then studied the room more closely. "Is there anything missing or out of place?"

Harrington looked around. "Not as far as I can tell. I wouldn't know what personal effects she had. Diane might know."

Naomi examined the body from several feet away. "She's been dead no more than a couple of hours. I'd estimate no less than an hour."

"She was last seen at three-thirty by George and Lydia. Ryan fought with her," Harrington remarked. "So that would put her death between three-thirty and four-thirty."

"That will help. I wonder if anyone had an alibi for that time," Naomi asked more to herself.

"Mr. Westinghouse and Mr. Christman were playing pool in the billiard room up until they heard about Joanne," Harrington informed her.

Naomi entered the bathroom. Two towels were hanging on the towel rack. Naomi approached the towels and touched them. One was still wet. There was a brown residue on the towel. She looked into the tub. There was a brown stain on the bottom. Harrington now stood behind her.

"What do you make of that?" Harrington asked.

"It's not blood," Naomi replied "Could be iron from the water or maybe even dirt."

"Dirt from the cemetery perhaps?" Harrington asked then appeared curious. "Can we assume the killer is male?"

"There's no indication that she'd been sexually assaulted. I don't think we should assume anything." Naomi looked around the bathroom. "By the looks of the scene, I'd say she was asleep when she was attacked. Whether or not she'd been alone before that, I couldn't say."

Harrington inhaled nervously. "I think we should speak to the staff. Someone should know something."

§

Everyone gathered in the lounge a little after six that morning. Diane was sobbing on Harrington's shoulder while he comforted her. Lydia smoked one cigarette after another, and Barney continued to drink despite the early hour. Barney finally glared at Diane and slammed down the bottle with apparent irritation.

"Give it a rest, Diane," he lashed out.

Diane lifted her head and looked at Barney as she sniffed. "My sister's dead. Show a little respect!"

"You hated your sister," Barney announced simply then smiled slyly. "I wouldn't doubt you killed her yourself. So spare us the grieving sister act."

"How dare you accuse me of killing her!" Diane cried out in rage.

Harrington groaned irritably. "Leave her alone," he announced firmly.

Barney snorted a laugh. "You aren't falling for her dry weeping, are you?" he demanded. "You know if there's anyone guilty of killing Joanne, it's Diane."

Harrington released the grieving maid and stood. All attention was on the butler. "If anyone is going to start pointing fingers, it'll be me."

Barney returned to the bar without further comment.

Harrington looked around the room with a hardened expression. "I'd like to know where everyone was between three-thirty and four-thirty."

"This is ridiculous," Lydia proclaimed and crushed her cigarette with aggression. "You're just the butler. We don't have to answer to you."

"If you haven't anything to hide, you shouldn't mind answering the question," Naomi remarked coldly.

"I had no reason to kill Joanne. I didn't even know her," Lydia scoffed then turned toward Harrington. "George and I saw Ryan and Joanne fighting in the hallway outside her room. It was about three-thirty. She went back into her room then Ryan and George went downstairs for a drink."

"What time did she take a shower?" Harrington asked.

Lydia appeared baffled while staring at him. "What's that got to do with anything?"

"It could help place the exact time of the murder," Harrington informed her.

"I'm not sure. It must've been shortly after she returned to her room," Lydia replied.

"And you didn't hear anything after that?" Harrington pressed her for more information.

"No," Lydia scoffed while glaring at him. "I went to bed shortly after." She lit another cigarette. "I didn't kill her. Why should I want to?"

George leaned forward and raised a cocky brow. "I have nothing to hide," he announced casually. "Ryan and I were playing pool right up until Joanne was discovered dead."

"That's the truth," Ryan confirmed.

Harrington eyed Ryan then turned to Frank. "Where were you?"

Frank was a bit hesitant then leaned back in his chair. "I was with Diane," he remarked. "She'd been upset about something personal and needed to talk to someone."

"Frank and I talked from the time I'd left your quarters until I went to wake Joanne for her morning duties at four-thirty," Diane said sadly.

"I suppose I was the only one actually sleeping during that time," Donna muttered.

"Me too," Bradly remarked. "I didn't wake until I'd heard Diane screaming."

Barney drank the whiskey from his glass. "I was asleep as well." He raised a cocky brow and glared at Harrington. "What about you, Harrington? Where were you?"

Harrington straightened proudly and clasped his hands behind his back. "I was alone in the servant's wing."

Frank laughed loudly. "Not entirely alone."

Harrington shot a glare at Frank. "What's that supposed to mean?"

He smirked deviously and shrugged. "Just that I heard you were hiding out all night in the servant's wing with Miss Remus," Frank remarked.

Harrington's eyes narrowed with anger. "Watch it, Frank," he growled.

Frank took a step toward Harrington with a mocking smile on his face. "Why? In a couple of hours the police are going to be here," he informed him. "And who do you think will be their prime suspect?" Frank raised his brows and smiled. "That's right--you. The police suspected you of murdering Duke Alden."

"Is there anything else you'd care to add?" Harrington asked lowly. "It may be your last chance."

"Is that a threat, Harrington?" Frank asked almost humored with a mocking smile.

"As a matter-of-fact, it is," Harrington replied dryly while glaring at Frank. "I suspect we'll be finding a new groundskeeper very shortly."

Barney sprang to his feet, stepped between the two, and attempted a smile. "We're all under a lot of stress right now. Let's not make any hostile decisions."

Diane stood and clung to Harrington's arm. "Harrington, would you take me back to my room?"

"Yeah, sure," Harrington muttered his response then escorted her from the room.

"What an actress," Frank chuckled.

"How can you be so cruel?" Donna demanded while placing her hands on her hips. "She's just lost her sister. Don't you think she could be genuinely upset about it?"

"Doubtful," Barney replied simply.

"She turned on the tears for Harrington's sake," Frank remarked. "She'd like for everyone to believe she's a saint. The woman's evil to the core."

"Some friend you are," Naomi replied. "She comes to you for comfort, and you stab her in the back the moment she leaves the room."

"Don't give me more credit than I deserve, Naomi," Frank replied. "I only wanted to take advantage of her."

"You're sick," Donna scoffed.

Frank removed his gold pocket watch and looked at the time. Barney seemed curious to see the time as well.

"Well, I don't suppose we'll be getting any sleep now," Frank said then looked at Barney. "Wanna play a few rounds of pool?"

Barney beamed with enthusiasm. "You rack 'em, and I'll pour the drinks."

Chapter Fourteen

*N*aomi entered the silent, empty kitchen and prepared the teakettle for her morning tea. As she searched through the cupboards for a teacup, she could hear someone approaching from the back, kitchen stairs. Naomi glanced behind her and saw Harrington walk across the large kitchen toward her.

"You shouldn't be running about the castle on your own. It's not safe," he informed her.

"It's not exactly safe in the lounge either," she replied. "Bradly and Ryan are fighting over poker."

"As long as they don't get Frank and Barney involved," he remarked. "Whenever they fight, they destroy entire rooms at a time."

Naomi removed the sugar bowl and stared at it a moment. "How's Diane?"

"She's resting now," he replied. "I think the sedative finally took effect." He sighed deeply. "I suppose, despite all their cat fights, they still cared for each other."

"Were their fights violent?" she asked.

Harrington eyed her. "You mean enough for Diane to want Joanne dead? Diane isn't like that. She couldn't possibly murder her own sister."

"But yours is a bias opinion," Naomi informed him.

"What do you mean?" Harrington asked with a look of confusion.

"You and Diane," she replied and raised her brows. "You wouldn't side against her."

"Are you insinuating Diane and I are lovers?" he asked with surprise.

"Aren't you?" Naomi asked then immediately tensed. "I mean, it's none of my business."

"No, we're not lovers," he growled lowly, "and I certainly hope she didn't imply that we were."

"Maybe a little." Naomi forced a tiny smile. "I mean, she's an attractive woman. It wouldn't be completely inconceivable."

"Diane has a very unattractive personality," Harrington remarked. "If I had a type, she'd be the farthest from it."

"Sounds like you don't get out enough," Naomi replied.

"I don't have time for relationships," he insisted. "The idea of chasing women sounds all too tiring."

"How sad."

He met her gaze as they stared at each other in silence. There was a faint crash from the billiard room. Harrington turned with surprise and ran for the kitchen door. Naomi hurried after him and down the hallway. A chair flew from the billiard room and crashed into a hall table. Harrington ran for the doorway, skidded around the corner, and entered the room. Naomi stopped before the doorway and watched. There were the sounds of men punching each other and women screaming. Naomi cringed and turned her head. Harrington was thrown from the room and collided with the opposing hall wall. He straightened proudly and proceeded back inside. There were more punches and groans.

Frank flew from the room and crashed into the hall table. He narrowly missed a suit of armor. Barney tumbled from the room and dove into the armor. It crashed to the floor with a metallic clang. Both men straightened and marched back into the billiard room. Naomi looked at the pile of armor near the table. Most of the pieces were still connected. Something gold lay on the floor just near the armor. Naomi picked up the gold pocket watch and stared at it with great interest. Harrington was tossed from the room and collided with her. Both slammed into the wall and fell to the floor, leaving Naomi slightly dazed. Harrington moved to his knees and dabbed the blood on the corner of his mouth then looked at her.

"Are you all right, madam?"

Naomi slowly sat up while holding her head. "Yeah," she muttered then became angry and glared at him. "Are you going to let them get away with that?"

Harrington stood and helped her to her feet. He removed his jacket, handed it to her, and returned to the billiard room. There were several punches, crashes, groans, and screams. Naomi cringed once more. Frank and Barney dragged Harrington from the room and tossed him into a nearby broom closet. They locked the door with the key that had been in the lock and returned to the billiard room for another round. Naomi hurried to the closet while Harrington pounded on the door yelling British profanities. Naomi unlocked the door and opened it.

"Acht, that'd be cheating," Barney said from behind, although she never saw him, and shoved her into the closet as well.

Naomi collided with Harrington, tossing both against the back wall of the rather large closet. They heard the door lock behind them. Harrington pushed past Naomi and threw himself against the door. He cried out painfully and again cursed.

"The door opens inward," Naomi scoffed. "Any more brilliant ideas?"

Harrington glared at her through the dim lighting beneath the door. "Just the one where I throw you into the moat." He leaned against the door and relaxed. "We'll just wait until someone comes along."

An hour later. Naomi sat on the floor of the closet and attempted to examine the pocket watch. Harrington leaned against the closet door and rubbed his sore jaw.

"Isn't there a light in here?" Naomi asked.

"No," Harrington said sternly. "Some incompetent fool never replaced the burnt bulb."

"You?" Naomi asked simply.

"Yeah, that would be me," he moaned.

"Isn't there a candle or flashlight in here?" she persisted.

"There might be one on the shelf in the back," Harrington said with a defeated sigh. He moved across the closet and almost stepped on her while rummaging through the upper shelf.

Naomi slapped his calf. "Sit down, before you hurt me."

Harrington continued to rustle through the shelf. A small light appeared and lit the entire closet. Harrington sat beside her with his flashlight and shined it on the object in her hand. Naomi examined the gold pocket watch.

Harrington stared at the watch with surprise as his brow arched. "Where'd you get that?"

"I found it in the hallway," she informed him. "I thought it was yours."

Harrington snatched it from her and studied it. "This belonged to Duke Alden." He opened it. "It's inscribed by the duchess."

Naomi grabbed the flashlight and shined it around the closet. "That proves the duke was down here."

"No, this watch disappeared the night Duke Alden was murdered," he announced while caressing the watch. "I thought it had been stolen."

"That would mean one of the staff murdered the duke," Naomi announced.

Harrington stared across the closet with narrow eyes and shut off the flashlight. "Yes." He groaned and leaned his head against the wall. "More bad publicity."

"People have been slain in this castle for centuries. It's not as if the castle had a reputation to maintain," Naomi remarked simply.

"That's different," he said then moaned. "I can see the headlines now. Castle Bloodshed; a dead time for all."

"You're overreacting just a little," she said simply.

"I just don't want it to end like this," he said softly. "The castle can't support itself. Even the tours don't really help. Without the duke's will, there's no telling what will happen." He was silent a moment then spoke timidly. "This is all I know."

Another hour passed, and both had become sleepy. Naomi woke, although she wasn't sure what woke her. She slowly looked around the dark closet then at Harrington alongside her. She rested against him while he slept with his arm securely around her. Naomi studied him a moment and gently touched his face. She pulled her hand away when he woke. Harrington looked around with some disorientation then rolled his eyes closed.

"Bloody hell," he groaned. "I thought it was just a bad dream."

Harrington removed his arm from her shoulder and smiled with embarrassment. "Sorry."

The flashlight came on allowing him to see his wristwatch. He groaned in response. Naomi stared at the door then grabbed the light from him. She shined the light on a pool of blood collecting just beneath the door. Naomi gasped with horror as both sprang to their feet and backed away from the door.

"Harrington--?"

He stepped to the side of the blood and pounded on the door. "Someone unlock this bloody door!"

There was movement in the hallway.

"Someone's coming," Naomi whispered.

Harrington grabbed her around the waist and pulled her to the back of the closet. He stood before her with the flashlight raised above his head, prepared to protect her from the person in the hall. Once the key turned in the lock, silence followed. Harrington slowly approached the door and pulled it open. Barney lay dead in the hallway near the closet door. His throat had been slit, and there was a large pool of blood surrounding the body. They looked around, but there was no one to be found. The disabled suit of armor was now intact and back at its original post.

"I think I know who did it," Naomi suddenly gasped.

Harrington turned toward her with a look of surprise. "Who?"

"Frank had the duke's watch," she informed him. "Barney saw him with it. I bet he recognized it as the duke's and attempted to blackmail Frank."

"Then Frank killed the duke as well," Harrington remarked.

"It's very likely that would be the case," she agreed. "He did have the watch, which was last seen the night he was murdered."

"We need to find him," Harrington said firmly.

"If he's the killer, we can't catch him ourselves," Naomi protested. "He's a dangerous man."

Harrington appeared distant then looked back at Naomi and nodded. "You're right. Why don't you wait in the study and lock the door behind you," he announced firmly. "I'll find the others and meet you back here."

Naomi stared at him with a concerned look. "I don't think we should separate."

"You'll be safe in the study," Harrington replied. "I'll be right back."

Harrington turned and walked down the hallway. Naomi watched him head into the kitchen. Something just didn't feel right.

Chapter Fifteen

Naomi hurried into the duke's bedroom and studied the sword mounted on the wall along the king-sized bed. She removed it then approached the writing desk near the large window. Naomi laid the sword on the desk and sat in the chair. Only a few moments passed. The door to the bedroom opened. Harrington entered without even noticing her and immediately darted for the wall where the sword had been mounted. He stopped when he saw the blank space on the wall.

Naomi picked up the sword. "I had hoped I was wrong with my suspicion, but it would appear I wasn't."

Harrington was startled by her voice. He spun around then glared at her. "This doesn't concern you."

"You're not thinking about defending yourself, Harrington," Naomi snapped. "All you want is revenge. You intend to kill Frank in cold blood."

"Cold blood?" he demanded. "You think destroying a man who's murdered five people isn't justified?"

"We don't have any real proof he killed anyone," she protested. "It's just my theory." Her look turned hard and cold. "I won't allow you to simply kill him."

"Madam--" he snorted. "I have always been a gentleman, but not tonight. Give me the sword, go back to your room, lock your door, and don't come back out until I say so."

Naomi stared at him with some apprehension. She clutched the sword nervously and raised it. "No, I won't," she announced, summoning all her courage. "Avenging the duke won't bring him back."

Harrington stared at her with an icy look on his face. For a moment, she could only hear the ticking of the grandfather clock. He casually turned and approached the master chamber door. Naomi shifted uncomfortably and watched him with apprehension. Her heart nearly stopped when Harrington locked the door. Naomi's expression shattered while her hands trembled as she clutched the sword. He turned and walked toward her with a psychotic look on his face.

"You just stay away! I'm warning you," she cried out.

"I suggest you put down the sword," Harrington said firmly. "Don't make me take it from you."

Naomi backed across the room. "I won't allow you to do it, Harrington."

"I've asked nicely."

Harrington lunged at her. Naomi darted out of his path and faced him while breathing heavily. She wouldn't swing despite fearing for her life. She understood his thinking, but she wasn't about to let him go through with his plot for revenge. He lunged at her again. She attempted to jump from his path and bolted across the room, but he caught her around the waist. She dropped the sword, grabbed his arm, and threw herself to one knee, flipping him over her hip. As he struck the floor, Harrington was left momentarily dazed. Naomi leaped for the discarded sword. Harrington jumped to his feet and grabbed the long handle as well. They struggled for possession of the sword.

Naomi clung to the sword despite Harrington's strength. She was tossed around the room several times but still didn't let go. Harrington yanked harshly, tearing the sword from her hands. The blade scratched her forearm as it was pulled back. Naomi cried out with surprise and pain while clutching her bleeding arm. Harrington stared at her a moment while remaining motionless. Naomi backed up a step as blood seeped between her fingers from the wound. She couldn't control the tears of pain streaking her face from the intense burning sensation. She feared even looking at the wound. There was a metallic clang as the sword fell to the floor. Harrington stared at her bleeding arm with a horrified look on his face.

"I-I didn't mean to hurt you." He took a step toward her. "Let me see how bad--"

Naomi glared at him with hatred and anguish in her eyes. "Just stay the hell away from me, you son-of-a-bitch! You've won. It's yours. Take your revenge!"

She stormed across the room and entered the master bath, leaving a trail of blood droplets. Naomi stopped before the sink, nervously removed her hand from the wound, and ran cold water over it before even pausing to assess the damage. The amount of blood-tinged water running down the drain was frightening at first.

She finally looked at her injured arm. The cut was two inches long but, despite all the blood, it wasn't very deep. She endured the pain and allowed the cold water to flush it clean. Naomi looked in the mirror. Harrington was now standing behind her with genuine concern on his face.

"Are you all right, Miss Remus?" he asked gently.

Naomi looked back at her arm and scoffed, "I'll live."

"I'm so sorry," Harrington whispered.

"Leave me alone," she growled and avoided looking at his reflection in the mirror behind her.

Harrington lowered his head and left the bathroom. She was fortunate enough to find a medical kit in the bathroom medicine cabinet and tended to her injury. It required some creative patchwork, but she managed to wrap it securely. Fortunately, it seemed as if the bleeding had stopped as well. Naomi left the bathroom a little while later and paused just within the bedroom. The sword had been returned to its rightful spot on the wall near the bed with her blood remaining on the blade. Naomi was surprised Harrington hadn't cleaned the blade, considering the sword's symbolism to him.

§

Naomi, Donna, Lydia, and Diane waited in the lounge nearly an hour for the men to return. The four men entered the lounge with matching looks of disgust on their faces. Harrington immediately approached the window and stared outside. George collapsed on the sofa beside Naomi and patted her leg. Bradly and Ryan headed to the bar and poured themselves some coffee.

"So where's Frank?" Lydia asked.

"We couldn't find him anywhere," Ryan reported with a groan. "He wasn't in his room; he wasn't in the dungeon; he wasn't in the cemetery. The guy just disappeared."

"Or he's dead," Bradly remarked.

Donna looked at the butler's back. "How long until someone comes out here to check on us, Harrington?"

"The mainland dock will wonder where Mark is about noon today," he informed her. "When they try to call and can't get through, they'll send someone out to investigate."

"I suggest we hunt him down," Ryan announced boldly.

Harrington turned and gave Ryan a stern look. "We should remain together. He knows this castle far better than you do. He could hide anywhere." He looked back out the window with little expression. "We should wait for the police."

"Screw that! I say we find him before he finds us," Bradly launched hotly. "I don't know about the rest of you, but I don't want him sneaking out when help arrives."

Ryan finished his coffee and slammed the mug on the bar. "Come on, Bradly. Let's arm ourselves and find the bastard."

Ryan and Bradly left the room on their hunting expedition, where they were potentially the hunted.

George sighed and playfully slapped Naomi's thigh. "Someone needs to keep an eye on those two," he announced. "Will you be okay here with the others?"

"Don't go with them, George," Naomi moaned. "They're just being stupid."

"Don't worry about me," he announced with a grin. "I've had combat training. I'll be fine."

"I think you should wait for the police," Naomi said with a frown. "But I know you won't listen to me."

"You're right," he said with a mocking smile.

George stood and left the room, following the others. Harrington remained by the window, staring into the distance. Diane finally approached him, and they talked quietly.

A few minutes passed before Lydia groaned and stood. "I need to freshen up." She turned to Donna. "Will you come with me to the ladies' room down the hall?"

Donna nodded and left the lounge with Lydia. Harrington finally turned away from Diane and approached the small bar. He poured himself a glass of whiskey, which was the first time he'd drank any alcohol during their visit.

Diane joined him at the bar. "Are you all right, Avery?" she asked gently.

"I'm fine," Harrington growled.

"I could give you a massage," she cooed and touched his arm. "You'd feel better."

Harrington pulled away from her and glared through hateful, angry eyes. "Leave me alone."

Diane appeared surprised by his hostile outburst. "What's wrong with you? Why are you acting like this toward me?" She suddenly pointed at Naomi. "It's because of her, isn't' it?"

Naomi was a little surprised by the insinuation, but she knew she shouldn't have been. She immediately stood and groaned.

"I've had just about enough of you, Diane," she launched.

Diane turned toward Naomi and glared back at her. "That makes us about even."

"There's nothing between Harrington and me that could possibly concern you," Naomi launched hotly. "Stick your nose in my business, and you're liable to get it punched."

Diane turned toward Harrington with her mouth hanging open. "Are you going to allow her to talk to me like that?"

Harrington's look was cold and angry. "I'd like to know where you get off telling people we're lovers."

"I never--" Diane cried out.

"Don't bother lying to me, Diane," Harrington snapped. "I know what you've been up to. There's never been anything between us, and there never will be."

Diane slapped him across the face and stormed from the room. Naomi and Harrington exchanged looks. She turned and left the room as well. Harrington suddenly came to life and hurried after her, catching her good arm.

"Wait--"

Naomi spun with a look of anger. "Do you really want to be slapped twice in one day?"

Harrington released her arm and took a step back. Naomi walked along the hallway and hurried up the stairs to the third floor. She was almost surprised Harrington didn't follow. She walked along the hallway and paused by the suit of armor near her old bedroom. She inhaled deeply, lowered her head, and sighed. Perhaps she'd been a little unfair toward Harrington. She turned back toward the stairs. Naomi was suddenly struck on the back of the head. She clutched her head and fell to her knees while turning toward the knight, believing he'd attacked her. To her surprise, it wasn't the knight who'd struck her. Diane stood behind her with a dagger in her hand. Naomi slowly pulled her hand from her head and looked at the small amount of blood on her fingers.

"Did you really think I'd just let you take Avery away from me?" Diane spat in anger.

Naomi couldn't deny she was in pain and felt dizzy, but she wasn't about to let that stop her from lashing out. "I don't know what you're talking about," she snarled. "There's nothing between Harrington and me."

"I know what you're up to," Diane growled. "I know why you want him. When those jewels are found, I'm going to see that Avery gets them. He's going to be mine, the jewels will be mine, and this castle *will* be mine."

"You're out of your mind," Naomi said and touched her head once more. "This castle will never be yours. It doesn't belong to you, and you have no claim to it."

"That's where you're wrong," Diane said with a smirk. "I know where Duke Alden's will is hidden. I hid it the night he was murdered. I had to withhold it, or everything would be ruined."

"This is insane," Naomi said in an attempt to save her own life. "Harrington isn't interested in me. Put the knife down, and I'll forget about this whole incident."

Diane smiled evilly. "I'm not taking any chances. I've made too many deals to stop now."

Naomi's mouth fell open as she stared at the woman with horror. "You murdered the others?"

"Not exactly--"

Naomi's vision blurred and she could no longer control her dizziness. She sank against the wall. Diane raised the dagger and lunged for the defenseless woman. Naomi shielded her face with a gasp and waited for the sting of the dagger. There was a loud, metallic clang. Naomi managed to open her eyes and saw a silver blur standing before her. Everything suddenly went dark.

Chapter Sixteen

Frank turned the unlit dungeon torch sideways to reveal the hidden compartment within the stone. The small treasure chest sat in the compartment. He removed it with some effort and almost dropped it to the floor from the weight. He opened the chest to reveal many precious stones and gold coins. He grinned then closed the chest, shut the compartment, and lit the torch. He removed an envelope from his pocket. The decorative writing on the front read, Last Will and Testament. He extended the envelope to the flame. Footfalls echoed in another corridor.

Frank appeared concerned then placed the envelope down the helmet of a nearby knight with a dented shoulder. He grabbed the wooden chest and carried it away as quickly as possible, entering a room off to the right. Frank approached an opening in the stone floor and opened the small oubliette chamber, which was only four foot by seven foot. An oubliette was often used as a place to put prisoners and forget about them. A jousting pole struck him across the back of his head, splitting the pole in two. Frank gasped in agony and fell alongside the oubliette. The other half of the pole was tossed aside, and Frank was then pushed into the small pit, where he landed with a thud.

Naomi woke and saw Harrington sitting on the king-sized bed alongside her. She looked around the duke's master chamber with some confusion then eyed Harrington.

"What happened?" she asked and attempted to sit up. She cringed, clutched her head, and fell back down onto the comforter. "Oh, my head!"

"I was hoping you could tell me," Harrington replied. "It was just blind luck I found you in here."

Naomi stared at him with a puzzled look. "You found me in here? You didn't bring me here?"

"No, of course not."

Naomi held her head a moment and looked around with confusion. "Then how did I get here?" She looked back at Harrington. "Diane hit me on the head and tried to kill me. I must've passed out."

"Diane?" he gasped with surprise. "You can't be serious."

"She talked some nonsense about the jewels and the duke's will," Naomi remarked while clutching her aching head.

"His will? But that was never--" Harrington shook his head. "I suppose there was more going on than I'll ever know." He stared at her as his concerns shifted. "I'm really sorry about what had happened earlier. I didn't mean to hurt you."

Naomi attempted a warm smile. "I know. I shouldn't have been so cold to you when you were trying to apologize."

"No, I deserved it," he replied firmly. "I could've hurt you a lot worse." He looked down with shame. "As much as I wanted to avenge Duke Alden, I couldn't live with myself if I'd hurt you to achieve it."

Naomi held back her pleased smile. "I think that's about the nicest thing you've said to me this entire tour."

Harrington grimaced with some embarrassment. "I need to work on that too, I suppose," he replied. "I've been a bit of a bastard to you."

"I'd probably have to agree with that," Naomi replied with a tiny laugh.

Harrington took her hand, surprising her. "You have every right," he replied then gently kissed the back of her hand. It was far more passionate than the average, suave greeting. "Get some rest. I'll check on you in a little while." Harrington released her hand and left the room.

Naomi watched him leave with a stunned look on her face. She looked at the back of her hand and appeared baffled. She wondered if her face was as red as it felt. She finally lay down on the bed, smiled contentedly, and cuddled the pillow. Her hand accidentally hit the headboard, forcing her to turn her head. There was a small opening in the wood. Naomi lifted herself, despite the pain in her head, and pushed on the opening. It opened to reveal a secret compartment. She reached inside, removed the duke's journal, and paged through it. The last entry read, "I found the missing jewels in the dungeon. They are--" She turned to the next page, but it had been torn out. Naomi sat up in bed and immediately clutched her head, regretting the action. She then opened her eyes and looked toward the door.

"Harrington!"

§

*N*aomi walked beside Harrington through the dimly lit, eerie basement corridor. "Why do you suppose Frank felt it necessary to trap us here?" she asked. "Why not look for the jewels during the week when there were fewer witnesses?"

"Perhaps the jewels aren't the prime motive," Harrington replied. "If the real intent had been murder, he would want to establish an alibi to protect himself." Harrington then raised a brow. "To the other extreme; perhaps one of the guests is a partner and needed a way in."

"Wouldn't you recognize them though?" Naomi asked.

"I never went ashore on weekends with the others. I have no idea with whom they'd associated," he replied. Harrington paused outside the armor repair shop.

"What's this place?" Naomi asked.

"Just one of Frank's work areas," he said simply. "Also one of the few places we hadn't searched recently."

Harrington cautiously opened the door. There were piles of dented armor scattered about the room. Harrington entered the messy workshop and shook his head. "Frank's a poor worker. Look at this place."

Naomi looked past the pile of armor to the door near the back. It was almost completely obstructed by boxes. "Where does that go?"

"Storage," Harrington replied.

He approached the door, pushed it open, and turned on the light. There were several crates, although some were open. Valuable castle objects were partially packed within the crates.

"That can't be the missing treasure, can it?" she asked with surprise.

Harrington frowned. "No, apparently Frank's been stealing from the castle for months " He sank into thought then guided her back to the door. "I think we'd better return to the others. This may not be a safe place to be right now."

"Perhaps Duke Alden was aware that Frank was stealing and that's why he killed him," Naomi suggested.

Harrington glared at her then became angry. "He called for me that night just before he was killed. He'd taken a walk. According to the journal, he'd been down here and found the jewels. It's possible he intended to fire Frank." He sank into his own thoughts. "I think I need to have another look at that journal."

§

*H*arrington sat on the duke's bed while reading the journal then finally shut it and set it on the nightstand. He appeared deep in thought. Naomi sat on the bed alongside him and awaited an explanation.

"I'm positive he ran into Frank in the dungeon and fired him himself."

"I just can't understand why your ghosts would save me and not the duke," she said with some confusion.

Harrington glared at her. "What are you talking about?"

Naomi nervously bit her lower lip. "That knight in the hall saved me from Diane."

"I thought you said you'd passed out," Harrington remarked.

Naomi smiled with embarrassment. "I did. I just skipped the part about the knight protecting me from Diane."

He stared at her a moment while oddly silent. "I think they enjoy playing with you. They must like you," he replied simply.

Naomi stared at him in disbelief. "I thought you didn't believe in ghosts?"

"I lied," he replied with a devious smile meant to mock her. "You're correct. I know most of them by name."

"I can't believe you allowed me to think I was crazy!"

Harrington inhaled deeply and smiled. "I've learned a long time ago never to speak of the castle ghosts. I wasn't sure why they chose to torment you. They usually have their reasons. Perhaps they chose you because you write. Ghost knights have huge egos."

"I can't believe you!"

"It's not easy for me to admit this to you," he said simply. "I've never mentioned the ghosts to anyone--not even Duke Alden. Though I think he knew they existed."

"What are we going to do about Frank?" Naomi asked. "I don't know that any of us are safe particularly you."

Harrington sighed. "I can't allow him to slip out when the police arrive."

"You can't go after him, Harrington. He'll be expecting it," Naomi said sternly.

"You'd better rest."

Harrington stood and left the room. Naomi sprang from the bed and hurried after him, stopping him in the hallway just outside the master chamber.

"I don't know what's running through that thick, British head of yours, Harrington, but you can't be serious," she announced. "This is not a game."

"I'm aware of the situation, madam," he replied simply. "If Frank wants to get out of this castle when help arrives, he's going to go through me to get away. He hates me anyway. I may as well face him, don't you agree?"

"So you're going to go looking for him?" she announced in anger. "You can't do that!"

"Why not?"

Naomi stared into his eyes and searched for an answer to his question. Without thought, she moved toward him and kissed him passionately on the mouth. Harrington tensed with surprise. Naomi pulled away just as quickly. She blushed then hurried back down the hall.

Chapter Seventeen

*F*rank hung limp from shackles attached to the wall. He slowly woke with disorientation as blood matted the hair near the side of his head. As a shadow moved past him, he watched with apparent confusion.

"What are you doing?" Frank gasped nervously and pulled on the shackles. "Get me out of these!"

The duke's sword was raised.

"What are you doing? Are you crazy?" Frank cried out with a look of horror on his face.

The broadsword was swung at Frank as he struggled against the shackles. Frank saw the sword coming at him and cried out only briefly. Then there was silence.

*T*here was a loud explosion, immediately followed by another. Seconds passed before the third explosion. Harrington stood behind the cannon on the roof of the castle in the cool, damp night air. Everyone ran across the roof and slowed when they saw him. Harrington saw the others approaching and casually leaned on the cannon.

"Sorry, did I wake you?"

"What the hell's going on?" Lydia demanded to know. "What are you trying to do? Kill someone?"

"No," Harrington replied while eyeing the others. "That's already been done for me." He stared at the small group. "Moments ago, I found Frank dead in the dungeon. He'd been decapitated with the duke's sword."

Ryan snorted and smiled bitterly. "You expect us to believe that? If Frank was killed with the duke's sword, then you're the one who killed him."

"That was the killer's intention," Harrington replied. "To make me look guilty."

"What's with the cannon?" Donna asked.

"A last chance effort to call for help," Harrington replied. "Someone from the mainland should hear it and report it to the police."

"Are you saying someone's framing you for Frank's death?" George suddenly asked.

"It would be logical. Everyone here knows I would avenge the duke," Harrington replied then eyed the remaining group. "I know what's going on in this castle. While I've been searching for the killer, the rest of you have been searching for the missing jewels. Jewels I'd have sworn never existed." He raised a cold brow. "It would appear I was wrong. Duke Alden discovered the jewels the night he was murdered. Frank found their location from the duke's journal, and that's why he was killed."

"You're insane," Ryan burst out then laughed. "How can you accuse us? None of us knew about those jewels before we'd arrived. Just a myth, remember?"

Donna folded her arms across her chest and glared at Ryan. "That's a lie!" She looked at Harrington. "Ryan came here for the sole purpose of finding those jewels. I didn't know anything about his plan until after we'd arrived."

"Donna," Ryan gasped.

"I'm not covering for you. I know exactly what your intentions were in Joanne's room," Donna snarled. "You wanted to extract information from her and seduce her."

"So he murdered her," Bradly deducted with enthusiasm.

"It would've been impossible for him to have murdered Joanne," Harrington replied. "He was seen by Ms. Beller and Mr. Westinghouse while Joanne was still alive. After that, he had an alibi."

"What about Diane?" Bradly asked. "You said she'd tried to kill Naomi. She's the logical suspect."

"It would've been impossible for Diane to move a man of Frank's size. Someone here is her accomplice," Harrington announced simply then stared at Bradly. "I saw you coming from the dungeon stairs just before I'd gone down them. Did you happen to run into Frank?"

"I didn't kill him!" Bradly looked around at the others. "Okay. You want to know everything I know? I was in a bar about two months ago. It was a small, quiet place just off the docks. While I was there, I overheard a conversation at the table behind my barstool. There were three people at that table. Frank, Diane, and Joanne. They were drunk and talked a little loud. Frank was talking to Joanne about the jewels. I listened to them plan and plot to steal the jewels and came up with my own plan." He raised his head proudly. "I'm a wimp by nature. I wouldn't have gotten involved had I suspected anyone would die."

Naomi glared at George. "A bar near the docks?"

George rolled his eyes and groaned. "I was bartending earlier that night. I had just finished my shift and overheard their conversation." He looked around defensively. "Who couldn't? They were loud enough."

"George," Naomi gasped with surprise then anger.

George frowned and appeared embarrassed. "It wasn't like that, Naomi. I wasn't out to hurt anyone." He then eyed the others. "Nothing was *ever* mentioned about hurting anyone. I thought they intended to steal the jewels." He glared at Harrington. "Naomi knew nothing about the jewels."

Harrington remained cold. "I suggest everyone return to their rooms and not leave until the police arrive."

§

Donna read a book while casually sitting on her bed with her back to the headboard. She turned the page while sighing softly. Someone could be heard walking in the hallway. She lowered the book and stared at the door with concern. The old-fashioned deadbolt was across the door, allowing her to relax a little. Donna inhaled nervously then returned to her book. She then heard a faint creak from within the walls. Donna sat forward and looked around the room. When she didn't hear anything else, she leaned back and returned to her book. She heard another faint creak. The panel in the wall just near the bed opened. Donna suddenly tensed and turned her head toward the opened panel. Her eyes widened with a look of horror.

§

*N*aomi stood with George in the first floor grand hallway and stared at him while shaking her head with disappointment. "I can't believe you're acting this way. What possessed you even to consider taking those jewels?" she demanded.

"I owe people money, Naomi. I need to pay them," George said then held his breath. "I had to do something."

Naomi's look didn't soften. "You could've come to me. You know I'd give you the money."

George lowered his head with shame. "I was embarrassed. I didn't want to be like your other so-called friends always asking for money."

"When we get back, I'll give you the money you need to pay this guy," Naomi told him firmly.

"Thank you," George said timidly.

Bradly ran down the steps with excitement then rushed past them and up the foyer steps toward the doors. "There are men at the gate!"

Naomi and George chased after him into the courtyard. Two men stood on the opposite side of the gate and studied it. Harrington was already at the gate talking with them.

"This is pretty thick," the one man announced. "It'll take a while to cut through it."

"There's an old gate around back in the cemetery," Harrington informed the worker. "It was welded shut six months ago. You could cut through that one in less time. I'd prefer you cut that one anyway."

"If you could wait until morning--" the man began.

"No, it can't wait," Harrington said firmly. "I'll pay you extra to get it done tonight."

"How much?" the second man asked.

"Name your price. Just get the gate open," Harrington remarked.

The first man grinned. "Sure, we'll get her open. We have to go back for our cutting torches. It'll probably be about two hours until we can get you out."

Harrington appeared nervous. "Is that the soonest you can have it opened?"

"I'm afraid so. Is there a problem?" the man asked and appeared slightly concerned.

"Just a domestic dispute," Harrington replied simply. "Kindly bring the police with you. I'd like their assistance when the gate is opened."

"Are you sure there isn't something we should know about?" the second man asked.

"No, nothing that would concern you. Just bring the police with you." Harrington turned and walked past Naomi, George, and Bradly.

"Moody bastard, eh?" George scoffed.

"I'm going to tell the others about the workers," Bradly announced cheerfully then turned and hurried into the castle.

Naomi looked at George. "I need to talk to Harrington."

"Must you?" George asked.

"Yes," she replied firmly.

Chapter Eighteen

Harrington sat behind the desk in the study staring at the computer monitor while seemingly engrossed in his work. Naomi gently tapped on the open door and entered. Harrington briefly looked up then returned to the computer.

"I'm very busy, Miss Remus," he announced coldly.

Naomi approached the desk. "Is everything okay?"

Harrington glared at her. "No, everything is not okay. I'm about to be arrested for murder." He looked back at the computer. "I've lost control somewhere along the way, and I don't know how to deal with the situation."

Naomi rounded the desk and glanced at the screen. Harrington was playing solitaire. "You didn't kill Frank," she insisted. "They'll find out who the real killer is."

Harrington suddenly glared at her. "How do you know I didn't kill him?"

"You wouldn't have left the sword there if you wanted to get away with it," she insisted. "Or you'd be proud of the fact and admit it openly."

Harrington leaned back in his chair but didn't look at her. "I'm very tired," he announced gently. "Please, just go back to your room. I'd prefer to be left alone."

Naomi stared at him and shook her head in disgust. "Does anything penetrate that concrete wall you've built around yourself?" she demanded. "I'm trying to help you. Why do you keep pushing me away?"

Harrington stared at the computer without a word.

Naomi frowned and huffed with annoyance. "Fine. I've just about exhausted myself trying to figure you out," she remarked. "It's obvious I'll never get through."

Naomi turned and walked toward the study door. Harrington suddenly stood and hurried after her. He slammed the door shut from behind just before she reached it. Naomi turned with surprise and looked at him.

Harrington stared into her eyes with a gentle look. "You've gotten through." He touched her cheek. "I thought I could resist you, but I'm not that strong."

Naomi smiled warmly as her cheeks reddened. She moved closer to him and ran her hand along his tie with an innocent look on her face. "Then don't resist."

Harrington stared at her a long moment, seeming more nervous than she was. He lowered his mouth to hers and gently kissed her. Naomi sank into his arms and immediately returned the kiss. The kiss swiftly turned more passionate.

Harrington moaned then pulled away and fidgeted. "Would you consider staying after the others have gone?"

"I'd like that very much."

Harrington smiled with some embarrassment, again fidgeted, and then pulled her against him, kissing her passionately.

§

Bradly hurried along the hallway while looking into several rooms. "Harrington! Harrington!"

The study door opened, surprising Bradly. Harrington slipped out with a flustered look on his face and appeared slightly out of breath. His hair was moderately rumpled, and his tie was crooked. He attempted to straighten his tie without Bradly noticing.

Bradly hurried toward him. "There you are. The men are here to fix the gate," he announced. "George is giving them directions to the cemetery. You're supposed to meet them at the cemetery gate." Bradly eyed him suspiciously. "Why are you out of breath?"

Harrington gently cleared his throat. "I was rearranging the study." He stepped past Bradly. "Excuse me."

Bradly watched him leave. Once he was gone, Bradly looked back at the study door and gently pushed it open. Naomi sat in front of the computer and looked up. Her cheeks were red, and her hair was slightly mussed.

"Care to play some solitaire?"

Bradly eyed her with confusion. "Uh, no, thanks. I can't find Donna anywhere. Do you know where she could be?"

Naomi stared at him with surprise and stopped pretending to play on the computer. "No. She must be around somewhere. Have you checked Ryan's room?"

"Ryan said he hadn't seen her," Bradly replied.

Naomi sprang to her feet. "We have to find her. I hope nothing's happened."

"I'll find George. He can help search," Bradly announced. "You should wait in your room where it's safe."

"I hardly think--" Naomi attempted to speak.

"The police will be here soon," Bradly announced simply. "There's no reason for all of us to put our necks on the line. Just wait in your room."

Naomi frowned as Bradly left the room. Once he was gone, she adjusted her shirt and slipped into her shoes that had been beneath the desk. She stuffed her bra into the top desk drawer and hurried from the room.

§

*H*arrington hurried through the dungeon with the duke's sword in his hand. As he passed the torture chamber, a shadow was cast on the wall behind him holding what appeared to be a crowbar. It crashed down on Harrington's head.

§

*N*aomi paced the small bedroom in the staff wing and stared at her watch. It had been nearly an hour since she returned to her room. She groaned and ran her fingers through her hair. There was a knock on the bedroom door causing her to jump nervously. She hurried to the door.

"Who is it?" she asked while feeling her heart pound.

"It's me," George said in a shaken voice. "Please let me in. Something's happened."

Naomi lunged for the door and fumbled with the lock before pulling it open. George stood in the doorway with a shaken look on his face.

"We found Harrington in the dungeon," he announced in a docile tone. "He's been killed."

Naomi's eyes were wide with horror. "There has to be some mistake."

"There's been no mistake. I saw him for myself in the torture chamber," George gently informed her then fidgeted. "He'd, uh, been beheaded."

Naomi gasped with wide, horrified eyes. "No!"

George attempted to hold her, but she was quick to push him away.

"I want to be alone, please," she sobbed.

George nodded and left the room.

Chapter Nineteen

Naomi walked through the dungeon carrying one of the antique swords from the wall. Her expression was hard and cold as hatred and anger consumed her. Knights were lined along the dimly lit corridor casting frightening shadows that could easily hide an ambush. She only cast brief glances at the knights and the dark corners. She was on a mission, and nothing would stop her. Naomi paused before the torture chamber door and peered inside. Harrington's body lay sprawled across the chopping block. The stained ax was still embedded in the blood-covered block before his neck. Naomi choked on her sobs as tears rolled down her cheeks. She sobbed for several minutes then opened her eyes, drew a deep breath, and approached the slain man. She lowered herself to her knees alongside him.

"Oh, Harrington--" she whispered and touched his outstretched hand.

She held back her tears and avoided looking at his severed neck above the shoulders, despite all the blood. As she held his hand, she noticed his ring was missing, and there wasn't the usual tale tell sign of the ring's indent on his finger. Naomi looked at the bloody basket almost certainly containing his head where it remained alongside the chopping block. She felt a strange pang. She slowly stood, inched her way closer, and peered into the bloody basket. She could only see the severed neck, which was enough to send chills down her spine. She had to know. Naomi held her breath, placed her foot on the edge of the basket, and toppled it. She heard the distinct sound of a head rolling across the stone floor. She had to force herself to look at the severed head. Despite being covered with blood, she could easily identify the man's head. It was Frank! Naomi was relieved yet confused.

Why put him in Harrington's uniform? She then considered the question and came to her own conclusions. If everyone thought he faked his own death, they wouldn't look for the real killer. Her eyes suddenly widened.

"They need him alive! He's not dead yet!"

Naomi stared at Frank's headless body and recognized Harrington's ruined uniform from the shaft the other day, explaining why the blood was dried on his shirt. The dried blood was almost brown in color. Brown. Brown stains in the tub? Not dirt; dye. Her eyes widened with a shocked realization. It wasn't Joanne arguing with Ryan; it was Diane with brown hair! She pretended to be her sister to give them an alibi. They'd already killed Joanne! Naomi ran from the torture chamber.

§

*H*arrington woke from where he lay on the stone floor within another part of the dungeon. As he slowly sat up, he placed a hand on his throbbing head. Diane stood over him and twirled the duke's sword.

"I'm glad you're alive," Diane said gently with a tiny smile. "For a moment, I thought I'd killed you."

Harrington held his head while staring at her. "That wasn't your intention?"

"If you tell me where the jewels are, I'll let you live," Diane remarked.

Harrington snorted a laugh. "I'm not that stupid. Either way, I'm going to die," he remarked then sneered at her. "I may as well die leaving you bloody well pissed at me."

"Don't make me kill you, Avery. I don't want to do it," Diane scoffed.

"Your partner won't allow me to live," Harrington informed her. "I'm the perfect scapegoat."

Diane smiled wickedly. "I have plans of my own." She lowered herself before him, turning more affectionate. "If you cooperate, we could be rich together."

"And your partner?"

"How do you know I have a partner?" she asked.

"There isn't a brain between you and Frank," he replied without emotion.

Diane frowned, obviously not happy with the insult. "It's not important." Her smile then returned. "You and I don't need partners. We have each other. Join me, Avery, and we'll have it all."

Harrington glared at her without emotion.

"There's not much time to decide. Naomi's about to become the bait for your complete cooperation," Diane announced. "It's not too late to stop him from hurting her."

Harrington's look turned hard and angry. "What have you done with Naomi?"

Diane frowned with disapproval. "Oh, now it's Naomi?" She became angry. "I knew there was more between you two than you led on."

Harrington grabbed the sword blade with his right hand and slowly stood with anger in his eyes. Diane appeared surprised and attempted to pull the sword from his clenched hand. Even though blood ran down his hand, he didn't release the sword or take his eyes off her. Harrington grabbed for her with his free hand. Diane gasped in horror and released the sword. Despite his injury, he flipped the sword through the air and caught the handle in his bloodied hand. Diane removed a gun from the back of her pants and aimed it at him. Her look was horrified then stiffened to something resembling anger.

"Poor choice," she scoffed.

"If Ryan so much as touches Naomi, I'll show you just how much I know about medieval torture," Harrington growled while glaring into her eyes.

Harrington turned, ignoring the gun she held, and walked toward the door. Diane pulled the trigger. The shot echoed through the room. Harrington clutched his left thigh then turned and hit the wall with his back. He looked at the bullet graze on his leg but didn't advance any closer to Diane. She aimed the gun at his head with a little more confidence.

"I didn't want to have to do it, but you gave me no choice!" Diane inhaled deeply then relaxed. "I suppose it wasn't too hard to put it together about Ryan. Frank killed Jake and Mark after cutting the chain to the gate, but Joanne nearly ruined everything with her petty jealousy of Donna, so I pretended to be Joanne to give us an alibi during her death. It was the perfect plan." She sneered her anger. "I could stop him from harming you, but you just won't listen."

Harrington shifted in pain. "Was it really necessary to kill Duke Alden?"

Diane frowned, although she didn't seem proud of the fact. "Yes, it was. He ran into Frank that night," she replied. "Duke Alden fired him on the spot. Unfortunately, for the duke, he wasn't aware that Frank hadn't been down here alone. Ryan went up to the duke's chamber and killed him."

"How does Ryan figure into all of this?" Harrington asked while tilting his head.

"He and Joanne were married. That's why Joanne was so upset about Donna." Diane smiled lightly. "It's not too late to change your mind, Avery. Naomi doesn't have to die. We can kill Ryan and take the jewels for ourselves." She smiled slyly. "I know you have the jewels."

Harrington leaned against the wall with less hostility. "I'd assume hang myself than spend a moment with you."

She sneered at him. "You give me no choice but to kill you," Diane said coldly.

Harrington shrugged with little regard. "That might be difficult, considering you have a sword aimed at your back."

"Come on, I'm not that stupid," Diane remarked while sneering at him.

"Sure you are," Naomi casually announced from where she stood behind Diane.

She spun around with alarm, saw Naomi behind her, and attempted to aim the gun at her. Naomi thrust her sword into Diane's mid-section. She cried out while clutching her abdomen, dropping the gun. Their eyes met for a moment. Naomi's stare was cold as she pulled the sword free, allowing Diane to sink to the floor. Naomi shut her eyes, exhaled, and dropped the sword. Harrington stood with some discomfort. She looked at him with relief and rushed into his arms. Harrington held her against him while burying his face into her hair.

"Thank God you're alive," Harrington gasped.

Naomi pulled back while looking at him as she sniffed and added a tiny smile. "Me? You should see the length they went to make me think you were dead!"

"The police should be through the gate any minute now," Harrington announced. "Let's go upstairs and wait with the others. I'm through avenging the deceased."

"Wise decision," Ryan replied from the doorway.

Both turned. Ryan picked up Diane's gun and aimed it at them. He reached for the duke's discarded sword and held it in his free hand. He looked at Diane's lifeless body on the floor and shook his head with mild disappointment.

"She really was a stupid girl," he remarked then looked at Harrington and Naomi. "What do you say we go upstairs and have a look at those jewels?"

"He doesn't have them," Naomi boldly announced.

Ryan laughed. "That's where you're wrong. They were hidden in the cannon," he remarked. "After his signal for help, they were gone. He purposely made himself a target to flush me out. Unfortunately for him, it worked."

Naomi eyed Harrington with surprise. Ryan showed little expression as he motioned them from the room. As they entered the corridor, they could hear someone pounding on the cemetery door. The police made it through, but there was no one to let them into the dungeon.

Chapter Twenty

Naomi and Harrington walked quietly through the first floor hallway with Ryan following them. He had the sword in one hand and the gun in the other. Harrington stopped just outside the study and turned to face Ryan.

"This is where I stop, Ryan," Harrington informed him. "The jewels are in the safe. Only I have the combination. You can have the jewels, but you must let Naomi go first."

"You must be out of your mind. As long as I have her, you'll do what I say," he remarked with a low chuckle. "You'll retaliate the moment she's free. The staff had warned me about your reputation."

"I could allow you to kill me without giving you the jewels as well, but I'm willing to bargain for Naomi's life," Harrington said. "If you don't set her free now, I know you'll kill her."

"She'll be set free after the safe is opened," Ryan casually informed him.

Harrington glared at Ryan and sighed. "You give me no choice." He made a fist and exposed the ring on his pinkie. "This ring belonged to the daughter of King Chasity," he remarked simply. "It's a symbol of royalty. Many centuries ago, the knights in the castle vowed to protect their king. A vow they were unable to keep."

"All right, history class is over," Ryan groaned while rolling his eyes. "If you intend to resist, do it now, so I can shoot you and get it over with."

Harrington shrugged with little emotion. "I have no intentions of fighting you. I was just explaining that I'm of royal descent," he casually replied. "See, the knights of Wesley Castle are under my command."

Naomi rolled her eyes and muttered something under her breath. She didn't know what he was up to, but it had to be the worst bluff in history.

Ryan burst out laughing, humored by the comment. "If the ghost knights could've protected anyone, they'd have saved Duke Alden. They didn't do a very good job protecting him."

"Oh? So what happened to the knight at Duke Alden's bedside?" Harrington asked.

Ryan's smile faded, obviously traumatized by whatever had happened. "That was my imagination; nothing more."

"There's something you should know about the knights in this castle. They would protect the duke, certainly, but they were the king's knights." Harrington looked around the hall. "Upon my royal command, I order every knight to come forth and seek vengeance upon this man for the murder of Duke Alden Wesley."

Naomi looked around the hallway and cringed slightly at his words. Naturally, nothing moved. Harrington didn't appear concerned.

Ryan casually looked around as well then smirked and laughed. "Enough fun and games, Harrington. Into the study."

Harrington frowned and entered the study with Naomi. Ryan entered behind them and shut the door so that they wouldn't be disturbed. Harrington eyed Naomi, indicating she should sit on the sofa. Naomi slowly sat where indicated and looked at Ryan. Harrington approached the painting of the duchess and pulled it away from the wall to reveal a wall safe. They heard the sound of clanking steel from outside the room. Naomi looked around with some confusion.

Ryan glared at her, not hearing anything. "What's with you?"

"I thought I heard something," she replied nervously.

"That won't work on me," Ryan growled.

Harrington looked into the safe and appeared stunned. "It's gone!"

Ryan grabbed Naomi, pulled her to her feet, and forced her to join Harrington by the safe. Harrington gathered Naomi into his arms and moved toward the bookcase just out of Ryan's way. Ryan looked into the empty safe and removed a folded piece of paper. He appeared bewildered and opened it.

He read the note aloud. "The jewels belong to me. Leave my castle or die. Duke Alden Wesley." He dropped the note and glared at Harrington. "Very funny. Where are they?"

Harrington stared at Ryan with wide eyes. "I'd never disrespect the duke by leaving that sort of note. It had to be his ghost. We never found his body. His spirit is restless."

The sound of metal clanking in the hallway was getting louder and possibly closer. Ryan looked toward the hall door, having heard the sound that time.

"What's that sound?" he asked.

"It's the knights," Harrington replied simply while clinging to Naomi. "They're coming for you."

"Sure they are," Ryan remarked with a nervous smile then pointed the gun at them. "Stay there."

Ryan backed up to the door and opened it. A sword struck the doorframe and became embedded in the wood. Ryan gasped, slammed the door, and looked at them with horror.

"You're going to get me out of here!"

Harrington pointed across the room. "There's a secret passageway behind the fireplace."

As Ryan looked at the fireplace, Harrington pulled on a book within the bookcase behind him. The case popped away from the wall next to them. Without warning, he shoved Naomi through the opening. Ryan saw them and fired the gun at them just as Harrington closed the bookcase, trapping Ryan on the other side. The secret opening took them into the weapons room. As she stared into the room, shock and horror crossed Naomi's face. They watched empty suits of armor milling about the room gathering swords and shields from the walls. Harrington guided Naomi toward the door and looked into the hallway. Seventy ghost knights in hollow armor marched in rows along the hallway. Ryan appeared from the study and shot at the knights marching toward him, bullets ricocheting off their metal chests until the gun clicked empty. As Ryan ran down the hall, Harrington slipped into the hallway and entered the study next door. He returned with the duke's sword.

"Go to the dungeon entrance and let the police in," he firmly instructed.

"What about you?" she asked.

"I'll be fine," Harrington replied and grinned. "I have an army on my side."

Harrington pushed past the knights and raised his sword. "After him!"

The ghost knights jogged behind Harrington into battle. The metallic clanking was almost deafening. Naomi attempted to make her way to the kitchen while nearly being crushed by the knight's broad, metal shoulders. She ran around the corner in the hall and collided with George. Both fell to the floor. Naomi sprang to her feet, but George remained in a sitting position.

"Did you see what I just saw?" he cried out.

"I'm afraid I did," Naomi replied as she helped him to his feet. "George, you have to go to the dungeon and let the police inside. I have to help Harrington."

George appeared shocked while staring at her. "Naomi, he's dead, remember?"

"No, he's alive," she told him. "That was Frank's body. It's a long story."

Naomi ran along the hallway in the direction Harrington had gone with his ghost army.

§

Ryan entered the lounge, slammed the door behind him, and panted while fumbling with the lock. Metal could be heard striking the door. A sword splintered the wood near Ryan's face. He cried out and jumped away from the door. He looked around nervously and ran for the bookcase toward the back of the room. He had to remove several books before triggering the secret passageway, allowing the bookcase to open. Ryan hurried into the passageway and shut it behind him.

Moments later, the panel alongside the fireplace opened in Duke Alden's master chamber. Ryan hurried through the opening and looked around the room. The remaining suit of armor alongside the bed was now missing as well. The rumbling from the lower floors became louder as the ghost knights ran through the castle, although they seemed to be on the first and second floors. He felt fairly safe on the third floor. The sound of whispering voices filled the chamber, causing Ryan to look around. He hurried across the room and removed a sword from the wall. Dozens of ghostly apparitions materialized and whizzed past him, circling the room. Ryan stared in horror at the specters as they flew past his face attempting to frighten him. It worked! He cried out while backing across the room and into the bedpost.

As Ryan spun around, he stared in horror upon seeing Duke Alden standing before him. He was clearly dead but somehow standing before him. Ryan gasped as the duke grabbed him by the throat and slammed him against the bedpost with surprising force for an old dead man. The duke raised the gold dagger in his right hand. Ryan gasped and pulled free just as the dagger was thrust downward. The dagger sliced his arm and struck the bedpost. Ryan screamed with surprise and pain then ran across the room. When he turned and looked behind him, Duke Alden approached with the bloody dagger in his hand. Ryan cried out with horror and ran from the master chamber.

Chapter Twenty-one

*N*aomi stood in the kitchen and stared at the ceiling while listening to the sounds seemingly echoing from every corner of the castle. The knights in armor could be heard from the floor above her. The entire castle appeared to vibrate along with the deafening sound. She jumped nervously while attempting to follow the sounds of clanking metal from every direction. She heard someone on the kitchen stairs. Naomi spun around and nearly collided with Ryan as he appeared from the staircase. Her eyes widened, but she held back her gasp.

He grabbed her wrist and yanked her harshly while staring into her eyes with fear. "You're getting me out of here," Ryan cried out while darting looks around him.

"I don't think so," she casually replied.

"You don't really have a choice," he announced as his fear turned to hostility.

Naomi stomped on his foot then kicked him in the shin. He yelped then swung his sword at her as she turned to run. Naomi came face-to-face with the knight from the dungeon with the dented shoulder. The knight swung its sword at her. She cried out and ducked then heard a loud, metallic clash above her head. The knight blocked Ryan's sword that had nearly cut her in half. Naomi rolled out of their path. The knight aggressively swung at Ryan while he blocked several blows before he turned and ran from the kitchen. Naomi stared with surprise at the knight from where she sat on the kitchen floor. The knight extended its metal hand to her. She uncertainly accepted it and allowed it to help her to her feet.

§

*H*arrington stepped into the hallway and cautiously approached the foyer. Ryan sprang out from the dining room and swung the heavy sword for Harrington's head. Harrington blocked the blow with his own sword. The force of the blow nearly sent Harrington to his knees. Ryan backed up and swung again. Their swords collided with a loud clash as sparks flew. Harrington pulled back and struck again. Ryan blocked the blow but was thrown back against the wall. He straightened and ran for the front door with Harrington chasing after him. Several knights appeared in the hallway and followed them into the courtyard.

Both men ran across the courtyard. Harrington chased Ryan up the courtyard steps to the ledge on the wall overlooking the moat. Several knights followed Harrington up the small, stone steps. Others went to the opposite side, scaled a second set of steps, and approached Ryan from behind, cutting off his path. There was a huge block missing along the walkway, trapping Ryan. Ryan gripped his sword and looked around, attempting to plot a way around the missing block.

"Give it up, Ryan," Harrington growled. "There's no way off except down."

"Or through you," Ryan replied and leveled his sword. "What happens if I kill you? Do the ghosts just die with you? I think it's worth finding out."

"You don't want to fight me," Harrington announced in a calm tone.

"I'm skilled at fencing," Ryan said with a mocking smile. "I can take you."

Harrington stood his ground and lifted his sword. Ryan swung the heavy sword while Harrington easily blocked the blow. Ryan made several more attempts to strike the armed butler, but Harrington skillfully stopped each swing without much exertion. Ryan was panting and losing strength.

"You seem to forget. I was raised in this castle," Harrington announced and twirled the sword in his hand. "Antique swords make wonderful toys for a bored little boy. Slightly heavier than your fencing foils, wouldn't you say?"

Ryan swung at Harrington. They again battled with the swords. Naomi watched from the courtyard below as the two men clashed swords on the high wall. Ryan blocked Harrington's sword and kicked him in the abdomen then came back at him with the tip of the sword. Harrington managed to block the deadly blow and nearly lost his balance. He fell against the three-foot wall overlooking the moat.

Naomi ran past the knights watching the fight and hurried up the steps to the walkway. She was directly behind the two knights nearest Harrington.

Harrington recovered quickly and stopped the next blow from Ryan's sword. Ryan grunted with each swing, the weight of the sword wearing him down. Steel clashed with each blow. Naomi looked down to the courtyard below. Bradly, George, and the two police officers ran across the courtyard and looked up at them. She looked down at the moat on the other side of the half wall. Something surfaced then sank below the murky waters. Could it be the moat monster? Harrington nearly lost his footing on the ledge by the aggressive swings of the tiring Ryan. Naomi feared for Harrington. She climbed onto the half wall and crawled along it past the first knight. She teetered a moment and looked at the moat below. She then looked at the castle and saw a woman in the tower window watching the battle. Could it be the princess?

Ryan continued to swing hard. He swung high and nearly decapitated Harrington. Harrington struck back with his own series of blows. Ryan was almost out of energy. He made a hasty swing. Harrington leveled his sword, lunged forward, and drove the sword into Ryan. Ryan gasped with agony and froze while staring into Harrington's eyes. Harrington pulled the blade back and straightened. Ryan dropped his sword, clutched his bleeding stomach, and fell from the wall to the courtyard below. Naomi relaxed with a relieved sigh from where she was positioned on the half wall. The knight before her turned. Its broad shoulder struck her, and she toppled off the ledge. Naomi screamed as she plummeted into the moat below. There was a loud splash as she entered the water.

"Naomi!" Harrington cried over the ledge.

Harrington tossed the duke's sword aside, removed his jacket, and jumped over the wall into the moat. The knights on the castle wall peered into the moat below. Naomi struggled to swim to the surface after having touched the murky bottom. She was tangled in plant life and couldn't break free. Something big, brown, and green pulled her free and pushed her to the surface. Naomi appeared above the water and gasped for air. She looked around the dirty moat. Harrington surfaced after her, but she knew he hadn't been the one who saved her.

"Are you okay?" Harrington gasped.

Naomi looked around the dirty water. "There's something down there!"

Harrington gave her a puzzled look then dove under the water. A moment passed before he resurfaced and shook his head. "I wouldn't believe it if I hadn't seen it for myself."

Naomi appeared horrified. "What is it?"

"It's the missing knight from the duke's chamber," he informed her. "It was missing the night he died. When it attempted to defend Duke Alden, Ryan must've cast it out the window."

Chapter Twenty-two

The remaining guests gathered in the lounge along with the police and emergency technicians. A paramedic finished wrapping Harrington's hand and leg while the other guests talked with the police, describing their ordeal. The knight with the dented shoulder was still within the lounge, guarding the doorway and refusing to leave Naomi's side. Detective Addams entered the lounge and suspiciously eyed the knight.

"Everything seems to check out with the stories you've given," Addams announced then cleared his throat. "I may have trouble explaining the ghosts to my superiors though."

"The duke's body is still missing. We don't know what became of him," Harrington informed him with moderate concern.

"We've checked into that for you," Addams remarked. "I assure you, he's in his casket where he belongs."

Harrington appeared confused as he stared at the detective. "But he wasn't there, I swear," he announced.

"We all saw it," George confirmed.

Addams shrugged. "Well, he's there now. Two officers swear they saw seventy ghost knights return to their posts," the detective informed him. "I'm willing to believe the duke took himself back to his casket at this point."

"I suppose it was a bit crowded for him earlier," Harrington said with a sigh.

"Donna's still missing," Naomi announced with concern. "Has anyone found her?"

"We're still looking for her," Addams replied. "It'll take some time to cover the entire castle."

An officer entered the lounge with Donna, who appeared worn and dirty. Harrington and Naomi sprang to their feet and hurried toward her.

"You're alive," Harrington proclaimed.

"Of course I am," she replied firmly then glared at Naomi. "What took you so long to send help? You saw me in the tower window."

Naomi appeared surprised. "That was you? I thought--" She smiled with embarrassment. "Never mind."

"How did you get locked in the tower?" Harrington asked with surprise.

"Ryan abducted me from my room and locked me in there when I realized what he was up to," Donna remarked. "I don't know why he didn't just kill me."

"Maybe he really did care about you," Naomi gently informed her.

"I don't think he was ever capable of feelings," Donna remarked. She was then was escorted from the room where she would be taken to an awaiting boat.

George approached Naomi and indicated one of the officers. "Our boat is waiting," he announced then eyed Harrington and looked back at his friend. "Did you want a moment?"

She nodded then watched her friend leave the lounge. Naomi and Harrington were finally alone for the first time in hours. He appeared nervous and fidgeted.

"We should probably join the others on the boat," he announced and straightened proudly.

She stared at him with surprise. "You want to return to the mainland?" Naomi asked.

"Don't you?" Harrington countered.

Naomi smiled gently. "I don't mind staying here. I can deal with the ghosts." Naomi cocked her head to one side. "Though I am curious about something."

"What's that?" Harrington asked.

"Who left the note in the safe? And what happened to the jewels?"

Harrington smiled and chuckled. "Oh, that's quite simple. I knew the safe would be the first place someone would look, so I wrote the note and hid the jewels in a very safe place."

Naomi appeared surprised while staring at him. "You had the jewels the entire time?"

"I had to make sure there weren't any balls in the cannon before I fired it. Wouldn't want to accidentally sink any boats in the harbor," he informed her while grinning. "Just pure luck that I'd found them, I assure you."

Naomi shook her head and laughed. "So where did you hide the jewels?"

"The one place no one would ever think to look for them," he announced then smiled deviously. "The vacuum sweeper."

Naomi laughed.

Harrington nodded toward her knight. "It would seem your guardian knight has failed to return to his post." He smiled at her. "I guess he'll only listen to you."

Naomi smiled warmly then stood and turned toward the knight. "That will be all, gallant knight."

The knight remained standing by the door. Harrington and Naomi exchanged puzzled looks. When Naomi looked back at the knight, he removed an envelope from his metal plated chest. Naomi slowly approached and accepted the envelope. The knight turned and left the room. Harrington approached and looked over her shoulder. To their surprise, it was Duke Alden's will. They exchanged stunned looks.

"It's the duke's will," Harrington gasped. "How did it get there?"

"Diane said she knew where it was. Perhaps she hid it there for safekeeping," Naomi suggested. "Should we open it?"

Harrington forced a tiny smile and chuckled. "I don't know. I may be out of a job."

"You'll find something else. Something you'll enjoy more," Naomi replied gently.

"Where will I stay?" Harrington asked while eying her.

"I have plenty of room," Naomi replied as her smile brightened. "You could stay with me."

Harrington tilted his head and raised his brows. "Do you mean that? You'd make that sort of commitment?"

Naomi smiled and blushed. "Yes. I love you, Avery."

Harrington remained motionless. A tiny smile crossed his face. "I'd never believe a woman like you could ever want someone like me."

"It's not often a girl finds a genuine butler of royal descent," she replied. "I think you'd be quite an inspiration to my writing."

Harrington smiled warmly and set the will aside. "It's not necessary to read the will."

"Why not?" she asked.

"I know what it says." A tiny smile crossed his face. "Duke Alden left the entire estate to me. He showed it to me a couple of months before he died. Diane must've removed it after his death."

"Why would she do that?" Naomi asked.

"It would've ruined her plans to sweep me off my feet," he said simply. "She didn't know I already knew what was in the will. The police had some suspicions about my involvement in the murder. When the will turned up missing, I thought it was in my best interest that it stayed missing. They'd see it as a motive for murder."

"So what now?" Naomi asked.

Harrington sighed and grinned. "I think it's time I retired. Maybe I'll find a nice, young writer and settle down."

Naomi hid her smile. Harrington gently pulled her into his arms while staring into her eyes a brief moment then kissed her warmly on the lips. Naomi returned the kiss.

§

The sun was setting in the distant harbor where Wesley Castle remained picturesque in the sunset. The portcullis was lowered, and the drawbridge was raised. Two suits of armor stood guard outside the master chamber door. A champagne cork popped from within the room. Naomi was heard giggling. The giggling ceased and was replaced with soft moans. Both knights leaned toward the door and listened.

The End

Fleshies

Chapter One

The elegant castle on American soil was nestled in the well-maintained field beyond a thick forest. An early morning fog lent an eerie atmosphere to what was left of the old structure. Only the main building remained intact. The left wing was left in a pile of ruins. A large, chained gate secured the driveway and deterred anyone from venturing up to the castle. An expensive, black sedan pulled up to the gate, stopped, and shut off. A mysterious man in a long trench coat and fedora got out of the car and unlocked the smaller gate. Once he entered, he closed the gate behind him and began his long walk up the driveway to the castle. The dark-haired man in his late twenties stood nearly six foot tall and had a slightly lean build. Jules Carrington wasn't excessively handsome, but he was charismatic, and his expensive attire garnered attention. He paused before the massive, double doors and used the old, brass knocker to announce his arrival.

Within moments, one door creaked as it opened. Jules inhaled a deep breath, managed an insincere smile, and then entered. As he stood in the foyer, he looked down the four steps to the grand hallway. The grand hall appeared to extend across the entire castle, and as its name suggested, it was massive and tall. A well-dressed man in his late thirties shut the door behind Jules and offered a pleasant smile.

"You're late," he announced then turned and headed down the grand hall.

Jules withheld his sigh of defeat and followed his Uncle Rutger Carrington along the impressive, silent hallway. "You must go insane all alone in this place."

"I have little choice in the matter," Rutger replied, although remaining cheerful. "Besides, I have your bi-weekly visits on Monday mornings and Friday evenings. How much company do I really need?"

They entered through a set of double doors to the room on the right. The library was massive and looked as if it'd been taken straight out of a fairy tale. It extended from the first floor up to the third with balconies, bookshelves, and ladders on rollers in each section.

"That's what I wanted to talk to you about," Jules announced. "Perhaps this weekend--"

Rutger turned to face him with a stern look as if knowing what he intended to say. "Absolutely not," he abruptly announced then resumed his calm demeanor. "I know you're looking out for my best interest, but I don't want any company. The rules are very simple and perfectly clear."

"I can't stand seeing you like this," Jules protested.

Rutger collapsed into a comfortable antique chair by a blazing fire within the marble walk-in fireplace. A book lay on the end table along with a half-filled cup of tea. He smiled pleasantly while eying his nephew.

"Like what?" he asked while looking around with a grin on his face. "I'm not exactly suffering." Rutger picked up the book and smiled cheerfully. "Just received my latest Becka Stone novel. As long as the book club doesn't cancel my membership, I'm in great shape."

Jules appeared slightly annoyed by his uncle's enthusiasm. "I don't know how you can sit there so calm and read."

"What would you suggest I do?" he asked while eying him. "Roller skate about the house?" He chuckled. "Calm is good. Calm maintains harmony in this home. Hatred, anger, and rage bring out the worst in this place. Solitude is sometimes a blessed thing." Rutger studied the cover of the book he held and seemed to sink into his own thoughts. "Have you read any of her books?"

Jules frowned and avoided looking at him as he collapsed onto the expensive, tacky red settee. "I don't care for romantic drivel written by women who've never been on a date." He then muttered. "Probably fat and ugly."

"The cover is simple and lacks artistic appeal, but the words are incredibly beautiful," Rutger informed him while affectionately touching the cover. "Besides, they aren't romance novels." He flipped the book over and flashed the photo on the back cover while grinning. "And she's very easy on the eyes."

Jules glanced at the photo on the back cover. The young author posed in a bold but sensual position, conveying a commanding yet stunning presence. Rutger turned the cover back toward him and smiled contentedly.

"Think she'd have morning tea with me if I'd ask nicely?" he remarked almost to himself.

"You're getting off the subject, Uncle Rutger."

He eyed Jules with a slightly curious look. "I thought Becka *was* the subject."

"I want to get you away from this place," Jules insisted. "Hear me out."

"No, no, no," he adamantly protested. "Out of the question. It's impossible even to suggest." Rutger looked back at the author's photo and smiled. "Perhaps I'll ask her over for Friday evening drinks. A fine cognac."

"I'm trying to help, and you're lusting after some psychotic lesbian," Jules snarled.

Rutger glared at Jules with annoyance. "It's not lust; it's fantasizing," he corrected then glared his disapproval. "And she's *not* a lesbian."

"You've been lost so long in fantasy land; you've mistaken cybersex for the real thing," Jules scoffed while sinking in the settee. "Work with me here."

Rutger appeared offended and pointed a warning finger at his nephew. "And that's another thing," he announced in a stern, commanding tone. "I found out what cybersex means, and I'm not humored. I'm beginning to wonder where you come up with this vulgar stuff."

"If your Becka was on the receiving end you might feel differently," Jules teased.

Rutger held the back cover of the book to his chest as if to spare the author Jules' sexual insinuation. "My dearest Becka is an angelic creature with a warm, compassionate heart. I would treat her with the respect that she deserves."

"I think you're losing it, Uncle Rutger," Jules remarked. "Pretty soon, there won't be a reason to take you away." He appeared defeated and sighed. "Were your supplies delivered on time?"

Rutger casually set the book aside. "Everything but my cupcakes," he replied. "I think one of those plump little deliverymen must've eaten them. If you'd find a bulb for my E-Z Bake Oven, I could make my own."

Jules groaned and refrained from losing patience. "I'll bring more cupcakes on Friday." He shook his head. "You and your cupcakes."

"Will Friday be formal or casual?"

Jules shifted in his seat as if contemplating the odd question. "What the hell. Why not go formal?" he replied. "You can set a place setting for your book and one for the date I'll never have on a Friday night."

"Don't be silly," Rutger announced. "I'm not setting a place at the table for a book." He then paused a moment and tapped the arm of the chair. "I've got a framed photo from a man on the internet. I'll set that out."

Jules stared at him a moment with disbelief then attempted a smile as he stood. "It's getting late," he announced. "I have to get to work, and it's an hour's drive. I'll see you on Friday."

Rutger sprang to his feet. "Don't forget my cupcakes. The chocolate ones with the cream inside."

Jules gave him a slight wave and left the room. "Yeah, yeah," he muttered. "I won't forget your cupcakes."

Rutger slowly returned to his chair. "He has to learn to relax. Must get that from his mother's side." He picked up his teacup and discovered it was empty. Rutger sighed, set the cup down, and then looked at Becka's photo on the back of the book. "Allow me to refill my cup then I'll give you my undivided attention, darling."

He reached beneath his chair and removed a pair of roller blades. As he removed his shoes, he hummed the theme song from "Mr. Roger's neighborhood".

Chapter Two

Friday evening. Every light within the castle's first floor was lit as well as a series of outside lights, which brightened the massive property. Jules' black sedan pulled up to the locked gates and stopped as usual. Jules climbed out of the driver's side. He was dressed in an expensive black suit with a bold, maroon vest. He approached the passenger side door and opened it, extending his hand to his guest.

"Sorry," he remarked to his passenger. "We'll have to walk the rest of the way."

A young woman accepted his hand and got out of the expensive car. Becka Stone was as beautiful as her book cover suggested. Beneath her long, black trench coat, she wore a formal, black evening dress with just enough leg and cleavage to draw attention to her already attention-grabbing body. She wore her long dark hair up in a French twist, adding the perfect, classy touch to her beauty. Becka took a few steps closer to the locked gates and stared at the distant castle. She appeared slightly apprehensive.

Jules stood behind her and noted the uneasy look on her face. "My Uncle Rutger is a very sick man," he informed her timidly. "He refuses to see a doctor, and he'll freak out if you even mention his condition."

Becka glanced back at Jules and appeared sympathetic. "How long does he have?"

"Could be years; could be hours," Jules remarked with a soft, dramatic sigh. "Whatever happens, don't let his eccentric behavior startle you. He has sharp mood swings."

She appeared surprised while staring at him. "He's not violent, I hope."

"No, no. Not at all," Jules quickly covered and offered a charming smile. His smile almost immediately faded. "Although he does have a nasty habit of saying what he thinks. He can become offensive at times, but certainly not toward you. That's more my burden."

"Is he mentally ill?"

"No, just a side effect of his medication," Jules easily lied then opened the gate, extending his hand for her to enter.

She again eyed the castle and uncertainly stepped through the open gate. Jules pulled the gate shut but for once didn't bother locking it.

§

*B*ecka stood in the foyer and looked around with great interest at the amazing detail of the massive hallway and the grand staircase. Despite her interest, she revealed some discomfort as well. Jules hung her full-length trench coat in the foyer closet then looked around himself.

"He's usually here to greet me," Jules informed her, seeming a little surprised by his uncle's absence. "Uncle Rutger?" There was no response. He smiled covering his concern. "He's probably in the kitchen preparing dinner. It's a big place, and he probably won't hear me calling. Why don't you wait in the library while I get him? You can surprise him."

"All right."

Jules escorted her to the library and opened the double doors for her. She uncertainly entered and looked around while marveling at its size and grandeur. Being she was a writer, the massive library was practically paradise to her.

"I'll be right back," Jules announced and shut the doors behind her.

Becka clutched her small, black purse and walked around the enormous library, taking in its beauty. Her high heels clopped against the marble floor as she walked. She strained her neck looking up at the third floor high above her. There was a stained glass skylight on the ceiling. Becka then approached the massive, marble fireplace with a roaring fire despite the warm evening. The castle was slightly drafty, so it actually felt rather pleasant. She ran her finger along the marble mantle and admired the amazing detail and the antique trinkets on top.   She heard voices in the hallway.   Becka looked at the comfortable chair near the fireplace with her book lying face down on the table alongside it.   Jules and Rutger talked outside the door, although it sounded more like an argument.

Becka made herself comfortable in the chair, crossed her legs, and picked up the book.   She opened it to the marked page and observed the bookmarker, which was a laminated photo of her. Concern crossed her face.   Had she agreed to have dinner with a crazed fan?   The library door opened, causing her to jump slightly. She casually set the book down and looked up, preparing to meet Jules' deranged uncle.   The men entered with Jules practically shoving his uncle into the library.

Rutger's head remained turned toward his nephew.   "I don't care for surprises.   If dinner burns--"   He glanced at his chair, eyed Becka, and then looked back at his nephew.   "Duck is very temperamental."

He stared at Jules as if what he saw suddenly registered, causing him to fall silent.   He slowly turned his head back toward his chair and eyed Becka.   She stood, clutching her bag, and smiled warmly. Rutger looked back at Jules and rubbed his finger along his temple.

"I think I'm having some sort of attack," Rutger muttered.   "I'm seeing things."

Jules smiled proudly and indicated the attractive woman across the room.   "Don't be rude, Uncle Rutger," he announced cheerfully. "You have a guest."

Rutger turned back toward his chair with a strange look.   "I'm not imagining--?"

Becka observed both men then attempted another smile.   She was becoming more concerned now.   Rutger hesitantly approached her with long but cautious strides.   He stopped several feet before her and smiled with increasing delight then extended his hand, which she accepted despite her concerns.

"Ms. Stone, I apologize for my rudeness," he announced with enthusiasm.   "Sometimes I see things that aren't--"   He embraced her hand as if he wouldn't let go.   "Forgive me.   My nephew hadn't prepared me, or I would've--"   He suddenly hesitated and looked at Jules with concern.   "The duck!   Go check the duck!"

Jules flashed a smile and left the room, closing the doors behind him.   Rutger stared at Becka a moment longer while gently caressing her hand, which he refused to release.   He suddenly broke his trance and jerked.

"Where are my manners?" he announced politely.   "Please, have a seat."   He guided her toward the plush loveseat and finally released her hand.

She sat without response, although attempting to maintain her pleasant smile despite her concerns. Rutger slowly sat on the edge of the loveseat half facing her.

"Can I get you something to drink?" he asked then grinned almost boyishly. "Cognac, perhaps?"

"No, thank you," she replied. "I'm fine."

He stared at her a moment longer then shook his head while grinning. "How did my nephew manage to lure you here?" His smile faded slightly. "He really is a naughty boy. I'll probably have to kill him later tonight."

Becka attempted a smile and shifted uncomfortably, hoping his last comment was just a joke. "A friend of my agent's introduced us this past week," she replied. "He said you don't get out much and would enjoy having dinner. He was quite persuasive."

Rutger laughed lowly and shifted uncomfortably. "In other words, he told you it was a dying man's last request."

She forced a smile and looked away, remembering she was told not to bring it up.

"No, it's okay, really," Rutger politely informed her. "My nephew tends to exaggerate. Perhaps you'll want to kill him for me."

Becka looked back at him with some surprise. "You mean you aren't dying?"

"No immediate plans, but you've certainly improved my spirits," he teased.

"I'll take it up with Jules on the way home," she remarked pleasantly through gritted teeth.

"Let's not allow it to ruin our dinner, which if we want it fit to eat, I'd better return to it." He sighed with defeat. "Jules has no kitchen etiquette." Rutger stood and extended his hand. "I'll escort you to the dining room."

She accepted his hand, which he linked onto his arm and guided her from the library.

Chapter Three

Rutger entered the kitchen as Jules removed the small roasting pan from the oven and placed it on the stove. He saw his uncle enter, set his hot pads aside, and looked at Rutger while grinning slyly.

"Well, are you impressed?"

Rutger paused near the counter and leaned his back against it while firmly gripping the countertop. His mood appeared hostile as he stared with an icy look across the kitchen at nothing in particular. Jules noted his mood but didn't seem concerned.

"You know my rules about guests," Rutger remarked in a low, angry voice.

Jules appeared surprised by the gruffness of his tone and stared at the hostility in his profile.

"Why did you bring her here?" his uncle demanded.

"Because you like her," Jules announced while straightening. "I thought it'd make you happy."

He glared at his nephew. "You told her I was dying!"

"How else was I going to get her here?" Jules remarked then waved him off. "Just play along and enjoy yourself."

"I've already told her the truth," Rutger announced then glared at his nephew. "Don't ever pull a stunt like that again. I mean it. Now get out of my kitchen."

Jules frowned and walked toward the swinging door.

Rutger shook his head in disgust. "Ask him to bring cupcakes, and he brings me angel food," he muttered.

Rutger cheerfully entered the dining room while pushing a wooden cart with covered dishes upon it. Despite his earlier outburst in the kitchen, he appeared to be in good spirits. Becka sat to the right of the head of the table and watched the uncomfortable exchange between the two men.

Jules poured wine and attempted a smile at his uncle. "The duck smells good."

"Perhaps, but you're getting microwave chicken nuggets," Rutger casually informed him. "It's your own fault for surprising me at the last minute."

Rutger served Becka her covered platter while grinning like a schoolboy. She mocked Jules while nibbling on a celery stick. She didn't feel the least bit sorry for him after the lie he'd pulled on her as well.

"Please, don't wait on us," he announced to her.

Rutger eyed Jules into his seat with a nasty look. Jules frowned and flopped into his chair to the left of the head of the table. Rutger served Jules his covered plate then returned to his place at the head of the table. He hesitated then moved his entire place setting to the seat alongside Becka so he could sit closer to her. Both Becka and Jules watched as Rutger centered the candle between him and Becka, as though they were having an intimate, candlelit dinner for two. He then made himself comfortable alongside her.

Rutger raised his wineglass to Becka. "To our beautiful and talented guest, Ms. Stone."

She clinked her glass to his. "Please, call me Becka."

Both sipped their wine. Jules rolled his eyes and shook his head before taking a large swallow from his glass. Rutger set his glass down and glanced at Becka while she picked at her duck complimented with baby red potatoes and asparagus.

"I read about that unfortunate proposal made to you by that man in California," Rutger remarked with a scowl on his face.

She glanced at him and shifted, uncomfortable with the subject. "It wasn't made directly to me, thankfully, so I'm not that upset about it."

Jules appeared curious and eyed her from across the table. "What proposal was that?"

His uncle didn't respond.

Becka again shifted in her chair. "A man in California met with my agent and offered a million dollars if I'd sleep with him." She managed a smile and leaned back while sipping her wine. "She threw him out of the office, but unfortunately, the details were leaked to the media."

Rutger attempted an awkward smile. "My nephew hadn't made a similar offer, I hope."

Jules appeared horrified and stared at him with his mouth hanging open. "Uncle Rutger--"

She was equally surprised by the suggestion and stared at Rutger. "No, he didn't."

"Then perhaps he'll live to see tomorrow after all," he replied.

Rutger returned to his meal as if nothing had happened. Becka eyed Jules. He gestured with his eyes, which only partially relaxed her. They both proceeded with their meal. Once they'd finished with dinner, Rutger sat back in his chair and looked at the clock on the dining room fireplace mantel. It was nearly nine o'clock. Rutger's chair seemed to be positioned closer to Becka's than it had been when the meal had started. He'd obviously been creeping closer.

"We have just enough time for drinks in the lounge before Jules takes you home." Rutger stood and pulled her chair out for her. "Jules will clean up so that I might enjoy your company these last few minutes."

He suavely extended his hand to her. She placed her hand in his and stood, enjoying his charming manners. He again linked her hand to his arm and guided her from the dining room.

Chapter Four

Becka and Rutger entered the elegant formal lounge, which contained several antique sofas, chairs, a small bar, and other frilly antiques. Becka joined him at the small bar and sat on one of the stools while he poured two glasses of cognac.

"Are you sure you wouldn't prefer to sit on the sofa?" he asked. "It's more comfortable."

"This is fine."

He walked around the bar and sat on the stool alongside her. "After reading all your novels, I must ask where you get your inspiration."

"Any number of places," she replied. "My dreams, watching people, movies, songs--"

"Perhaps you'd be inspired by this place," he informed her. "Absolutely rich in history and scandal."

"I'll admit, I am intrigued by this place," she replied. "Jules promised you'd give me a tour."

"Jules also told you I was dying," he teased with a mocking smile. He glanced at the grandfather clock and smiled pleasantly. "It's nearly time for you to leave. I'm afraid a tour would be impossible. Maybe another time."

She looked at the grandfather clock then at Rutger. "It's only going on ten o'clock," she teased, although she was a little surprised he wanted her out so quickly. "I don't turn into a pumpkin until well after midnight."

"All guests must leave by midnight," he informed her. "If you're out by ten, it's less stress on me."

"Why must all guests be gone by midnight?" she questioned while tilting her head.

"Those are the rules."

She stared at him with some confusion, but he seemed reluctant to explain his odd statement. She brushed the comment aside and again attempted a smile.

"Jules told me the castle is haunted," she remarked.

His smile vanished as he stared at her without response. She'd obviously hit a sore subject.

"He said that's why you don't like company," she continued. "My curiosity was aroused. Why don't you give me a quick tour? I'd like to see for myself."

He continued to fidget and avoided looking at her.

She studied him a long moment while awaiting a response. "Well, Rutger?"

He tapped his fingers on top of the bar then met her gaze with a strange look in his eyes, almost as if his entire personality changed before her eyes.

"I've lived alone in celibacy in this house for the past five years," he casually informed her. "I could give you a guided tour, but I can't guarantee I won't *eat* that dress right off you." His stare was piercing and almost frightening. "Are you willing to take that chance?"

Becka slowly stood and adjusted her dress to minimize her exposed cleavage. "You've been charming company until now, Rutger, so I'll refrain from slapping you out of respect for the duck." She attempted to retain her dignity. "Please tell Jules I'll be waiting in the car. Goodnight."

Rutger stood as she turned and walked toward the lounge doors. He frowned, ran his fingers through his short hair, and sighed with defeat.

"I'll slap myself later," he muttered to himself. "At least it was effective."

He walked across the room to the lounge doors and hurried into the grand hallway after her. Rutger entered the hallway with his hands insecurely in his pockets while watching Becka snatch her trench coat from the hall closet. She then turned to the door to leave. Rutger fidgeted then trotted up the steps to the foyer and cast himself before the door. He smiled warmly despite her hostility.

"Please accept my apologies," he announced in a timid, sincere tone. "If I have to read your novels knowing you hate me, I'd probably hang myself."

She glared at him and attempted to control her hostility. "I don't hate you, Rutger," she informed him. "I just don't appreciate the sexual remarks."

"Understood and noted." He tilted his head and managed a timid smile. "Did you really find my company charming up until that unfortunate moment in the lounge?"

She glared at him with limited patience. "Will you move away from the door?"

"Would you leave me with one small kiss, if I promise my hands will remain in my pockets?" he asked then grinned. "Think of it as a dying man's last request."

"You aren't dying."

"I will be one day."

She groaned and appeared defeated. "Will you get out of my way, if I do?"

"I'll even open the door for you."

Becka stared at him a moment then cautiously moved closer to him. He leaned toward her, prepared to meet her halfway. She pulled back and hesitated.

He flashed a timid smile. "Sorry--"

She braced her hand against his chest to hold him back and quickly kissed him on the lips. As she pulled back his mouth followed hers, attempting to prolong the kiss. She held him back and met his gaze. Their lips were only inches apart.

"I've held up my end of the bargain," she remarked without flinching.

"So you have."

He made another attempt to put his lips to hers. She smirked and backed away from him.

"The door, if you don't mind," she remarked.

Rutger managed a smile, although clearly disappointed, then removed his hands from his pockets, and opened the door. He stood to the side and bowed like a respectable butler. Becka passed through the open door and paused on the other side. He looked up and met her gaze. She managed a tiny smile then left. Rutger grinned, although she couldn't see it, and shut the door behind her. He leaned his back against the door, shut his eyes, and sighed.

Jules approached from the farthest end of the grand hallway and looked around with surprise. "Where's Becka?"

Rutger dramatically placed his hands on his chest. "She took my heart and left."

"Left? I drove. How could she leave?" He glared his annoyance at his uncle. "What did you say to her?"

Rutger straightened and casually shrugged. "Just that I liked her dress," he replied. "Then she kissed me and left."

"*She* kissed *you?*"

"Umm, hmm. She's waiting for you in the car."

Rutger casually walked away from the door and headed for the broad staircase.

Jules watched him. "Where are you going?"

Rutger caught the banister, swung gracefully to face Jules, and smiled. "I'm going to take a hot bubble bath with a double scotch and pretend I'm not alone."

Jules watched his uncle trot up the stairs like a schoolboy in love.

With each step, he chanted. "Becka, Becka, Becka."

Jules rolled his eyes and shook his head. "Have fun."

There was a knock on the door, startling Jules.

Rutger could be heard shouting from halfway up the stairs. "Becka!"

Thundering feet ran down the grand staircase. Rutger jumped the last few steps, ran past Jules, leaped up the foyer steps, and whipped open the door. His smile faded at the sight of five strangers in their early twenties standing on the covered porch. The rain poured down outside, and all five were soaking wet. Rutger stood in the doorway and stared at them with some surprise.

"Our van broke down about half a mile from here, and there's no reception on our cell phones," Jamie, the sole woman in the group, informed him with a sweet smile. "Could we use your phone?"

"I don't have a phone," Rutger retorted and attempted to close the door on them.

Jules pulled his uncle from the doorway and smiled at the five strangers. "You'll have to excuse my uncle; he's not right in the head."

Rutger glared at Jules.

"There's a phone in the hall," Jules offered. "I could give you a lift back to your van then."

Rutger continued to glare at the four wet young men and one woman as they entered the foyer. Jules shut the door behind them. Rutger cast himself against the closed door with his arms across his chest and an annoyed expression on his face. Jules led the first man to the hall phone.

"It's getting late," Rutger snarled at his nephew.

Jules glanced at the hall clock and waved him off. "It's not even ten o'clock. We'll be out of here shortly."

Jamie attempted to fix her wet, blonde hair. She was an attractive young woman. She was teenager thin, giving the appearance of someone who didn't eat enough, revealing little muscle mass on her petite frame. Despite being soaked, her makeup seemed to hold, almost looking freshly applied. She seemed more concerned about her wildly mussed hair than their situation with their disabled vehicle.

She shifted her look between Jules and Rutger and smiled sweetly. "Think I could use your bathroom?"

Rutger continued to glare with annoyance. "I don't have a bathroom."

Jules glared at his uncle then smiled at the young, attractive woman. "Ignore him. It's just down the hall," he informed her. "Fourth door on the left."

Jamie walked down the grand hall, straining to look at the elegant art on the walls. "This is some place," she commented while heading toward the bathroom.

Bryan followed behind Jamie in the direction of the bathroom as well. He was a stocky young man who quite possibly played football in high school. His dark hair was nearly shoulder length, and, unlike Jamie, he wasn't nearly as concerned about his appearance. Out of the four young men, he was dressed more shabbily, not caring if his pants and shirt had holes, tears, and stains. Rutger's arms fell to his sides as irritation crossed his face. He straightened and walked down the hall behind them but at a slow, leisurely pace. He saw the bathroom door close, indicating the girl had gone into the powder room, but Bryan wasn't anywhere to be found. He looked around then entered the nearby room. Bryan stood in the trophy room and looked at the swords and spears decorating the walls.

Rutger entered behind him with the same unpredictable look on his face. "Looking for something?"

Bryan turned with some surprise then indicated the few animal heads mounted on the walls. "This is some collection," he announced.

"Perhaps you'd like to see the dungeon," Rutger announced. "It's where I keep the leftover parts."

Bryan looked back at Rutger with some concern. He attempted a smile then hurried past him and out of the room. Rutger casually followed while grinning, proud of himself. Jamie stood in the hallway before the hall mirror and fixed her makeup. Rutger approached her from behind. She glanced at him through the mirror and smiled but didn't stop applying lip-gloss.

"What a horrible night to run into a ditch," Jamie announced and made kissy faces in the mirror, admiring her lip-gloss. "It's nice of you to let us use your phone."

Rutger smiled charmingly while staring at her through the mirror. "You have nice hair."

Jamie smiled at him through the mirror. "Thanks. It's looked better though."

"Did you see that movie?" he asked. "The one where that psycho killer scalped that blonde woman and wore her hair for a wig?"

Jamie eyed the strange man through the mirror with a look of concern.

Rutger grinned almost psychotically. "Then he ground her into hamburger and fed her to his dogs." He smiled deviously. "You remind me of her before she was hamburger." He appeared curious. "Do you think that would really work? Grounding someone into hamburger?" His look then turned serious. "What do you suppose they did with the head? Mount it on the wall or keep it in a jar to preserve it?"

Jamie stared at him through the mirror, forced a smile, and then hurried to join the others. Stanley stood by the phone on the hall table and made his call to rescue their stranded vehicle. Stanley was moderately handsome and stood over six-foot-two with an athletic build. His dark hair wasn't nearly as long as Bryan's, but he obviously spent more time tending to his luscious, thick locks. The clock struck ten as Stanley hung up the phone.

"They won't send anyone out until morning," Stanley announced. "We'd better call a cab."

Stanley again reached for the phone on the table. Rutger witnessed Jules standing before the foyer door as he reached for the doorknob. Rutger appeared concerned and looked from the chiming clock in the hall to his wristwatch. His watch indicated it was already midnight.

Rutger's expression became horrified as he looked at his unwelcome guests. "Out! Everyone out!"

Jamie and Bryan jumped with alarm. Jules pulled on the door, but it wouldn't open. Rutger ran for the door, shoved Jules aside, and pulled harshly on it. It didn't budge. He turned and glared at Jules, who stared back with a stunned look. Rutger placed his hands in his pockets and walked casually down the foyer steps. Everyone watched him enter the library and shut the door behind him. Jamie and Bryan ran to the door and took turns trying to open it.

Jules jumped around with hostility. "Fuck!" He cast his back to the wall and slid down it while holding his head.

"How do we get out of here?" Jamie demanded.

"We don't," Jules muttered while holding his head and staring blankly at the floor.

Stanley stared at Jules where he sat on the floor and appeared surprised. "What do you mean?" he demanded. "Come on, man. Open the door."

The remaining two men from their group, Phil and Harold, appeared equally alarmed.

"What's going on?" Bryan demanded.

"They won't open again until six o'clock Monday morning," Jules muttered.

Jamie glared at Jules. "But it's Friday night," she squawked with horror. "What the hell are we supposed to do in this museum all weekend?"

"You don't want to know," Jules muttered.

All five soaking wet strangers looked at one another, uncertain what to make of the comment.

Chapter Five

Phil and Harold stood by the outer kitchen door and attempted to open it with a screwdriver. The screwdriver slipped, slicing into Phil's hand. He clutched his bleeding hand and cursed. Phil was seemingly average by all accounts. He was an average height and build. He was neither handsome nor homely. His nearly black hair and darker complexion indicated he was Latino, possibly of Columbian descent. Despite slicing his hand, he seemed to handle the stress better than his counterpart, Harold. Harold was a much shorter, leaner man than Phil. The stress of being stranded within the creepy castle had already taken its toll on the young man. He was already ripping out his excessively blonde hair at a staggering rate. Considering his tough appearance, Harold revealed he wasn't so tough after all. Stanley ran into the kitchen carrying an antique ax from the trophy room wall.

"I got this," he cried out, obviously not handling his incarceration well. "Get back!"

Harold and Phil saw him with the ax and leaped away from the door. Stanley swung the ax for the glass near the jam. There was a tremendous crack as it hit the glass, snapping the wooden handle in half, and throwing the broad head behind him. Harold and Phil darted from the flying projectile's path. All three stared at the broken ax then looked at one another. Stanley dropped the broken handle as all three backed away from the door.

"There's something not right about this place," Phil informed them.

"I knew it wasn't going to be a good day," Harold muttered. "What are we going to do?"

"We should find Jules," Phil suggested. "There has to be a way out of here."

"Well, he's convinced there's not," Stanley snapped.

"What about that other guy, Rutger," Phil suggested. "We haven't heard a peep out of him."

"No, we'll just keep our distance from him," Stanley announced. "He's a little off the wall."

"He lives here," Phil reminded them. "Maybe he knows something."

"I say we beat it out of him," Harold launched while making a fist.

"Jamie and Bryan are trying to flag down that woman in Jules' car, but she's pretty far down the road," Stanley informed them. "If we can get her attention, she can take Jules' car for help."

"Brilliant idea," Phil huffed under his breath. "Jules' car keys are in his pocket. I doubt she's getting very far without them."

Bryan entered the kitchen while clutching Jamie's arm, pulling her along as she protested through gritted teeth.

"Let me go," she cried out. "I won't do it."

"Jamie and I have an idea," Bryan announced while ignoring the thrashing woman.

"You're supposed to be getting the attention of that woman outside," Stanley reminded her.

She glared at him while yanking her arm free from Bryan. "Tell that to the Neanderthal here."

"What's your idea?" Harold asked Bryan.

"I'm not doing it," Jamie blurted out. "I'm not going anywhere near that guy--especially alone."

"Jules says he's harmless," Bryan reminded her with little concern to her fears.

"Jules knew and never warned us," Stanley remarked, turning hostile. "Do you honestly trust him?"

"I'm not doing it," Jamie again insisted while folding her arms across her chest. "He's going to grind me into hamburger and feed me to the dogs. He said so."

"Be serious," Bryan lashed back with annoyance. "Do you see any dogs?"

Jamie glared at Bryan.

§

Rutger sat before the fireplace in his plush chair. His hands were clasped together near his mouth as he remained hunched over, staring into the fire. The library door opened and Jules cautiously entered.

"Uncle Rutger? Can I talk to you?"

Rutger didn't bother looking up. "There's nothing to discuss."

"I did it for you."

"You brought them to their deaths," Rutger remarked with little emotion. "You knew what would happen to them, yet you brought them here anyway."

"Without them, you won't be free," Jules protested while approaching his chair.

"I didn't ask for your help." Rutger turned in his chair and gave his nephew a hostile look. "I only wanted some cupcakes!" Rutger regained his calm demeanor and looked back at the fire. "You know they're going to die; you're going to die, and there's nothing I can do about it."

"One will survive."

"How comforting," Rutger muttered and cast a look at him. "Perhaps you'd like to share the good news with them. Clever thing you did, changing all my clocks so I wouldn't know what time it was. Becka was a lovely distraction." He shook his head while frowning. "Would you leave me? I have to think."

"Uncle Rutger--"

"Leave me," he announced in a firmer tone.

Jules appeared defeated and left the room. Rutger sat back in his plush chair and shut his eyes. Only a moment passed when the door was heard opening. His eyes opened as he looked across the room. Jamie hesitantly approached him. Rutger barely eyed her as he reached for his drink and finished it. He casually set the glass down and looked back at her.

"What do you want?"

"The guys nominated me to find out what's going on," Jamie replied.

"Would you like all the unpleasant details?"

"What's happening?" she asked gently. "Won't you tell us anything? Won't you help us get out?"

"You can't get out." Rutger stood and studied her. "There's nothing to tell." He approached the fireplace and leaned his arm against the mantel. "There's a monster lurking within the walls of this house. It only comes out at night, and it only stalks hatred and fear. If your mind is weak, then you will be its feast."

Jamie didn't appear convinced, although she subconsciously shivered. "Monster? Have you seen it?"

"Many times. I'm its slave," he informed her. "It communicates through me. Sometimes positive and sometimes negative."

"Can we defeat it?"

"No," he replied without hesitation. "It feeds on hate and fear. Don't feed it, and you may just survive."

Jamie stared at him a long moment in silence. When he offered nothing more, she turned and left.

§

Jules paced before the five stranded travelers where they had gathered in the lounge. They all appeared a little anxious and with good reason.

"We'd probably be better off if we'd just lock ourselves in the bedrooms and sleep," Jules informed them then muttered, "if we can."

"We should stay together," Jamie insisted while wrenching her hands together.

"She has a point," Bryan remarked. "I'm not sure I want to be alone in a bedroom. If there is something in this house, we should probably stick together."

"Well, there are six of us," Jules remarked. "We could split into pairs and lock ourselves in the bedrooms. That way we could take turns sleeping."

"Sounds like I'm getting the short end here as the only girl," Jamie remarked. She then eyed Bryan. "If you can keep your hands to yourself--"

"Believe me," Bryan scoffed. "Sex is the last thing on my mind."

"If I could only explain the ax, I wouldn't buy into any of this," Stanley remarked.

"I assure you, this isn't some story made up by my uncle to scare his guests," Jules informed them. "He went from a workaholic tycoon to a monk in the first year. Something changed him. They never did find the bodies."

"Bodies?" Phil suddenly gasped while staring at him.

"My uncle and a few investors came here five years ago to look the place over after buying it sight unseen," Jules explained. "By the end of the weekend, he was the only one left. His orders to me were to send his personal belongings." Jules took a swallow of his drink. "The local police won't even come out here. They wouldn't even come out to investigate his missing partners. All I could ever get out of him was they were dead, and he could never leave the house because he was cursed. He's never talked about it much since then."

"And you brought us here because--?" Stanley almost demanded.

"I'd hoped *it* would allow him to leave if it had someone else," Jules informed them while lowering his head shamefully.

"Of course," Phil scoffed and laughed. "No one invites thieves to rob their house."

"You're taking this rather well," Jules remarked.

"Probably because we intend to take some antiques with us when we leave Monday," Stanley announced.

"Don't you mean *if* we leave?" Jamie snapped.

Stanley glared at her.

She ignored his look and eyed the others. "His uncle is convinced there's something evil here," Jamie informed them. "We should consider the possibility that he's telling the truth."

"We'll just need to be a little more cautious, that's all," Stanley informed them. "Anyone want a nightcap?"

Jamie and Bryan were the only ones who declined.

Chapter Six

Rutger sat in his plush chair before the fireplace and stared into the aggressive flames. He held Becka's book on his lap, back cover facing up, and ran his forefinger lovingly along her picture. He was lost in his own world when there was a soft knock on the door. Rutger jerked slightly from the disturbance and looked at the door as it opened. Becka uncertainly stepped into the doorway and almost immediately looked toward his chair. Rutger's expression suddenly shattered as he bolted upright in his chair.

"It's after midnight," she informed him. "Did Jules forget about me? I was worried something had happened."

Rutger sprang to his feet and stared at her with the same horrified expression then slowly approached her. The way he stared at her made her uneasy, and she attempted to keep her distance from the strange man.

"You shouldn't have come back inside," he practically gasped, unable to take his eyes off her.

"I couldn't wait out there all night," she replied. "Where's Jules? I want to go home."

"I'm afraid that's impossible," he gently informed her. He nearly choked on his words. "You're trapped here with the rest of us."

"Excuse me?" She forced a tense smile and backed away from him. "I'll just call for a cab and wait outside."

"None will come, and the phones stopped working at midnight," he replied.

Becka gave him an odd look and hurried from the room. Rutger ran into the hall after her. She picked up the phone from the table and dialed the operator. Rutger entered the hallway but kept his distance. She repeatedly hit the button but couldn't get a dial tone.

"You can't get out," he timidly informed her. "The doors and windows have been sealed by the evil force that controls this house. We've covered all this earlier."

Rutger attempted to approach her. She backed away several steps and glared at him with distrust. He stopped, obviously noting the fear in her eyes.

"If you'll permit me to explain, I'll tell you everything you need to know," he informed her. "Including why I had to offend you so you'd leave."

He extended his hand, indicating the library. She stared at him a long moment then slowly walked past him and entered the library. Several minutes later, Becka sat on the loveseat while facing Rutger, who sat alongside her maintaining a comfortable distance so as not to frighten her. She stared at him with a strange look of either disbelief or horror.

"So you're a slave to some evil spirit who controls this house," she repeated his words while raising her brows. She wanted to laugh, but it was obvious he was mentally unstable. "He wants to collect our souls and eat our flesh. Do I have it right so far?"

"You have it correct, but your tone mocks me," he announced gently.

"I'm sorry, but I just find all of this a little hard to believe," she scoffed and leaned back on the loveseat.

"You could ask the others, but I'd prefer if you took my word for it." He sank into his own thoughts. "They're a shady bunch. I suspect they came here to steal the silverware."

She stared at him in disbelief. He belonged in a straightjacket. "Actually, I'm too tired to argue at this point," she muttered while scratching her head.

"Would you like someplace to lie down?" he asked eager to please her. "The master bedroom is exceptionally comfortable, and I don't sleep much."

She eyed him and almost laughed at the irony. "Didn't you make a similar proposal earlier tonight?" Becka demanded. "I believe you intended to eat my dress."

"I told you, that was just to get you out of the house," he reassured her. "There's little difference if you sleep on the sofa down here with me watching over you, or if you sleep in the master bedroom."

"Whatever, Rutger," she groaned while holding her head. "I just want to get some sleep."

"I'll take you up in the elevator," he announced while springing to his feet. "You can avoid interacting with my nephew's low-life associates."

She reluctantly left the library and walked along the grand hall with him. They entered the antique elevator with the elegant, carved door. The door slid shut, and the elevator jerked into motion. Becka jumped with surprise and anxiously looked around.

He looked at her and smiled with some humor. "It's safe, I promise."

The elevator bucked to a stop on the third floor and the doors opened. The elevator had stopped a little below the third floor, leaving a slight step up. Rutger stepped out of the elevator and assisted her up the step. He didn't release her hand once they were outside the elevator and led her along the elegant hallway toward the master bedroom.

"You'll be very comfortable here," he announced cheerfully. "Only the best--"

Rutger paused before the double doors and opened them together. The massive master bedroom contained every lavish comfort for a king. The huge canopy bed seemed to extend forever with three wooden steps leading up to it because of its height, and the bed curtains could be closed for that cozy feel. Rutger stepped into the room and stood to the side, allowing Becka to enter. There was a fire already blazing in the hand carved fireplace. Every detail was breathtaking.

"It has its own whirlpool tub in the master bath," he informed her. "If you feel like soaking, there are bubbles or scented oils."

Becka looked around the room and marveled at its elegance. She looked back at him and smiled warmly. "I've always wanted a room like this."

He smiled pleasantly. "It's yours," he announced without hesitation. "I'll remain on the sofa tonight to ensure your safety." He then hesitated and tilted his head. "Would you like some tea? I was just about to get myself some."

"That would be nice, thank you."

"Feel free to help yourself to anything you might need to sleep in," he informed her. "I'll be right back."

"Take your time. I'll be in the tub." Her look turned threatening. "No peeking."

He snorted a laugh. "I wouldn't dream of it, but if it makes you feel better, there's a lock on the inside."

Rutger approached the bedroom door, paused to look at her standing in his room, and then groaned to himself. He left the room, locking the door from the outside. Becka heard the locking sound and immediately bolted to the door. It took only a second to realize she could easily unlock it from her side.

Chapter Seven

Becka lounged in the whirlpool tub filled with bubbles within the massive bathroom. The tub was centered in front of a large stained glass window, which took up the entire wall. With her hair still up in the French twist, she relaxed up to her neck in bubbles. A shadow moved past her. Her eyes opened, having sensed something, and she quickly looked around. There was no one there. She stared a moment longer then returned to relaxing in the tub, although not nearly as relaxed now. A gentle breeze blew a stray lock of hair from her shoulder, and the water shimmered beneath the bubbles. Becka jumped with a gasp and looked around. The whirling water unnaturally rocked the bubbles, alarming her. Something brushed past her bare thigh. She let out a scream and jumped to her feet while tossing the towel around her.

"Rutger!"

She heard keys outside the bathroom door. Bubbles and water splashed over the side of the tub where she had stood immobile, watching something moving beneath the water. Becka screamed and sprang from the tub.

"Rutger!"

The door was unlocked, and Rutger immediately charged inside with a look of surprise. "What? What happened?"

He looked around the room then eyed the frightened woman, where she stood near the back of the bathroom while clinging to her wet towel.

"There was something in the tub," she cried out. "It touched me."

He approached the tub, peered inside, and then hit the release lever. The water began to drain. Becka grabbed a shirt from the dressing table and slipped into it without releasing the towel while Rutger watched the draining water. She didn't even care that she wasn't alone while slipping into the shirt. Once the tub was completely drained, he washed down the bubbles. She hurried alongside him while buttoning the shirt and looked into the tub just over his shoulder. There was nothing there. He looked back at her in silent question.

Her eyes widened in horror. "Something *touched* me," she proclaimed. "I'm not lying!"

"We'd discussed remaining calm," he gently informed her. "You need to relax no matter what." He searched her eyes. "I believe you."

She held her breath and attempted to do as he asked. "What was in that tub?" she growled under her breath.

"I don't know, but it's not there now." He directed her to the door. "I've brought you some tea. Let's get you relaxed before bedtime."

"I'll need something stronger than tea to accomplish that," she grumbled.

As Becka and Rutger entered the bedroom, she collapsed on the sofa. Her shirt clung to her wet body, but she didn't seem to notice or care. She tucked her feet beneath her and rested her head in her hand. Rutger poured her some tea then sat down alongside her and extended the cup.

"Your tea."

She eyed the cup, nervously laughed, and then accepted it. Rutger watched her with great interest then allowed his eyes to fall to the clinging shirt. He appeared slightly uncomfortable for staring and fidgeted.

"Okay, so on the off chance that what you told me about this flesh-eating creature is true," she announced, "does this mean that I'm it's next meal?"

"No, no," he informed her. "It wouldn't have any reason to come after you unless you were agitated while soaking."

"I wasn't anything," she muttered while glaring at him. "I was practically asleep."

"I don't understand it," Rutger remarked then considered the comment. "Perhaps it was just probing you."

"Copping a feel?" she suddenly gasped and nearly shot up in her seat while casting her teacup onto the coffee table. "You can't be serious."

"Just speculation," he informed her gently. "Can you please remain calm?"

"You're telling me some evil entity wants to make me it's girlfriend, and you expect me to remain calm?"

"If you don't remain calm, it could be worse," he informed her in a reassuring tone and again offered her the teacup. "Will you trust me?"

She groaned, held her head a moment, and again accepted the china teacup. "It appears I don't have much choice."

Rutger moved closer to her and stared into her eyes with sincerity. "Believe that I'd never allow anything to happen to you if I can help it."

She stared into his eyes a long moment. For the first time she wasn't uncomfortable by his closeness. "You really mean that, don't you?"

"Yes."

She groaned and peered into the rose-colored tea within her cup. "You don't even know me."

"Five years of near insanity; stuck alone in this house, but never truly alone," he informed her, causing her to meet his gaze. "You've kept me going, even in the face of the demon. There must be part of you in what you write; therefore, I know enough."

"I don't understand you, Rutger, but I feel better knowing you're on my side," she replied then sighed with defeat and again set her teacup down without drinking from it. "What do I do now? Can I reason with it? Will it continue to bother me?"

"I'm not sure what its intentions are, but I can attempt to find out," he informed her. His look turned serious. "You need to understand something, Becka. This evil is my master, and I am its slave. Our relationship is unnatural, but it can't survive without me or someone. If I die, it will simply wait for its next host. We communicate, in depth. I am its only friend. It doesn't always like me, but I know it feels my emotion." He straightened proudly. "I can't keep it from destroying if it wanted to, but I can make requests. I'll do what I can, but I can't promise it will respond favorably."

Becka took his hand in hers with a glimmer of hope. "Then it might let us go. You can convince it."

"It likes having me around," he informed her, although enjoying her hand grasping his. "It'll never let me go." He reluctantly released her hand and stood. "I must meet with the evil one now. While I'm in conference, it cannot hurt you."

She stared at him with surprise, somehow not doubting a word he said. "Where must you go?"

"Right here will work," he replied and indicated the nearby chair. "It comes to me when it feels like it. There are no rules for it. Please, try to get some rest." Rutger's eyes again strayed to the nearly see-through shirt clinging to her wet body. "That shirt has never looked better."

He turned away to avoid embarrassment then moved to a plush chair near the fireplace. She looked down, realizing the shirt was nearly see-through while it clung to her wet body. She shifted uncomfortably and folded her arms across her chest with embarrassment. Nearly an hour later, Becka had changed into dry clothes and paced the bedroom. She cast several looks at Rutger where he sat peacefully in his chair with his eyes shut. There was a knock on the door. Surprisingly, Rutger didn't wake. Becka hurried to the door.

"Uncle, we need to talk," Jules announced through the door while attempting to open it, but the lock prevented him from entering.

Becka unlocked and opened the door. When he saw her in the doorway, he appeared surprised.

"What are you doing here?" he suddenly demanded. "How did you get inside the house after midnight?"

"The door was open," she replied. "At least from the outside." She folded her arms across her chest and glared at him. "Thanks for warning me, you bastard."

"I didn't know that was possible," he informed her and shook his head. "I'm sorry, Becka. I didn't mean for you to be stuck here with the rest of us." He sharply raised a brow and glanced inside the master bedroom. "But what are you doing *here*?"

"Rutger insisted I stay in the master bedroom," she informed him. "He thinks he can keep me safe."

Jules looked from the shirt she wore to Rutger sitting in the chair by the fire. He attempted to enter the room, but she stopped him.

"Don't disturb him," she announced firmly. "He's in conference."

Jules glared at her then shook his head. "With his inner demons?" he scoffed then frowned. "I've been giving this whole situation some thought, and I'm not sure we can trust my uncle. He isn't the same man he used to be. He may be more closely united with this evil than we think." He shifted uncomfortably while studying her. "You should probably stay with us. You can share a room with Jamie."

"Let's not jump to conclusions, Jules," she announced. "I think Rutger's sincere about wanting to help us."

"Help? The only thing he wants is to get you alone in his room, and he's obviously succeeded in that," Jules scoffed while forcing a tense smile. "He's only thinking of himself and what he can get from you."

"I appreciate the warning, but there's something more sinister going on than your uncle trying to get me in his bed," she informed him then tensed. "Something came after me tonight. Whatever it was, I couldn't see it, but I could certainly feel it. I know for a fact it wasn't Rutger." She gently pushed him out the door. "We can discuss this in the morning."

He attempted to protest. Becka shut the door, nearly hitting Jules in the face, and then locked it behind him. She walked back to the sitting area and sat on the sofa while keeping her eyes locked on Rutger.

His eyes suddenly opened and he looked at her as if nothing had happened. "Couldn't sleep?"

She gave him a strange look and shook her head.

He sat forward and rested his chin on his hands. "I'm afraid my interest in you piqued *his* interest in you. He wants to make you my replacement."

"I don't think so," she proclaimed.

"I told him so much."

"Now what?"

"I suggest you get some sleep," Rutger replied. "I'll remain awake."

Becka thought about it only a moment, realized how tired she was, and then approached the bed. Rutger watched her climb beneath the sheets then turned down the lights and returned to the sofa, making himself comfortable.

Chapter Eight

The game room was a less formal social gathering room. In addition to an expensive, wood carved pool table; there was a massive, marble top bar big enough to seat ten people. The room had several sitting areas containing sofas, chairs, and a few pub tables. Despite the late hour, Stanley and Phil played pool and had a few drinks while Harold and Jules remained at the bar nursing a bottle of whiskey. The lights flickered causing all four to tense and look around with shared concern. Jules frowned, easily became disinterested, and finished his drink. He immediately poured another without regard to his already drunken condition.

"Wouldn't doubt he killed her," he muttered into his glass then took a large swallow. "She was hot too."

Harold appeared surprised while staring at Jules. "What are you talking about?"

"My uncle," Jules remarked without emotion. "He's not the same man I remember. Maybe that demon possessed him. Either way, I feel sorry for the girl."

"What girl?" Phil asked and no longer paid attention to the pool game he was obviously losing.

"Becka," Jules replied. "The one you were attempting to flag down at the bottom of the driveway. She showed up."

"But the doors were locked," Harold insisted, becoming interested. "How did she get in?"

"*It* let her in," Jules replied with little emotion. "She said something attacked her earlier, and she insists it wasn't my uncle." He groaned and took another large swallow of whiskey. "I don't know what to believe anymore."

"Should we check on her," Phil asked, showing more concern than Jules.

143

"If it or he has already gotten to her, there's not much point," Jules casually replied. "From what I'm told, it's very unpleasant. Eats the flesh right off you."

The three men cringed at the thought.

"Maybe we should arm ourselves," Harold suggested while casting looks at the others. "There are some pretty impressive weapons in the trophy room."

"Those weapons won't work on the demon," Jules remarked. "And it'll probably piss him off."

"What will work on this demon?" Harold demanded becoming impatient with the drunken man.

"Apparently nothing works."

Harold finished his drink and slammed his glass on the bar with irritation. "I'm going to bed. I've had enough of this bullshit for one night."

As Harold left the room, Stanley and Phil returned to their game and Jules returned to drinking.

§

*H*arold entered the brightly lit trophy room, looked around a moment, and then approached the case of large, elegant daggers. He removed a lock pick device from his pocket and easily forced his way into the case. He removed a large, jagged dagger from the case and admired it. Harold then placed the dagger into its sheath and clipped it to his pants. As he shut the case and turned, he came face-to-face with Rutger. Rutger attempted a smile, but it came off oddly sinister.

"You don't really think that'll do you any good, do you?" Rutger remarked.

"Makes me feel better."

"I feel I must warn you, it only makes him angrier," Rutger informed him. "Had you thought of that?"

"What is this thing anyway?" Harold demanded while glaring at the odd man. "How is it you've been here so long, and it hasn't killed you?"

"You don't cut off your right hand," he casually informed him then raised his brows along with a sinister grin. "You should be more concerned about Jules."

"Jules?"

"He brought you here knowing you would be killed," Rutger informed him while casually placing his hands in his pockets. "Does he just dislike the bunch of you, or do you think it was nothing personal?"

"You're a strange man, Rutger." Harold walked past him and approached the door.

Rutger followed him and stopped near the door. "What were your intentions, Harold?" he finally asked and removed his hands from his pockets. "Were you and your friends just going to rob the place or did you intend to kill me as well?"

Harold removed the knife from its sheath and held it to Rutger's face. "I still might kill you, if you don't go away."

"Anger, hatred, and fear feed the monster," Rutger reminded him with an almost teasing grin. "You're presenting an excellent display. Tell me, Harold; do you think I'm setting you up right now? Do you think you could cut me with that large knife and get away with it?"

Harold suddenly thrust the dagger forward and stabbed him in the midsection. Rutger clutched his bleeding abdomen with surprise and genuine agony, sinking to his knees as Harold pulled the dagger free.

"Yes, I do," he scoffed with a sneer. "One less freak to worry about."

Harold casually left the trophy room, crossed the hall, and entered the bathroom where he rinsed the blood from the dagger. He returned to the hallway from the bathroom and saw Rutger standing in his path. Despite the blood saturating his abdomen, he looked calm and unfazed.

Harold stared with horror and disbelief. "What the--?"

Rutger grinned revealing a mouth full of sharp teeth. "My turn," he hissed.

Harold opened his mouth to scream when Rutger lunged for his throat, sinking his teeth into his flesh. The scream never came. Harold didn't even have time to defend himself as he gurgled a gasp, spitting up blood while Rutger tore out his throat.

§

Becka jerked beneath the covers in her sleep from her torturous nightmare. A shadow moved past the bed where she slept restlessly.

She allowed a soft cry to escape her throat as she thrashed. A stray lock of hair was gently brushed from her temple. Becka jerked with a gasp and woke. She looked at Rutger, who lay casually on top of the comforter, propped on his left elbow facing her. She sprang up into a sitting position. She attempted to relax but found it difficult between the nightmare and waking up to find Rutger in her bed.

"What are you doing?" she gasped, still rattled from her nightmare.

"You were having a bad dream," he informed her. "I promised to protect you." He grinned playfully. "Even from the evil men in your head."

"Mission complete. They're gone," she announced firmly. "Off the bed, Romeo."

He grinned playfully and teased, "But it's my bed."

"Would you like me to leave?" she asked while raising a clever brow.

"No. I rather enjoy watching you nestle beneath the covers," he replied in a soothing, gentle tone. "I won't change the sheets again until that wonderful lavender scent fades away."

Becka clung to her knees overtop the comforter and stared at him in mild disbelief. "Are you really that charming or just completely insane?" A teasing smile crossed her face as she studied him. "I'd really love to know."

"Possibly a little of both," he replied with a chuckle. "I could tell you a little bedtime story."

He patted the pillow near his arm.

She studied him a long moment, hid her smile, and shook her head. "I hope I don't regret this."

Becka lay back down on her side to face him, propping her head on her hand.

"Once upon a time--" He pulled the covers up to her chest and tucked her in. "There was a wealthy, self-centered business tycoon who only had time for work. He was an evil man." Rutger lay on his side with his head propped on his hand as well, so they were in the same position. "Until one day, he was locked away by his own greed. He suffered in his prison alone and in silence." His brows dramatically rose. "In his solitude, he was able to take a long, hard look at himself. All the money, all the greed, all the anger--where had it gotten him? The prison he found himself living in was not that different from the one he'd already created for himself years ago."

There was a long silence. Becka waited a moment with a curious look. "Well? How does the story end?"

Rutger brushed the hair from her brow. "The story doesn't have an ending yet," he teased. "Perhaps he spends his life alone with his own thoughts for all eternity." A warm smile crossed his face. "Or maybe he meets a beautiful writer and lives happily ever after." His grin turned bold while studying her. "I opt for ending number two."

Becka placed her hand on his between them. He stared into her eyes with an admiration rarely ever seen.

"Would you lay with me until I fall asleep?" she asked timidly.

"I'd love nothing more."

She shut her eyes and held his hand.

Chapter Nine

Morning. An unusual rolling sound echoed through the first floor hallway. Rutger rollerbladed at a leisurely pace along the marble hallway while pushing a rolling cart containing a silver teapot, two teacups, and a covered dish. Stanley suddenly stepped out of the lounge and in front of him, catching the cart. Rutger and the cart were jolted roughly, causing the teacups to clatter. He appeared surprised by the unprovoked attack then studied the hostile look on Stanley's face.

"Harold's missing," Stanley snarled with a drunken, exhausted look in his eyes. "Where is he?"

"I really couldn't say," Rutger replied without taking his eyes off the irate man. "When did you last see him?"

Stanley became angry and gave the cart a shove into Rutger, jolting him. "Don't play games with me. Something happened to him, and I think you know what it was."

Phil stepped out from the game room looking equally tired and hung-over. "Give it a rest, Stanley," he wearily announced while approaching them. "He didn't do anything with Harold. I wouldn't doubt he passed out somewhere." He placed a hand on Stanley's shoulder. "Come on, leave him alone."

Stanley glared into Rutger's eyes in an attempt at silent intimidation, but Rutger stared back with his own evil, icy glare. Stanley tensed from the stare and moved out of his path. Rutger continued to push the cart along the hall toward the elevator. As he passed the grand staircase, Jules came down the steps and eyed the cart.

"Entertaining early this morning?" Jules asked.

He eyed his nephew and grinned cheerfully. "There's an angel in my bed," he announced. "Have you ever held an angel, Jules?"

Jules considered the question then shrugged. "No, but I held a belly dancer once."

"If I die tomorrow, it'd all have been worth it," Rutger informed him then cheerfully pushed the cart into the decorative elevator.

As the elevator door closed, Jules sighed and shook his head. "I guess someone got some last night."

§

Becka attempted to open the balcony doors then frowned with disgust when they wouldn't budge. She'd already forgotten she was a prisoner. It was a beautiful sunny morning, and she couldn't even enjoy the fresh air. She pulled open the curtains and allowed light to flood into the room. She stretched in the warm sunlight. The bedroom door was heard closing. She quickly gathered herself mid-stretch and looked behind her. Rutger leaned against the bedroom door with a sly grin on his face while admiring her morning ritual. He appeared almost embarrassed.

"Don't let me interrupt your morning stretch," he announced with a sigh.

Becka attempted a smile, although she was embarrassed herself, and approached the sofa. She casually sat on it with her legs tucked beneath her. Rutger pushed the cart toward her, leisurely rollerblading across the area rugs. He left the cart near her then cast himself into a nearby chair where he removed the skates and replaced his shoes.

"You're going to break your neck in those things," she teased.

"Actually, I'm getting rather good at it."

He sprang to his feet and placed a covered platter on the coffee table before her. He removed the lid to reveal waffles with strawberries and powdered sugar.

"Don't be too impressed," he announced while grinning boyishly. "They're frozen."

"I could get used to all this attention."

He placed a teacup on the coffee table, eyed her, and then filled the cup. "I'm completely devoted, my dearest Becka."

He poured himself a cup of tea in the delicate teacup and sat alongside her on the sofa. Becka studied him a long moment, almost uncertain what to make of the unusual man. She picked up the waffle and extended it toward his mouth. He hesitated a moment, hid his grin, and took a bite of it. She smiled warmly then proceeded to take a bite herself.

"So are we safe for a couple of hours?" she asked while enjoying her lavishly decorated frozen waffle.

"From the evil? Yes, quite safe," he replied then grinned deviously. "Everyone can be angry and hateful for another seventeen hours."

She eyed him suspiciously. "Is there a problem?"

"I'm on the castle's most wanted list right now," he informed her. "Apparently, during a drinking binge, one of the guys disappeared." Rutger sank into his own thoughts. "He may have just passed out somewhere."

"You don't think--?"

"No," he announced a little too quickly. "What would the evil want with someone who's eighty proof?"

"We should probably look for him, don't you think?" she offered.

"As you wish," he replied then grinned. "Right after breakfast."

Becka held the waffle out to him. He moved closer with his hands on the sofa like a stalking predator, not even looking at the waffle.

She eyed him sternly. "Down boy."

Rutger stopped mid-stride, moved back, and bit from the pastry. He sat back on his right leg and casually picked up his teacup.

"Not half bad for frozen." He cast a devious glance at her. "Would've preferred what I'd been aiming for though."

He returned to sipping his tea and avoided looking at her, attempting to play innocent. Becka removed one of the strawberries and moved onto her knees closer to him. She placed her left hand on his shoulder and held the strawberry before his mouth while seductively leaning over him.

"Be a doll and find me a pair of pants," she cooed while dangling the strawberry in front of him.

He eyed the strawberry, grinned with pleasure, and placed his mouth over it, taking her fingers as well. She had to pull her fingers back out with some effort.

Rutger sprang to his feet, turned toward her where she kneeled on the sofa, and kissed her passionately but briefly. She immediately tensed. Despite her surprise, he pulled away before she could react.

"I'm allergic, but thanks anyway," he announced.

As he turned and headed across the room for the closet, Becka ate the strawberry that had mysteriously found its way into her mouth. Rutger removed a pair of pants from the closet and approached her.

"You do know I'd have little objections to spending the rest of the morning making love to you," he casually informed her. "You don't have to be afraid to ask."

She rested her elbow on the back of the sofa and placed her temple to the back of her hand. "I hate to ruin the entire seduction scene for you, but I'm a virgin," she reported. "That means I don't do that sort of thing."

Rutger suddenly pounced onto the sofa alongside her with enthusiasm and grinned deviously. "Better extend that straight through until evening then," he announced with delight. "Neatness counts."

She leaned closer, unable to contain her smile, and gently smacked his face. "No."

He frowned and dropped the pants on her lap. "Tease."

She collected the pants then stood and turned to face him. "I'm quite satisfied with the emotional stimulation," she informed him and flashed a smile. "That's the difference between men and women." She kissed him quickly on the nose and walked toward the bathroom.

"It was just a suggestion," he called after her while watching her as she entered the bathroom.

The door closed and the shower could be heard running. Rutger sprang from the sofa, approached the door, and knocked lightly.

"Could I join you?" he asked through the door. "Or at least watch?"

The bathroom door opened, surprising him. He jumped back then grinned with eagerness. A wet sponge flew out and hit him in the face. The door shut and locked. Rutger picked up the wet sponge and again tapped lightly on the door.

"I could wash your back." He groaned and slid down the doorframe, sitting with his legs stretched in front of the closed bathroom door. He scratched softly at the bottom of the door. "Becka--?"

Chapter Ten

Stanley, Phil, and Bryan entered the trophy room and looked around a moment before finally setting their eyes upon the case of daggers. Phil approached the unlocked case and eyed the assortment of knives. The jagged-edged dagger had been returned to the case, giving no indication it had recently been used. Jules entered the trophy room after the three men, paused in the doorway, and eyed them suspiciously.

"What are you doing in here?" Jules demanded and eyed them with distrust. "I thought we were going to check the bedrooms and the dungeon."

"We were thinking about arming ourselves before going to the dungeon," Stanley casually replied.

"But there's nothing around during the day," Jules informed them. "You don't need weapons."

"Harold's missing," Bryan remarked while glaring at him, "and we haven't exactly ruled out your uncle just yet."

"I hate to ruin your conspiracy theory, but it would appear my uncle was with Becka all night."

"I won't believe that until I hear it from her," Stanley remarked and returned his attention to the knives on display. "Do you honestly think some big-time novelist would fall for a lunatic like Rutger?"

"He's not a lunatic," Jules protested then seemed to fumble over his words. "He's been under some pressure, that's all. How would you react if you were locked up for five years?"

"They'd put me away for three once," Stanley offered and raised a clever brow. "I didn't go insane."

"You also weren't isolated and forced to live with some demon," Jules snapped.

"I'm still not convinced there's a demon," Stanley informed him and opened the knife case. "How do we know your uncle didn't just make it all up? He could have rigged the doors and windows to trap us here so that he can kill us one by one."

"And he just chose to remain here by himself for the last five years?" Jules demanded then rolled his eyes. "Give me a break." He then seemed to realize Stanley was in the knife case. "That was locked."

"No, it wasn't," Stanley replied.

"Crazy people do strange things, Jules," Bryan remarked.

"I'm telling you, he's not crazy."

§

*B*ecka walked along the hallway while rolling up the sleeves of her borrowed shirt. Rutger remained by her side with his hands in his pockets while giving her his full attention.

"I could give you the grand tour while we look for Harold," he announced cheerfully. "Where would you like to start first?"

She seemed surprised by the offer. "Actually, I'd like to check out the dungeon."

"Really?" Rutger stopped in the hallway and stared at her with surprise.

Becka realized he'd stopped then paused to look back at him. "Something wrong with that?"

"I just didn't imagine you were into the darker side of humanity."

"I write thrillers, Rutger," she reminded him. "A dungeon is right up my alley." She studied him a moment and appeared curious. "Are you disappointed?"

He considered the comment then smiled warmly while chuckling. "No. I just can't figure out how to make a trip to the dungeon romantic."

She groaned softly. "Will you give it a rest before you strain something?"

The dungeon remained dimly lit with modern lights in the form of old torches to keep with the creepy theme. There were several cells with shackles attached to the walls and a torture area filled with frightening devices. Stanley and Bryan walked along the stone corridor and glanced into each cell as they passed. They acted bold, but it was easy to see both were slightly apprehensive about the entire area.

"Harold?"

"It's really no use, Stanley," Bryan announced in a tone of defeat. "He's gone."

Stanley became angry and shoved Bryan against the wall, jolting him. "We don't know that." He released Bryan and relaxed. "Maybe that bastard has him locked away down here."

They continued through the torture chamber area and paused before an old, large door. Stanley attempted to open the door, but it wouldn't budge.

Bryan looked around with increasing concern. "Come on. Let's get out of here."

Stanley pulled the door again with a little, added vigor. It finally creaked open. A foul smell poured out causing both men to gag and cough. Stanley looked into the room and stared with horror. There was a large pile of human remains, which must have contained dozens of bodies. The remains of Harold's partially eaten body were carelessly thrown on top of the heap. Stanley and Bryan screamed, slammed the door, and ran from the dungeon.

Chapter Eleven

Becka and Rutger approached the dungeon door at the back of the hallway. Despite their macabre reason for visiting the dungeon, both seemed to be in a good mood. The door suddenly flew open, startling both. They were lucky the door opened inward or both would have been struck. Their luck didn't hold out long as Stanley and Bryan ran through the doorway from the stairs and collided with them, knocking them to the floor. All four were dazed, but none were injured. Rutger pulled himself to his feet then helped Becka to hers. Stanley and Bryan sprang to their feet and glared demandingly at Rutger.

"Would you like to tell me what happened to Harold now?" Stanley demanded while breathing heavily obviously upset.

Rutger stared at him with surprise and innocently shook his head. "I have no idea what you're talking about."

Stanley suddenly grabbed him by the shirt and shook him several times. "He's dead," Stanley cried out. "Half-eaten on a pile of dead bodies in the basement!"

"Unhand me," Rutger snarled with little emotion as if not hearing the news about the bodies.

Stanley slammed him against the nearby wall and held him immobile. "I want the truth!"

Rutger stared into Stanley's eyes without appearing ruffled by the incident and made no attempt to fight back. "The truth is if you don't unhand me, you'll be sorry."

Stanley punched him in the abdomen, causing him to double over with pain.

Becka cried out with surprise then leaped for Stanley. "Leave him alone!"

Bryan grabbed her around the waist and kept her from interfering. "Your boyfriend is a killer," he announced. "How can you defend him?"

Rutger slowly straightened while glaring into Stanley's eyes with an evil, angry look. He suddenly grabbed Stanley by the throat and squeezed. Stanley gasped, unable to breathe, clawing against the hand cutting off his air. With little exertion, Rutger cast Stanley across the hall and into the opposing wall. Stanley clutched his throat and gasped for air. Rutger then turned his attention to Bryan, who immediately released Becka and backed away.

He pointed a threatening finger at Bryan. "Touch her again, and I'll kill you," Rutger snarled while glaring into his eyes. "Do you understand me?"

Bryan backed up to Stanley as Becka moved alongside Rutger and clung to his arm. She kept her eyes on both men, fearful of their next move.

Despite his hostility, Rutger composed himself. "Show me where you found Harold."

"Fuck you," Stanley shouted while rubbing his throat then turned and walked away.

Rutger cast a look at Bryan and raised his brow in silent question.

"At the end of the dungeon corridor," Bryan informed him. "There's a door to the back of the room." He then hurried after Stanley.

Rutger sighed then turned to Becka. "Would you prefer to wait here?"

She clung to his arm despite her apprehension. "I'll go with you if it's all the same."

§

Jamie placed a plate filled with scrambled eggs and several pieces of toast on a silver serving tray then set it on the kitchen table before Phil and Jules. Both men helped themselves to the brunch as Jamie joined them at the table. The kitchen door slammed against the cupboards, startling all three, as Bryan and Stanley ran into the room. Despite their surprise, Jamie attempted to act as if nothing had happened.

"Brunch?" she asked.

Stanley ignored the question and immediately approached Jules where he sat at the table. "Something has to be done about your uncle."

Jules groaned with annoyance, his brunch officially ruined. "Not that again."

"Harold's dead," Stanley informed them, becoming animated. "We found his half-eaten body in the dungeon along with rotting bodies of a dozen others."

All three dropped their forks onto their plates with looks of nausea and pushed their breakfast away.

"I already told you, he was with Becka all night," Jules informed him.

"I'm sure she fell asleep at some point," Stanley remarked. "He could've come back down."

"He hasn't been around a woman in over five years," Jules informed them while leaning back in his chair. "Believe me; he didn't let her sleep."

"No, I don't believe you," Stanley snarled, about ready to lunge. "A man has been butchered, and your uncle is behind it." He turned to the others and glared at them with hostility. "We need to get him before he gets us."

Jules abruptly stood and tossed his napkin aside. "Wait just a minute--"

Stanley glared at Jules. "I don't mean kill him," he snarled. "I mean lock him up somewhere until Monday."

"And if he is behind this, that would mean he locked the doors and windows," Phil informed his friend. "In which case, we won't be leaving Monday either."

Stanley glared at Jules and pointed an accusing finger. "You need to find out how he locked us in."

"He didn't lock you in," Jules informed them with a bored groan. "He was in the hall with us when the place was locked down. The house sealed itself. I told you that. Why won't you listen?"

"Because it's not possible. Your uncle is the devil himself, and he needs to be stopped," Stanley lashed out. "If you're not with us, you're against us."

Rutger led Becka past several torture devices within the dingy, dark dungeon. Becka studied each device with great interest despite Rutger's desire to reach the back of the room and investigate what

Stanley and Bryan had found. He stopped at the door near the back and pulled the old door open with some effort. The hideous creaking sound was enough to cause Becka to shiver. She fidgeted with nervous anticipation to what they were about to see as the door opened. Both stared inside the large, empty room. They didn't find any bodies and no traces of blood. There was no stench of decay either, just the smell of musty, stale air. They exchanged confused looks.

"I was threatened over an empty room?" he demanded. "I am correct. The room's empty, right?"

"I certainly don't see a pile of dead, rotting bodies," she remarked. "Could they have been mistaken where the door was located? Is there another room?"

Rutger pushed the heavy door shut. "Not in here," he replied then shook his head. "I think those guys either drank too much or found something much stronger." He then sighed and looked at Becka. "Would you like to return upstairs or continue our search for Harold and the dead bodies?"

"We're down here now," she announced as her mood lightened. "Give me the grand tour."

A strange grin crossed his face. "Would you prefer the audio tour or the hands-on version?"

She stared at him with some surprise while folding her arms across her chest as she hid her smile. "You're dreaming if you think you're getting me on the rack or shackling me to the wall."

Although his look indicated he'd taken a moment to consider her comment with great pleasure, he gave her an innocent smile. "I wouldn't dream of torturing you," he announced without hesitation. "Although, the thought of you half-naked, shackled to the wall does sound somewhat appealing."

"And you wonder why I locked you out of the bathroom this morning."

He led her through the chamber and grinned at the comment. "My dearest Becka, you could be completely naked, and I wouldn't touch you without permission."

She laughed as they left the first chamber. "I actually believe you."

They entered the connecting room, which contained shackles on the walls and the stretching rack. Rutger hoisted himself into a sitting position on the old, wooden rack and looked around the room while indicating the torture devices.

"These are all replicas," he informed her. "They function to a degree, but the spikes were filed down to dull nubs so they wouldn't cause injury." He eyed her and raised his brows suggestively. "You know, in case someone like me was to play with them. The castle was built in the early 1900's by some wealthy European. It was claimed he dabbled in black magic and worshiped Satan. For all I know, he may be the same one who speaks to me."

Becka joined him on the rack and sat alongside him. "So when the doors open Monday morning, will you be able to walk out a free man if someone else is forced to stay?"

"I'm only assuming that's how it works," he informed her. "I arrived here with four other men. At the end of five days, I was all that was left." He hesitated then sank into thought. "I never found them dead or alive."

"But who was here before you?"

"I don't recall seeing anyone else," he replied.

"Then how do you know someone has to remain here?" she asked.

"*He* told me I was the castle keeper, and that there would always be someone to oversee the place," Rutger replied while considering the comment. "I may have made some assumptions about the meaning, and I suspect I could be wrong about a great many things. I am, however, convinced he killed the others."

"What makes you think he won't kill you?"

"He said he wouldn't. He needs me here," he insisted while studying her. "I know you can't understand it, Becka, but I believe him when he says he won't kill me."

"I don't understand," she insisted. "If he's completely evil, why would he care if he killed you too? Lies come easy for bad men."

"He doesn't hate me," he informed her. "You don't spend five years as someone's only companion and not leave with something from them." He sighed deeply. "I thought he was learning to care about people, but I'd like to find Harold first before assuming anything."

"You think he's dead, don't you?"

"If he doesn't turn up by lunchtime, I'd be pretty confident that he is."

She shivered slightly and rubbed her chilled shoulders. "We should go back upstairs."

Rutger jumped off the rack and suavely assisted her down even though she didn't need help. He proudly held her hand in his as they walked out of the room together.

Chapter Twelve

Becka and Rutger continued along the dungeon corridor and walked past several mostly dark cells. Stanley jumped out of a cell behind them. As Rutger turned, he was struck on the side of the head with a brass candlestick. He staggered along the corridor with disorientation while clutching his bleeding head. Becka lunged for Stanley to stop the assault when Bryan grabbed her from behind and placed his hand over her mouth. She struggled against him. Despite his injury, Rutger turned angry and lunged for Stanley. Stanley punched him in the face, having the advantage. Rutger struck the stone wall across the corridor. Stanley aggressively punched him in the back then tossed him into a nearby cell, casting him to the damp stone floor. Becka bit Bryan's hand, causing him to release her mouth. Bryan screamed with surprise and pain. Stanley backhanded Becka across the face, momentarily stunning her. Rutger became agitated and attempted to stand but fell back down.

Stanley stood inches from Becka and stared into her eyes. "Be nice, or I'll show you how nasty I can be."

He kissed her harshly on the mouth then pulled away while grinning with satisfaction. Becka used Bryan's hold on her to brace herself as she thrust both her feet into Stanley's groin. As he doubled over, she threw her head back, smacking Bryan in the nose. Bryan's head snapped back and struck the wall behind him. She again used Bryan as leverage and kicked Stanley in the face. As Stanley fell to the floor, Bryan threw Becka into the cell with Rutger. She stumbled over Stanley's writhing body and fell forward into the cell. Bryan clutched his bleeding nose while slamming the door behind her then helped Stanley to his feet.

Stanley glared through the bars at Becka with rage. "You're going to pay for that, you bitch!"

She slowly pulled herself to her hands and knees, slightly dazed. Bryan forced Stanley away from their cell. Rutger slid across the cell to Becka and lovingly brushed the hair from her face while staring at her with concern

"Are you all right?" he asked then examined the red mark on her cheek. His concern turned to rage. "He'll be sorry he did this to you."

Becka moved to her knees and sat on her feet. She looked at Rutger with her own concern and gently touched his bleeding temple. "You're hurt far worse than I am."

"I'm not worried about me." He watched her fuss over his bleeding temple. "You're quite the fighter."

"I had four older brothers," she informed him. "If I didn't learn to fight, I would have been beaten on a daily basis."

"Remind me not to piss you off."

She looked around and groaned with defeat. "So, how do we get out of here?"

"It's a prison cell," he informed her. "You're not meant to get out." Rutger held his head a moment then snorted a soft laugh and grinned teasingly. "Fortunately for us, this place is only a replica, so I believe there's a passageway out." He indicated the walls. "Start pushing on stones. I just need a few minutes to keep my head from splitting in two."

He attempted to stand but immediately collapsed to the floor. Becka gasped and slid closer to his side.

§

Stanley and Bryan walked around the lounge that evening and looked at several paintings along the walls. They were taking inventory of valuable items within the castle, debating what they'd take with them when they were able to leave on Monday.

"Think they're worth anything?" Bryan asked while indicating the paintings.

"I don't know," Stanley replied and frowned. "Art's not really my specialty. Maybe there's a safe." He then looked around and appeared curious. "Where are Phil and Jamie?"

"They're pouting over what we did to Rutger and Becka," Bryan remarked with some irritation then shook his head in disgust at his friends. "Apparently they've stolen a conscience somewhere along the way."

"Better watch them," Stanley announced. "They could ruin the whole thing."

"I told you not to bring Phil. He's more of a conman and petty thief. Home invasion isn't really his thing," Bryan informed him then sank into thought while Stanley looked over a vase on the hall table. "I don't know what's gotten into Jamie though," Bryan continued. "She shouldn't be too upset. She stole from her own grandmother."

"Let's try the study," Stanley suggested. "There might be a safe in there."

As Stanley and Bryan left the room, the grandfather clock struck midnight.

§

*B*ecka sat against the cold stone cell wall and held Rutger's head to her chest while gently stroking his hair. He finally woke, nuzzled the exposed cleavage above the opening in her shirt, and spoke softly into her chest.

"You smell good," he remarked. "Did I die and go to heaven?"

"Hardly. I think we're in hell," she informed him while continuing to stroke his hair. She attempted to look at him where he was comfortably reclined, although the dim lighting made it difficult. "Are you feeling better?"

"The room stopped spinning, but I feel so cold," he informed her.

Becka looked down at his nose buried in her chest. "Yes, I can feel your cold nose."

He nestled his cheek into her chest then sighed as his lips pressed against her cleavage. He eyed her bosom before him. "This must be heaven. I can't remember being this content." There was a moment of silence. "Tell me, Becka. Do I do anything for you?"

She hesitated a moment from the question then kissed the top of his head. "More than I care to admit."

He again nuzzled his lips to her bosom. "Why can't you admit it? Are you afraid I might ravish you?"

"Just afraid," she replied then sank into thought. "I'm not sure who or what you are. I don't think you even know the answer."

Rutger's eyes suddenly opened. He slowly lifted his head away from her chest and looked her in the eyes with some surprise. "You think I'm the monster?"

"I really don't know," she replied while staring back at him. "Are you sure you're not?"

Rutger stared at her a long moment as if contemplating the question. He wasn't upset or concerned. He simply returned his head to her bosom. "I don't think I am, so that must mean I'm not. If I was a monster, Stanley never would've touched you. I'm sure I could've stopped it."

"Maybe there's hope then."

"Would you be terribly disappointed if I killed Stanley?" he asked with little emotion.

"Killing him would be a bit severe."

"You're probably right. I suppose I'd only feel better for a little while." He glanced up at her and grinned with enthusiasm. "Can I beat him within an inch of his life?"

"Almost the same difference," she replied then sighed. "It's over. Revenge won't change what's happened. Besides, I don't think he's feeling so good right now either."

Rutger kissed her bosom then straightened with some discomfort before she could protest and looked around the dimly lit cell. "The back wall would be the best place to start poking at stones. Anywhere from the waist up to eye level."

"Are you sure you're feeling well enough?"

"As tempting as it is to remain with my head to your bosom, I'd rather not spend the entire night down here."

He slowly pulled himself to his feet, although he had to hold the wall a moment for support. Becka quickly stood and held onto his arm. He pointed at the back wall. They approached the wall from opposite ends and began pushing on stones. Becka pushed on one causing it to move inward. A section of the wall slid open an inch.

Rutger looked at her and smiled. "That wasn't so difficult." He then took her hand. "I'd better lead. It's going to be dark and full of nasty cobwebs."

"With spiders?"

"You aren't afraid of little spiders, are you?" he asked with a strange look on his face.

She fidgeted slightly then forced a confident smile. "No, of course not."

"Good, because I've seen them the size of baseballs." Rutger entered the narrow stairs and pulled on her. "You should hear them crunch when you step on them."

Becka appeared horrified just before being pulled into the passageway behind him. They traveled through the dark passageway for several minutes, taking it slow. Becka was afraid to touch the damp, stone walls in fear of touching something creepy and crawly. They traveled up a set of stone steps, which wasn't pleasant in the darkness. When they reached the end, Rutger was able to open the exit. He looked into the empty, first floor hallway then led her out behind him. Once they were in the light, she could see Rutger was covered with thick, spider webs. A few meaty spiders crawled along his body, although he didn't seem to notice or care. He looked casually back at Becka, who pulled webs off her and danced around while batting at a large spider.

"Oh, yuk!" She jumped away from the spiders racing around the floor.

Rutger pointed down the hall as a meaty spider ran up his arm toward his shoulder. "We'll take the elevator upstairs so that you can shower."

She pulled away from him and glared at his web-coated body. "Will you do something about *them*?"

Rutger looked back at himself and the coating of webs and spiders covering him. He casually removed the webbing and brushed off the large spiders. Becka watched the hearty creatures run back to the dark passageway before Rutger closed the doorway. They approached the elevator and rode to the upper floor then headed for the master bedroom. Rutger allowed Becka to enter then waited just within the doorway.

"I'll get some tea to warm us before bed," he informed her. "Would you like some brandy in yours?"

"Actually, I think I would," she announced with a sigh then gave him a serious look. "Go light on the tea and heavy on the brandy."

He chuckled. "Certainly. Save me room in the shower. I'll join you when I get back."

"Nice try, but you can forget it."

Rutger flashed a teasing smile then left the room, locking the door behind him.

Stanley stood before a wall safe hidden behind a painting within the study. Bryan handed him a small screwdriver and a hammer, actually believing they'd be able to open the safe that way. While

Stanley worked on the safe, Bryan kept watch on the remainder of the study to alert him to any unwanted visitors. Stanley pounded on the screwdriver with the hammer several times before hitting his finger.

"Fuck!"

Bryan didn't bother looking back at his friend, having lost his patience for the vain attempt to open the safe. "Why don't you just get the combination from Rutger? I'm sure he'd cooperate if we had his girlfriend."

Stanley concentrated on the safe and made another attempt to open it with the hammer and screwdriver. "He's not going to tell us anything."

"You're just afraid she'll give you another beating," Bryan teased while briefly glancing back at his friend.

"Oh, very funny," Stanley snapped without turning to face Bryan. "I'm sure I won that round."

Bryan suddenly let out a loud and dramatic gasp. Stanley was obviously annoyed by the distraction and turned toward his friend.

"What's the drama about this time?" Stanley demanded with a groan.

Bryan clutched his throat, attempting to stop the blood pouring from a deep tear through his jugular. Stanley watched in horror as his friend collapsed to the floor, blood spilling across the area rug. There was no one else in the room, stunning Stanley. He then heard a sound between him and the safe. Stanley spun around and saw Rutger standing before him with blood covering his chin and mouth. Stanley jumped back with surprise and horror and held up the hammer and screwdriver defensively.

"It *was* you," he cried out then appeared alarmed as if suddenly considering something important. "How'd you get out of the dungeon?" Without waiting for an answer, Stanley darted behind the library desk.

Rutger casually approached Stanley and the desk, stepping on Bryan's chest as he gasped his last few breaths.

"There's a very funny story that explains everything, Stanley," he informed him while chuckling, "but I doubt you'd find it amusing."

Stanley cast the screwdriver aside and pulled a switchblade from his back pocket. The blade popped out.

Rutger eyed the small but sharpened knife with some amusement then met Stanley's gaze. "Harold had a much bigger knife, yet it did him little good when I tore out his throat."

Rutger suddenly lunged across the desk for Stanley. He slashed with his knife, slitting Rutger's throat. Rutger gasped as blood poured from his neck, and he fell off the desk onto the floor. Stanley jumped back several feet and stared at the motionless man a moment, watching his blood spill from his neck wound and create a puddle on the floor beneath him. When he was convinced Rutger was dead, he slowly moved closer and stared at him. His confidence soon returned while he waved the bloodied, switchblade knife.

"Want to fuck with me?" Stanley demanded in an arrogant tone. "That's what happens when you fuck with me!"

Stanley kicked Rutger's motionless body as he walked past him. Rutger's eyes suddenly opened.

Chapter Thirteen

Becka's silhouette was seen through the frosted glass shower door as she soaked under the hot stream of water. She had her hair tied up to avoid getting it wet, allowing the water to relax her shoulders. A shadow moved past the shower, though she didn't appear to notice. She heard a faint clunk. Becka came back to life and looked at the frosted doors while listening intently.

"Rutger? Are you out there?"

There was no response, alarming her. Becka grabbed the towel hanging over the shower door, wrapped it around her wet body, and shut off the water. She heard a distinct popping sound coming from the bathroom. Becka grabbed a back scrubber brush and threw open the shower door with the scrubber in her hand, prepared to strike. Rutger sat on the edge of the whirlpool tub with a glass of champagne in his hand. He smiled warmly while watching her with the deadly scrubber in her hand.

She frowned and lowered the brush. "I wish you wouldn't do that." She cast the brush aside and stepped out of the shower.

"I couldn't resist the temptation of watching your sexy silhouette in the shower," he informed her. "I hope you aren't too angry. I brought champagne as a peace offering."

He picked up the second glass and approached her with it. She eyed both him and the glass.

"That's very romantic of you, but do you suppose I could get dressed first?"

He playfully pouted. "Kind of takes the fun out of it."

"Tough."

He resumed his smile, collected the bottle of champagne, and left the bathroom. Once she was changed, Becka entered the bedroom wearing one of Rutger's clean shirts. She removed the clip from her hair and allowed her mildly damp hair to fall free. Rutger leaned suavely on the sofa holding both glasses, patiently awaiting her. Becka couldn't help but shake her head at his undying dedication. She approached, sat down alongside him, and accepted the glass. She hesitated a moment then glared at him.

"Oh, no," he muttered, appearing scolded. "I'm in trouble now."

"You just don't stop," she remarked with a groan. "What will it take for you to turn it down a notch?"

"Well, I suppose if you threw me down and repeatedly made love to me, that might slow me down for a few hours," he announced cheerfully. "You could tell me I repulse you and you never want to see me again." He frowned while considering the comment. "That would work, although I'd probably throw myself into the fire."

Becka set her glass down and placed her hand on his. "I appreciate the romantic gesture, Rutger, but I'm not the type to sleep around," she informed him with a sincere look in her eyes. "I'm not looking for a whirlwind romance. I'm looking for a long-term commitment."

"No one's more committed to you than I am. It's not even about sex, Becka," he informed her. "I'd be satisfied with whatever you're willing to give me. I'd be happy just to hold you in my arms all night." He smiled almost dreamily. "I'd marry you tomorrow if I could. My intentions couldn't be purer."

She studied him from where she sat on the sofa. He set his glass down and leaned closer to her. Becka didn't move away and watched him with anticipation. He gently kissed her on the lips. She uncertainly returned the gentle kiss.

He slowly pulled away and smiled. "See, I'm not the monster. I'm just a crazy man in love."

Becka slowly leaned closer to him, touched his face, and stared into his eyes. "I bet you're a great lover."

"I could be--with you."

Rutger lowered his mouth to hers and kissed her gently but passionately. Despite her better judgement, she clung to him and returned the kiss. He slowly lowered her to the sofa, running his hand along her side and to her bare leg. His hand traveled up her thigh and beneath the shirt. His mouth left hers, and he immediately began kissing her neck and throat. Becka clung to his neck and ran her fingers through his hair. He suddenly hesitated. She opened her eyes and attempted to look at him.

"Is something wrong?"

Whatever caused him to hesitate immediately vanished. Rutger continued to kiss her neck and managed a tiny laugh. "Just a little nervous, but I'm not sure why."

"You're not the only one."

He pulled back to meet her gaze, smiled warmly as he gently touched her face, and then eagerly kissed her.

§

Jules, Phil, and Jamie sat at the game room bar drinking and looking pathetic. Each had sedate looks on their faces with their heads propped on their fists. Stanley ran into the game room and slammed the doors behind him, bracing them closed with his body. He was out of breath while clutching his bloody switchblade.

"What happened to you?" Jamie gasped.

"It's Rutger," Stanley cried out. "He killed Bryan right in front of me. I stabbed him in the throat, but it didn't even faze him!" He breathed heavily and appeared frightened. "He's after me, and he's pissed!"

Stanley bolted across the room and attempted to pull a table in front of the doors.

Jules approached with a look of concern and some disbelief. "Calm down, Stanley."

Stanley raised the knife to Jules in a threatening manner. His eyes were wide and wild. "No one leaves," he cried out. "He won't die! You can't let him in!"

"He's my uncle," Jules remarked with surprise then frowned. "Do you really think he'd hurt me?"

"Yes, now back off!"

"I thought you said you'd locked him in the dungeon with that woman," Jamie remarked, seemingly unfazed by his outrage. The alcohol may have helped.

"Easily solved," Jules announced. "The dungeon cells are non-functional. Replicas. In other words, they're not real. They're designed with passageways out. Even I know that."

"See," Stanley cried out and darted looks around the room. "I told you it was him!"

"I saw him taking a bottle of bubbly upstairs along with two glasses," Jules casually informed Stanley. "I think he wants a piece of Becka more than he wants a piece of you."

Stanley became angry and threw his arms around wildly, concerning everyone with the bloody knife he still held. "It's all a hoax. She's probably already dead!"

"He wants to screw her; not kill her," Jules responded. "The man's obsessed with her. The only way you'd need to worry about him is if you'd hurt her."

Stanley stared at him with a look of guilt and fidgeted.

Jules saw the look on his face then rolled his eyes and groaned. "You idiot!"

Phil finally stood and approached them, staring down Stanley. "What now? Do you want us to stay in here all night like caged animals?"

"He's not human," Stanley cried out with fear and anger. "I'm telling you!"

"Let me talk to him," Jules announced and offered a bored sigh. "He'll listen to me."

Stanley waved his bloody knife near his face, causing Jules to jump back. "If you go out there, I'm locking the door behind you," he cried out. "You're on your own."

Jules rolled his eyes and waved him off. "Yeah, okay. Whatever. I'll talk to him and straighten this entire matter out," he remarked. "I'm not afraid of Uncle Rutger."

Stanley moved the table away from the door and quickly backed away from it. Jules opened the door, peered into the hallway with some apprehension, and then left. Stanley immediately closed the doors and returned the table in front of them.

Chapter Fourteen

Several minutes had passed since Jules left the others in the game room. Stanley paced the large room near the barricaded door. There was a soft tapping on the door, alarming him. Stanley eased his way closer to the door while clinging to his switchblade knife.

"Stanley, open up," Jules casually announced through the door.

"Is he gone?"

"Yeah, I'd say," Jules remarked through the door. "There's no one in the study. Not Rutger; not Bryan; not even a trace of blood."

Stanley appeared shocked by the news. He pulled the table away with amazing strength and threw open the door.

Jules stood in the doorway and stared at him while shaking his head in disbelief. "You're two for two, Stanley."

Stanley ran from the room, hurried to the nearby study, and stopped in the doorway. He looked around the nearly spotless room with a baffled look. He suddenly gritted his teeth and spun to face the others, who had followed and now stood behind him.

"Bryan was dead," he proclaimed becoming animated. "Rutger killed him. I saw him do it! He ripped his throat out with his teeth. I stabbed him, but he wouldn't die!"

"I'd love to believe you, Stanley, but there should be some blood, you know, with all that ripping going on," Phil remarked then looked around. "How could he have cleaned up all that blood so quickly?"

"Shut up!"

"Remember, we're not supposed to become angry," Jules informed him. "It brings the demon."

"Demon my ass," Stanley cried out while slinging his knife in the air. "There's no demon, only a man with a sick sense of humor and psychotic tendencies."

"You're being completely irrational," Jamie informed him while keeping an eye on the knife in his hand. "Bryan's playing a trick on you."

"I'm going upstairs to get that bastard myself," Stanley cried out.

Jules jumped in front of him and stared into his eyes. "That would be a mistake," he announced. "You don't want to bother him. Interrupt whatever he has going with Becka, and you may actually see that psychotic side."

"He killed two of my friends and nearly killed me," Stanley lashed out. "I don't care what I interrupt. I'm going to kill that bastard!"

Stanley pushed past them and hurried from the study. All three ran after him.

Rutger and Becka gently moved against each other beneath the covers on the large, canopy bed. He held her hands to the mattress as they kissed warmly but passionately. The movement beneath the covers continued as Becka gasped without opening her eyes. Rutger's eyes remained open while watching her reaction to their lovemaking with great pleasure. He released her hands and clung to her. She ran her hands along his back and moaned to his movement. After their passionate lovemaking, he held her in his arms and affectionately kissed her neck and shoulders. She smiled with contentment and opened her eyes to see him studying her expression.

"You are divine, my dear Becka," he announced warmly, unable to take his eyes off her.

She pushed him onto his back, and half lay on top of him while smiling deviously. "And you are incredible."

"I'll interpret that as you won't mind losing sleep tonight," he teased.

She kissed him on the nose and grinned. "We can discuss it over champagne in the hot tub."

Rutger chuckled, although obviously delighted at the suggestion. "I think I've corrupted you, my dear."

He pulled her against him and kissed her passionately. They heard angry voices in the hallway not far from the bedroom door. Rutger became alerted to the voices, pulled back, and looked into her eyes.

"I think we're about to have company," Rutger remarked.

They could hear their voices in the hallway. "Should've let me kill him when I wanted to," Stanley cried out.

Becka suddenly eyed Rutger with concern as both sat up. "What do you suggest?"

"You may want to put some clothes on," he mildly suggested.

Outside the master bedroom, Stanley pounded on Rutger's door. Jules, Phil, and Jamie remained nearby with looks of disgrace to his hostility.

"Open up, Rutger!"

When there was no response, Stanley kicked the door several times until it cracked and flew open. All four looked around the dimly lit room giving off a romantic glow. The room was empty, although the sheets remained mussed, indicating they had been there not long ago. Stanley ran across the room and stormed into the bathroom. He stopped in the doorway and frowned with disappointment when he didn't find anyone. Jules casually entered the room and looked around, paying particular attention to the mussed bed.

Stanley approached him from the bathroom still carrying his bloody knife and held it before Jules' face. "When I find your uncle, I'm going to kill him." Stanley stormed toward the door and paused near Phil. "Let's go get this guy."

Phil stared at him with surprise and shook his head. "No way. I think you're all nuts!" He turned and left the room.

Stanley was surprised by his reaction then looked at Jamie. She gave him an appalled look, folded her arms across her chest, and shook her head. Stanley pushed past her without a word. Jules approached Jamie and placed his hands in his pockets while staring after Stanley.

"Do you think he could have killed Harold and Bryan?" Jules asked, indicating Stanley.

"Stanley's a real hot head at times," Jamie informed him, "but I don't think he's killed anyone before. I can't say I know him that well though." She hesitated while staring back at him. "Do you really think your uncle *didn't* kill them?"

"The man has really changed since his tycoon days," Jules insisted. "There was a time I may have believed it was possible, but over the past few years, he's become almost saintly. All he seems to care about is love and cupcakes."

"Cupcakes?"

"Yeah, he has a real addiction."

"But what happened to Bryan and Harold?" she asked. "They must be dead, don't you think?"

"I don't know, but I don't intend to run around this place at night to find out either," Jules informed her then tensed slightly. "We'd better settle in somewhere for the night. I'd feel safer if we locked ourselves in a room away from Stanley."

"I think I'd rather take my chances with you than being anywhere near Stanley right now."

Chapter Fifteen

The dimly lit attic stretched the entire distance of the castle in a never-ending sea of clutter. Many items were as old as the castle itself and probably worth a small fortune. Thick cobwebs and dust coated most of the stored items, giving the attic a cluttered, creepy appeal. Rutger held Becka's hand as he led her across the attic along a narrow path.

"This certainly is creepy," she remarked while eyeing the thick cobwebs and the few meaty spiders attempting to hide within them. Why did she feel as if they were watching her, sizing her up for their meal?

He grinned at her with delight. "You like?"

She laughed in response. "It's fascinating."

"No one would ever think to look for us up here. I found that secret passageway years ago," he informed her. "There's also one that leads to the study, but they'd probably find us if we hid in there." He pulled her along the attic. "Since we're here, and we have time; there's something I'd like to show you."

They walked halfway across the attic, which was a rather long haul. Rutger stopped her by a chest that resembled something from a pirate's ship. He opened the chest and showed her an old, antique box decorated in gold and silver. Its value could only be imagined. He set the box on top of the chest and opened it to reveal a shimmering silver sphere that appeared to be suspended in mid-air. Becka stared at the sphere and marveled at its ability to float in suspended animation.

"What is it?" she practically gasped, having never seen anything like it before.

"I'm not sure, but you can hold it in your hands and yet never touch it," he informed her with a childlike enthusiasm. "There's this

175

warm sensation that sweeps through you. You feel as if you're flying."

He removed it from the box and placed the glowing silver sphere into her outstretched hands. Her entire body was surrounded by the bright light, fascinating her. Rutger placed his hands over top of the ball in her hands. He too was engulfed by the brilliant light. They felt the sensation of flying above a thick mist. The mist cleared, and they saw the castle and its estate far below. They almost appeared to be flying overhead without ever leaving the attic floor. Voices seemed to surround them in their state of bliss. Most couldn't be made out, but they soon heard familiar ones.

"You think I'm the monster?" Rutger's voice echoed softly in the mist.

"Are you sure you're not?" Becka was heard responding to his question.

There was a brilliant flash of light. It was frightening at first, but oddly warm and comforting. They were transported to another place and another time. They witnessed Rutger and four men sitting around the dining room table while staring at the sphere in the center. There was another flash of Rutger holding the sphere and chanting. As one image faded away, another flash revealed Rutger killing the four men, one at a time. During the final flash, Becka swung the decorative sword at Rutger, connecting with his neck, and nearly decapitating him. Both gasped at the image and released the ball. It fell gently to the floor and sat dormant without ever hitting the dusty wooden planks. Becka and Rutger stared at each other, sharing the same expression.

"What was that?" she suddenly cried out.

"That can't be a premonition," he announced with concern. "It just can't. You wouldn't kill me."

"You killed those men?" she suddenly gasped. "They were your business partners, weren't they?"

"They were my business partners, but I didn't kill them, I swear," he insisted defensively.

Becka slowly pulled her hands from his while staring at him with a frightened look.

His expression shattered as he stared back at her. "Becka, don't do this."

"I-I just need a few minutes alone to sort this out," she announced while backing away from him.

"It wasn't me, I swear."

She continued to back away from him, unable to take her eyes off him.

"Please, don't leave me," he gasped while staring at her with a frightened look.

"I just need some time," she gasped, the fear flooding her senses. "Please, understand." She turned and ran across the cluttered attic.

"Becka, don't go," he called after her but didn't dare follow. "Becka, don't leave me!"

Rutger grabbed the floating sphere, looked at it with hostility, and then angrily cast it across the attic. It flew back to him like a softball pitch and nearly knocked him down. He caught the sphere, held onto it with both hands, and stared into it.

"What does this mean?" he demanded with anger. "I can't lose her! I'm not the monster!"

§

Jamie walked across the library and paused halfway to the raging fire within the massive fireplace. Rutger sat in his chair before the fire with his temple resting against his fist. He appeared distant while staring into the flames. Jamie hesitated, drew a deep, nervous breath, and took a few steps closer.

"I was hoping to have a moment alone with you," she announced, breaking the silence.

Rutger didn't look up and showed no interest in her presence. "We've nothing to discuss," he muttered without emotion. "I have no use for you."

She slowly approached and paused a few feet before him. "None at all?"

"What use would you like me to have for you?" he muttered without looking at her.

"I was hoping you'd want me for a lover."

Her words caught his attention. He lifted his head and stared at her a moment, although his expression didn't change. "What about Becka?"

"I thought maybe if you'd grown tired of her, you'd like to try me."

He continued to stare at her then stood like a stalking predator. "Try you?" He approached her with a strange look on his face. "In what way?"

Jamie grinned lustfully. "In *that* way."

Rutger paused before her, studying her a long moment, then tilted his head with a strange look. "Why?"

She hesitated, almost as if frightened by what she had to do, then ran her hands in a caressing manner along his chest. "Because there's more to you than meets the eye."

"Oh? You think I have some special gift? That I can control the stars and moon?" he asked while touching her arm then caressed her skin. "And you'd like to be connected to a man of great power, even if it's for evil?"

"I find it intriguing, I'll admit."

"And what about Becka?" he asked while tilting his head with a curious look. "What would I do with her?"

"Get rid of her," Jamie replied a little too quickly. "You don't need her when you have me."

Rutger studied her a moment then pulled her against him and kissed her roughly on the mouth. Jamie returned the aggressive kiss. She suddenly tensed, allowing a muffled gasp to escape, and attempted to push him away. He continued to kiss her and wouldn't release her. She muffled a scream as blood ran down her chin and panic swept over her face.

§

Jules approached the closed library door, hesitated a moment, drew a deep, tense breath, and then opened the door. He took one step inside while speaking. "Uncle Rutger--?"

He suddenly stopped when he saw Rutger holding Jamie limp as a ragdoll in his arms. Her lips were torn away from her face, her throat was ripped open, and she was covered in blood. Rutger looked at Jules as blood ran down his chin from bloodied, sharp fangs. He snarled at his nephew as if smiling. Jules stared horrified at the sight then ducked back into the hall, slamming the door shut behind him. Jules stared at the closed library door a moment then looked around the hall in panic. Becka hurried down the stairs, appeared relieved to see him, and approached.

"Oh, Jules. Thank God," she gasped. "I don't know what to do."

Jules ran toward her and grabbed her hand while staring into her eyes with fear. "Run."

"What?"

He pulled her down the hall and into the trophy room, slamming the door behind them. Jules released Becka once they entered the trophy room and frantically worked on barricading the door.

She watched with alarm as he pushed heavy objects in front of the door. "Jules, what's gotten into you?"

Jules backed away from the blocked door and removed a sword from the wall. He stood several feet from the door, stared at it, and clutched the sword, prepared to strike.

"Stanley was right," Jules cried out while trembling. "My God; was he ever right!"

"Right? About what?" she demanded with surprise. "What's going on?"

"My uncle--he's gone mad," Jules cried out. "I saw him in the library. He killed poor Jamie!"

Becka stared at him with surprise as her mouth hung open. "That's impossible," she gasped while her mind was reeling. "I just left Rutger in the attic not five minutes ago. He couldn't have gotten down here that fast."

"Trust me, Becka. I know my uncle when I see him," he informed her in sheer panic. "I also know that any man with fangs isn't a good thing." He shook his head. "I should have believed Stanley. He told me he killed Bryan in the study, but I didn't believe him. Oh, Becka, we're in so much trouble."

"Killed Bryan?" she gasped. "That's impossible. Apart from a few minutes, we were together all evening."

"Well, I'm telling you, less than an hour ago, my uncle killed Bryan and attacked Stanley," Jules informed her. "We went up to the master bedroom to find him. I wasn't going to let him harm my uncle, but he was right."

"Less than an hour ago, I was with Rutger in the master bedroom," she informed him and folded her arms across her chest. "We heard you approaching and went to the attic. We were together the entire time before and after."

"He couldn't be two places at once," Jules informed her. "He must've killed Bryan right before I saw him with the champagne." He then considered. "That hardly seems right either. He didn't have any blood on him."

Becka stared at Jules a long moment then became alarmed. "I need to find Rutger. We need to go to the attic. He may still be there."

"No, he was in the library right before I ran into you," Jules insisted.

Becka looked around the room then saw the decorative sword from her vision hanging on the wall. She snatched the sword and returned to Jules where he stood staring at her.

"We have to hurry," she informed him with concern.

Jules eyed her with surprise.

Chapter Sixteen

Phil routed through the refrigerator looking for a snack. He removed some leftover fried chicken from lunch and carried the wrapped plate to the table where he sat down. Stanley entered the kitchen in a whirlwind of fury with one of the daggers from the trophy room. Phil held the drumstick to his mouth, mid-bite, and watched Stanley with some surprise. Stanley looked around the kitchen while breathing heavily then finally rested his eyes on Phil. Phil bit into the chicken leg and continued to watch Stanley with a curious look.

"You're going to help me get this psycho," Stanley launched in a state near hysterics while removing a butcher knife from the block. "He has to be destroyed." Stanley rammed the butcher knife into the wooden table near Phil.

Phil stared at the knife embedded in the wood then continued to eat. "No way, man."

"This is your ass too!"

Phil sat back, wiped his hands on a napkin, and sighed. "I have a theory about that, you see. Okay, so maybe Rutger's some monster, and maybe he killed Harold and Bryan," Phil announced then eyed his friend. "Do you remember what Rutger said about the monster? It feeds on fear and anger." He cleverly raised his brows. "You haven't exactly been first-class guests, plotting to steal and especially going after Becka." He shook his head. "No. I'm going to take his advice."

"He's going to kill you too. You're not exactly innocent in all this," Stanley cried out. "You're a thief just like us."

"No, not just like you," Phil corrected while wagging his finger at Stanley. "I made a few mistakes, but I can still correct them." He removed a cross necklace hidden beneath his shirt. "And if I get out of this alive, I'm going to become a pastor just like my father wanted me to be."

"You're insane."

"Not insane, Stanley," he replied. "A long time ago, you made a deal with the devil; now he's coming to collect. Last night, I made a deal with God. It's not too late for you too, you know. Choose the right path, and you too will be saved."

Stanley glared at his friend and raised his brows. "You're going to die; you know that?"

"Maybe so, but at least I know where I'm going," Phil casually replied.

Phil returned to his chicken and didn't give Stanley another glance. Stanley pointed the dagger into Phil's face, but it didn't even rile him enough to look up from his chicken leg.

"Maybe I'll help you get there a little faster," Stanley snarled with rage.

Phil cast a look at Stanley and patiently waited. Stanley sneered and pulled the dagger away from his face. He turned to leave when Rutger entered at the same moment. Stanley jumped with surprise then turned aggressive and attempted to stab Rutger. Phil jumped up from the table, knocking his chair over, and backed away. Rutger easily blocked the dagger and tackled Stanley against the counter. Phil watched in horror while practically tripping over his fallen chair. Rutger suddenly tore into Stanley's throat with his mouth full of sharpened fangs, leaving a massive, bleeding gash. He casually released him.

Stanley twitched, gurgled up blood, and gasped while falling to the floor. Rutger turned toward Phil, who stared at the bloodied fangs and the blood running down the monster's chin. He then looked at the butcher knife within his reach. He clutched the cross necklace instead. Rutger slowly approached Phil as blood dripped from his chin. Phil shut his eyes a moment and said a little prayer. Rutger stood directly before him. Phil slowly opened his eyes and saw Rutger's large, bloodied fangs before his face. Rutger moved to Phil's throat. Phil once more shut his eyes and chanted a prayer. When he opened his eyes, both Rutger and Stanley were gone. There was no blood to be found. Phil trembled slightly and looked around the kitchen for any signs of blood, but there wasn't any.

Becka and Jules walked along the massive, cluttered attic and stopped before the familiar area with the crate. Becka approached the crate and opened the lid. The expensive, decorative box was gone. She looked around with concern.

"I wish you'd tell me what you're looking for," Jules announced.

"A ball," she informed him. "A mystical ball."

Jules groaned and looked away. "Sorry I asked," he muttered.

Becka turned to Jules and stared at him with a strange look on her face. "Tell me what your uncle used to be like; before he was stranded here."

"Oh, he was a cutthroat business tycoon," Jules replied with little forethought. "Made lots of money. Owned people. Complete asshole."

"Then he changed," she remarked. "He was stuck here and became mellow and compassionate."

"Exactly."

Becka sank into thought then looked at Jules with an odd look of knowing. "I think I know how he was in two places at once," she boldly announced.

"Tell me."

"We need to find him and fast."

"This place is huge," Jules protested while indicating the clutter. "How will we know where to look?"

"We don't have to look. He'll come to us." Becka hurried across the attic.

Jules ran after her with a look of surprise. "How?"

§

Jules paced the hallway before the master bedroom then finally paused and knocked on the door. It was obvious he was becoming tense while waiting out in the open.

"Come on, Becka," he announced while shifting looks both directions in the second floor hallway. "This is very unnerving out here alone."

The door finally opened to reveal Becka in her black evening dress from the day she arrived. She looked as stunning as the first day she'd met Rutger. Her hair and makeup were flawless. Jules stared at her a moment with some confusion.

"Did I miss something?" he asked while giving her a quick once-over. "My uncle will come to us because you're dressed like that?"

"If I'm correct, it won't take him long to find me," she replied without hesitation.

He leaned closer and sniffed her. "You smell strong of lilacs."

"I didn't have time to soak in the tub," she replied while fidgeting. "I had to rub the oil on my skin."

"I don't get where you're going with this," he announced with confusion.

"Let's go to the library."

"Why the library?"

"Because that's where he's most comfortable," she informed him then headed down the hall.

"Unless my uncle has become a bloodhound, I don't know why you think this will work," Jules announced and hurried to catch up with her.

"Don't forget my sword," she called back.

Jules hesitated and returned to the bedroom doorway for the sword she'd chosen. As she approached the elevator, Jules caught up with her and gave her a concerned look.

"You intend to kill him?"

Chapter Seventeen

Jules paced before the fireplace while Becka sat seductively reclined on the sofa with her exposed legs stretched alongside her. She looked as if she was posing for the cover of a magazine or one of her book covers. Jules looked at her and shook his head still not understanding her reasoning.

"You can't turn him on if he's not in the room," he remarked then cast another glance at her. "And maybe you should've tried a teddy or a thong." He then muttered while looking away, "I know it would've helped me."

"Will you sit down somewhere and keep quiet," she announced with limited patience.

Jules frowned and cast himself into his uncle's chair by the fireplace. Becka repositioned herself on the sofa and gently ran her finger along the neckline of her dress. Jules watched with surprise then hid his smile and looked away with embarrassment.

"I guess I shouldn't complain," he muttered.

The library door suddenly opened as if on command. Rutger hurried inside, saw Jules in his chair, and then immediately looked at Becka reclined on the sofa. Jules straightened in the chair but resisted standing. Without comment, Rutger approached Becka and sat on the edge of the sofa, taking her hand in his and lovingly kissing it several times.

"Oh, my darling," he announced affectionately. "Please tell me I'm forgiven. I don't want you mad at me again."

Becka smiled warmly and gently touched his face. "It's you who should forgive me."

Rutger appeared puzzled although he enjoyed her hand on his face. "I don't understand," he announced while stroking her hand touching his face. "You've done nothing wrong."

Jules quietly stood with his sword in his hand and approached his uncle from behind.

Rutger held his finger in the air toward Jules without looking behind him. "It is so important that you don't complete that thought."

Jules stopped mid-stride and looked at Becka with some surprise. She didn't even bother looking at him but instead kept her attention focused on Rutger. He affectionately continued to kiss her hand, as if unable to control himself.

"I think I know what's been happening around here," she informed Rutger. "I can even explain that vision we saw in the sphere."

Rutger stopped ravishing her hand and studied her a moment. "It hit me too," he announced then muttered, "very hard, as a matter-of-fact." He appeared momentarily excited. "The demon killed them, and he made himself look like me in order to move around unnoticed."

"Almost right."

"If that's not it, then what other explanation is there?" Rutger suddenly asked.

"You aren't really Rutger."

He stared at her with a horrified look but refrained from bolting up from the sofa or releasing her hand. "You still think I'm the monster?"

"There never was a monster," she replied.

Both Jules and Rutger were now confused as they stared at her.

"But I saw it," Jules firmly protested. "I saw my Uncle Rutger kill Jamie."

"Yes, your uncle came here and discovered the sphere and the power it contained," she informed Jules then drew a deep breath. "He also killed the men who came here with him by using the power from the sphere."

Rutger stared at her and appeared equally confused. "Then who am I?"

She shifted her attention to him. "I'm not sure. I was hoping you could tell me," she replied. "That sphere has something to do with it. I'm just not sure what."

Rutger scratched his head as he sank into thought. He seemed to drift out as he had so many times before.

"So my uncle really did kill the others?" Jules gasped.

Becka glanced at Jules and nodded. "I'm afraid so, he was always a corrupt man," she replied. "When he found unbridled power within that sphere, he became something more evil and unstoppable."

Rutger continued to stare at the floor while deep in thought. "Light."

Both looked at him.

"What was that?" Becka asked.

Rutger suddenly looked at her with an odd realization. "I was a force of light," he practically gasped. "The product of a greater entity from the sphere. When Rutger found me in my box, he wanted to possess my power. I wanted to be free. I wanted to live as a mortal," he explained. "I gave him my power in exchange for his mortal body. Unknowingly, I made him into a monster." He stared at them with surprise and horror as his mouth fell open. "It's my fault. What have I done?"

Becka gently held his face and stared into his eyes. "It's not your fault, Rutger," she informed him. "You didn't know what would happen. You were incapable of seeing the darker side of humanity. You were pure and innocent."

A tremendous weight lifted from him as he smiled while staring into her eyes. "Thank you for understanding."

"But we need to stop him," she insisted and turned serious. "What do we do?"

"The sphere," Rutger announced with enthusiasm. "It will tell us what to do."

"Where is the sphere?" Jules asked.

"In the attic. It rolled away somewhere," he replied and sprang up from the sofa. "I'll get it."

"I'll come with you," Becka announced.

"No, it's too dangerous. If he knows, he could try to stop me," he informed her. "I can't risk you getting in the middle. He knows my weakness for human life, particularly yours. Stay with Jules. Whatever happens; don't show anger or aggression. He can't touch you if you don't give him any power."

They watched as Rutger ran from the room.

Jules exhaled and shook his head. "That was pretty weird," he remarked. "Do we trust him?"

"Yes."

He eyed her with surprise and almost laughed at the irony. "No hesitation with that, huh?"

"None."

"I'm glad you have faith," Jules muttered and studied the sword in his hand. "So that wasn't my uncle? No wonder I'd grown fond of him the last few years."

Several minutes passed before the library door opened and Rutger returned with the sphere in his hands.

Jules stared at the sphere with some surprise. "That's unusual."

Becka jumped to her feet as Rutger approached with the ball. Jules moved closer to it, attempting to get a better look. Becka suddenly grabbed Jules and pulled him back, surprising him.

"That's not Rutger," she gasped.

"What?"

The demon identical to Rutger stared at her and grinned almost as if humored. "How could you tell?"

She stared into his eyes without flinching. "I know evil when I see it."

Jules clutched his sword and raised it. The demon immediately moved toward him.

"Jules, drop it," Becka shouted with alarm.

Jules stared back at her with a terrified look while clutching the sword. "Are you insane?"

"Aggression!"

Jules dropped the sword with a look of horror then stared at his demon uncle with concern. "Any ideas?"

She pulled him back as they stepped away from him. "Don't panic."

"Too late," Jules muttered.

Becka stepped in front of Jules while facing the Rutger demon. He smiled in the most sinister manner.

"This sphere possesses all the power you could imagine, Becka," he informed her in a moderately seductive tone. "Join me, and we can rule together."

"Doesn't look too impressive to me," she remarked with little interest. "What can it do?"

"It can give you everything you want," the demon informed her. "Once I destroy it, all its power will transfer to me, and it'll rid me of Rutger forever."

"Why would you want to destroy him?" she asked while feeling her body twitch with anxiety. "He's stood by you all these years."

"He didn't stand by me, he stood in my way," the Rutger demon snarled. "He was pure, even for a mortal, until you tainted him with mortal pleasures. That's when I was finally allowed inside his thoughts. He'd kept the sphere hidden from me all these years deep inside his mind, so deep, even he'd forgotten about it." He took a step closer to her. "He subconsciously kept himself confined within this castle to prevent me from ever leaving. If he didn't leave, I couldn't leave. The sphere connects us. By finally being able to enter his mind, I can obtain the power of the sphere. Then I can destroy the sphere and him with it. I'll be free to leave here with you by my side."

"Me?" she announced then chuckled softly. "I'm not leaving with you."

"Then you can die with him," the Rutger demon snarled.

"You can't kill me," she informed him. "You can't kill what doesn't hate."

The demon moved closer to her and exposed his fangs close to her face. Becka turned her head and looked away. He moved for her throat.

Jules grabbed his sword. "No, Becka, look out!"

Becka's eyes open with horror as Jules lunged forward with the sword. "Jules! No!"

Jules plunged the sword into his uncle demon's midsection. Despite the sword impaling him, it didn't affect him. The Rutger demon suddenly grabbed Jules by the throat. Becka grabbed the sword and pulled it from his midsection. She held the blade to the demon's face. The Rutger demon looked at the cold look in the eyes of the young woman holding the sword. He suddenly tossed Jules across the room and spun to face Becka. She clutched the sword while backing away. The Rutger demon attempted to grab her.

"No!" Becka cried out and swung the sword, severing the hand holding the sphere.

The hand and the sphere fell to the floor and rolled across the thick padding of light surrounding them. The demon looked at Becka with a mocking smile then reached for her. She stood defensively with the sword raised. As he lunged for her, Rutger bolted into the room and tackled his demon likeness to the floor. Jules scrambled across the floor on his hands and knees and grabbed the sphere, pulling it from the severed hand. Rutger kicked the demon off him and across the floor. Both jumped to their feet in a face-off of identical men. The only way to tell them apart was the missing hand on the demon. Rutger saw his nephew with the sphere.

"Jules," Rutger cried out and pointed to the fireplace. "Destroy the sphere! Throw it in the fire!"

"Jules, no," Becka screamed with horror.

"Do it!"

The demon lunged for Rutger with a mouth full of fangs exposed. Becka swung the sword, slicing halfway through the demon's neck as Jules tossed the sphere into the fire.

The Rutger demon struggled to recover while reattaching his head, healing the gaping wound, and laughed at Becka.

"I'll enjoy making you pay--"

The sphere glowed red hot in the fire. Jules saw the condition of the sphere and gasped with alarm. He threw himself against the wall and covered his face. The sphere suddenly exploded. The demon lunged for Becka. Halfway to her, he exploded, and his body parts flew across the room in bloody chunks. Both Becka and Rutger shielded their faces. The room suddenly became a large vacuum. All the blood and body parts of the demon were sucked across the room and into the fire. Rutger grabbed Becka and clung to her as the heavy suction pulled on them. The room suddenly became still. The sphere rolled out of the fire on its metal base, no longer shielded by a protective light. Jules lifted his head and watched as it stopped rolling. Becka looked at Rutger clinging to her. He slowly lowered his arms and looked at his hands with surprise.

"Hmm," he remarked and ran his hands over his body. "That's interesting."

Becka studied him with the same surprise. "But he said destroying the sphere would destroy you."

"He only knew what he could see in my mind," Rutger informed her then managed a smile. "I'd like to believe I'm smarter than he is."

"But I thought you were part of the sphere," she remarked with surprise.

"We'd traded places, although I maintained control of the sphere. I couldn't allow him to have my power and freedom. He'd be a plague," he informed her then seemed to recall the day many years ago. "I wanted so much to be human, that I banished all other thoughts from my head, including who I really was. I'd invented the story surrounding Rutger's reason for never being able to leave as a means of rationalizing why I had to remain. I had to stay in order to keep my monster contained. I was my own prisoner. Destroying the sphere destroyed the one attached to it, not necessarily the one controlling it."

"Does that mean you're free?" she asked while feeling her heart racing at the thought.

"There's no energy surrounding this place," he informed her while feeling the air. He then grinned and almost laughed. "I've achieved mortality."

Phil ran into the library doorway and slid to a stop. "The doors suddenly opened," he cried out. "We can leave! Let's get out of here!"

Jules ran from the room after him. Rutger took Becka's hand and led her to the library door. Instead of following the others, he shut the door and pulled her into his arms.

"Can I hold you to your promise?" he asked while gently cocking his head in question.

"Which promise?"

"That you'll love me forever?"

She smiled warmly. "I can do that."

"Even without knowing *what* I really am?" he asked with a curious look.

Becka kissed him warmly on the lips. "I'm willing to take the chance."

Chapter Eighteen

Phil ran out the front door and for the main gate at the end of the driveway. He didn't stop until he reached Jules sedan just outside the gates. Jules paused on the porch and watched as Rutger and Becka stepped out of the house. For Rutger, it was the first time he'd ever left the house. Rutger squeezed her hand and smiled proudly.

"It's dawned on me, that I've really never experienced anything firsthand," he informed her. "There are so many things you'll need to teach me."

Becka laughed at the first thought that came to mind. "I don't know. You certainly seemed to figure out sex in a hurry," she remarked while grinning. "How does a pure entity know about these things?"

"Extensive reading. Guess I was a virgin too," he teased. "Thank God I didn't know I had no experience. I'd still be upstairs trying to figure it out."

"Nothing wrong with that," Becka replied then grinned. "Sounds like fun."

Rutger smiled lustfully. "Perhaps we need to go back upstairs and experiment further."

She clung to his arm and smiled her response. As they turned back toward the house, Jules approached them.

"Incidentally, Rutger," he announced, attempting to tackle the conversation delicately. "What do we do about the business and finances? You're technically entitled to them. I certainly can't explain any of this. Without my uncle's body, no one will ever believe he's dead. It'll be a nightmare."

"What do you suggest?"

"Well, you should continue to be Rutger Carrington for legal purposes," Jules informed him. "It'll make life a whole lot easier on all of us."

"I really want no part of Rutger's lifestyle," he informed him. "I doubt I'd much enjoy that."

"How about half the cash and the castle?" Jules offered without thinking twice.

Rutger looked at Becka for advice. She shrugged with little concern. He looked back at Jules. "If it seems fair to you."

"Oh, very fair," Jules announced while grinning.

"Throw in some cupcakes, and I'll sign the papers in the morning."

"I'll bring you a whole case of cupcakes," he announced with enthusiasm then grinned, "Uncle Rutger." Jules turned and hurried down the driveway where Phil motioned for him to hurry.

Rutger looked at Becka and smiled brightly. "A whole case of cupcakes and the woman of my dreams," he announced. "I must be in heaven."

"Is that all it takes to make you happy?" she teased. "Sex and cupcakes?"

"Pretty much." Rutger pulled Becka into his arms just short of the doorway. He smiled warmly. "There may be one or two things I neglected to mention about my returning memory. A few leftover entity side effects."

"Such as?"

He kissed her warmly and grinned. "We'll discuss it over a hot bath."

Becka smiled and entered the castle. Rutger was about to follow then paused and looked at the garden. Several flowers burst out of the ground and rapidly filled the entire garden. Rutger smiled and shut the door behind him. The entire exterior of the castle erupted into a bright, new finish.

The End

Demon Island

Chapter One

Day one. A young redheaded woman wandered through the island jungle along the worn path while cautiously looking around. The island was peaceful with only the sounds of exotic birds singing to one another. Vicki scanned the area as her confidence and arrogance faded to concern.

"Well, I'm here," she announced while looking for any signs of life. "You wanted to talk to me, so let's talk."

There was no response. Vicki insecurely rubbed her arms beneath her white, short-sleeved shirt. The birds suddenly squawked loudly, frightening her. She gasped and looked around, concern clearly on her face.

"Fine, if you don't want to show yourself, I'm going back to the beach with the others," she bellowed.

A twig snapped from behind. Vicki turned around with a look of irritation on her youthful face.

"Well, it's about--"

Vicki stared with horror and let out a terrified scream. She ran down the path, realizing too late that she was heading in the opposite direction of the beach. Someone could be heard chasing her through the woods. Vicki glanced back only once, and despite her hiking boots, she nearly fell to the ground. She stumbled, caught herself, and continued running along the path while screaming. She skidded to a stop and caught her balance while staring at the pool of quicksand before her. She bolted from the path, avoiding the life-threatening substance, and screamed as her attacker was nearly on top of her. She ran through the woods back the way she had come, now slowed by the rocks and vegetation. By the sounds of rustling and twigs snapping, the person chasing her was just a few yards behind.

She could just about see the beach through the part in the trees almost one hundred yards ahead. She veered toward the path without slowing. Vicki no sooner set foot on the path before she was roughly tackled to the ground. She and her attacker rolled several feet and back into the woods on the other side of the trail. Vicki attempted to scramble to her feet when a fourteen-inch dagger plunged into her calf. She screamed and fell to the ground, clutching her bleeding leg. She rolled onto her back while attempting to get back on her feet when the dagger thrust downward, repeatedly striking her in the chest, saturating her once white shirt in bright red blood. She screamed during the first two strikes then gasped and attempted to look at her attacker. The dagger plunged into her throat and went straight through her flesh and bone into the ground beneath her, silencing her screams. She wheezed as blood spilled from her neck. Her eyes remained fixated on her attacker as the knife was pulled free.

§

"I'll be damned if I'm just going to sit here and wait for an explanation," Carrie Goddard said as she stood abruptly from the white, sandy beach.

Her younger sister stood and held her back. "I don't think you should go off on your own," Kera informed her, seeming tense. "There's no telling what's lurking around on this island. Besides, the Parkers are already exploring. We should just wait for them to return."

"It's been three hours since that scurvy boat captain dumped us on this deserted beach, Kera," Carrie scoffed, stating the obvious. "He never even told us why we were left here, or if someone was coming for us. Hell, we don't even know if anyone lives on the island."

If not for their dire situation, the white tropical beach on the warm sunny day would be the perfect island paradise. Instead, Carrie was forced to wait for an explanation or a rescue, possibly even a slow death by starvation. Kera's eyes pleaded with her. Carrie glared at her younger sister, who just barely made the legal drinking age. Kera's dark, shoulder length hair was pulled back into a ponytail, giving her an even younger appearance. She was a natural beauty. Her skin was makeup free and glowed, only enhancing her sparkling hazel eyes accentuated with thick, dark lashes. Despite that Carrie and Kera were the same height; Kera had a slimmer build than her more athletic sister. Carrie groaned with defeat, knowing her less aggressive sister was just as frustrated as she was.

"I'll stay for now," Carrie finally huffed, "but if they're not back soon, I'm going out on my own."

Kera nodded seeming relieved she was able to control her sometimes uncontrollable sister. Carrie cast herself onto the sand and tapped her fingers to her thighs. At twenty-three years old, Carrie was self-confident, very much her own woman, and managed to find trouble everywhere she went. She glanced at Kera, already feeling bad for giving her a hard time. She didn't know why she allowed herself to get so out of hand. She'd looked after her sister ever since a car accident claimed their parents' lives five years ago. Turning eighteen and suddenly finding herself responsible for her sixteen-year-old sister was frightening. She sometimes forgot how much Kera still emotionally depended upon her. Carrie drew a deep breath and raked her fingers through her long, dark hair, attempting to relax for her sister's benefit. Unlike Carrie, Kera didn't seem bothered by the outburst. She'd apparently grown used to it. Carrie didn't like to be tied down, so being stranded on an island surrounded by nothingness was going to be difficult for her.

"Who is this Chester Milton anyway?" Kera finally asked, attempting to lighten the mood.

"I'm sure he must have been a client for the ad agency," Carrie replied. "The name sounded familiar, though I don't know why he'd mention me in his will."

"And the letter said you had to come to this island to inherit what was left to you?" she questioned, although they'd been through it all before.

Carrie nodded then looked back at the ocean. "Considering our present situation, I'd say we've been had."

"You did your research," Kera defended her. "The legal firm is legitimate, and Chester Milton had died a month ago. Mr. Ruvim, his lawyer, was supposed to meet us here." Kera stretched her legs on the beach and rested on her hands behind her. "Maybe he was just delayed."

Carrie was almost certain that was wishful thinking on her sister's behalf. There had been twelve passengers dumped on the beach of the remote, tropical island, but nine grew impatient and decided to explore the island. Carrie looked past her sister at the only other person who chose to stay on the beach with them. Before their first official introduction, Carrie thought Barbie Allender seemed like a nice woman. Barbie was just a tick over five-foot-one and sported a tiny frame, resembling a young teenage girl, although she had to be in her late twenties. Her light brown hair was perfectly styled, and her face was hidden behind a layer of pancake makeup. She appeared very attractive on the surface, as most women did when excessively dolled up. Her slightly curled-up nose gave her the look of a model, and her long fingernails were professionally manicured. Her expensive gold watch with diamond accents was eye-catching even to Carrie, who was somewhat of a tomboy. Barbie obviously came from wealth.

After Carrie spoke with Barbie an hour earlier, her opinion of the petite woman had changed. Barbie was a snob and came across as an annoying, yippy little dog. The conversation proved to be a failed attempt at kindness, and it ended with Barbie looking down her nose at Carrie then clucking her tongue in disgust. Carrie was always one to make a friendly attempt, but she wasn't the best person in the world to piss off. One of the men finally returned. Carrie glanced over her shoulder and watched Danny Boxlander approach then sit down next to Kera. Although they had never met prior to the dock on the mainland, they seemed to hit it off on the boat ride to the island. Danny was traveling alone and possibly just needed a companion.

"I didn't run into anyone," Danny informed the sisters. "I don't know where the others got to."

Danny had only been gone an hour, but the others had been gone nearly two and a half. As he talked with Kera, Carrie ignored their conversation when it became more general and pertained less to their current situation. When Kera laughed, Carrie felt compelled to look at them.

"Are you always this funny?" Kera asked.

"I should hope so," Danny teased. "I'm a comedian. Though for the purpose of this trip, I'm a writer."

"A writer?"

"My best friend is an author. He was invited here but couldn't make it. He's always traveling somewhere being inspired," Danny announced dramatically. "Anyway, I decided to come in his place. It sounded exciting. I don't have many opportunities to visit a private island."

"Did you know Chester Milton?" Kera asked.

"Nah. Probably some friend of Drake's," he replied.

He sat back on the sand and continued his conversation with Kera. Danny made a lasting impression on those on the ship by impersonating the captain and singing pirate songs. He topped off his impromptu show by faking a fall down a flight of stairs, a stunt he was rather good at. Danny was a tall, lanky six-foot-two and was possibly in his mid-thirties. He had sandy brown, shoulder length hair pulled back into a small ponytail and bangs to his brows. His voice seemed to wail when he spoke. Possibly just Carrie's opinion, but he reminded her of Shaggy from the "Scooby Doo" cartoons. Carrie actually liked him. It would appear most people did. He wasn't shy, and he seemed to say what was on his mind no matter how offensive. He managed to get away with his comments since he used humor to achieve them. Carrie then heard Danny speak louder, forcing her to look at him.

"And I said to him, is that a toupee or did something die on your head?" Danny remarked.

Kera laughed at Danny's antics, although Carrie saw Barbie roll her eyes at their conversation. The snobby woman obviously didn't like Danny. She didn't seem to like anyone. Barbie's upper lip curled, and she clucked her tongue with disgust at the lively man. Carrie felt like hitting the woman and knew she had to remove herself from the situation before she actually followed through with her thoughts. Carrie stood and brushed sand from her backside, immediately catching her sister's attention.

"Going somewhere?" Kera asked.

"I have to take a walk or something," she remarked, not telling her the real reason she needed to get away. "I can't just sit here and do nothing."

"Will you stay on the beach?"

Carrie groaned and rolled her eyes.

"Don't roll your eyes at me," Kera huffed. "I could remind you of an earlier incident with one of the other passengers. The man you helped over the ship's rail."

"No, you needn't remind me," she hissed. "I'm only going for a walk. What trouble could I possibly get into?"

"Famous last words," Kera grumbled.

Carrie walked along the beach and found her way to the edge of the woods. She could see a small, well-worn path, possibly created by some animal that roamed the island. She followed it and kept a watchful eye on everything around her. She hoped the path she traveled might lead to somewhere of importance. There had to be more to the island than what met the eye. She paused and watched a snake slither past her. Although it was non-poisonous, she knew her sister would freak out at the mere sight of it. Kera had a classic fear of things that slithered. It seemed silly that her sister was frightened of non-poisonous snakes. She could understand if her sister was afraid of something truly frightening such as spiders. While keeping a mindful watch for spiders, Carrie noticed a red spot on the path. There was another one on a nearby rock. She knelt beside the rock and ran her finger over the red spot. She stared at the blood on her finger. It would appear as if something was recently killed. She wondered what type of predators stalked the woods. Carrie straightened and wiped her finger on a nearby tree then looked around the jungle. Birds sang continuously, keeping her from hearing much else.

Carrie saw something shining five feet in the woods. She considered walking away then changed her mind and went toward the silver object. She paused in the woods and stared at the decorative handle to something buried partially under the brush. She picked it up and lifted it a foot from the ground before discovering it was a dagger covered with blood. Carrie screamed, dropped the dagger, and jumped back a step. Her heartbeat quickened to the frightening find. She stared at the bloodstained fourteen-inch dagger with the tip broken. She shot looks around the area with concern then looked back at the knife and the surrounding area. Carrie's eyes followed a trail of blood just two feet from the knife.

A thin, pale, female hand was exposed from under some brush. Carrie's eyes widened in fear as her mouth fell open. She backed away then turned and ran down the path. She thought she heard someone behind her. Carrie looked back but didn't see anyone. When she turned her head, she collided with someone in front of her. Carrie jumped back a step, nearly falling, and screamed. She stared at one of her fellow castaways, Nicholas Parker.

"I suppose I shouldn't be surprised to find you out here," he scoffed.

Panic filled her as her mind reeled with the new information. Was it a coincidence that he was in the area of a recently murdered woman?

Nick noted her expression and tilted his head. "Is something wrong?"

Carrie was speechless a moment then nervously shook her head and backed up another step.

"You're acting strange," he remarked.

She didn't take her eyes from him and considered his potential involvement in the unidentified woman's death. If he hadn't been involved, she was being ridiculous. Carrie nervously pointed back the way she'd come.

"There's a body in the woods."

Nick stared at her with surprise. "A body? Where?"

"About forty feet from here," she informed him. "Just off the path."

His look hardened, indicating he didn't believe her. "Show me," Nick demanded.

"Are you crazy?" she gasped. "I'm not going back there!"

Carrie could tell Nick was a powerful man, and she didn't want to put herself in a situation where she had to defend herself against him. He was intimidating in both actions and appearance. He stood over six feet and was built solid with broad shoulders. He seemed unusually stern and serious all the time. The tone he used with her was the tone he used with his brother. His voice was very authoritative and commanding, almost guaranteeing cooperation from others. In Carrie's opinion, Nick lacked compassion.

"I used to work for the FBI," he informed her, noting her apprehension regarding his presence. "I assure you, I'm safe."

Carrie was skeptical but gave in and showed him the way to what she'd found.

Chapter Two

Kera looked around the beach with rising insecurity, obviously upset that Carrie had wandered off. Barbie waded in the water up to her knees and appeared to have little interest in anything. Kera looked back at Danny, who was reading a novel written by his friend. It seemed as if Kera was the only one in panic mode. Bart and Cindy Galloway approached from the north. Kera had met the couple on the ship. Cindy was a pleasant woman in her mid-thirties with long, golden blonde hair and blue eyes. She was rather large busted with a slim waistline, easily catching plenty of male attention. Cindy always remained a foot or more behind her husband and was reluctant to talk much. Her husband's dominating personality may have had something to do with it.

Her husband, Bart, was in his late thirties. He was average height although moderately heavyset. He had dirty blonde hair that had receded several inches, and the hair he did have was thinning. His eyes were pale blue and set close together, giving him a beady look about him. Kera looked across the beach and hoped Carrie would return soon. She didn't like being alone with people she didn't know, and it was difficult for her to talk to strangers. She was always the shy one and that only intensified after the death of their parents. She caught a glimpse of a man approaching them. She didn't recognize him at first, but when she saw the large, timber wolf trotting alongside him, she knew he was one of the men from their group.

Duke Wedemeyer was easily remembered, though he barely said a word. Devlin, the exceedingly large, silver wolf often by his side, seemed to attract more than his share of attention. Kera strayed away from the group to avoid contact with him. She didn't want any part of the strange, quiet man; particularly one traveling with a dangerous wild animal. She sat on a large rock and found herself watching him from a distance. Despite her distrust, she couldn't seem to take her eyes off the man. Duke was somewhere in his mid to late thirties, but his gray hair gave him a slightly older appearance. A relatively soft-spoken man, he looked sophisticated and mature. Kera thought he had kind eyes, although they were hidden behind wire-rimmed glasses. Duke only stood five-foot-eight and had a lean, medium build. Danny cast his book aside, sprang to his feet with enthusiasm, and met Duke halfway.

"Did you find anything?" he asked.

"I found the dock not far from here," Duke said and adjusted his glasses. "Beyond the dock, there's a path that leads to a hotel, of all things."

"Who would put a hotel on an island?" Danny asked.

"The rich, eccentric type," Bart replied, moving in on their conversation.

"What are we waiting for?" Danny announced excitedly. "Lead the way."

Kera watched Cindy, Bart, and Barbie join Duke and Danny as they walked down the beach with their bags. Kera looked toward the woods with concern and near horror. Were they just going to leave without Carrie? What about the others? She was suddenly torn with what to do. When she looked back, Danny jogged toward her and extended his hand.

"Come on, Kera," he announced reassuringly. "We'll come back for Carrie."

She held her breath, then smiled and accepted Danny's hand. He pulled her from the rock, kept hold of her hand, and forced her to run behind him like a couple of schoolkids to catch up with the others.

§

Nick examined the dead woman while Carrie observed him from a safe distance. He kneeled on the ground alongside the body and touched her as little as possible so that he wouldn't destroy evidence. From her position nearly ten feet away, Carrie could see blood covering the woman's white shirt just below her sternum and along her throat, although she couldn't make out the wound beneath the caked blood.

"It's Vicki, isn't it?" Carrie asked while fidgeting.

She didn't know the woman personally, but she had seen her on the ship several times. Her red hair was a dead giveaway. It saddened her to see the woman left like that, and it sickened her to think someone they were traveling with was responsible.

"I believe so," he said then patted her pockets.

"What are you looking for?"

"Anything that might tell us why someone wanted to kill her." He sighed and straightened. "There's nothing here. There's no evidence of a struggle, and her pockets are empty." He proceeded to check her fingernails.

"Are you looking for blood?"

"Yes, but I don't see any under her fingernails. Apart from her skinned knees, there's no sign of a struggle," Nick announced although more to himself. "Her attacker must have gotten the slip on her pretty fast." He sat back on his feet and looked at the position of the body. "She was dragged here. The position of the body is unnatural."

Carrie noticed the covered marks on the ground and the dirt on the heels of her hiking boots. "Why would someone want to kill Vicki?"

"Good question," he replied then stared at the dead woman and scratched his head. "Judging by the freshness of the blood and the temperature of the body, I'd estimate she's been dead no longer than an hour and a half."

Carrie looked at her watch with a baffled look. They'd been at the scene nearly a half an hour already. That meant Vicki was murdered only an hour before Carrie found her. She looked up and saw Nick staring at her.

"Who was on the beach when you left?" he asked.

Carrie hesitated and considered the question. "Just Kera, Barbie, and me. Oh, Danny returned before I left."

He nodded then stood. Nick walked toward the dagger and paused to pick it up with his handkerchief. He examined the knife as he walked toward her.

"The blade must have broken off when she was stabbed the fourth and last time. One wound to her calf, two in the chest, and one to the throat. The two to the chest would have been fatal, but I'm guessing she was making some noise, so the killer stabbed her in the throat to silence her." He studied the knife. "The knife itself is a work of art." He wiped the blood onto some moss then showed her the handle. "This is a replica of a medieval dagger. Note the wire wrapped handle."

Carrie peered at the dagger then looked at him. "How could someone hide a knife that size on them?"

"It wouldn't be easy, but it's possible," he said. "Some of the guys were carrying backpacks." Nick gave her a serious look. "I need a favor from you, Carrie."

She eyed him suspiciously. "What sort of favor?"

"Don't tell anyone about Vicki until I've had a chance to investigate her death. I don't see a reason to upset everyone, especially the person who killed her. Once we discover who killed her, we can remove him or her quietly."

Carrie nodded. "All right. I won't say anything to the others, but solve this quickly, okay?"

"Don't worry. I intend to."

§

*N*ick and Carrie walked onto the beach in silence. Carrie allowed her mind to process the information while secretly deducing which of her fellow castaways may have murdered the young woman. Nick still carried the dagger wrapped in a handkerchief. His expression revealed nothing that may have been on his mind. Carrie didn't know how someone could be so emotionless, particularly after finding a woman murdered. When they reached the portion of the beach they were certain they'd left the others, they found the beach empty. Even their bags were gone. At first, Carrie swore they must have made a wrong turn, but there was some evidence the others had been on that particular stretch of beach.

"Where's Kera?" Carrie asked while looking around with concern.

Nick walked past her without a word. She watched him and remained puzzled then saw a man jogging toward them. Nick hurried toward him. Carrie studied the two men together. Jerry was Nick's brother, which wasn't difficult to believe. Jerry favored Nick in size and build. He stood approximately six foot, but his build was less impressive than Nick's muscle mass. Neither was exceedingly muscular, but they were built solid. Jerry was in either his late twenties or early thirties, being Nick's younger brother. Both men had short, dark hair, although Nick's hair was slightly shorter than Jerry's. Jerry seemed more outgoing than Nick and was also the man whom Carrie helped overboard. He was a little *too* friendly, in her personal opinion. Carrie approached the two men, wanting to hear their conversation.

"The others are at the island mansion. Well, actually, it's more of a hotel than a mansion," Jerry said and glanced at the dagger Nick carried. "Where have you been?"

"I'll tell you later," Nick announced then frowned. "It's a long, interesting story."

"Fine. I'll take you back to the hotel. We took all the bags with us. Wait until you see this place," Jerry said with a dry laugh. "It's called Demon Island Hotel."

§

The path to the hotel was well maintained with stones lining the entire walkway, which started at the edge of the beach just beyond a sturdy dock. The path was five feet wide with limited rocks and few vines to obstruct it. It was at least a hundred and fifty yards from the beach to the clearing where the hotel was situated. A large sign hung above the porch. As Jerry informed them, it read, Demon Island Hotel. The wood siding was old, though well-preserved on the plantation style home with a wrap-around porch. An old iron fence surrounded the clearing beyond the hotel, but most of it had fallen down over the years. There was a stone wall beyond that, with a sturdy iron gate across the opening.

"What's that?" Carrie asked, indicating the area beyond the hotel grounds.

Jerry snorted a laugh. "That's an old zoo," he informed her. "Mostly empty cages except for a couple of wolves and a tiger."

They approached the porch and walked up five steps to the front door. The double doors appeared to be the only new thing on the hotel. They followed Jerry through the main entrance. The inside of the hotel was even more spacious than the outside indicated. The foyer and the stairs were secluded from the lobby. Carrie approached the stairs and ran her hand along the polished, wooden banister with a decorative, ten-inch ball on top. The wooden steps had multicolored carpet on them leading up to the second floor. There was also an old elevator beyond the staircase. The hallway had hardwood flooring throughout.

Nick stuck the knife in a nearby flowerpot to conceal it from anyone they might run into. As they entered the lobby, Carrie remained a couple of feet behind and paused to look down the long hallway. She could see several rooms on either side, all with double doors. Most of the rooms had either one or both doors open. She entered the lobby behind Nick. The lobby was decorated with antique furniture. The many sofas and chairs were upholstered in a gray and pink flowered pattern with sculpted wood legs. There was enough seating for fifty or more guests. Toward the center of the lobby, there was a large, walk-in fireplace made of stone and wood with a marble mantle. The carpet was a tacky red and yellow with traces of green in the large, outdated pattern. The front desk toward the back wall was made from sculpted mahogany and had an old register book lying open on top. Behind the desk, there was a door, undoubtedly to the manager's office.

"Wait until you meet Troy," Jerry said with a laugh.

"Troy?" Nick asked.

"Troy Milton. He's Chester's nephew," Jerry remarked. "Pleasant fellow with beady eyes."

"I heard that," Troy said from across the room.

All four looked at the man in his mid-thirties standing in the archway to the lobby. He smiled with long, white teeth, and walked toward them.

"But since you were good enough to add 'pleasant fellow', I'll forgive you," Troy remarked.

Jerry laughed, although it was somewhat sinister. "Troy, I'd like you to meet my brother, Nick. And this is Carrie."

The men shook hands.

Troy gave Carrie a lengthy once-over and grinned. "Is this your beautiful wife?" he asked Nick then took Carrie's hand in his as if about to kiss it.

Carrie glared at him with distrust.

"No, she's not my wife. One of us wouldn't survive the experience," Nick remarked.

"Better yet," Troy said while grinning and raised Carrie's hand to his lips.

Carrie wasn't charmed. She pulled her hand away, keeping him from kissing it. Troy was taken aback, but he seemed to expect the reaction. Carrie thought he had a sinister smile. Troy had light brown eyes that appeared to be too small for his face, giving them a beady appearance. His light brown hair was tied back in a four-inch ponytail. Troy was taller and more muscular than Nick, but not nearly as handsome. In fact, Carrie found him slightly repulsive, and it didn't seem to have anything to do with his physical features. Troy walked behind the desk, turned the register book toward them, and smiled.

"If you'll check in, I'll give you your room keys, and you can get settled before dinner," Troy announced cheerfully. "Attorney Ruvim should be along any moment. Lawyers are generally very punctual."

Chapter Three

The eleven guests gathered in the dining room for dinner at seven o'clock that evening. It was the first time everyone from the ship had been together since they arrived. No one seemed to notice Vicki was missing, and Carrie wasn't about to mention it. The dining room was slightly smaller than the lobby. It had ten round tables, which seated eight each. Two of the ten tables were set for dinner to accommodate the guests. A buffet style dinner was laid out for them on a long, sideboard near the kitchen. Troy entered from the kitchen as the eleven guests uncertainly congregated around the room.

"Please, help yourselves," Troy announced through a toothy smile Carrie had already come to hate. "I must apologize, but we don't have any help this weekend. There was a slight mix-up with the staff, but that shouldn't concern you."

No one appeared eager to start first, but Danny's hunger got the best of him, prompting him to approach the buffet table. Carrie and Kera reluctantly joined him, although Carrie didn't have much of an appetite after finding Vicki's body. She walked past several appetizers without touching anything then glanced back at Troy. Nick was now standing with him, but she couldn't hear their conversation. Carrie looked back at Danny as he piled roast beef onto his plate and smothered it with gravy. Carrie felt her stomach churn.

"Why don't I trust him?" Carrie muttered.

"Who?" Danny asked.

"Troy," she replied.

Kera then spoke from behind Carrie. "Because he's a sleazy pervert," her sister scoffed. "I caught him looking down my shirt earlier."

Carrie looked at her sister and noted she had very little on her plate as well.

"Maybe someone should ask him about the will," Carrie suggested.

"I want to know what happened to the lawyer," Kera remarked with concern.

Carrie glanced back at Troy and Nick. Whatever their conversation, Troy was still smiling. She looked back at Danny as he piled some mashed potatoes onto his plate and poured more gravy over them.

"How do we know the lawyer isn't dead somewhere?" Carrie whispered.

"We don't, but I suspect Nick is getting information from Troy. He seems fairly competent," Danny bluntly informed her. They finally reached the end of the buffet line. "Just relax and let Nick handle it."

Carrie frowned at Danny's lack of concern for their situation, whatever that exactly was. He stood alongside her and looked at her plate.

"Are you going to eat all that?"

Carrie looked at her plate and realized there was nothing on it. She groaned, placed her empty plate on the table, then joined Danny and Kera. She sat at the table and looked around the dining room. Troy was now at the buffet table while Nick joined his brother at the table across from them. She wondered what information he had gained from Troy. He sat beside Jerry and leaned toward him to talk confidentially. What sort of secrets was he telling him? Carrie wished she knew what they talked about.

"Stop staring before they see you," Kera whispered.

Carrie leaned toward Kera but didn't look at her. "What do you make of them?"

"The Parkers? They're strange, to say the least," Kera said. "They make me nervous. I feel like they're watching everything everyone does."

"I'm sure they are," Carrie remarked softly. "They're private detectives, you know."

Kera sat back in her chair and stared at her sister with surprise. "No, I didn't."

§

*C*arrie walked around the trophy room and looked at the various animal heads mounted on the wall and grimaced slightly. She assumed Chester Milton was the great hunter. There were at least ten animal heads. Skins lined the floor and the walls, and spears hung above the fireplace. There was a gun cabinet filled with rifles and shotguns, while another cabinet contained several handguns. Carrie paused by the case that contained an extensive knife collection. She looked at the various knives and daggers, then noticed an empty spot, indicating one was missing.

The knife case wasn't locked. Carrie opened the lid and removed one of the wire-handled daggers. The dagger looked very similar to the one she had found in the woods near Vicki's body. She returned it to the case, closed the lid, and looked around the room once more. If that dagger came from the hotel, it would mean someone had been to the hotel earlier and removed the knife, either that or Troy murdered Vicki. But that couldn't be possible. Troy didn't know Vicki. Carrie tensed while deep in thought then left the room. She walked down the hall and paused outside the billiard room to look inside. Karl Ruben was behind the bar against the far wall, pouring himself a drink. Carrie looked around the room and didn't see anyone else.

"Come in and join me, Carrie," Karl said cheerfully. "I'll buy you a drink."

Carrie cautiously entered while checking out the room and sat on a stool before the bar.

Karl leaned on the bar as if he was a bartender. "So, what can I get you?" he asked pleasantly.

She didn't know what to make of Karl, although he seemed to be a nice and cheerful fellow. Carrie returned the smile with some distrust. She didn't exactly trust anyone since she found Vicki murdered.

"A little brandy just to make me sleepy," she replied while attempting to make herself comfortable on the tall chair.

He found the bottle and poured her a drink while she studied him. He was in his mid-thirties and stood a tick under six feet with a medium build. Karl had thinning, light brown hair, and a short mustache that was showing some gray. Her eyes fell to the old scar on his chin just below his lower lip. Carrie didn't find him particularly attractive, but he was a neat dresser, and he wore a fragrant cologne. So at least he smelled good.

"So did you know Chester?" Karl asked.

"I assume so, but I don't particularly remember him," Carrie replied. "What about you?"

"I'm afraid I don't remember him by name either," Karl remarked. "I'd have to see a picture."

"What do you do for a living?" Carrie asked.

"Insurance."

Carrie hid her smile and chuckled. "You aren't going to try to sell me some, are you?"

"No, I don't make sales," he teased cheerfully. "I'm an adjuster. I'm the guy who rejects your claims."

Karl was pleasant enough, but Carrie knew he would soon bore her.

"Do you travel a lot?" Carrie asked, hoping to find a common interest.

"Actually, I just returned from Arabia," Karl informed her. "It's an interesting place."

"Oh? Do you speak Arabic?"

"Sure," Karl replied. "I can speak Arabic and Hebrew too. It's not a commonly used language here, but it comes in handy occasionally."

Carrie was losing interest in his conversation. His ability to speak foreign languages was of little interest.

"This is some place, huh?" he remarked, possibly changing the subject to keep from boring her.

Carrie surveyed the room. There was a slate top pool table with broad, pedestal legs, an old phonograph in the back corner, a felt top card table, and two antique slot machines. The bar was tall enough to stand at with comfort. There was a brass rail that went around the top of the bar as well as the bottom. The glasses hung upside down under a rafter above the bar.

"But not very accessible to visit," Carrie commented.

Karl laughed. "No, I guess it isn't."

As if on cue, the remaining woman from their group entered the billiard room, saving Carrie from her boring conversation with Karl. Kristy Freud was an attractive woman in her mid to late twenties. She was down-to-earth and more to Carrie's liking than Barbie. She had auburn hair, which she wore down, and wore little to no makeup on her girl-next-door face. Close to Carrie in height, the young woman was built lean with slightly broad hips giving way to a generous, round bottom. Kristy didn't get nearly as much attention entering a room as she did while leaving. Carrie earlier caught Troy staring at Kristy's backside, practically mesmerized by it. It didn't take a genius to figure out what he'd been thinking.

"Hey, Karl," Kristy announced cheerfully then teased. "I didn't know you worked here."

Karl chuckled and offered her a drink. As Karl and Kristy made small talk, Carrie decided she'd found the perfect opportunity to duck out. She finished her drink, thanked Karl, and left the room. Carrie entered the hallway as Nick was approaching from the stairs. She was glad to have run into him.

"Nick, I have to show you something." She grabbed his arm, practically dragged him into the trophy room, and showed him the knife cabinet.

Nick stared through the glass and tilted his head. "This can't be good."

"Do you think that dagger came from this case?" Carrie asked with a curious look.

"It's very possible," he said then eyed her. "It's important that you say nothing to the others about this. We don't need to cause panic."

"Do you think Troy killed Vicki?" Carrie asked nervously while scanning the knife case.

"I don't know, but I suggest you lock your bedroom door tonight," he replied.

Chapter Four

Day two. Most of the guests were awake by nine o'clock the following morning. Carrie entered the lobby where she found Kera and Danny, who were both engrossed in their books. Carrie casually collapsed on the sofa alongside her sister.

Kera lowered her book and eyed her sister. "I'm surprised you're up. I heard you tossing and turning half the night," she announced. "Didn't you sleep well?"

Carrie shook her head and ran her fingers through her hair. "No, not really," she remarked. "Sound really travels in this place. Someone down here was making noise half the night."

"Down here?" Danny asked with surprise. "I wonder who that was. I was up with Jerry until midnight. We were the last to turn in. We didn't make that much noise."

"No, this was about two in the morning until at least five," Carrie informed him.

"I didn't hear anything," Kera countered.

Voices could be heard by the front door. Carrie turned her head and looked toward the foyer, but it was an obstructed view. The voices were familiar. Carrie sprang to her feet and walked across the lobby until the foyer came into view beyond the archway. She saw Nick and Duke standing near the front doors.

"I would consider this a problem," Duke remarked with annoyance.

Devlin sniffed Nick's hand, although he ignored the impressive large wolf.

Nick glanced at Carrie then returned his attention to Duke. "I'm not thrilled about our situation either. Lawyers don't just fail to show," Nick stated.

"There's something wrong, and I don't enjoy not having a way off the island," Duke responded as his serious look turned moderately angry. "There aren't any phones or even a radio that I've seen. I suggest we look for a way off, preferably without Troy's knowledge."

Carrie assumed Duke knew nothing about the murder or he'd be reacting worse. Carrie decided not to tell Kera about it either. She didn't want to upset her sister. Carrie wondered what had Duke upset.

"I'll gather a few of the others," Nick informed him, sounding oddly casual. "We'll explore the island in two groups and see if there's a way off."

"That would be helpful," Duke announced. "I'm going to the dock and look around. I saw a boathouse."

Carrie watched Duke leave the hotel through the front door with Devlin following. Nick looked at Carrie, frowned, and walked toward her.

"It would seem Duke found a hidden camera behind a mirror in his bedroom," Nick reluctantly explained. "We're being watched."

"I knew Troy couldn't be trusted," she snarled while folding her arms across her chest. "And what of the lawyer?"

"I doubt that there ever was one," Nick replied with disgust. "It's starting to look like Troy wanted us here for a darker reason. Vicki's murder seems to be a direct result."

"You don't think he invited us here to kill us one by one, do you?" Carrie asked nervously.

Nick turned his head, looking past her, and watched Troy walk down the stairs toward them.

"Good morning," Troy said joyfully. "Did the two of you sleep well?"

"Fine, thank you," Nick replied dryly.

"Glad to hear," Troy said in return.

"In fact, I was thinking about taking Carrie for a walk later this morning," Nick said and placed an arm over her shoulder.

She eyed Nick suspiciously and raised her brow. He seemed awfully comfy with his arm around her.

"Do you have a map of the island we could use?" Nick asked while remaining oddly cheerful.

"Sure. It's in the study," Troy replied, seeming almost too pleasant. "I'll get it for you right after lunch. Maybe I'll even join you."

Troy turned and walked toward the kitchen. Nick removed his arm from Carrie and looked at her.

"What a stroke of luck. He wants to chaperone our nature walk," Nick muttered sarcastically then groaned. "I'll search the study for the map. Think you can keep Troy in the kitchen for twenty minutes?"

"Yeah, sure," she replied.

§

Twenty minutes later, Carrie hurried up the back stairs from the kitchen. Entertaining Troy for the last twenty minutes was near torture and an experience she didn't wish to repeat. The man was a pervert and seemed to enjoy making women uncomfortable while undressing them with his eyes. Kera approached their bedroom from the opposite end of the hall, having taken the main stairs. They met at the bedroom door.

"I'm glad I ran into you. We're going to explore the island and look for a way off as a backup plan. Something's not right," Carrie informed her. "We need to meet Nick downstairs."

"I'm not going," Kera insisted.

Carrie gave her a stern look. "I don't think you should stay here by yourself."

"I don't feel like running around some creepy woods with a bunch of strangers," she remarked, allowing little room for argument. "Don't worry. I'll keep the bedroom door locked. I'll be fine."

Kera entered their room and locked the door behind her. Carrie considered taking a jacket along, but she didn't want to get into a debate with Kera. She could barely relate to her sister anymore. Kera was becoming more withdrawn each passing year since their parents died. Carrie continued down the hall toward the main stairs and headed down them. She was only partway down the staircase when she heard a woman scream from the bottom of the steps. Carrie ran down the stairs and stopped a few steps from the bottom. Danny held his stomach while slumped over the banister. Bart and Cindy were only a few feet away while screaming at each other. Carrie hurried to Danny's side and made sure he was all right.

"If you had stayed in the room like I told you to, I wouldn't have hit him," Bart yelled while pointing a thick, demanding finger at his wife. "This is your fault!"

"Danny didn't do anything. He was just talking to me, nothing more," Cindy protested, although it was obvious she didn't want to confront her husband.

"Danny? Oh, you're on first name basis, huh?" Bart grabbed Cindy by her arms. "What else have you been doing behind my back?"

Carrie's attention shifted to Bart. Bart shook Cindy roughly until she screamed with fear and winced in pain. Carrie's eyes narrowed as she took a bold step forward. Danny grabbed her arm and held her back, stopping her from getting involved.

"Let me go. You're hurting me," Cindy cried out.

"You should have thought about that before you disobeyed me," Bart yelled in anger.

Cindy sobbed from the pain he was causing. Carrie once more attempted to move closer to the couple as others appeared in the hallway. Carrie felt her heart racing as anger coursed through her veins. She managed to break free from Danny's grip. He lunged forward, grabbed her around the waist, and kept her from engaging the much bigger man. Nick joined them in the hallway and immediately interceded.

"Okay, Bart, loosen the grip," Nick announced in an oddly calm tone, although his right hand was already tightening into a fist. "She said nothing happened."

Bart glared at him with hateful eyes. "Go away. This is between my wife and me!"

"No," Cindy cried out. "Let me go!"

Bart faced her with a half-crazed look in his eyes and backhanded her across the face. As if by reflex, several men in the hallway jumped from where they stood and moved forward. Danny nearly released Carrie as his own instincts wanted to kick in as well. Nick, who had been the closest, threw his clenched fist directly into Bart's face, knocking the large man backward. Jerry moved closer to Nick, forming his backup posse. Carrie attempted to bolt forward, nearly knocking Danny to the floor. He clung to her waist from behind and could barely hold her back. Cindy darted behind the barricade of Parkers, while Bart recovered from the hard hit. He spit out blood.

"You're going to regret this, you little bitch," Bart lashed out at his wife while rubbing his sore jaw.

"You so much as lay a hand on her again," Nick said coldly while pointing a warning finger, "and you'll have more than just a bruised ego."

Bart glared his hostility for Nick, straightened slowly, and walked toward the stairs. Nick and Jerry turned, keeping their eyes on him. As Bart walked up the stairs past Carrie, she pulled against Danny, attempting to free herself from his grip. She wanted a piece of him. Bart glared at her and laughed with a dirty smile. Once Bart disappeared upstairs, Danny released Carrie. She spun to face Danny with anger in her eyes. He jumped back with a surprised look at the hostility she directed at him. She attempted to relax and avoided shouting at him since she knew he was only looking out for her welfare.

"And on that note," Nick announced, apparently feeling Carrie's tension. "We should get this field trip started."

Chapter Five

Jerry collected people to help search the island for a way off under the guise of exploring. It was a little before two o'clock that afternoon. They wanted to get as many people together as they could for safety in numbers. Cindy had locked herself in one of the rooms and refused to come out. No one bothered disturbing Bart since it would only encourage the others to fight with the big man. By the time they were ready to leave, Duke still hadn't returned. Carrie kept a watchful eye on Nick just to see what he would do next. She'd never admit it to anyone, but she enjoyed watching him take charge. It was a bit of a turn-on. Danny leaned toward Carrie while staring at the brothers.

"They look like a two-man SWAT team," he whispered.

Carrie again studied them with more than a passing interest. They were quite impressive, and masterful, to say the least. She suddenly felt subconscious for staring at the handsome brothers.

Nick then turned his attention to Jerry. "I'll take Carrie through the old zoo. The map I found shows a path leading to the beach on the other side of the island," he announced. "You'll go with Troy, Danny, Karl, Barbie, and Kristy to keep up appearances. Carrie and I will sneak out before Troy questions our decision to go off on our own."

"I assume I should keep our group heading in the direction of the dock," Jerry announced.

"Yes. Hopefully, you'll run into Duke," Nick replied and glanced at his scanned copy of the map. "He went that way a few hours ago, and still hasn't returned. If you don't find him, see if you can check out the boathouse. I'm a little concerned that he's been gone so long. According to the map, there are several quicksand pits."

Carrie felt a chill race down her spine. Did something happen to Duke? Before she could let the question consume her, Nick hurried her out the door and toward the old zoo just beyond the hotel. As they passed through the zoo's wrought iron gate, Carrie looked at the large webs between the cage bars. She hoped to avoid seeing the spider. She didn't mind snakes, but she feared spiders, especially those the size of softballs. The cages were spaced ten feet apart and set upon cement slabs nearly two feet thick. Only the fronts contained bars. The three remaining walls were in stone block for both protection and seclusion. Each cage had a small opening in the back, leading to a shelter of sorts. Carrie saw a tiger in the third cage on the left. It lay near the bars and watched them as they passed. The zoo itself wasn't very big, with five cages on each side, and a back gate only the size of a door. They passed through the back gate. Carrie hadn't seen the wolves Jerry mentioned, but she supposed they were in their shelter during the day.

§

An hour after Troy left with the second group, the hotel was quiet. Kera walked down the main staircase and entered the lobby, happy to have the hotel to herself. She then heard a scraping sound behind the desk. Kera cautiously approached the desk and paused when she saw Duke on his knees before the manager's office door. Kera shifted nervously and bumped the desk. Duke flinched and glanced over his shoulder at her then relaxed.

"You startled me," he said, then turned back to the door and inserted a small, metal device into the lock.

"What are you doing?" Kera asked with concern.

"Breaking and entering," he replied simply then looked back at her and offered a teasing smile.

She uncertainly looked around. "Did the others leave?"

"I assume so," he replied without looking at her. "I didn't see anyone else around when I returned."

"Did you find anything in the boathouse?" Kera asked.

"Yeah. A rotted floor and a leaky roof but no boat," Duke replied.

The lock sprang, and the door creaked open. Duke straightened and looked at her with a pleased expression on his face then entered the room. Kera had to smile at his boyish charm. She cautiously walked behind the desk and peered into the room while keeping a safe distance as she watched him. The room was tiny in comparison to the other rooms in the hotel. It appeared to be some sort of control room with assorted buttons and switches above a desk facing the left wall. Four T.V. monitors lined the wall above the desk with two full-backed, swivel chairs positioned before it.

"What's that equipment for?" Kera asked as she stepped into the room for a closer look.

Duke sighed with disgust. "It's used to spy on people."

Kera eyed him with surprise. "Is there something I'm not being told?" she asked with a concerned look. "Carrie has been acting strange since yesterday afternoon."

"That's what I intend to find out," Duke replied while looking around the room.

His eyes strayed to a door off to the side, possibly a bathroom. Duke approached the door and opened it. To both their surprise, they saw an older man in a wheelchair hiding in the bathroom. The older man looked at Duke, clearly stunned to see him.

Duke's eyes suddenly narrowed. "Chester Milton," he snarled with hostility.

The man stared at him a moment longer, allowing the surprise to wear off then smiled and laughed. "Duke Wedemeyer."

"You'd better explain what's going on," Duke demanded and blocked the doorway, intending to keep him captive until he got answers.

"This isn't the right time." He then nodded toward the monitor. "You better check on that woman. She appears to be in trouble."

Duke looked past the old man at the monitor. Within their bedroom, Bart had his hands on Cindy's arms and was violently shaking her while she screamed for him to stop. Duke looked at Chester, who raised a tiny smile, knowing he had him. Duke had no choice.

"Watch him," Duke informed Kera then ran from the room.

Duke bolted up the stairs and stopped in Cindy's bedroom doorway. Bart hit Cindy across the face, knocking her to the bed with a bounce. She sobbed from the hard hit.

"Now I'm going to teach you a lesson for defying me!" Bart cried out while removing his belt.

"Get away from her," Duke snarled.

Cindy slowly looked up from sheltering hands exposing her bruised face. Apparently, he'd been beating her for a while.

"Get out of here, before I knock you senseless, old man!"

"Do you really want to threaten me?" Duke snapped.

"And you think you're going to stop me?" Bart laughed, humored at the idea. Physically, Duke was much smaller than Bart. "Come and try it if you think you can. If you can't, then just get the hell out of here. You're wasting my time."

As Bart turned back toward his battered wife, the low snarling of the timber wolf was heard. Bart tensed and looked back at the doorway. Devlin now stood alongside Duke and snarled with exposed teeth. The hair on his back stood on end, and a vicious bark followed as saliva dripped from his jowls.

Duke glanced at the frightened woman cowering on the bed. "Mrs. Galloway, come to me."

Cindy did as he said and moved away from Bart, making a quick dash for Duke and his wolf counterpart. She hid behind him and waited for further instructions.

"Go downstairs to the lobby and wait for me," Duke informed her. "I promise you'll have no trouble out of this man." He cocked his head while raising an arrogant brow. "I don't think he wants his leg torn off."

Bart stared at the wolf without moving a muscle. Apparently, an angry wolf was just what he needed to be intimidated.

§

Kera and Cindy followed Chester as he wheeled himself into the kitchen. He stopped before the refrigerator and removed a can of soda. Cindy clung to Kera's arm while leaning into her and stared at the elderly man.

"He's supposed to be dead," Cindy gasped.

"I know," Kera remarked just loud enough for her to hear. "Where's Duke? He needs to be watched."

"Feeding his dog, I hope," Cindy muttered then eyed Kera. "Why would they lie about Chester being dead?"

"Don't bother whispering," Chester said as he closed the refrigerator door. "I can hear every word."

Kera walked up to Chester and placed her hands on either side of the wheelchair. "I demand to know what's going on, and you'd better tell me now."

Chester poked Kera sharply in the side with a two-foot-long stick containing a hook on the end of it. She jumped back a step with surprise.

"You just keep some distance, girl," Chester announced. "I may be old, but I'm not defenseless." He lowered his stick then spun around and wheeled toward the counter. Chester laid the stick across the armrests and took a banana from the counter.

"You've been watching us on hidden camera. Why?" Kera demanded.

Chester chuckled lowly. "I was curious."

"What sort of answer is that?" Kera snapped.

"The only answer you're going to get from me." Chester spun the chair to face her. "I'll see Nick Parker when he returns. If I'm going to be interrogated, I would like to get it from the head detective, not some little girl." He ate the banana while glaring at Kera.

"I may be young, but I'm clever enough to stick on your ass until Duke returns," she snapped. "We want off this island, and we won't let you hold us prisoner."

Chester wheeled himself past Kera and disappeared through the swinging door. Kera and Cindy exchanged looks then followed him back into the hall.

"There's a perfectly good radio transmitter in my study. Phone lines would have been too costly and unreliable," he said without looking at them as he rolled down the hallway. "I also have a yacht. I would have to be pretty stupid to live on an island without transportation."

Kera stopped Cindy in mid-stride. "Go into the study and look for a radio. If you find one, contact the mainland."

Cindy nodded and entered the study just before them on the right while Kera remained by Chester's side. Chester glared at her, becoming impatient.

"Are you still here?"

"I'm not leaving your side," Kera insisted.

Chester turned to the right, running over Kera's foot. When she jumped in pain, Chester rolled his chair into the library. He spun his chair around and closed the door in Kera's face. Kera took a step back, drew a breath, and reached for the doorknob. The door was locked. Duke hurried down the hall and stared at her.

"Was that Chester?"

"Yeah," she replied. "He locked the door on me."

Duke cursed and removed the lock pick from his pocket. It took him less than a minute to jolt the locking mechanism. He threw open the door.

"Did you really think--?"

Duke and Kera looked around the library. Chester was gone! Duke ran into the hallway, almost colliding with Cindy, who appeared from the study. Cindy jumped back a step with a startled gasp then closed her eyes and sighed.

"There's a radio transmitter, but it doesn't work," she informed him then looked around. "Where's the old man?"

"He's gone," Duke muttered. "He seemed to vanish from the library."

"A crippled man doesn't just vanish," she protested. "Are you sure he went into the library?"

"I was right behind him," Kera replied then insecurely rubbed her arms. "We have to find him."

"He's not going to show himself again, if he can avoid it," Duke remarked while shaking his head.

"He said he had a yacht," Kera informed him.

"I need to explore the island and see if I can find it. Maybe it'll have a radio." He then eyed the two women. "The two of you should probably lock yourselves in a room until I get back."

"I want to go along," Kera announced.

Duke hesitated and considered her bold request. "You should stay with Cindy."

"My father had an appliance store," Cindy informed him. "I may be able to fix the radio. Take Kera with you. I'll be fine. I'll lock myself in the study."

Duke didn't appear completely convinced but gave in. "All right then," he announced and removed a semiautomatic from his shoulder holster. He checked the magazine, slammed it back in, then cocked the gun, and replaced it. He looked at Kera. "Ready to go?"

Kera flattened herself against the wall and stared at the gun that had already disappeared. Perhaps she'd been mistaken about Duke being trustworthy.

"Relax, Miss Goddard," he said with a chuckle, "that's not for you."

Chapter Six

Nick led Carrie around the east side of the island. The island was approximately four square miles with winding trails. They had passed a stream, a pond, and two patches of quicksand, clearly marked with signs. The east side of the island was less scenic than the west. Rocks and cliffs created a small beach. The cliffs were close to the ocean not fifty feet from the path leading back to the hotel. Below the cliff were scattered rocks embedded in the sand. Although there was little noticeable wildlife, birds could be heard singing within the trees, and an occasional tarantula scurried along the edge of the woods. Carrie shuddered at the sight of the hairy, black creatures. She drew a deep breath and clung to Nick's arm.

"I don't like tropical islands," she muttered. "The wildlife leaves something to be desired."

Nick appeared humored and patted her arm. "They're more afraid of you."

"I doubt that," she retorted. Carrie studied the cliff they were approaching. It was at least thirty feet high. She released Nick's arm and shook her head. "I wouldn't suggest diving off that."

"I'd like to visit the murder scene again," Nick informed her. "I want to make sure I didn't overlook anything."

"I don't suppose Troy has an alibi."

"No, he was alone on the island when we arrived. We can only assume there's no one else here," Nick informed her. "Jerry searched Vicki's bags and came up empty."

"If there was a lawyer, I wouldn't doubt he's dead too."

"Quite possible," Nick agreed. "He could easily throw a dead man into quicksand not forty yards from the hotel. No one would ever know."

Carrie shuddered at the thought and rubbed her chilled arms. It was morbid but made for a convincing theory. She again looked at Nick's handsome profile. "Why do you think we were brought here?"

Nick looked back at her and raised his brows. "Honestly?"

She nodded nervously.

"I think we were brought here to be executed."

§

"And here's one of the more interesting sights of Demon Island," Troy said proudly.

Danny and Jerry peered into the pit and saw it was halfway filled with hundreds of snakes slithering in a massive ball. There were several kinds and many sizes, most of which were poisonous. The others stared into the pit as well, sharing the same horrified expression.

Danny slowly straightened, took a step back, and cleared his throat. "That would be a wrong step."

"How many are in there?" Karl asked.

Barbie cringed and rubbed her chilled shoulders. "Who cares. They're disgusting," she gasped. "Let's get out of here before they get out."

"They're trapped in there," Troy replied. "They just slither into the pit and never get out."

Karl backed away from the pit and looked at Troy. "What about the other animals?"

"They sometimes fall into the pit. That's how the snakes survive," Troy announced.

"What kinds of animals live on the island?" Kristy asked while remaining several feet away from the snake pit.

"Only small animals. My uncle hunted most of the bigger ones. He trapped some and put them in his zoo but most didn't survive longer than a year," he replied. "The wolves, the Siberian tiger, and her cub are all that remain. There had been a male tiger, but I guess it died."

They walked along the path through the woods with the beach to their left, visible through the tree line. The paths seemed to cross each other, creating an endless circle.

"I wouldn't doubt you could get lost in here for weeks," Danny said to Jerry.

Jerry looked toward the front of the group. Troy was sweet-talking Kristy, attempting to charm her. "I don't doubt that," Jerry replied then stopped on the path.

Danny seemed surprised and stared at him. "What's wrong?"

"Troy's been leading us around in circles," Jerry remarked.

"How do you know?" Danny asked while looking around.

"We've passed that snake pit before, but we passed it from a different direction. Either he's purposely leading us in circles, or he's lost," Jerry remarked. "I'm certain I should keep an eye on him, yet I'd like to explore the beach for a way off the island."

"I can keep an eye on Troy," Danny informed him, "if you want to go off on your own."

"Are you sure?" Jerry asked. "It's important that he's watched closely."

"Not a problem," Danny replied.

Jerry looked at the beach beyond the woods then looked back at Danny. "I'm counting on you," he announced.

Danny saluted him. Jerry walked through the woods and headed to the beach. Danny hurried to catch up to the others and walked beside Barbie. Barbie kept her attention on Troy, Karl, and Kristy several feet in front of them. Kristy laughed and tossed her auburn hair over her shoulder.

"She's really enjoying all the attention," Danny muttered. "I suppose they'll fight over her company tonight."

Barbie looked at Danny as her upper lip curled, and she clucked her tongue. "Let's get something straight, Danny," she snapped. "I don't like you, and I certainly don't want to talk to you. So why don't you just stay the hell away from me."

Danny's expression dropped with surprise. "Well, that's the direct approach," he said. "What did I ever do to you?"

"You just disgust me," she replied. "I don't like the sight of you, and you have an offensive personality. But I suppose someone of your class can't help it."

"My class?" Danny asked sternly. "What class is that?"

She looked down her nose at him and slung her head back. "Don't be offended," she snapped. "I just don't associate with common people."

"Maybe you shouldn't have come on this walk," he retorted. "It's full of common people."

"No, just you and Kristy," she replied. "Troy and Karl are both in my class. Rich and important."

"Uh, huh," he remarked casually. "Too bad for you they prefer Kristy's company to yours. Snobby bitches must not be their type." He then walked past her.

§

Duke led Kera through the woods until they reached the white, sandy beach. A fallen tree blocked their path. Devlin jumped over it and ran toward the waves that gently lapped onto shore. Duke stepped onto the fallen tree and assisted Kera. He jumped down to the other side and once more took her hand to help her down. He didn't release her hand when they reached the other side. Duke was almost boyishly pleasant. He talked gently, as a man of great passion would, holding her interest. Kera studied him while he spoke of his beach house in Hawaii. She noted his warm tone and, for once, she felt as if she was being treated like an adult. That was something Carrie rarely did. Kera looked young and innocent, so everyone treated her that way.

"You certainly have a fondness for the beach," she remarked.

"There's nothing more beautiful than the sun setting on the horizon over the ocean," he informed her. "I spend a lot of my evenings on the beach just relaxing and admiring the waves."

Kera smiled while studying him and laughed at herself for worrying about the gun he carried. The man seemed so kind and gentle; she was certain he didn't have a malicious bone in his body.

"So are you a beachcomber?" she teased then almost hit herself for making an immature remark. Now he'd reconsider her age and take on a fatherly attitude.

Duke glanced at her and smiled warmly. "No, I have a self-grooming beach." He chuckled at his own response.

Kera was relieved that he found that entertaining. They continued to walk hand in hand with Devlin running along the shore ahead of them, every so often jumping into the waves that were barely a foot high. Duke told her when high tide would come, and showed her, by the beach erosion, how far inland it extended. Carrie would have found him boring, but Kera thought he was fascinating and intelligent. She also thought it was romantic that he lived on a beach in Hawaii.

"I bet Hawaii is beautiful," Kera remarked. "Except for this trip, I've never really been anywhere."

"I'd be more than happy to have you and your family come stay with me if you want to visit Hawaii," he informed her. "I have plenty of room."

Kera hid her smile, feeling somewhat embarrassed by the invitation. "Actually, I would love that." She was silent a moment as her thoughts strayed to their situation. Duke's pleasant attitude aside, she knew something was off with their island visit. "What's going on around here, Duke? It seems like everyone is keeping secrets."

"There's no cause to worry just yet," Duke replied. "Right now we need to be a little cautious, that's all. We're looking for a way off the island, in case it becomes necessary to leave in a hurry."

Something caught his attention. He paused then looked around the beach with some concern, causing her to do the same.

"What's wrong?" she asked.

"Devlin's gone," he said then sighed. "I suppose he'll turn up eventually. That wolf never misses a meal."

Chapter Seven

The boathouse was built against the dock on pillars. The half-rotted building had an interior walkway along with a small dock for boats. The only boat docked in the boathouse was a rowboat. The bottom half was rotted and filled with water. The rope attached to the dock seemed to be the only reason it stayed afloat. Jerry walked through the dimly lit boathouse while shaking his head. The floor itself was beginning to rot, and the boards creaked under his body weight. Several tools hung on the wall just behind him, and there were old wooden crates on the floor. He looked at the crates as he walked further into the unstable building. Fishing nets and life preservers hung from the ceiling just above him with cobwebs connecting the objects. Jerry turned toward the dirt-coated window, which only provided a small amount of light to the dingy interior.

As he looked out the window, a large, hairy spider crawled along its web just before his face. Jerry jumped back a step, and his foot went through a rotted floorboard. He lost his balance, bracing his fall with his hands while cringing in pain. He attempted to pull his foot back through the rotted floorboard and out of the water below, but the splintered wood caught his leg. He cursed softly then looked around. A crowbar lay on one of the crates just two feet away from him. Jerry reached for the crowbar and touched it with his fingertips. He paused and looked at the crate just before him. Upside down was the word 'dynamite'. Jerry's eyes widened, and a gasp escaped his throat.

"Oh, shit," he murmured.

He grasped for the crowbar once more and knocked it off the crate and onto the floor. Jerry grabbed it and broke away the splintered wood surrounding his knee. A shadow passed by the rotted slats in the wall just outside, catching his attention. Jerry remained immobile a moment. He reached inside his jacket and removed his Magnum revolver then watched the shadow as it approached the partially open door. He aimed his gun. Devlin's gray and silver nose poked through the opening. The wolf's head tilted to the side as its eyes remained fixed on Jerry. Devlin barked. Jerry groaned and replaced his gun. He retrieved the crowbar and continued to free himself.

Devlin trotted into the boathouse, stopped before him, and happily licked his face. Jerry cringed and pushed the wolf away with his right hand that held the crowbar. Devlin's tail wagged as he grabbed the crowbar in his mouth and pulled back with a soft, playful growl.

"Stop it," Jerry said and pulled back.

Devlin took a better hold on the bar and leaned back on his haunches, pulling with tremendous force. Jerry looked around and reached for a discarded fishing pole handle. He waved the two-inch stick near the wolf.

"Wanna play?" He tossed the stick across the boathouse floor. "Fetch!"

Devlin barked and excitedly pounced after the stick. Jerry hurried to free himself, breaking enough wood to pull his leg out. Devlin returned to him as he stood. Jerry looked at the wolf as he wagged his tail and held a stick of dynamite in his mouth. Jerry jumped backward with concern then uncertainly extended his hand to Devlin.

"Good boy. Now give it to me," he said and reached for the explosive.

Devlin growled and pulled back. Jerry quickly released it then backed up a step and reached into his pocket. He pulled his hand out with closed fingers.

"Wanna treat?"

Devlin wagged his tail excitedly.

"Sit."

The wolf obeyed and continued to wag his tail.

"Speak."

Devlin dropped the dynamite and let out a deep, loud bark of enthusiasm while wagging his tail. Jerry kicked the dynamite away from the wolf and into the water. He lowered his hand and exposed his empty palm.

"Oh, sorry, nothing there."

Devlin snarled, revealing sharp teeth. Jerry wasn't the least bit concerned as he turned and walked out of the boathouse. Devlin barked loudly, expressing his displeasure. Jerry looked back and saw

Devlin running toward him. His eyes widened with concern as he turned and ran.

§

Danny looked at the pool of quicksand they had passed multiple times already then eyed Troy, who walked beside Kristy with his arm around her. His leadership skills left something to be desired, and Danny was becoming irritated. It was nearly six o'clock that evening, and their little tour still lingered.

"How did you sleep last night? If your bed isn't comfortable enough, perhaps mine is more to your liking," Troy teased not caring that he embarrassed the woman.

Kristy giggled at what must have passed for charm. "No, the bed was fine. My sleep was just interrupted by the insensitive soul who took a late night walk," she informed him then offered a tiny smile. "My room is right above the kitchen. The door has a terrible creak to it."

"I'll be sure to fix it when we get back," Troy informed her without hesitation.

Danny rolled his eyes then walked directly behind Troy. "I don't mean to interrupt you while you're putting the moves on Kristy, but do you know where we're going? We've been circling the same area for nearly two hours."

Troy looked at Danny and flashed his long, white teeth. "I know exactly where we are, and we have not been going in circles. You just don't know the jungle as I do," Troy informed him. "It sometimes appears to look the same."

Danny shifted his eyes to the sign by the snake pit and looked at the familiar dollar bill placed between the face of the sign and the stick.

"That's really amazing because I placed that dollar bill on that sign when we passed it thirty-five minutes ago," Danny informed him while glaring demandingly.

Troy looked at the sign, noticed the dollar, and then glared at Danny while frowning. He didn't seem to be happy that he'd been caught at his incompetence or perhaps in a lie.

"You think you're a real funny man, don't you?" Troy launched hotly.

Danny grinned with some irritation. "I'd like to think so." His lips then twisted into a frown. "I think it's time you led us back to the hotel. I've had enough of this trek."

Troy spun to face Danny and poked a finger into his bony chest. "You're welcome to go back anytime you want," he snarled with annoyance.

Danny backed up a step while glaring at Troy then turned and walked away.

Troy smiled slyly then laughed at how easily he'd chased away Danny. "What a wimp," he remarked then looked at Kristy. "I have no respect for his type."

"I like Danny," Kristy replied, seeming a little surprised by the comment.

Troy let out a hearty laugh. "Sure, he's good for a laugh, but he's weak and useless." He nodded at Danny's back as he walked further away from them. "Look at him," Troy scoffed. "He even walks like a sissy."

Karl and Barbie looked behind them as well. Kristy stared at Danny as he disappeared beyond the bend by the quicksand then she frowned slightly.

Troy again placed his arm around Kristy and guided her in the opposite direction. "Where were we?"

Karl leaned closer to Barbie and whispered, "I don't exactly trust him."

Barbie frowned in response then folded her arms across her chest. "He does leave something to be desired, but I bet he's worth a small fortune."

"I'm uncomfortable with this entire situation," Karl insisted. "Kristy said she heard someone leave the hotel in the middle of the night. I wonder if the Parkers know something and they're just keeping it to themselves."

"I don't know what secrets are being kept around here, but I don't trust Danny."

Karl looked at her with surprise. "Danny? Why don't you trust him?"

She rolled her eyes, maintaining her snobbish look. "He's repulsive, and he's never serious. He's like a big, dumb kid," she scoffed. "We made fun of his kind when I went to school. I can't help being repulsed."

Karl's lips curled into a cold smile. "I thought you were above that childish stuff," he remarked. "The other kids always made fun of me; now I'm a successful businessman. I could rub it in when I see them working at fast-food restaurants, but instead, I choose to feel sorry for them. I'm sure you'd like Danny if you gave him a chance." Karl hurried to catch up to Troy and Kristy. "Troy, I'm heading back to the hotel. I've had enough quicksand and snake pits for one day."

"Do what you want," Troy remarked and waved him off without care.

Barbie and Kristy turned and watched Karl walk away. Both women appeared concerned with their new situation.

"Maybe we should go back. We've been out here for a while," Kristy finally announced, starting to become concerned by the others' lack of faith in Troy as their tour guide. "In a couple of hours, it'll be dark."

"Don't you worry yourself, Kristy," Troy announced while flashing a moderately creepy smile while clinging to her. "You're with me. I'll get you back in time for dinner and maybe even a hot shower for two."

"Oh, please," Barbie moaned with disgust. "You're making me sick with your lack of tack and blunt perversion."

Troy glared at Barbie, turning angry. "Then I suggest you join Karl." He pulled Kristy to his side. "We might decide to get down and dirty right here."

"Maybe I will," Barbie said and looked down her nose at Troy. "You're nothing but a barbaric pig."

Troy laughed as she walked away. Kristy suddenly seemed concerned that she was left alone with Troy. Troy turned her in the direction they'd been heading and forced her to keep walking. He finally stopped Kristy near the base of a hill with a path leading upward. She looked at the steep path.

Troy grinned deviously. "I know a secluded spot just beyond this path. It leads to the cliff overlooking the ocean," he informed her. "It's breathtaking."

Kristy now appeared nervous and fidgeted. "I think we better go back to the hotel with the others," she said while staring at him. "The jungle is starting to give me the creeps."

"There's nothing to worry about. You're here with me," Troy again insisted.

"I just want to go back," Kristy announced and pulled away from him.

Troy's expression became angry, assuming he'd been rejected. "Suit yourself, sweetheart. There are plenty of other women around," he snapped hotly. "I don't need to waste my time on you. You can find your own way back." He stormed away in anger, leaving her alone in the woods.

Kristy watched him leave, wanting to put some distance between them, and then leaned against a tree. She shook her head and mumbled under her breath.

"Bastard."

Chapter Eight

Kera walked alongside Duke in silence as they continued their hike along the beach. There was still no sign of Devlin, and he'd been gone quite some time.

"I wonder where he is," Duke remarked. "He could have marked the entire island as his territory by now."

"You don't suppose he got into quicksand," she gasped with alarm. "I heard Troy mention something about several pits on the island."

Duke looked at her sharply, apparently not pleased with the conversation. "Keep your distance from Troy Milton," he announced firmly. "I don't trust him." He then looked away and drew a deep breath.

Kera cocked her head to one side while staring at his profile. "There has to be a good reason why no one trusts Troy. I know why women shouldn't trust him, but why you? Why is everything such a secret?" she demanded to know.

Duke paused and turned to face her. "You have every right to know what's suspected," he announced. "Didn't Carrie tell you anything?"

Kera frowned at the comment and folded her arms across her chest. "Carrie doesn't think I can handle problems. She's been trying to shelter me ever since our parents died," she remarked. "I can handle more than she thinks. I'm not some child, despite what she says."

Duke smiled warmly. "I'll agree with you there."

"Damn it, tell me if there's a problem," she insisted. "I'll deal with it in my own way. It's no wonder I have a problem with people. Everyone keeps me in the dark."

"Allow me to shed some light on the circumstances of our trip," Duke informed her. "I knew Chester Milton. He was a corrupt and villainous man."

"I don't understand. Why would he leave you in his will?" Kera suddenly asked. She then considered the question. "Then again; why would he pretend to be dead?"

"This has always been about revenge," Duke informed her. "About ten years ago, when I was working for a special government task force, Chester forced me into a kill or be killed situation. I'm the reason he was confined to a wheelchair, so when I received the letter, I had to settle my curiosity."

"So this was a setup from the start?" she gasped. "No one else seems to remember him. Why didn't you say something about this sooner?"

"I assumed everyone else was involved in dirty dealings with him," Duke informed her. "Everyone is a suspect in my book. I wasn't about to say anything."

"Do you think Troy is up to something?" she asked. "Maybe seeking revenge while assisting his uncle?"

"We're uncertain. But when I searched my room, I found a hidden camera," he replied. "We're being watched. You saw the equipment in the security office."

"Is there some sort of danger involved?" she asked with concern. "Is that why Nick wants to find a way off the island?"

"If there's been trouble already, I wasn't told about it," Duke informed her. "I just know my relationship with Chester wasn't a pleasant one."

"There's something going on," Kera said firmly while eyeing him. "Carrie knows something, and it has to be more than just hidden cameras."

"Nick's not talking about it; I assure you that," Duke stated. "I'll find out what they're hiding eventually."

"Carrie said something about the lawyer possibly being dead," she informed him then appeared curious. "Could that be what they're hiding?"

"I doubt if there ever was a lawyer, Kera," Duke remarked simply. "Chester wasn't even dead."

"There had to be a lawyer," Kera protested. "Carrie checked into the law firm. There *was* a lawyer."

"She undoubtedly called the number on the letter," Duke insisted then raised his brow. "If you're going to put a phone number on a false document, you put a number that will come to you when someone calls it."

"I think she dug a little deeper than that," she remarked with a knowing smile. "Carrie isn't exactly trusting. What else do you know?"

Duke took a deep breath and stared at her a moment as if debating what he wanted to say. "Just that a woman from our group has been missing since we've arrived on the island. I seem to be the only one who's noticed her disappearance."

Kera's mouth fell open as horror filled her. "Someone's missing? Who?"

"Vicki Manner."

"I don't remember her, but I didn't pay much attention to anyone onboard."

"I generally keep close watch of people I don't know, especially in questionable situations," Duke informed her.

"What do you suppose happened to her?" Kera gasped.

Duke frowned and looked toward the ocean a moment then looked back at her. "I think she's dead," he replied. "I think she was murdered, the Parkers found out, and they're keeping it from us."

Kera's mouth dropped open. "Murdered? No, they wouldn't keep something like that a secret." Kera was silent a moment. "Would they?"

"It would be understandable," he insisted. "Trapped on a remote island like this; discovering someone has been murdered could be unhealthy for all of us."

Her eyes widened while putting it together. "I wouldn't doubt that's why Carrie's been acting so strange."

"It's possible, but we mustn't say anything about what we suspect," he insisted. "As I said, if it's true, it's being kept a secret for a very good reason. We don't want to be responsible for lighting a killer's fuse."

Kera nodded and shivered coldly. "I won't say anything. Despite my concern, I really appreciate you being honest with me, Duke."

He managed a warm, reassuring smile. "You have nothing to fear," he insisted as they entered the woods. He strayed ahead of her to move a branch from their path. "I won't let anything happen to you."

Kera suddenly gasped then fell silent. When Duke looked back, she was gone.

§

Nick searched the entire area surrounding the murder scene, which was now minus one body. He straightened and raked his fingers through his hair then looked at Carrie.

"I just don't understand it. Why would someone remove the body?" he practically demanded. "The killer couldn't have suspected we knew."

"Perhaps it was part of the plan to dispose of the body at a more convenient time," she remarked while nervously looking around. "You said so yourself. Quicksand would be an effective way to dispose of a corpse."

Nick shook his head in disgust then became angry. "Son-of-a-bitch!"

Carrie leaned against a tree, feeling tired from their lengthy hike. "Is there quicksand nearby?"

"The map seems to indicate there is, but I haven't seen it myself." He muttered something under his breath then looked around the jungle and back at her. "We should start heading back. It's going to be dark soon, and I don't want to be out here in the dark."

Carrie nodded, having had enough of the great outdoors for one day. They walked through the woods for nearly an hour. As Carrie looked around the jungle, it was all starting to look similar to her. She cast a look at Nick's profile.

"Do you know where we're going?" she finally asked.

Nick drew a deep breath and groaned while crumpling the map. "No, not especially. It's getting too dark to make out any landmarks."

Carrie eyed him with surprise. "Are we lost?"

"It's possible," he replied matter-of-factly. "I don't think we're going to get any further tonight."

"What?" Carrie suddenly gasped and stopped him. "Isn't there any chance of getting back to the hotel?" She ran her hands along her chilled arms. "I really despise tarantulas. I mean it. If one touches me, I'm going homicidal."

"I'm not overly fond of snakes myself, but it's too dangerous to keep wandering around with all the quicksand," he informed her. "We can barely see where we're going."

Nick gathered some sticks and twigs to start a fire then cleared a spot in the woods.

"Couldn't we at least find the beach?" Carrie asked while insecurely looking around.

He removed his lighter and started some brush on fire. "I'd gladly take us to the beach if you care to point me in the right direction."

"Some Boy Scout you turned out to be."

The fire caught hold and began to burn. Nick threw on some bigger sticks then sat on the ground near the fire. Carrie just glared at him. He finally looked at her where she remained standing.

"Are you planning on standing all night?"

Carrie frowned, hesitantly approached, and sat near him on the ground. The fire helped warm her, but she was more concerned about the wildlife that might explore them while they slept. She wasn't kidding about tarantulas. If she caught one probing her body, she'd turn into a girl and run away screaming.

"What about poisonous snakes?" she asked, attempting to keep her mind off spiders.

"What about them?" he demanded, obviously not wanting to think about them.

"What if they decide to visit our little campsite tonight?" she practically demanded. "Don't you think that's dangerous?"

Nick tensed, possibly at the thought of snakes, then groaned and finally gave in. "Fine, we'll rest here for a little while, then we'll continue our search for the beach or the hotel, but you had better stick close to me," he warned her. "If the jungle wasn't so thick, we might be able to see by the light of the moon."

"I'm willing to handcuff myself to you if it gets us out of here," Carrie remarked.

Nick didn't respond to the comment. Both were unusually silent for a few minutes. Carrie glanced at him and studied his profile through the dim light of the fire. He was truly a handsome man; she had to admit. It was such a shame he was so cold and unfeeling. Carrie turned her attention back to the fire and hugged her knees for added warmth. She hadn't anticipated a cold evening in the woods. Her shorts and short-sleeved shirt wasn't going to keep her very warm. Nick glanced at her a moment then removed his jacket and put it over her shoulders. Carrie jumped slightly and looked at him.

Perhaps she would have argued with him at a different place and time, but for now, she was cold, and his jacket was warm.

"Thank you," she whispered.

Her eyes scanned over the shoulder holster, which was now exposed, and the semiautomatic within it. He caught her staring, and their eyes finally met. She was slightly embarrassed that she was caught staring at him, even if it was just his holster. His smile almost mocked her before he resumed looking at the fire. Carrie slipped into his jacket and zipped it up. There was enough room for her to tuck her knees up and under the jacket as well. She slipped her hands into the pockets and played with the objects she found within them. She felt the lighter he carried although he didn't smoke, a few bullets, and a piece of paper in the one pocket. In the other pocket was a pair of handcuffs but no keys, and a small nylon case. Carrie removed the case and opened it. He cast a look at her but didn't comment as she rummaged through his belongings. She glanced at the strange metal device with some confusion.

"What's this?" she asked.

"A lock pick."

She eyed him suspiciously. "Private detectives are allowed to pick locks?"

"No, but I do what it takes to get a case solved," he replied. "I don't always play by the rules."

"So I've noticed." She replaced the lock pick and returned the case back to the jacket pocket. There was a pause as she thought then spoke once more. "My cousin doesn't have anything this interesting in his pockets," she announced while removing the handcuffs and played with them. "He only has condoms in his. You know--in case of an emergency."

Nick removed the handcuffs from her. "That's more Jerry's style," he remarked. "You'd find his handcuffs very close to his condoms."

Carrie eyed him then let a slight laugh escape.

Chapter Nine

Jerry grumbled as he walked with a slight limp along the east beach that would eventually lead back to the old zoo. He was only half an hour from the hotel and warmth. The beach was dimly lit by what little moon poked through the thick night clouds. He had been lost for nearly two hours while searching the jungle for his brother. The ocean waves crashed loudly onto shore then rushed back out again. It was almost high tide. A woman's shrill scream interrupted the tranquil sound of the crashing waves. He froze for a moment and looked toward the nearby cliff just in time to see a woman plummet. Jerry ran across the beach and rounded several large rocks that were embedded in the sand. He stopped about twenty feet away from the scene. An auburn-haired woman lay draped, limp and broken, over a large rock. Jerry ran toward the unidentified woman then finally saw her face. It was Kristy! He sank to his knees alongside her as she barely breathed. She gasped and spit up blood as her eyes rolled slightly.

"Kristy," Jerry gasped with surprise but was mostly horrified that she was even alive.

It was disrespectful to leave her on the rock like that, although moving her might cause more pain. It was obvious her back was broken, but he couldn't just leave her like that. He gently slid her off the rock and onto the sand and his thighs. She gasped, but it didn't appear he'd caused her any additional pain. There was no point leaving her to get help since she would be dead before he even reached the hotel.

"Kristy, what happened?" Jerry asked gently while clasping her hand.

Her hand didn't squeeze his back, indicating she had lost all feeling from the neck down. She gasped and attempted to speak.

"Finger--pushed--Vicki--dead--"

Jerry stared at her not understanding her words. "Kristy," he announced in a firm tone. "Who did this to you?"

She gasped several times as more blood seeped from her mouth. Kristy wheezed as her eyes rolled back and her head fell limp to the side. Jerry stared at her for a long moment, knowing she was dead. He finally tensed while inhaling deeply then gently lay her down on the sand and closed her eyes. He looked up at the cliff, which contained little more than jagged rock, and then glanced at his watch for time of death. It was twenty after nine. Jerry stared at the dead woman with remorse, drew a deep breath, and groaned with defeat.

§

Nick and Carrie finally found the beach and headed in the direction they thought would take them back to the hotel. The moon provided enough light to see most of the beach before them. Carrie was unusually quiet. She was somewhat tired, which probably added to her silence, but mostly she found herself casting stray glances at Nick while they walked. She eyed his sturdy build and scanned over his shoulder holster once more. She had to admit; there was something about a man in a shoulder holster that intrigued her. Perhaps she was just fascinated with the dangerous look. To her surprise, Nick grabbed her arm and stopped her. She gave him a puzzled glance then noticed he was staring at something further along the beach. Carrie glanced in the same direction and saw what looked like a person lying on the sand near the rocks.

"Wait here," Nick said then headed toward the motionless person.

Carrie followed despite his order for her to wait for him. As they neared the body, she peered around him and recognized the dead woman as Kristy. Nick felt the woman's outstretched hand then shook his head before looking up the ledge as he straightened.

"She'd been in Troy's group," Nick muttered.

"Do you think she slipped?"

"She's been dead less than two hours," he remarked. "What was she doing out here alone in the dark?"

"I'm guessing she wasn't alone," Carrie announced while feeling slightly sickened by the condition of the dead woman.

"Someone moved the body," he announced then indicated the nearby rock. "She landed on that rock."

Carrie glanced at the rock and noticed it had some blood on it. The sight caused her to grimace.

Nick took Carrie's wrist and pulled her behind him. "Come on; we'd better return to the hotel."

§

The hotel basement was dimly lit with two hanging lightbulbs. Cobwebs hung from the ceiling, attached to the support beams. The basement was cluttered and dirty, unlike the upstairs floors. There were wine racks in what could be considered a wine cellar of sorts lining the back wall, which were also covered in cobwebs. Cindy walked through the basement, darting concerned looks at the shadows dancing on the walls. She groaned and continued past several stacked boxes. There was a creak from the wine rack, causing Cindy to stop in mid-stride and shift her gaze around the basement. Everything was now silent. She continued walking then paused before the first wine rack. She peered around the rack and saw Chester near the back wall.

Chester carefully pulled a bottle from its slot and reached inside the opening. The rack beside it slid open. He replaced the bottle then wheeled himself through the opening into a small, hidden elevator. When the door slid shut, Cindy walked around the rack she'd been hiding behind and looked at the one against the wall. Only one bottle of wine had no dust or webs attached to it. She took a deep breath and listened to the sound of the elevator moving. Once the sound ceased, she waited another minute, then removed the bottle from the rack and pressed the button inside the slot. Nothing happened. The elevator was then heard moving once more. Cindy stepped back and watched the wine rack with nervous anticipation. The sound ceased, and the rack slid open.

She took a deep breath and entered, flattening herself against the back of the small elevator. She placed a hand on her chest, exhaled, and pushed the bottom button on the small panel. The door slid shut, and the elevator jolted before descending. Cindy nervously stared at the doors before her until they finally opened revealing a dimly lit area. She cautiously stepped out of the elevator onto the concrete walkway and looked around for signs of Chester. There was a wall to her left and a rail to her right. Beyond the rail was an underground pond. She walked along the walkway then stopped. A yacht was docked just thirty feet away. There were several crates along the rail not five feet from her. Cindy slipped behind the crates, kneeling on the walkway, and looked between the wooden boxes. Chester wheeled himself up the ramp and onto the dark yacht deck. As he wheeled closer to the control room, his head quickly turned to the left just behind him.

"Damn it; you startled me," Chester scoffed, talking to someone who must have appeared on deck with him. "Stop fooling around and make yourself useful."

Cindy gently bit her fingernails as she watched Chester, who obviously wasn't alone. Chester turned his wheelchair in her direction, although he didn't seem to notice she was there. She held her breath and remained still. Someone grabbed Chester from behind, pulling his head backward, and dragged a dagger across his throat. Blood spilled from the gaping wound. Cindy gasped then quickly covered her mouth to stifle the sound. She kept low and backed away from the crates. Once she was clear, she turned and ran back the way she'd come. She jumped into the hidden elevator and pressed the button. As the door began to close, she panted heavily with relief. A knife slashed through the closing door and cut her lower arm. Cindy cried out and clutched her bleeding arm. She kicked the hand sticking through the opening, allowing the elevator door to shut. She held her bleeding arm while the elevator made its upward trip.

When the door opened within the wine cellar, she bolted from the elevator and ran across the basement. She retraced her steps and easily found the main elevator. She pressed the button several times and fidgeted while waiting for the doors to open. As soon as the doors opened, she sprang inside the elevator and repeatedly hit the first floor button.

Chapter Ten

It was almost eleven o'clock at night by the time Nick and Carrie reached the well-lit hotel. Jerry paced while waiting impatiently in the lobby. As soon as Carrie and Nick entered the hotel, Jerry darted toward them.

"Nick, I'm glad you're back. Kera and Cindy ran into Chester Milton--alive and in person," Jerry informed him. "Cindy said he was spying on us through the security monitors in the manager's office."

Nick stared at Jerry as if he didn't understand what he said. "Whoa, wait. Chester's alive?" he repeated with some surprise.

Carrie looked back and forth between Nick and Jerry. "But Troy said--"

Nick didn't take his eyes off Jerry. "Where is he?"

Carrie raised her brows. "Will someone please tell me what's going on?"

Nick shifted his attention briefly to Carrie then returned it to Jerry. "I think I'd better speak to him."

"Cindy said he went into the library and vanished," Jerry remarked. "There has to be a passageway somewhere, but I couldn't find it."

Nick raked his fingers through his hair and groaned with disgust. "I want that man found. If he's dead, I want him brought back to life," he announced firmly. "I want an explanation from him, and I don't care how you have to get it."

"That's not the worst of it," Jerry remarked with some hesitation. "I spoke with Kristy just before she died."

"Kristy? We just came from there," Nick announced.

"It's worse than you think, Nick. She muttered something about Vicki's death," Jerry remarked. "I don't know how she knew about Vicki unless she witnessed something."

Nick looked away and sighed. "We have two murdered women and a supposedly dead old man, who may have some answers, now among the missing." He glanced back at Jerry. "I want to know when Chester disappeared and what time you found Kristy. I would also like a list of who was here when you got back, and what time the others returned to the hotel." Nick gave Jerry a curious look. "Is there anyone else missing?"

"Yeah, according to Cindy; Kera and Duke went out earlier, but they haven't returned," Jerry informed him. "Cindy disappeared on me too."

"Great," he muttered. "I want to know where Troy was during all this, and if he was anywhere near Kristy."

Jerry nodded.

"Anyone else MIA?" Nick demanded.

"Danny and Karl left about forty minutes ago," Jerry replied. "They were worried about Carrie and Kera."

Nick took a deep breath and studied his brother. Jerry appeared to be waiting for further instructions.

"Well? What are you waiting for?" Nick demanded and waved him away. "You're a detective, go detect!"

Jerry nodded and took off. Carrie wanted answers, and she was tired of waiting. She placed her hand firmly on Nick's lower arm, forcing him to meet her gaze.

"What's going on around here, Nick," Carrie suddenly demanded. "If you know something, I think the rest of us have a right to know. That's my sister out there."

Nick's lips curved into a frown. "I don't know any more than you. There are two dead women and three missing people," Nick announced. "After my conversation with Duke, I remembered Chester Milton. I never suspected him as the revenge-seeking type, but I suppose I'd underestimated him."

"Who is Chester Milton?" she finally asked.

"I knew him as the father of a terrorist, or so I thought. It was back when I was with the FBI. I was a young, know-it-all," Nick remarked. "Chester's son was involved with several others in a plot to blow up a federal building. When we apprehended the suspects, there was a shootout, and I shot his son. He died nine days later in the hospital."

"So that's why you believe Chester wants revenge on you?" she asked then turned curious. "What about the rest of us? Why were we brought here?"

"Duke told me he crippled Chester in an incident similar to the one his son committed. He was known to have influential friends involved in drug trafficking as well," Nick informed her. "I don't think Chester brought us here for a couple of drinks and a few laughs about old times."

"But I don't understand," she pressed with concern. "Maybe he wants revenge on you for something that happened to his son, and on Duke for putting him in a wheelchair, but why me and the others? Why are we here?"

"You have to figure that one out," Nick replied, offering little comfort. "I wouldn't doubt that everyone invited here was on Chester's hit list."

Carrie shook her head. "No, that's not possible," she protested. "When would I have crossed Chester? I lead a boring life."

"You got an invitation."

Carrie became concerned and immediately fidgeted. "We have to find Kera."

"We will, but first, we must keep our wits. If we were brought here to be systematically murdered, we'll need our own plan for survival," Nick informed her. "We'll need transportation off the island, and we'll need to stick together. Once Jerry reports back to me, we may have a better understanding of what we're up against." He considered the conversation. "I doubt Chester is physically capable of committing the murders himself. As his relative and keeper of the hotel, Troy would be the most logical suspect, but I'm not limiting myself."

"So how do I know I can trust you?" She recalled how he was conveniently close by when she found Vicki's body.

"Sometimes blind faith needs to be applied," Nick remarked while cocking his head.

"Of course, blind faith could also get a girl killed," Carrie said with a cleverly raised brow.

Nick was silent a moment then spoke, breaking the tension. "I'll take you to your room. I suggest you keep your door locked. When I find your sister, I'll let you know."

"If it's all the same, I would prefer to wait for her down here."

"It's not all the same," Nick announced then took her by the arm and led her to the elevator.

She considered protesting but wasn't up for the battle. Nick pushed the button, and they waited for the elevator. Jerry trotted down the stairs and swung around the banister. He approached Nick and Carrie.

"Troy isn't in his room," he announced. "The lights in the zoo are lit. Should I check there?"

"Not by yourself," Nick informed him. "I'm taking Carrie back to her room. I'll go with you when I return."

"I could escort Carrie to her room," Jerry suggested a little too eagerly.

Carrie glared at him. "I don't think so."

Nick looked back at the elevator and shook his head as the doors opened. All three peered into the elevator and simultaneously froze. Blood covered the elevator walls and streaked downward to the woman, who lay face down in a pool of blood. Blood saturated Cindy's long, blonde hair. Carrie let out a small, horrified scream and turned away. Both detectives stared at the dead woman. Nick slowly entered the elevator and looked over the body then glanced at Jerry.

"Break the news to Bart," Nick instructed.

Jerry nodded and hurried toward the stairs. Carrie slowly turned around and held her breath. She could barely look at the butchered woman. Nick's eyes met hers.

"Carrie, please wait in the lobby," Nick announced. "You shouldn't have to see this."

Carrie took a deep breath and shuddered. "I'm fine, Nick," she replied.

Cindy had been dead for an hour or more. The blood was dried and her body was cold and starting to stiffen. Nick slowly lowered himself alongside the butchered woman in the elevator. He gently rolled her onto her back to examine the wounds. Carrie felt her body tense and her stomach turn.

"Judging by the wounds, it would appear the weapon was something similar to a hunting knife. It had a blade at least an inch wide," Nick announced although possibly more to himself. "Possibly a knife similar to the one used on Vicki. She'd been stabbed once in the abdomen, and, judging by the cuts on her hands and arms, she put up a good struggle." Although he didn't say it, the slit across her throat indicated that was what ultimately killed her.

"Such a bloody slaying," Carrie whispered.

Nick glanced around the elevator for any other sign of clues but didn't find any. Troy appeared in the hallway from the kitchen and looked into the elevator. He stared at the dead woman with wide, horrified eyes.

"Oh, my--what happened?" Troy gasped.

"She's been murdered," Nick said dryly as he looked over his shoulder.

"Who did it?"

Nick glared at Troy with some disbelief. "If I knew who killed her, I wouldn't be inspecting the crime scene."

"It had to be that husband of hers," Troy insisted. "Vulgar, disgusting bastard."

"We don't know that," Nick remarked and straightened. "But I suppose I wouldn't be completely out of line if I asked where you were the past two hours."

Carrie held her breath, surprised by Nick's forward question, and uncertainly glanced at Troy waiting for the explosion.

"You have your nerve," Troy cried out. "How do I know you didn't kill her?"

"I have an alibi for the entire evening," Nick casually replied. "Do you?"

Troy didn't reply but instead walked away before Nick could ask any more questions.

"That's what I thought," Nick snarled then returned to inspecting the blood in the elevator.

Jerry soon appeared and stared at the scene a minute or two before Nick even noticed him.

"What a mess," Jerry muttered while flexing his hand.

Nick didn't look away from the dead woman despite his brother's remark. "Did you find Bart?"

"Yeah, nearly broke my hand," Jerry informed him. "The guy went insane. I'm pretty sure he thinks I was accusing him of killing her. He didn't actually seem too torn up over her death as much as fear of being accused."

"Is everything under control with Bart?" Nick asked as he kneeled down and searched Cindy's pockets.

"Yeah, I'd say. The wall broke Bart's fall," Jerry remarked. "He's resting comfortably now."

Carrie was slightly surprised at Jerry's callousness.

"Good," Nick muttered. "I suppose we can't keep quiet about this any longer." He glanced at his brother with a stern expression. "Can I depend on you to inform the others about the murder of Kristy and Cindy? They'll need to know." His brow sharply rose. "*And* use a little tact."

Jerry smiled lightly. "Don't I always?"

Nick frowned as Jerry jogged toward the lounge. "That's why I mentioned it," he muttered then straightened and looked at Carrie. "Are you all right?"

Carrie nodded. He walked toward her and gently guided her down the hall to the lounge after his brother. When they entered the lounge, Barbie turned away from Jerry and stared at Nick with wide, concerned eyes.

"Is it true? Cindy's been murdered?" Barbie practically cried out. "What's this about blood everywhere?"

Nick glared at Jerry. "I knew I could count on you to handle the situation tactfully."

"I thought I handled it rather well," Jerry remarked.

Nick was about to speak when they heard a harsh pounding on the front door, alarming everyone. They ran from the room to the foyer. Before they could reach the main entrance, the door was thrown open, and Danny darted inside. He violently slammed the door behind him and threw his body against it to hold it shut. He was breathing harshly, and his pants legs were shredded, though he appeared to be fine physically.

"What happened, Danny?" Carrie cried out with concern.

Just then, there was pounding on the door so violent that it vibrated Danny's body. It sounded as if the person on the other end would break it down.

"Let me in," Karl cried from the other side.

Danny spun around, opened the door, and pulled Karl into the foyer. He again slammed the door, and both men braced themselves against it.

"Wolves," Danny cried while gasping for air. "Hundreds of wolves!"

Troy ran to the foyer to check on the commotion within the hallway. Jerry hurried to the window alongside the door and looked out. Five wolves ran toward the hotel and jumped onto the porch, sniffing the area.

"Your wolves decreased by a couple hundred," Jerry remarked dryly.

Troy ran down the hallway then returned carrying a rifle. He opened the door just wide enough to fire several shots in the air. The wolves ran away. Troy closed the door and turned toward the others.

"Those wolves were in my uncle's zoo," he remarked with a frown. "I noticed they were missing when I went to feed tonight. Someone must've left them out."

"Oh, great," Barbie moaned with hostility. "Now we're trapped inside the hotel."

Carrie watched Barbie bite her stubby fingernails. She must have been biting them a while since they were all down to the nubs.

"No, I have a dart gun," Troy replied. "I'll collect them tomorrow morning."

As Troy returned to the trophy room to replace his rifle, Carrie thought about Kera then nervously looked out the thin window alongside the front door. She was out there somewhere. What if the wolves attacked her?

Nick spun to face his brother and gave him a stern look. "I want you to inspect the knives in the trophy room. See if all the daggers are there," he ordered. "I want to know if any have traces of blood on them. There's also a gun cabinet. Remove the weapons, even if it means breaking the glass. Put them someplace safe."

Chapter Eleven

The underground tunnel was dark and damp. The water had been steadily rising around Kera's feet as she uncertainly walked in one direction, hoping it would lead somewhere. It had to be after midnight already, although it seemed like forever since she fell into the underground tunnel through a trapdoor. There were many turns within the tunnel, and she didn't know how long she'd been walking or where she was even going. Despite her somewhat desperate situation, Kera wasn't nearly as panicked as she thought she should have been. Devlin's familiar bark echoed through the tunnel. Kera's heartbeat quickened when she heard the wolf.

"Devlin," she called, hoping he'd locate her.

Surprisingly, he barked in response. She could hear the wolf splashing through the six-inch deep water toward her.

"Here boy," she called even though she couldn't see him in the nearly pitch-black tunnel.

Devlin's cold nose touched her hand, momentarily startling her. He rubbed his wet body against her legs, allowing her to feel the dampness through her pants. She patted the wolf with relief, no longer feeling alone and frightened.

"I'm glad you're here," she said with a relieved sigh. "Now, if I only knew where *here* was."

Devlin barked again and splashed through the water, heading away from her. She attempted to follow the splashing sound in hopes he knew a way out. There was a bang, followed by a loud splash. Devlin barked excitedly. Kera ran through the darkness to locate the wolf. She could hear Duke's familiar voice and slowed her pace as his voice got louder while speaking to Devlin.

"So this is where you've been," he said then laughed. "Down boy."

"It's good of you to join us," Kera remarked.

"Kera?" Duke gasped. "Is that you?"

"Yeah, it's me."

Duke bumped into her in the darkness, nearly knocking her down. To her surprise, he put his arms around her and pulled her against his saturated body. She was slightly startled, not used to being held by strange men, although she found his embrace comforting.

"Thank God I found you," he said and refused to release her. "I was worried something had happened to you."

When he pulled away, she returned to the reality of the tunnel. "The water's rising," she informed him. "I've been looking for a way out with no success. I don't know how high the tide gets, but I'm afraid this entire tunnel may fill with water soon."

Devlin barked and led the way down the tunnel, happily splashing ahead of them. They could hear his bark as it echoed, leading them onward.

"Where do you suppose he's going?" Kera asked.

"I don't know," Duke remarked, "but I trust his sense of direction over mine."

They followed the sound of Devlin's barking. Duke and Kera walked about twenty minutes with the water now above their knees. There seemed to be light up ahead. As they got closer, they noticed a curve in the tunnel and more light. They rounded the corner and saw the entire tunnel was lit.

"It's dark outside," Duke commented as they walked. "I wonder what that light could be."

They continued to splash through the water a little faster, reaching the end of the tunnel. Kera saw a large opening before them. It formed an underground pond. Devlin swam across the water and headed toward the yacht docked against an underground pier. They found a way off the island!

"I'll be damned," Duke said softly and shook his head.

They could see a bigger opening to the left of the tunnel they now stood within. That had to be the way the boat went out, even during high tide. They jumped into the water and swam for the dock, being the only way to reach the boat and safety from the rising water in the tunnel. Excitement and coldness of the water enabled them to swim faster. They reached the ladder to the dock that was five feet above them. Devlin was already on the dock, shaking water from his thick, gray coat. Just as Kera was about to climb the ladder, something hit her leg. She let out a terrified scream. In panic, she jumped onto the ladder, wanting to get out of the water as soon as possible. Duke climbed up behind her and looked back to the water.

"Wait for me on the dock," he ordered. "I'll be right back."

Before she could protest, Duke jumped back into the water. Kera stood on the dock and stared at the dark pool of water, not seeing Duke. Something floated past the ladder from under the pier. She kneeled on the dock and strained to see the floating object. A dead man floated face down past the ladder. Kera screamed and fell onto her backside then scrambled to her feet just as Duke surfaced.

"Duke! Behind you!"

Duke whirled around in the water, wiping the water from his eyes and his glasses. Chester's dead body drifted into him. Duke gasped then swam backward to the ladder and joined Kera on the dock.

"Oh, my God," Kera gasped. "Was that the missing lawyer? Do you think he drowned?"

Duke placed an arm around Kera's shoulder while she shivered, and half turned her. "That's not the missing lawyer," he announced. "That's Chester Milton, and judging by the slit in his throat, I would say he was dead before he hit the water."

Kera's eyes widened, and she attempted to look back to see for herself. Duke didn't allow her to look back but instead forced her along the dock and toward the boat.

"You mean he was murdered?"

"We need to check the boat," Duke insisted. "If my suspicions are correct, the boat won't work."

They boarded the yacht, soaking wet, and entered the control room. Duke glanced over the controls then attempted to start the engine. The engine didn't make a sound.

"Are you sure you know what you're doing?" Kera asked while shivering in her wet clothes.

"I know my way around boats," he informed her. "This one isn't going anywhere."

Kera followed Duke across the ship's deck and stopped as he paused near a pool of blood. He then followed a streak to the stern and ran his finger along the rail, revealing more blood.

"We have to tell Nick what we found if he doesn't already know," he informed her.

He hurried Kera from the yacht and across the dock. There was an iron door to their right and an elevator in front of them. They chose the elevator, which took them to the basement. Duke stepped out of the secret elevator and looked around, appearing somewhat disoriented in the wine cellar. Kera looked at the wine rack and noticed a bloody, female handprint.

"Duke," Kera whispered and indicated the blood.

§

*C*arrie sat in the lobby reading a book even though it was nearly two-thirty in the morning. She was tired, but she wanted to stay up a while longer in case Kera returned. Jerry was in the back room behind the hotel's registration desk watching the security monitors, so she knew she wasn't alone. A strange sloshing sound from the hallway startled her. Carrie looked up from her book and saw Duke, Kera, and Devlin standing near the stairs. They stared back at her, all three soaking wet. Carrie dropped her book and sprang to her feet.

"Kera!" she cried out and ran to her sister. Carrie threw her arms around Kera and hugged her wet body. "I'm so glad you're alive."

"Me too," Kera mumbled.

Before Carrie could convince them to go upstairs, Jerry came out of the back room and saw the soaking wet couple.

"What happened to you?" Jerry practically gasped.

"Duke and I found a boat," Kera explained with little emotion, fighting her chill.

"You found a boat?" Carrie exclaimed.

"Don't bother packing just yet," Duke informed them with the same lack of emotion. "The boat's been sabotaged. It isn't going anywhere. Then there's the other thing."

"What other thing?" Jerry asked.

"We also found Chester Milton. He's been murdered," Duke replied.

Jerry and Carrie looked at each other and then drew deep breaths. Carrie remained silent and fidgeted.

Kera noted their odd reactions. "What happened?" she gasped.

"Why are you people acting so strange?" Duke demanded.

"Cindy and Kristy were murdered sometime this evening," Jerry told them in a gentle tone.

Duke closed his eyes and groaned while shaking his head. "Somehow, I'm not surprised."

Kera placed a damp hand to her forehead and sighed. "This can't be happening," she whispered then eyed Duke. "I don't think I can handle one more shock tonight."

She turned away from him and walked toward the elevator. Duke instinctively followed her with Devlin by his side.

Carrie looked at Jerry with concern. "Did anyone remove Cindy's body from the elevator?"

Jerry shrugged then ran with Carrie for the elevator as the doors opened. "Kera," they called out while running. "Don't use the elevator."

"Why not?"

Kera then turned and stepped inside the empty elevator. Cindy's body was no longer there, and most of the blood had been cleaned, although some stains remained. Duke and Devlin joined her in the elevator just before the doors closed. Jerry appeared baffled then exchanged bewildered looks with Carrie.

Chapter Twelve

Day three. By afternoon the following day, Troy announced that he had successfully returned the wolves to their cages in the old zoo. Despite their capture, none of the guests felt comfortable venturing outside the hotel. They'd been through a lot the previous day, and most were still recovering from the news of the murdered women. Several guests turned in early that evening since they still lacked sleep from the night before. A few others went back to their rooms to relax without fear of someone slitting their throats when they weren't looking. Despite her lack of sleep, Kera sat on the edge of the desk in the study and watched while Duke searched through the drawers.

"What are you looking for anyway?" Kera asked.

Duke sorted through some papers then stuffed them back into the drawer with mild disgust. "Anything that might shed some light on our friend, Troy."

"He may be your friend, but he's certainly not mine," Kera replied then looked around the room with a curious expression. "Where's Devlin?"

"Outside, taking care of some business." Duke collapsed in the chair and sighed.

"Didn't find what you're looking for?"

"No, there's nothing here," he replied with defeat. "Perhaps the Parkers will have better luck searching Chester's room." He cast a look at her. "I assume the others turned in."

"A while ago, I believe," Kera replied.

"It is getting late," he remarked. "I'll walk you to your room on the way to mine."

Duke stood from behind the desk and walked with Kera into the hallway. He stopped her by the stairs.

"Wait here," he announced then indicated the front door. "I should check on Devlin."

She watched Duke head into the foyer and out the front door. Kera waited with some insecurity by the bottom of the stairs for him to return. Troy staggered from the lounge with a bottle of whiskey in one hand and a black book in the other. The stench of whiskey lingered as he approached her and the stairs. He gave her a moderately creepy smile, which was magnified by his drunken condition.

"Looking for me?" he teased.

"No," Kera replied. "I'm pretty sure I wasn't."

He laughed softly. "Well, you found me anyway." He cast a lustful sweeping glance over her. "You certainly are a gorgeous, young thing. Why don't we go up to my room for a little fun," he said and caressed her shoulder, allowing his hand to stray toward her chest.

Kera pulled away from him with irritation. "You're drunk, Troy."

"Yes, I know. Care to join me in a bottle?" he chuckled. "We can celebrate life, or in our case, death."

Kera stared at him with bewilderment. "What are you talking about?"

Troy moved closer to her. She attempted to back away from him but backed into the banister instead. The corners of his mouth were raised in a drunken, psychotic manner.

"I found my uncle's journal this afternoon," Troy informed her and raised the black, leather book. "He intended to kill everyone on the island, including me, his only nephew." He chuckled. "Can you believe the nerve of that bastard? If he wasn't already dead, I'd kill him myself."

He tossed the journal aside and took another swig from the bottle. Kera stared at him and attempted to make sense of his drunken ramblings.

"I don't understand," she remarked. "You think your uncle killed those women?"

He lowered the bottle and shook his head as whiskey dripped from his lips. "No," he told her then moved closer, setting the bottle on the step behind her head and rested his arms on the banister, trapping her. "He wasn't the type to bloody his own hands."

Kera decided he was too drunk to know what he was talking about. His closeness and the smell of booze on his breath frightened her. "That's really very fascinating, but I think I had better return to my room before Carrie comes looking for me."

She attempted to move past him. Troy grabbed her by the arm and pulled her back, now pinning her between the banister and his body.

"There aren't any consequences to our actions anymore," Troy whispered. "I can do whatever I want."

Kera was shocked by his words, knowing he believed it to be true. Before she could call for Duke, Troy kissed her harshly on the mouth. Kera pushed against his shoulders in a poor attempt to hold him back. She could taste the whiskey on his breath while struggling to push him away, but she couldn't break free with her head pinned against the banister. Troy was roughly torn away from her and thrown against the opposite wall. Kera jumped with surprise then saw it was Duke who stood between them. His look was oddly calm, but the lack of emotion in his eyes almost chilled her. Troy slowly straightened while keeping his eyes on Duke.

"What's your problem, old man?" he cried out.

"Don't touch her again," Duke growled.

The two men locked eyes in a standoff of sorts. Troy was drunk and hostile while Duke remained calm and cold.

"I could take you on any day," Troy snarled.

Duke spun into a high, roundhouse kick for the large, round ball on top of the banister. The ball broke off its base and catapulted across the stairs, striking the opposing wall. Duke returned to center from the kick, facing Troy.

"Do you really think so?" Duke scoffed. "Bring it, boy."

Troy stared at the banister and its missing decorative ball, revealing concern and fear on his face. Devlin was suddenly between Duke and Troy, snarling at the drunken man with his teeth bared and the scruff on his back standing on end. The wolf's aggression even frightened Kera.

"I suggest you take your bottle and go back to your room," Duke remarked showing little emotion.

Troy kept his eyes on Devlin then backed away from them and down the hall. He didn't bother stopping for the bottle. Once he was far enough, he turned and ran away from them. Devlin made a motion to chase him, but Duke stopped the wolf with a slight motion of his hand. The snarling immediately stopped, and the playful wolf returned. Duke placed his hand on Kera's shoulder and studied her with concern.

"Are you all right?"

Kera nodded, still astonished by what had happened, then threw her arms around Duke's neck and clung to him. "I'm so glad you were here," she gasped while shaking.

"I'm not about to let anything happen to you," he replied gently, his warm breath near her ear.

Despite his closeness and the warmth of his embrace, Kera pulled away, remembering something important. She saw the journal on the floor and picked it up.

"What's that?" Duke asked with surprise.

She handed him the black journal. "I think this may be what you were looking for."

Chapter Thirteen

It was four in the morning. Devlin trotted down the main stairs and entered the lobby. Indicated by the light in the room beyond the front desk, someone was on night duty. Devlin was about to approach the desk when there was a faint knock on the front door. The wolf was immediately alerted, stopped mid-stride, and stared at the main door, snarling softly. As the front door opened, Devlin silently crept closer to the foyer. A handsome man in his early thirties stood in the doorway, immediately saw the large, intimidating wolf, and remained nearly motionless. A nervous smile crossed his face.

"Nice doggie," he announced gently.

Devlin growled louder and let out a short bark.

"Maybe I should come back in the morning," the man with an English accent announced.

Devlin snarled, lunged for him, and snapped at his groin. The man gasped, dropped the envelope he held, then turned and ran into the woods. Devlin bounded after him and chased him down the path. He chased the man through the dimly lit woods and across the beach. Devlin stopped a few feet on the sand and watched as the man pushed a small rowboat into the water. As the man jumped into the rowboat, he looked back at the wolf while breathing harshly from his run. Devlin crouched down and barked viciously while standing in place, successfully chasing the intruder away. The handsome stranger rowed away from the beach and headed for the large yacht anchored just offshore. Devlin let out a low snarl then kicked up sand behind him, obviously proud of the job he'd done.

§

A loud crack of thunder interrupted the silence of the night. Carrie woke abruptly from her light sleep, her heart racing as she looked around the dark room. She could see Kera's outline in the bed located next to hers. Kera appeared oblivious to the rising storm. It was still off in the distance but sounded threatening all the same. Carrie was unable to sleep even though she'd been very tired earlier. It was only a little after four in the morning, but she couldn't bear to stay in the confines of the room. Carrie knew either Jerry or Nick were on duty in the back room of the lobby. She decided to go downstairs and join them. She locked the door behind her and headed downstairs. Carrie saw a light on in the billiard room, approached, and cast a glance inside. Nick sat at the bar sideways, in order to keep an eye on the doorway to prevent any surprise attacks. He held the black journal in his hand and had a drink sitting before him. Carrie entered and casually approached, eyeing the journal.

"What's that?" she asked.

"This is Chester Milton's personal journal," Nick replied and shook his head while skimming entries. "The man was completely insane. Duke showed this to me a couple of hours ago. He said Troy was muttering something about everyone dying. There are a couple of pages torn from the beginning but listen to the last entry." Nick raised a dark eyebrow and read from the journal. "It's complete. My ultimate plan has been set in motion. My enemies have arrived for sentencing. I sentence them to death. At noon on the ninth day, explosions will level my beloved Demon Island, taking all my enemies with it."

Carrie's mouth dropped open at the words he read. "I don't understand," she gasped. "We really were brought here to be executed?"

Nick shut the journal with added vigor and carelessly cast it aside. "That's correct. Ironically, Chester's son died nine days after I'd shot him. A coincidence? Perhaps. There are days I hate being right."

The lights flickered and went out. Carrie gasped and looked around the billiard room through the darkness.

"What happened?"

"Just a power outage from the approaching storm," Nick replied. "There's an emergency generator somewhere. I'd ask Troy to show me where it is, but he's passed out in his room."

Nick lit several candles to brighten the room. Carrie shivered at the newly found information. On that note, sleep was definitely out. She approached the pool table, found a pool stick, and lined her break shot by candlelight. She cast a look at Nick, who had been watching her while she leaned over the pool table. It occurred to her that he was possibly checking out her backside. When he casually looked away, she realized she had been correct. Carrie looked back at the pool table, smiled slyly, and then broke the pool balls. She straightened and glanced at Nick. He stood and walked around the table.

"Do you play?" she asked.

"I do, but I'm supposed to be watching the guests and perhaps prevent another murder," he remarked. "Now I also have to keep an eye on you."

Carrie straightened and looked back. "Keep an eye on me? Who said you need to watch me?" she demanded and approached him. "I can take care of myself."

"I don't know about that. Seems to me you're good at getting yourself into trouble," he announced, "but not nearly as good at getting out of it."

Carrie stood directly in front of him and stared without humor. "You're funny," she snarled then turned back to the pool table to line up her next shot. "You're about as compassionate as a hangman at the gallows."

"I don't know what you're basing that theory upon," he remarked.

"Nothing bothers you," she remarked in a callous tone. "Despite our somewhat unusual relationship, if I were killed tonight, you'd just continue as you have been. Solve the case. That's all that matters." She made her next shot and successfully sank the three ball. Carrie straightened and turned to face him. "We aren't people to you; we're just corpses in living bodies."

"I'd be upset if you were dead," he insisted.

Carrie smirked and nodded. "Sure you would. I saw how broken up you were over the others."

He cocked his head to one side. "I hardly knew them. This is what I do. It doesn't pay to get emotional."

Carrie laughed and shook her head. "Like I said, you're heartless."

Nick shook his head with a sigh. "There's just no arguing with you. It's late. I'll see you safely to your room."

"Charming as your company is, I think I can manage just fine without you."

Nick handed Carrie a candle. "All the same, I think I'll walk you to your room. Trouble is never far behind you."

"Then stop following me."

As he scooted her from the billiard room, she realized she wasn't going to win the argument. Now that the hotel was dark, she didn't exactly like the idea of remaining downstairs alone, although she'd never admit that to Nick. They left the billiard room together as the smell of extinguished candle smoke lingered behind. The hallway was still dark, but the faint light of day could be seen outside the narrow windows on either side of the front doors. They neared the stairs when a breeze blew out the candle. Nick looked toward the front door and noticed it was partially open.

The wind gently caused the door to sway. Nick approached the door and pulled it open, looking outside. The storm was gaining strength and would be onshore within the hour. He looked out into the darkness then down to the porch by his feet. A familiar envelope lay near the door. He picked it up. Carrie glanced past him to see what he had found. There was an unfamiliar name and address written on it, but it was the same invitation to Demon Island they'd all received.

"Drake Remington?" Nick read the name on the invitation then appeared puzzled. "Who do you suppose that is?"

"The name sounds familiar to me, but I don't know why," Carrie informed him.

Nick sank into thought while fiddling with the envelope. "This could mean a couple of different things," he remarked. "This man may have shown up when there was no one around, or the killer could have left this here to make us think we're not alone and someone else is responsible for killing those women."

"So if this man did actually come here, where is he now?" she asked with concern.

Nick sighed and stared out the front door a moment. "I don't know, but I'm going to check the beach, just in case there's a boat anchored."

"Let's go," she announced.

He glared back at her with doubt in his eyes. "I don't remember inviting you."

"It's a free island," she announced with little care. "I don't need your permission."

Nick groaned and rolled his eyes with defeat. "Why do I even bother?"

"I've asked myself that same question," she remarked.

Chapter Fourteen

The jungle was still fairly dark and would be for some time as storm clouds darkened the early morning sky. Nick and Carrie reached the beach and heard the distant thunder getting closer as the wind picked up. The waves seemed a little less friendly while violently crashing to shore. The sunrise attempted to shine through the dark sky, creating a purple horizon. Carrie followed Nick across the sand toward the dock, but they didn't see any boats. Nick checked the beach for any other signs of someone having been there, but anything that had been there was already washed away in the heavy surf. Carrie paused just before the tide's reach and stared at the horizon and the lightning in the distant sky.

"We better get back before that storm hits," Nick remarked with defeat that their exploration turned up nothing useful. "If there had been someone here, there aren't any signs."

"Are you afraid to get a little wet?" Carrie called after him as he walked toward the woods.

Nick paused and turned to face her. "No, but why should I if I don't have to?"

Carrie hid her smile while studying him. "You don't see a point to anything that doesn't pertain to the case at hand."

Nick groaned and walked a few feet closer to her. "I don't have a one-track mind if that's what you're suggesting."

She continued to smile. "I just want to enjoy the view." She indicated the horizon. "Doesn't that storm look impressive?"

Nick let a slight laugh escape. "I don't have time to stop and watch the tide," he replied. "There's a lot to be done, and I'm very tired."

"Don't be such a prude." Carrie extended her hand to him and smiled sweetly. "I'll share my tropical storm sunrise with you."

Nick looked from her hand then back at her warm expression. He forced a smile and laughed while shaking his head. "You can be charming when it serves your purpose," he said then accepted her hand.

Although she had offered her hand, somehow his hand holding hers surprised her. She stared into his eyes briefly and suddenly realized this was a defining moment for both of them. When was the last time she offered a man her hand? When was the last time she suspected Nick held a woman's hand? The way he looked back at her told her just about everything she wanted to know. In a split second, Carrie's attention shifted beyond Nick to a shadow she saw within the woods. Her expression dropped with possible confusion.

"There's someone in the woods," she remarked with some surprise.

Nick released her hand while simultaneously drawing his gun and spun toward the woods. In an instant, a gunshot rang out. Nick clutched his arm in reflex, although maintaining the grip on his gun. Carrie barely saw Nick grab his arm when she felt a sharp, burning sensation shoot through her left shoulder. She clutched her shoulder and cried out as she fell to her knees from the pain. She could feel something hot and sticky seeping between her fingers. When Carrie pulled her hand back and saw the blood, she realized she'd been shot. Nick sprang to her fallen side, shielding her from the shooter's line of fire, and turned toward the woods with his gun aimed. He fired twice into the woods at something that moved then remained motionless and fixated on the woods with no sound except his heavy breathing. There was no one there. Nick looked back at Carrie as she slumped over while clutching her bleeding shoulder and tears of pain streaking her face.

"Carrie--" he gasped. He saw the blood on her hand, and his expression became pale.

Carrie gasped while enduring the pain and pinched her eyes shut. Nick immediately picked her up and into his arms. She cried out in agony as he carried her.

"I have to get you back to the hotel. It's going to be all right," he whispered into her ear.

The wind was beginning to blow harder now, and the thunder was closer than before. He carried her toward the path in the woods with some caution. She clung to his neck with her good, right arm. He paused within the woods, his gun still in his hand under her legs, and made sure the shooter was gone. She buried her face into his neck and endured the pain as blood now covered her once white shirt.

"It's going to be all right," Nick chanted then stopped at the entrance to the path and stared at the small caliber semiautomatic lying on the ground.

"What's wrong?" Carrie gasped but couldn't open her eyes, fearful why he had stopped.

"The shooter left the gun," Nick gasped then looked around. There was blood on a nearby plant. "I injured him. He's probably halfway back to the hotel." He left the gun and hurried along the path. "We have to get back to the hotel and get some pressure on that wound," Nick said.

The rain started to pour harshly along with the blowing wind, immediately drenching them. The hotel was just ahead of them. Carrie let out a sharp gasp and dug her fingernails into his neck. Nick cringed from the pain.

"You're going to be just fine. Hang on," he announced. "Just a little further. Jerry can take care of you. He has emergency training. He'll know what to do. Just hang on."

Nick leaped onto the porch despite carrying her and attempted to open the door. It was locked!

"Damn it!" Nick cried out.

Nick set Carrie down on her feet but kept his left arm securely around her to hold her up. "Hold on," Nick said. "I have to break it down."

"I'm fine," she whispered while clutching her shoulder.

She closed her eyes and released her bleeding shoulder to clutch Nick's neck for support. Her knees buckled. Nick gripped her waist and held her against his side. Everything turned dark. A loud crack alarmed her. She opened her eyes and saw the front door fly open. Nick picked her up once more and entered the hotel, taking her up the stairs two at a time to the second floor. The upstairs hallway was dark. Carrie felt her head tingle.

*C*arrie opened her eyes and realized she was lying on a bed in one of the upstairs rooms. There wasn't much light except what came in the window from the stormy sky. The burning in her shoulder increased with each breath. She cried out and clutched the warm, sticky wound.

"Nick," she gasped as her head fell to the one side, "where the hell are we?"

"We're back in my room."

He pulled the sheet from the bed and applied pressure to her shoulder. Carrie cried out in pain.

"You have to hold this to stop the bleeding," Nick announced. "Can you do that for me? I have to get Jerry."

She slowly nodded and closed her eyes. When Carrie opened her eyes, she saw Jerry hovering over her. Jerry ripped her shirt where the bullet had passed through and observed the wound.

"It's not too deep. I can get the bullet out," he announced. "I'll need a very thin knife. Find a first-aid kit."

Nick nodded and hurried from the room.

"You're going to hurt me, aren't you?" she asked softly as her pain mysteriously seemed to lessen.

Jerry glanced at her and smiled reassuringly. "I'll try not to. Would you like me to get Kera?"

She groaned and closed her eyes. "No, I don't have the strength to hear her rant and rave right now."

Nick soon returned with a bottle of whiskey and a first aid kit. "This was all I could find."

He locked the door behind him and lit several candles to brighten the room. Jerry poured some whiskey into a large bowl with some linen Nick had gathered then handed the bottle to Carrie. Nick watched with concern.

"Take a couple of good swallows of this," he informed her. "It'll make you feel better."

Carrie sat up and did as Jerry directed. She took two swallows of the whiskey and gasped. "Oh, that's horrible!" She then proceeded to take a third swallow before falling back onto the bed.

"Nick, I'll need your lock pick," Jerry ordered.

"Why?"

"It's small enough to dig the bullet out and should cause her less pain."

Nick gave him the small metal pick with a slight curve to the thin end. Jerry sterilized it in the bowl of whiskey then took the bottle from Carrie, who was now on her fourth swig.

"I'm going to sterilize the site. This may hurt--" he announced then proceeded to pour some whiskey on the wound.

Pain shot through her entire body despite the numbness of her left shoulder. "Son-of-a-bitch!" Carrie cried out.

Nick quickly moved around Jerry and sat on the bed facing Carrie. He gently pushed her back down to the bed and rested on her good arm and shoulder.

"Just hold on," he announced reassuringly.

"This is going to hurt," Jerry said gently.

"Then don't do it," Carrie lashed out.

Jerry proceeded to probe into the bullet wound and dig out the bullet. Carrie cried out and shot upward, taking Nick with her, throwing her right arm around his neck while clinging to him. Jerry continued to dig the bullet out, despite the fact that she was in an upright position. Nick seemed to have a better hold on her now than he did before. As Carrie screamed into Nick's shoulder, he spoke gently in her ear. Tears of pain streaked her face, but his soothing voice allowed her to quiet down to a soft sob. She clung to Nick and dug her fingernails into his neck as the pain from her shoulder radiated throughout her entire body. Jerry moved away and dropped the bullet into a bowl near the bedside.

"Twenty-two caliber, huh?" Jerry questioned then stood. "It could've been a lot worse." He removed one of the linen cloths from the basin, wrung it out lightly, and then applied it to Carrie's shoulder.

She jumped slightly, but it didn't seem to hurt as bad.

"I better find more bandages," Jerry announced. "Do you have her, Nick?"

He nodded while gently rocking her. Carrie removed her fingernails from Nick's neck but remained in his arms.

She sniffed then whispered in his ear, "I guess you're not completely heartless after all."

Nick held her against him and snorted a laugh. "Don't tell anyone. You'll ruin my bad reputation."

Chapter Fifteen

Day four. The thunderstorm lasted a better part of the morning, leaving it miserable and dark outside. The wind blew fiercely, and the rain continued to pour. Just about everyone was up and about, but they weren't doing much since there was no power. Despite being daytime, most of the hotel's interior remained dark. Carrie and Nick were suspiciously absent. Despite Kera's persistent inquiries, Jerry wasn't offering any information on Carrie's whereabouts. By the time Kera located Duke to gain information, Jerry had conveniently disappeared as well.

The remaining guests had gathered in the lobby while Troy went out to the generator building to fix the power. With its big windows, the lobby was the only area offering enough natural light despite the stormy weather. Bart, having limited options for company, reluctantly joined Danny and Karl where they hung out near the front desk. A bored Barbie sat in a nearby chair while flipping through an old, outdated magazine. She'd successfully isolated herself from the other guests. None were willing to engage her in conversation, which shouldn't have been surprising. Kera hung out with Duke and Devlin on one of the sofas near the large, front window. They talked quietly and with an odd seriousness, giving the impression of co-conspirators plotting something sinister.

Despite Danny's earlier conflicts with Bart, Karl provided a buffer between the two, allowing the three men to have a jovial conversation. Karl was eager to share his tales from last night with his new friends.

"I'll tell you, someone must've been having a good night," Karl announced with a chuckle. "I heard one of the women screaming her head off last night."

Danny shook his head and laughed. "Lucky you. All I heard last night was Bart snoring in the next room."

"What the hell are you talking about?" Bart scoffed while glaring at Danny, obviously offended. "Your room isn't even next to mine. The princess' room is between our rooms."

Barbie unexpectedly entered their conversation and interrupted a potential fight. "I heard a woman last night too," she informed them. "I thought I was dreaming it. What I heard, though, sounded like someone in pain."

There was an odd silence among the four.

"Anyone missing?" Danny asked with concern while scanning the lobby to conduct a silent head count.

Kera overheard their conversation. Her expression dropped as her face turned pale. "I didn't see Carrie or Nick this morning." She eyed Duke and immediately fidgeted. "You don't think something's happened to her, do you?"

The group became quiet as they glanced at one another. Duke was about to speak when they heard the front door open. Their heads turned toward the archway in time to see Nick walk past the lobby. Without waiting for Duke, Kera bolted from the sofa, ran into the hall, and hurried after Nick. Duke and Danny attempted to follow Kera when Jerry appeared in the archway and prevented them from leaving. Devlin snarled his disapproval, although Duke shut him down with a slight wave of his hand.

"I can't let you leave," Jerry announced while folding his arms across his chest and taking a broad stance. "I have strict orders to keep everyone in the lobby for the next hour while Nick searches your rooms."

"Search our rooms?" Danny suddenly demanded. "Why would he need to search our rooms? We already know Troy's the one who murdered Cindy and Kristy."

"There have been questionable circumstances that might clear him," Jerry replied, offering little information.

Danny stared at him with horror on his face. "Has there been another murder?"

Duke stiffened and studied Jerry's expression. As Kera clearly pointed out, Carrie was the only one missing.

Jerry attempted to hide his emotions but drew a moderately shaken breath. "I'm not permitted to discuss the details at the moment."

Danny glared his contempt then reluctantly returned to the others on the far end of the lobby.

Karl gave Danny a strange look as he sat down. "That was a short trip," he remarked with surprise. "Is there a problem?"

Danny nodded while eyeing Jerry and Duke from across the room. "It would seem the Parkers are suspicious of the rest of us as well as Troy. I guess we've become the enemy."

"That's crazy," Karl replied. "Troy's the only possible killer. It was his uncle who brought us here. There's no doubt in my mind that Troy knew Chester wasn't dead the entire time, so he's an accessory to whatever evil scheme that old man plotted."

"He said something about circumstances that may clear him of involvement," Danny informed him. "I have a strange feeling something happened to Carrie last night. It's not right that they don't tell us."

"Carrie?" Karl gasped with concern, clearly stunned at the suggestion. "I can't believe that. I mean, she's been quite close to Nick since we've arrived. I seriously doubt he'd let any harm come to her."

"I'll talk to Kera later," Danny informed him.

Duke remained in the lobby entrance while standing before Jerry. Duke's cold stare was void of emotion as he glared into Jerry's eyes. His silent intimidation caused the younger Parker to flinch.

"I don't mind standing aside while you and your brother investigate the murders," Duke announced in a soft, low tone. "But if Carrie's been killed, I intend to be by Kera's side. If that's the case, you'll either get out of my way or I'll move you by force." He sharply raised his brows. "What will it be?"

Jerry tensed, somehow knowing he needed to tread lightly with the seemingly docile man. He gently cleared his throat. "Carrie's fine, I promise."

Duke tilted his head and managed a tiny smirk. "I'll take you at your word," he announced simply. "I'll leave you to your assignment."

As Duke and Devlin returned to the sofa by the window, Jerry released a slightly shaken breath.

§

*H*alf an hour had passed, and Jerry was having a hard time keeping everyone relaxed while being stuck in the lobby. They didn't want to be detained any longer, and most were a little irritated that Nick was searching their rooms.

"I don't know who the hell you Parkers think you are, but you have no right searching our bags," Bart said loudly. "You aren't the island police."

"Have something to hide, Bart?" Jerry asked while eyeing him suspiciously.

"Don't even try to accuse me of murder, Parker," Bart shouted and stood abruptly. He crossed the room toward Jerry and pointed a warning finger. "I'll kick your ass."

"Do you think you're above suspicion?" Jerry asked, showing little concern for the threat. "You beat your wife; now she's dead. I'd say you make a damned good suspect."

Danny groaned and placed his hand over his eyes while shaking his head. "That was a mistake," he muttered, concerned for Jerry's welfare.

"They're going to peel your ass off the wall, you rotten, little rent-a-dick," Bart shouted in anger then made a fist and swung for Jerry.

Jerry blocked the punch and returned it with his own hard fist, hitting Bart in the jaw. Bart's head snapped back, but he didn't go down. Bart angrily swung back, hitting Jerry in the stomach, doubling him over. The lights flickered and came on, but no one seemed to notice. Danny attempted to get into the fight, but Karl grabbed his arm and held him back. While attempting to keep Danny out of the fight, he caught a stray punch to his face. Karl was thrown across the room and flew over an empty sofa. Jerry managed to throw another punch and nailed Bart in the stomach. He gasped and doubled over but recovered rather quickly. Danny grabbed a nearby vase from one of the tables and prepared to take Bart down when the opportunity arose. Bart hit Jerry in the face, throwing him back a couple of steps. Troy, who had just entered the lobby, saw Danny with the vase and attempted to stop him from using the antique as a weapon. He was too late. Danny smashed the vase over Bart's head and knocked him out.

"Serves you right," Danny scoffed while sneering at him. "Rotten wife beater."

Danny turned with a satisfied smile only to be punched in the face by Troy. Jerry attempted to pull Troy away from Danny, but he spun around and hit Jerry as well. Duke cringed from where he sat in the corner and watched the grown men beat one another. Devlin lay down, put his paws over his eyes, and whined softly. Barbie scurried out of the way several times while the three men fought, and she screamed every time someone was hit. Danny was punched once more and fell to the floor then used his position to grab Troy by the ankles and pulled his feet out from underneath him. Troy landed harshly with a thud. Bart regained consciousness, climbed back to his feet, and immediately dove for Jerry. Both men sailed across the room and landed roughly on a coffee table, breaking it with a thunderous crack.

Karl recovered and approached the two men on the floor alongside the broken coffee table. Bart recovered first and pulled the slightly dazed Jerry to his feet by his shirt. Bart's fist flew for Jerry's face, but he ducked at the last second, allowing Karl to take the hit to his mouth instead. He was thrown back across the room and over the same sofa. Danny finally jumped back to his feet and tackled Troy to the floor. Jerry casually walked toward the small bar and poured himself a drink then glanced around the room, seemingly proud of what he'd accomplished. The four men continued to fight while Duke and Barbie steered clear of the chaos. Fists were flying, women were screaming, and bodies were becoming bruised. As promised, he kept everyone in the lobby. Jerry finished his drink, slammed the glass down on the bar with a grin, and then jumped back into the fight.

*C*arrie slowly opened her eyes to the sound of rain pouring against the bedroom window. The room was moderately dark for daytime since the storm outside didn't allow much light. She only napped a little after Kera's visit. Her sister was quick to point out Carrie's recklessness, so she was happy to send her on her way. Carrie attempted to sit up but was immediately reminded of the events of that morning by the shooting pain in her shoulder. She cringed and realized just how stiff she'd become. She couldn't even move her shoulder without feeling a terrible tugging against the wound.

She managed to pull herself into a sitting position with limited discomfort. When she looked around the room, she saw Nick asleep in the chair near the bedroom door. She looked at her watch and saw it was nearly noon. She was glad she had a nap since she didn't sleep much after the shooting. Carrie looked at Nick once more. It was best to let him sleep. She doubted that he'd even had two hours sleep. She knew he hadn't slept before she was shot. She glanced down at the shirt she wore. It wasn't hers, and she really didn't remember how she got into it. She remembered Jerry removing the bullet, but she didn't recall when he put the wrapping over her wound. Carrie reached under her shirt and felt the padded dressing with care. Jerry did a nice job. Nick stirred, opened his eyes, and glanced at her. He ran his fingers through his hair and straightened. He approached her, sat on the bed facing her, and forced a tiny, weary smile.

"How are you feeling?"

Carrie managed a smile. "Not too shabby considering I took a bullet for you last night."

Nick's mood suddenly changed and his smile faded. "I'm really sorry, Carrie."

"It wasn't your fault," she remarked. "Neither of us knew there was someone with a gun in the woods. It wasn't like you dodged out of the way and let them shoot me."

Nick shrugged slightly while looking down at the sheets. "I just keep thinking I could've done something differently. I never should've let you come along."

"If I hadn't come along, you might be dead," she informed him. "I wish I could have seen more than just a shadow, but it was too dark. If you hadn't turned, I'm sure you would have gotten it right in the back."

Nick managed a tiny smile. "I suppose I create my own trouble."

"I'm sure you do." She stared at him a moment then hesitated. "I was surprised how emotional you became when you thought I was going to die," she said while containing her grin. "Here I thought you didn't care."

"I didn't do anything for you that I wouldn't have done for a total stranger."

Carrie laughed. "Sure you didn't."

Nick smiled but didn't respond. Carrie moved across the bed and flipped the blanket over.

"You need some sleep," she said and patted the vacant spot alongside her.

Nick eyed the empty side of the bed where she patted then forced a tiny smile. He removed his shoes and wearily slipped under the covers with her.

"Just behave yourself," she reprimanded with a teasing grin. "I'm not allowed to fight with you for at least a week. Orders from Jerry."

Nick then turned on his side, propped himself on his elbow, and looked at her as a smile crept across his face. "Jerry's going to make a good wife someday."

"I'll be sure to tell him you said so."

Chapter Sixteen

Jerry entered Nick's bedroom, appearing exhausted and slightly battered from his afternoon. Carrie was now sitting up in bed while rummaging through Nick's wallet. Nick sat in the nearby chair and probed through a woman's purse. Jerry suspiciously eyed both, waved off their behavior, and collapsed on the bed, nearly crushing Carrie. She angrily pulled Nick's wallet out from under him. Nick eyed his brother with a strange look.

"What happened to you?" Nick asked.

Jerry groaned and closed his eyes while breathing heavily. "Crowd control sucks."

"Yeah? You look like you got your ass kicked," Nick remarked sternly.

Jerry opened an eye and looked at his brother. "I look better than Bart."

"Correct me if I'm wrong," Nick announced with a look of disapproval, "but didn't I simply ask you to keep everyone in the lobby for an hour or two?"

"And that's exactly what I did," Jerry replied with some annoyance to his brother's sarcasm. "They became unruly, so I had to give them something to do."

"So you started a fight?" Nick demanded.

"Of course not," Jerry insisted. "Bart started it; I merely finished it."

Nick shook his head.

"What did you find in Bart's room?" Jerry asked coming back to life.

"Just a kilo of cocaine," Nick replied simply.

"So that's why he didn't want his room searched," Jerry replied while snorting a laugh. "It's a good thing for him we're not interested in his personal habits as much as we are in murder." He then looked at Carrie near him on the bed and smiled cheaply. "You and Nick been having fun?"

"Leave her alone," Nick muttered. "We have important matters to discuss here."

"Did you find traces of blood from the shooter you injured last night?" Jerry asked.

"No, I didn't find anything with blood on it, but I did find Vicki's purse in Danny's room, of all places." He removed a letter from the zipper compartment, opened the paper, and read it aloud. "Dear Jen, the weather has been beautiful and sunny. The ship isn't exactly a cruise liner, but the food is good. You'll be shocked when I tell you who's onboard. You guessed it. Barbie Allender, that bitch."

Jerry and Carrie exchanged curious glances.

Nick continued to read the letter. "She pretended she didn't recognize me, so I didn't say anything to her. She's still the same. The really strange part is her boyfriend is onboard, but they haven't spoken two words to each other the entire time. Perhaps they had a fight. I hope so; he was always too good for her anyway. There's not much else to tell. I'll write more when we reach the island. Your sister, Vicki." Nick looked at Jerry. "So according to this letter, Vicki knew Barbie, and they didn't get along. Barbie also has a boyfriend, and it's clearly not Troy." He eyed his brother. "Do you remember seeing Barbie with anyone in particular?"

"I've seen her with Danny a lot," Carrie replied, "but they're usually arguing."

Jerry eyed Carrie and offered a teasing grin. "I think he meant more like a lover."

"She's absolutely right," Nick remarked and stood. "It's possible fighting is just a cover. When people leave the room, the conversation could change."

Carrie sneered at Jerry, mocking him. He didn't seem to mind and chuckled in response.

"Vicki's purse was in Danny's room, and he doesn't have an alibi during the murders," Nick announced then sighed deeply. "Are we any closer to fixing the boat?"

"It would appear there's a part missing," Jerry remarked with defeat. "There doesn't seem a way around replacing it either. We need that part."

"I want that part found," Nick announced. "We'll start at first light tomorrow. We'll search the boat, the underground dock, the generator shed, and the basement."

"What about Barbie?" Jerry asked as he sat up.

"We can't do anything right now. We have nothing to prove she killed Vicki," Nick replied. "I'd like her watched from a safe distance."

"I can do that," Carrie announced almost too eagerly.

Nick stared at Carrie with noted disapproval. "You're confined to this room until you're able to defend yourself properly."

"Not even married and he's already giving you orders," Jerry teased while chuckling.

Carrie jabbed Jerry in the side with her elbow, causing herself more pain than she caused him.

"Okay you two, cut it out," Nick snapped sharply then glared at Jerry. "Go back to your own room. You're starting to get on my nerves."

"And leave you two alone?" Jerry asked with a dirty smile.

"Go," Nick growled.

Jerry groaned, pulled himself up from the bed, and left the room. Nick locked the door behind him then turned toward Carrie and sighed.

"Barbie, huh," Nick muttered.

Carrie cocked her head slightly while studying him with great interest. "You know, Nick, there is something odd, now that I think about it."

"What's that?"

"Well, I remember Barbie had long fingernails when we met," Carrie informed him. "They must have been professionally manicured."

"Plenty of women have professionally manicured fingernails," he informed her with little emotion. "What does that have to do with murder?"

"Well, they're virtual stubs now," she insisted. "There would be no reason for her to cut her nails unless she broke one. Not that I speak from personal experience, but it would take a lot to break professionally manicured nails."

"You mean like pushing a woman off a cliff?"

"Exactly, and when you pay that kind of money to have those false nails applied, you probably wouldn't remove all of them just because you broke one," she announced. "Unless you *had* to cut them."

Nick smiled and chuckled lowly. "I think you may have something there."

"Now maybe you can answer a question for me," she said with a teasing smile.

"What's that?" he asked gently.

Carrie flashed a picture from his wallet. "Who's the attractive woman in this picture with you?"

Nick's smile brightened. "Jealous?"

"No, I was just wondering how someone like you got such an attractive woman," she remarked. "It couldn't possibly be that warm personality of yours."

He chuckled. "That's my mother."

Chapter Seventeen

Day five. Morning came, bringing a warm and sunny day. The sun had just barely come up when Carrie bugged Nick about leaving the room. Nick didn't want her running around yet, but Carrie wasn't about to stay much longer. Before the others got up, he took her downstairs to the small room behind the registration desk and allowed her to play with the monitors. Perhaps she could discover something pertaining to the murders. Once he had her settled into the security office, Nick removed a small semiautomatic and handed it to her. Carrie glanced at the .22 caliber gun and uncertainly accepted it.

"I get a gun?"

"You should be honored," he announced. "That was the one used to shoot you."

"Where did you get it?" she asked.

"I found it in the woods when I brought you back that morning," he informed her. "It was dropped there. Perhaps you don't remember."

"The smoking gun at the scene of the crime, huh?" she remarked. "That's a little strange, don't you think?"

"Yeah, the person who took a crack shot at us was only interested in getting one shot off," he replied. "Not much of a weapons expert either. A .22 semiautomatic wouldn't be my first choice if I wanted to assassinate someone. I intended to remove the guns from the trophy room cabinet without Troy's knowledge but discovered all the guns were already gone. It would seem everyone here is armed, so you should be too."

Carrie looked at the semiautomatic and aimed it at the monitor. "So does this mean I get to shoot someone?"

"Only in self-defense," he replied then turned serious. "And make sure you know who you're shooting."

"That kind of takes the fun out of it," she teased then looked at him and smiled warmly. "So does this make me an honorary Parker? Or must I actually shoot someone first?"

Nick hid his smile while watching her aim the gun at Troy's image on the security monitor. "Yeah, you can be an honorary Parker."

She glanced back at him with a curious look. "Are you staying here with me?"

"No," he replied. "I have to catch a killer, remember?"

"If you must."

Nick stared at her a moment longer, took a deep breath, then turned and walked toward the door. He paused and looked back at her.

"Remember to keep this door locked and don't open it for anyone but my brother or me," he warned her.

§

"I can't believe the dumb luck," Bart announced while sitting in the chair behind the study desk as he routed through drawers. "I'd never think Chester would want revenge over stolen drugs. I barely knew the guy."

"It doesn't matter anymore," Karl remarked with little interest. "Chester's dead. If we don't get off this island soon, we'll be dead too."

Troy entered the study causing both men to attempt innocent looks. "I've solved the murders," he announced proudly.

Both Bart and Karl glanced at each other then looked at Troy with surprise.

"Who do you think did it?" Karl asked.

"I found my uncle's guest list," Troy informed them. "A guy named Drake Remington never showed."

Karl sat forward from his position on the edge of the desk. "That's a very good point," he remarked. "An outsider could commit the murders without our knowledge. He might even be hiding in the hotel."

"Oh, shut up, Ruben," Bart scoffed. "We have several other suspects here who could just as easily commit murder. I think we should concentrate on them, and not worry about some man who never showed. By the time we narrow down the suspect list, there will probably only be three people left alive."

"Maybe so," Troy replied, "but will any of those remaining be us?"

"If it's a woman, I suggest you watch your back, Milton," Karl teased with a laugh."

"Don't be so stupid," Bart exclaimed. "It can't be a woman killing everyone. Women aren't smart enough or tough enough to commit those crimes and get away with it. I think those Parkers are in on it together."

Karl shook his head and stood. "I don't agree with you on either point, Bart," he announced. "The Parkers couldn't possibly be in on this together. If they wanted to kill us, we'd all be dead by now. Secondly, don't ever underestimate a woman. Women are crafty and deadly. Just because your wife never stabbed you in your sleep, you shouldn't assume all women are that docile. Never turn your back on an angry woman. She'll get you in the end, and it won't be pleasant."

"Agreed," Troy interjected. "And whatever you do, don't sleep with her sister." He shook his head as his eyes widened dramatically. "Only took me two times to learn that lesson."

"Only two times, huh?" Karl remarked while hiding his humored smile.

§

*C*arrie sat back in the chair behind the security monitor while paging through Chester's journal. There was a knock on the door, startling her. She jumped with surprise then turned to stare at the door but didn't respond.

"It's Nick," came the familiar voice from the other side of the door.

Carrie took a deep breath and sighed with relief while standing. She approached the door and unlocked it, allowing Nick to enter.

Carrie returned to the chair behind the monitor with Nick joining her.

"Learn anything interesting?" Nick asked.

"Bart thinks you and your brothers are the killers, and Karl thinks if you were, we'd all be dead by now," she informed him then grinned. "He has great faith in you as a murderer."

Nick shook his head with some humor. "Anything else?"

"I was reading Chester's journal and found something you must have skipped over," she announced.

"Oh? What's that?"

"A whole page on why he wanted revenge on those he invited," she replied while raising a clever brow. "As it turns out, I served on a jury that sent his wife to jail for attempted murder. She was later killed during a prison break." She cleverly raised her brows. "Interestingly enough, I served on that jury with a man named Drake Remington."

"Really?"

Carrie nodded as her eyes lit up. "That's not all. I finally remembered where I heard Drake's name mentioned before, and it wasn't from the trial. On the beach, Danny said he came in his friend's place. Drake Remington is his author friend who was out of the country."

"Danny, huh?" Nick asked now deep in thought. "That name seems to come up a lot lately. I'll need to have a little talk with him about Drake." He eyed her and appeared curious. "Anyone else I should know about on Chester's hit list?"

"Everyone invited was on Chester's hit list except Barbie," she informed him while hiding her grin. "She's the only one not mentioned anywhere in his journal."

"That's very interesting. I'm guessing this is where her mysterious boyfriend comes in." He pondered over the revelation then returned to their conversation. "I sent Jerry to work on the boat. It doesn't look very good though. If that journal is accurate, we have some bigger concerns."

"Is it actually possible to blow up an entire island?" Carrie asked him.

"I spoke with Troy about that yesterday," Nick replied and leaned back in his chair. "He claims the underground caverns are filled with methane gas. Bombs placed in the right location could trigger an explosion of that magnitude."

"So we're fucked?"

Nick looked at Carrie with surprise. "If you would like to put it that way, yes," he agreed. "It's best if I just concentrate on the murders for now. The rest is out of my control."

"How's that working out?"

"I do have a few leads, but I don't think they mean much," Nick replied. "They're more like misleads. It's not even worth mentioning." Nick looked at one of the monitors and nearly jumped from his chair. "I don't believe it!"

Carrie looked at the screen, which had been on the empty lounge. To her surprise, Barbie and Troy were having sex on one of the lounge sofas. Unlike Nick, Carrie thought it was humorous more than surprising.

"They seem well-suited for each other," Carrie casually remarked and leaned back in her chair while playfully smiling. "She's a bitch; he's a bastard. Imagine the suffering they saved two completely innocent people."

Nick shook his head while watching the screen. "He can't be the boyfriend Vicki mentioned," he said then sat back in his chair while deep in thought. "He wasn't on the ship. There's no way Vicki saw him onboard. Perhaps she's just looking for a good place to plunge a knife."

"Is that why you avoid women?" she teased. "You think they all want to kill you?"

He chuckled, amused by the comment. "Relationships and women require too much time and work. I have far more important things to worry about."

Carrie raised her brows as her mouth dropped open slightly. "If your mother would have heard you say that, she'd slap you right across the mouth."

"She might have done just that," he teased. "I guess I'm lucky she's not here."

"Most men seem to think women are a source of great pleasure," Carrie insisted. "Even the most pitiful man enjoys female companionship once in a while."

Nick raised an arrogant brow. "I'm not exactly neglecting you," he replied simply.

Carrie stood with some stiffness then leaned against the security desk. "That isn't what I meant," she retorted. "It's just, well; I can't understand a man your age not wanting to sleep with every woman he meets."

"Should I?" Nick asked with a humored smile.

"It's only natural for a man to want to seek and conquer," she insisted.

Nick suddenly grinned and chuckled. "You sound a little disappointed," he remarked.

Carrie stood up straight and glared at him. She felt her cheeks redden slightly, forcing her to look away and avoid his gaze. "You're delusional, Nicholas Parker."

Chapter Eighteen

Duke held Kera's hand as they took a romantic stroll in their bare feet along the beach not far from the hotel. Devlin was left behind so that he wouldn't wander off again. The island was too much temptation for the wolf and his instincts to roam. Duke helped Kera onto a large rock then sat beside her as they watched the waves crash to shore. The warm, salty breeze blew past her face while she stared at the ocean.

"I'd love to show you the beaches in Hawaii," Duke announced pleasantly. "They're spectacular."

Kera glanced at him and attempted to hide her embarrassed smile. "How is it you can be such a hopeless romantic and yet worked for some task force surrounded by violence?"

Duke laughed then gently brushed the hair from her eyes. "I get a little more sentimental every passing year," he informed her. "You appreciate life a lot more when you've seen so many die. That's why I didn't get involved in that fight. I don't want any more blood on my hands. It crushes your soul little by little." He gently stroked Kera's face while staring into her eyes. "I'd much rather watch the sunset with a beautiful woman in my arms."

As Kera stared at Duke, she felt her heart pound from his words. Even if he hadn't been sincere and was possibly conning her for his own selfish pleasure, she enjoyed listening to him. She couldn't help wishing he'd kiss her the way men kissed women in romance novels.

Duke lowered his hand from her face then looked away while shaking his head. "Listen to me, I sound like some crazy fool," he announced then managed a soft laugh. "What are you doing hanging out with some old man anyway?"

Kera stared at him with some surprise. She thought her intentions were quite clear, but maybe he thought he was misinterpreting them.

"I like hanging out with you," she informed him. "Why should your age matter?"

He hid his smile and looked away with embarrassment. "When you put it that way, I suppose it doesn't," he remarked. "There's no reason why we can't enjoy a walk on the beach together no matter our age difference."

Kera nodded, glad he agreed, but soon realized it didn't change the fact that he still wasn't going to kiss her. The bright, sunny afternoon was giving way to another storm brewing in the distance. She just hoped it wouldn't be as bad as the last one. Duke must have noticed her distant look and reassuringly squeezed her hand, forcing her to look at him. He offered a compassionate smile.

"Everything's going to work out, Kera," he informed her. "We'll survive this."

She managed a smile and allowed him to think that's what had been bothering her. Duke jumped off the rock and extended his hand to her. She uncertainly accepted it and allowed him to help her off the rock, landing softly in the sand.

"What you need is a confidence boost," he announced.

She gave him a strange look, wondering what that meant.

"Trust me," he informed her and chuckled. "Apart from a stiff drink, this is what you need most."

She eyed him suspiciously. "What do you expect me to do?"

"Defend yourself," he replied. "Defend yourself as if your life depends upon it because one day it might."

She watched while Duke showed her how to do karate kicks and punches. All things being equal, she would have preferred to be walking hand in hand with him on the beach. He had her kick and punch his hand held at chest level. Kera struck his hand several times with her fist and her foot. Once she got the hang of it, Duke finally stopped her.

"Now I'm going to show you your basic flip," he informed her.

She allowed Duke to place his hands on her and immediately tensed from his touch. She wanted to enjoy the moment, but before she even realized what had happened, he tossed her over his hip and onto the sand. She stared at him where she remain on her back then allowed him to help her to her feet.

"Now, you're going to flip me," he announced.

Kera looked at him doubtfully. "How can I possibly toss a full-grown man over my shoulder?" she asked with surprise. "You're bigger than I am."

"Have a little faith in balance and gravity," Duke replied. "I have tweeners in my martial arts class throwing me halfway across the mat."

He positioned himself behind her and placed an arm around her neck. Kera placed her hands where he instructed, listened to what he told her, and threw him over her and onto the sand. Kera gasped when she saw Duke lying on the sand.

He sprang to his feet and grinned. "See, I knew you could do it," he announced cheerfully. "But in your case, I'm going to recommend you follow through with a foot to the groin. Just stomp on his balls, or if opportunity has it, give a field goal kick."

Kera stared at him with horror. "You're suggesting I kick someone in the groin while they're down?"

"We're talking about survival here, especially survival of a woman versus a man with a weapon," he insisted. "In this particular situation, you aim to maim." He remained facing her. "Now I want to show you how to handle a frontal assault. I'll use an imaginary knife."

Duke picked up a broken shell and held it like a weapon. He then placed his arm around Kera's waist, pulled her against him, and held the shell near her face.

"Okay, I'm an attacker," he announced. "I have a knife aimed at your face. What's your next move?"

With his body against hers and his arm firmly around her waist, Kera couldn't even think about anything other than the dull ache sweeping through her body. She uncertainly eyed her situation, unable to focus, and then met Duke's gaze as he waited for her response. Kera hesitated only a moment before she rationalized her next move. She grabbed Duke's shirt with both hands and kissed him firmly on the lips. She pulled back almost as quickly, realizing what she had done, and stared at him moderately surprised with her own actions. Duke was possibly more stunned than she had been.

"Was that the right move?" she heard herself ask.

Duke stared at her with the same stunned look then cast the broken shell aside. "Close enough," he remarked then placed his hand behind her neck and kissed her passionately in response.

Kera wasted little time returning the kiss, since she was afraid Duke might come to his senses and turn fatherly again. The kiss turned more aggressive as Duke's hands firmly traveled her back and caressed her buttocks. As if the virgin alarm sounded, Duke suddenly broke off the kiss and pulled away, keeping her loosely in his arms. He immediately fumbled over himself and appeared embarrassed.

"I'm sorry," he announced with concern. "I don't know what came over me. I shouldn't have--"

"Why the hell not?" she suddenly demanded, not wanting to hear any more excuses regarding their age difference.

Duke stared into her eyes while gently caressing her face. "You deserve someone better than me," he replied then sighed. "If you knew the missions I'd been on--"

She was actually surprised to learn his reaction had nothing to do with her age and everything to do with his past. Kera had to think of some way to reassure him. "Are you that man anymore?" she asked while studying him.

"No," he replied. "But that's really not the point."

"What is the point?" she demanded.

He stared at her a moment then drew a deep breath. "Have you even been with a man?"

Kera fidgeted and pulled away from his arms. She couldn't even look at him knowing how he'd feel about the answer.

"That's what I thought," he replied gently.

A thousand thoughts and scenarios played out in her mind as she thought about what he'd just said. She finally looked at him and stared into his eyes without flinching.

"I know what I want," she insisted. "I'm old enough to understand the consequences of a fling."

Duke hid his smile and chuckled. "Not exactly where I was going with this conversation." His look turned moderately serious. "I've outgrown 'flings', and I like you too much to ever do that to you." He took her hand in his and smiled warmly. "You're not going to die on this island, Kera. There's no rush. If you really want this, come back to Hawaii with me when this is all over. We can take things at a comfortable pace."

She stared at him with surprise. "Really?"

"I'll be honest with you," he announced boldly. "I may be older than you and far from the man you deserve, but morality will only win so many times. I'm not strong enough to refuse you more than once."

Kera considered his words. "In that case," she announced, "that changes everything."

Without warning, she threw her arms around his neck and kissed him passionately with some pent-up lust. Duke tensed with surprise then pulled her against him and returned the aggressive kiss. Thunder was heard rumbling over the ocean, but neither seemed to notice nor care. Duke again pulled away, causing Kera's heart to pound with disappointment,

"My mother always told me never to argue with a woman," he remarked then took her hand and practically pulled her back toward the path where they'd left their shoes.

Chapter Nineteen

Day six. It was nearly eight o'clock the following evening. Troy, Bart, and Karl were sitting at the bar in the billiard room, while Kera and Danny played pool. Kera was feeling a little left out when Duke left the hotel unexpectedly and didn't offer to take her along. Nick had assigned Jerry to stay with Carrie in the security room behind the lobby desk while he went to the underground dock to check on the boat situation. Karl poured another round of drinks from behind the bar and shook his head while grinning at Troy, who was telling another one of his macho sex stories.

"You certainly get around for a man who lives on an island," Karl said to Troy.

"Truthfully, I haven't been here all that long," Troy remarked. "I moved into the house after my uncle died. I didn't have a job, so I decided to live rent-free for a while. I was only here two weeks before the rest of you arrived." He shook his head while frowning. "I didn't know my Uncle Chester was alive either. I didn't see him the entire two weeks I was here. The place was like a morgue."

"Now it's really a morgue," Danny remarked as he approached the bar to get drinks for him and Kera. "But you knew we were coming. You greeted us as if you were expecting our arrival."

"I didn't find out until the day before you arrived when a supply boat showed up with a dozen caterers," he informed them. "That's when I got a phone call from Uncle Chester's lawyer. He told me he was coming to discuss the will with those named in it. Until that moment, I assumed I was the only one mentioned in his will. I guess he didn't like me very much either, considering--"

"Considering what?" Bart chimed in.

Troy shook his head and looked at the glass on the bar. "Considering I was invited the same as the rest of you. He left me here to die as well. Honestly, I was just as shocked as the rest of you about the murders."

"Well, let me tell you," Bart announced while glaring at the three men. "If I had Cindy's killer in front of me right now, I'd make that bastard pay." He suddenly grinned deviously. "With cold, hard cash. Obviously, the guy has money, right? I'd want my share as compensation. If he refused to pay me; I'd expose his little operation."

"You're disgusting, Bart," Danny scoffed.

"Seconded," Karl muttered then looked at Troy and swiftly changed the subject to something less pitiful. "You were telling us about something that happened yesterday."

"Oh, yeah," Troy said while grinning. "I had a run-in with Barbie first thing yesterday morning. She warmed up to me real fast and threw herself at me right there in the lounge. That woman is a real vixen. I don't think I've ever had such wild sex in my life."

Danny tensed and shifted by the bar. "I don't think we really want to hear the steamy details," he remarked. "Not in front of--" Danny indicated Kera by the pool table as she racked the balls.

"I do," Bart snarled then looked back at Troy and grinned. "Tell us about your wild romp."

Troy chuckled in his throat. "I barely had to do anything, and she was on her knees," he insisted. "The lounge door was open the entire time too. Anyone could have walked past and caught us in the act. Believe me; I didn't even care by that point."

Danny snatched both drinks from the bar. "I find this entire conversation repulsive," he scoffed.

Bart looked at him and laughed. "Jealous?"

"No, just sickened at the thought of her face melting off in the heat of passion," Danny retorted then returned to the pool table to join Kera.

Troy and Bart laughed at Danny's hostility.

Within the security office, Jerry stared at the monitor revealing the scene in the billiard room and tensed from what he'd just witnessed. He practically jumped up from his chair while looking at Carrie.

"Did he seem a little jealous to you?" Jerry practically demanded.

Carrie grimaced and reluctantly nodded.

"Will you be all right by yourself for a few minutes?" he asked. "I think Nick should know about Danny's reaction to Troy's romp with Barbie."

"Yeah, I'll be fine," she replied and watched Jerry hurry from the room.

Carrie looked back at the monitor and listened to the remainder of the conversation. If she hadn't seen the incident with her own eyes, she would have found it hard to believe Danny could possibly be responsible. He looked somewhat guilty now. The conversation at the bar ended a few minutes later, and the three men talked about politics. Carrie knew Karl would ruin a good conversation once he spoke. She decided to check on Barbie's progress with her bubble bath and switched to the snobby woman's room. Barbie was now fully dressed while sitting on the bed, filing her short nails. A frown crossed Carrie's face as she stared at the woman's stubby fingernails. She was convinced she'd been right about Barbie. She watched the screen for several minutes then flipped back to the billiard room.

Through the security camera within the billiard room, she saw Danny and Kera had finished their game. Judging by both their expressions, it was obvious Kera had won. Carrie heard Karl laugh. She then watched him walk around the bar, slap Troy playfully on the back, and leave the billiard room. Troy and Bart eyed Danny and Kera. When they stood and approached, Carrie became suspicious. She watched only a moment longer before Bart attempted to start a fight with Danny. As Danny and Bart got into a shouting match, Kera attempted to stop the argument before it turned into a fight. Troy grabbed Kera around the waist from behind and laughed as he pulled her back, causing her to scream.

Carrie jumped out of her chair and ran from the back room. It only took her a few seconds to reach the billiard room. Bart was already punching Danny in the stomach and was about to hit him again. Carrie ran for Bart while grabbing a discarded pool stick on her way through. She spun her entire body into her swing with the stick, breaking it across Bart's back. He released Danny, who immediately fell to the floor. Bart gasped out in pain, but he didn't go down as she had assumed he would. He spun around with anger then laughed when he saw it was Carrie. He made a fist and threw a punch at her face. She gasped in surprise, ducked his roundhouse swing, and punched him in the crotch from her crouched position. Bart clutched himself and doubled over in pain.

Carrie immediately sank to her knees and clutched her injured left shoulder. She heard Kera screaming a warning to her. Carrie endured the pain in her shoulder and sprang to her feet. Before she could turn, Troy grabbed her injured left arm and spun her to face him.

"Not so tough now, are you?" Troy demanded while roughly shaking her by her arm.

Carrie winced in pain and once more clutched her left shoulder. The pain was so severe; she couldn't even verbally protest. Danny staggered to his feet with support from the pool table.

"Get your hands off her," Danny snarled.

Troy slung Carrie backward by her left arm, casting her against the pool table where she fell to her knees. Carrie gasped and removed her hand from her shoulder now seeing blood. When she looked up, she saw Troy tossing Danny across the pool table. Troy turned back to her with a devious grin on his face while Carrie stared at him, unable to defend herself. Kera grabbed a whiskey bottle from the bar and was about to lunge for Troy's turned back when Nick appeared from out of nowhere. He slammed Troy against the pool table, rattling the table and moving it several inches from its position. Before Troy could respond or protest, Nick punched him twice in the face, nearly knocking him unconscious. Troy didn't even have a chance to sink to the floor when Nick grabbed him by the throat and body slammed him on top of the pool table. He pinned him to the table with his hand clutching his throat. The look in Nick's eyes was threatening and nearly psychotic.

"You have a problem with her?" he snarled. "You take it up with me!"

Troy gasped while attempting to loosen Nick's grip on his throat as he thrashed his legs wildly. "Take it easy, Nick. I wasn't going to hurt her, I swear!"

Jerry entered the room and saw Carrie's bleeding shoulder as Danny and Kera kneeled alongside her. He ran to her side and immediately checked her injury.

"If I knew she was your girlfriend, I wouldn't have touched her. I swear," Troy cried out from beneath Nick's crushing hand on his throat.

"You're a lying bastard too," Nick lashed out. "You think laws of a civilized society don't apply to this island? Well, I'm the law now, and if either of you bastards so much as look at these women the wrong way, I'll be judge and executioner as well."

Jerry looked at his brother and the position that he held Troy on the pool table. Troy was unable to gasp for air and was turning a shade of blue.

"Nick!" Jerry scolded.

Nick sneered, released Troy's throat, and grabbed his shirt collar, pulling him off the pool table and to his feet. Troy gasped several times, attempting to breathe.

"Now you're going to answer some of my questions," Nick snarled, "and if I don't like the answers, I'm going to throw you through the fucking wall."

Nick slung Troy across the room and toward the door. He then took a step closer to where Carrie kneeled in agony, and his look immediately softened.

"Are you all right?" Nick asked gently.

Carrie stood with some assistance from Danny and Jerry and nodded in response.

"She tore her stitches," Jerry gently informed him while frowning. "She's going to need more stitches."

She groaned and dropped her head onto Danny's shoulder.

"Take her to her room," Nick commanded, revealing the irritation clearly in his tone. "I'll be up just as soon as I *interrogate* Troy."

Chapter Twenty

Carrie lay on her bed with her head turned away from Jerry as he placed a fresh dressing on her shoulder wound. Kera sat at the foot end of the bed and cringed, having witnessed Jerry suturing the reopened injury.

Kera gingerly rubbed her abdomen. "I think I'll check on Danny," she said and hurried from the room, fighting her urge to vomit.

Carrie was feeling a little better and allowed Jerry to help her sit up. She shifted slightly and eyed him. "Nick was really pissed, huh?"

"Just a little," Jerry replied then stared at her a moment before offering a tiny smile. "He's under some stress. He thinks everything is his own, personal battle."

"Then he has to deal with me," Carrie muttered while running her fingers through her hair. "I guess I'm dangerous to myself and others."

"You reacted appropriately, Carrie," Jerry informed her without hesitation. "You saw someone harming your family, and you took action. I'd do the same for my family."

She looked into his eyes and smiled with some embarrassment. "You've done so much for me considering the way I've treated you. I don't know how I could ever thank you enough."

Jerry smirked and shrugged. "A hug would be sufficient."

Carrie laughed then leaned toward him and placed her good arm around his neck. Jerry held her in a long, warm embrace. Nick stood in the bedroom doorway and cleared his throat. Jerry pulled away from Carrie and smiled with some embarrassment.

"Everything okay?" Nick asked while raising a curious brow.

"Yeah, everything's fine," Jerry replied then grinned. "The patient is restricted from fighting for at least a week, and there's no sign of infection."

"Good," Nick scoffed.

Carrie noted Nick's irritated mood and wondered if he was mad at her because she forced him to fight Troy. "What did Troy tell you?" she asked while shifting uncomfortably.

Nick closed the door and approached them where they both sat on the bed. Jerry immediately stood and nervously placed his hands in his pockets. He must've sensed Nick's annoyance as well.

"We had an interesting conversation about the dagger used to kill Vicki," Nick informed them. "He told me the dagger I had in my possession was definitely from his uncle's collection. He seemed surprised that it wasn't in the case with the others. He claimed it had been there when he arrived two weeks prior to our visit."

"If he didn't kill Vicki," Jerry began, "how did the killer get a hold of it?"

"That's a very good question," Nick remarked. "When I pressed him for an answer to that, he said Chester may have taken it. He claimed he didn't know his uncle was alive."

"So Chester murdered Vicki?" Carrie asked with disbelief. "That doesn't seem possible even if he wasn't confined to a wheelchair. If he'd been watching us from the moment we arrived and followed her into the woods, someone would have seen him." She then considered her own comment. "Besides, why would he want to kill Vicki if he intended to blow up the island anyway?"

"If we intend to keep the boyfriend theory in play," Nick announced, "that would mean someone onboard that ship had been here before, knew Chester had a collection of daggers, and stole one for the sole purpose to kill Vicki."

"But you don't think Troy killed them," Jerry interjected.

"No, I don't," Nick replied with a defeated sigh. "He didn't know anything about the underground dock. Chester was murdered on the boat. Judging by the blood I found on the railing; he was thrown overboard." He studied his brother and Carrie. "Cindy possibly witnessed the murder. We found her dead in the main elevator, but Kera had mentioned a small, bloody handprint in the sub-basement as well. I think she was initially attacked there."

"Did he tell you anything else?" Jerry asked.

"He told me his uncle had a dirty dealing with a drug lord in Columbia," Nick remarked. "Troy conveniently tore the pages from the beginning of the journal; the ones I discovered missing." Nick produced the pages. "They give an accurate account of the fight and tell of thousands of kilos of cocaine he'd stolen. It would appear Chester still has a small army on his payroll, and he had a good reason to play dead. The drug ship was raided and sank after an explosion. The drug lord in Columbia never suspected Chester. He was murdered himself not two weeks after the shipment failed to arrive at its destination."

"Busy old man," Carrie muttered.

"We need to investigate the dock a little more closely."

The bedroom door suddenly flew open, startling all three. Kera stood in the doorway while panting out of breath and a look of concern on her face.

"Nick, there's a problem," she nearly cried out.

"What happened?" Nick demanded, snapping to attention.

"Danny heard screaming from within the old zoo," Kera announced with concern. "I told him not to go out on his own and wait for you, but he didn't listen."

Nick and Jerry bolted from the room. Carrie jumped off the bed with a little less spring to her step then hurried after them. Kera watched her sister run from the room and shook her head.

*D*anny was already halfway to the old zoo when the trio, minus Kera, caught up with him. The gate was partially open, which it had been locked the last time they checked. Nick cautiously entered with Carrie, Jerry, and Danny following. The zoo was dimly lit with only a few lights near the two occupied cages. Apart from the wolves pacing their cage, the zoo appeared empty. Nick hesitated and stared at something in the middle of the walkway between the cages. It was possibly a butchered animal. As they got closer to the mangled and shredded creature, they saw the pile of flesh was Troy. Danny and Jerry ran toward the dead man but stopped short by several feet and cringed. Nick already had his gun in hand as he cautiously approached the dead man while attempting to keep Carrie back. Carrie inched her way closer until she actually saw the slain man. She gasped then looked away.

"My God, what did that?" Danny suddenly gasped while stealing peeks at the torn human remains.

Out of the corner of her eye, Carrie saw something move from the shadows. Her eyes suddenly widened at the sight of the frightening image.

"Tiger!" she screamed.

The three men suddenly spun around to see the tiger as it ran for Carrie and leaped into the air to pounce on her. Jerry pulled his gun, and both he and Nick fired at the attacking tiger. Carrie jumped from the cat's path while screaming. Nick and Jerry fired several rounds into the tiger before it finally fell to the ground. The men lowered their guns and stared at the dead animal with stunned looks on their faces. Both breathed heavily after the excitement. Jerry looked behind him to see if Carrie and Danny were okay. Carrie was clinging to one of the nearby cages, half-climbing up the bars, but Danny was gone.

"Where's Danny?" Jerry exclaimed and looked around.

Danny stood inside one of the empty cages while clinging to the bars from the inside. His eyes were wide, and it was possible he hadn't breathed for several seconds.

"What are you doing in there?" Jerry asked while replacing his gun.

Danny finally took several deep breaths and fidgeted. "Just checking the view," he replied and attempted to put on a tough front. "I wasn't scared or anything."

Nick shook his head. "Sure you weren't."

Something clawed Danny's leg. He yelled and spun around, slamming his back against the bars. When he looked down, a small tiger cub was clawing at his ankle. Danny rolled his eyes and laughed while running trembling fingers through his hair. He took several deep breaths then looked at the tiger cub.

"A compact version," Danny announced then reached down and picked up the cub. He held the cub against his chest and scratched its neck. The cub cuddled against him.

Chapter Twenty-one

Day seven. It was a little after eight o'clock in the morning. Barbie slowly woke to see Karl sitting at her bedside then looked around the room with an odd expression on her face. Jerry stood near her bedroom window and stared outside.

"What happened?" she gasped and gingerly touched her neck while looking at both.

"Apparently someone tried to kill you," Karl gently informed her.

She appeared stunned and stared at Karl. "Did you save me from the killer?"

"No, not me. I'm just keeping an eye on you," Karl informed her. "Danny found you on the bed with a robe sash around your neck."

"Danny?" she suddenly gasped. "What was he doing in my room in the first place?"

"According to him, he heard noise coming from your room," Karl informed her. "When he knocked and no one responded, he broke down the door."

"And you believe him?" she practically cried out.

"Why not? He probably scared the killer away. He must have escaped through the connecting door into the next room," Karl informed her. "You should be happy he was nearby when it happened."

"Nearby? Someone tried to strangle me," Barbie gasped. "I didn't see who it was, but I swear I heard Danny's voice!"

Jerry turned his head and looked at her with little expression.

Karl stared at her and fidgeted. "No, I don't think Danny tried to kill you. I don't think he's capable of harming a fly let alone another human being."

Barbie cringed in pain while rubbing her neck and became agitated with Karl. "Danny tried to kill me. He hates me. Isn't that motive enough?" She turned her head and looked at Jerry. "You tell Nick I want Danny locked up so he can't make another attempt on my life."

"You said you heard his voice," Jerry remarked and turned to face her. "What did he say?"

Barbie appeared puzzled while staring at him with disbelief. "What did he say?" she cried out. "What the hell difference does that make?"

"It could make a lot of difference," Jerry replied. "What did he say? Or don't you remember?"

"He was strangling me at the time," Barbie shouted. "I wasn't exactly taking notes. Are you going to tell Nick or not?"

Jerry stared at her a moment then finally nodded. "I'll speak to Nick about what happened," he replied. "We'll check Danny's alibi during the time of your attack. Beyond that, I can't promise anything."

"I thought you were supposed to be the sympathetic one," she lashed out.

"Not sure where you heard that," Jerry remarked casually. "We left the sympathetic one at home."

Karl eyed Jerry. "You mean there are more of you?"

"I have an identical twin," Jerry replied. "And then there's our younger brother."

"Your poor mother," Karl scoffed under his breath.

§

Danny sat in the lobby and played with the tiger cub he'd rescued from the old zoo. He obviously didn't want to see the motherless cub abandoned and left to fend for itself.

Kera was seated next to him and watched him cuddling the cub. She shook her head in amazement while smiling proudly. "I can't believe you saved Barbie from the hands of the killer," she announced. "Considering how she's treated you since we arrived, it's sort of ironic."

"Yeah, I guess it's a good thing I didn't stop to think about it first," Danny replied.

Nick entered the room with Jerry following and approached Danny where he sat on the sofa with the tiger cub.

"I heard what happened with Barbie," Nick announced.

Danny smirked and shook his head. "Yeah, how about that."

"She's saying it was you, Danny," Nick informed him. "She said you tried to kill her."

Danny stared at him with surprise and nearly jumped from his seat. "What? That's ridiculous," he bellowed. "I'll admit I don't like her very much, but I certainly didn't try to kill her."

"Why don't you tell me what happened?" Nick asked and sat on the arm of a nearby chair.

Danny took a deep breath and groaned with irritation. "I was in the hallway, heading toward the stairs, when I heard a loud thud. It was followed by a muffled scream. So, like an idiot, I checked to see if everything was all right," Danny informed him. "When no one answered, I thought there might be a problem, so I broke down the door." He shook his head in anger. "Now for my good deed of saving that little bitch, she's accusing me of trying to kill her. I tell you, I should've just kept on walking."

"Did you see anyone leaving the room when you entered?" Nick asked.

"No," Danny replied. "The room has a connecting door. I assume he went out that way. Barbie was already unconscious on the bed. Karl attempted to wake her while I ran for help. That's when I ran into Jerry."

"She didn't actually see Danny," Jerry explained. "She said she heard his voice, yet she can't remember what he said."

"The evidence isn't strong enough to warrant a house arrest," Nick remarked.

Danny sneered at Nick. "Don't worry; I'm not making any immediate plans to leave town just yet."

"There's a small matter of how you got here," Nick informed him. "I'm told you came here under an alias. Supposedly your best friend was the one invited."

"That's right," Danny replied. "He was out of town; I was bored, so I came in his place."

"Was your friend aware you were coming on his behalf?" Nick asked.

"No," Danny remarked with little concern. "He wasn't even home when the invitation arrived. He wasn't due back for another two weeks. I didn't think it'd matter if I came." He snorted a soft laugh. "Ironically, it sounded like fun."

Nick tossed the invitation onto the sofa near Danny. "Can you explain this?"

Danny released his tiger cub and looked at the name on the invitation. His eyes widened as he looked back at Nick. "This is Drake's invitation," Danny suddenly cried out. "I don't understand. I left this at the mansion."

"Are you sure that's the same invitation?" Nick asked with a curious look.

"I'm positive," Danny replied. "I spilled coffee on the bottom corner." He pointed to the light brown stain on the envelope. Danny's mouth fell open as he stared at Nick with horror. "You don't think Drake came out here looking for me?"

"That's what I suspect happened," Nick said and removed the invitation.

Danny looked down at the floor with concern that quickly turned to alarm. "I hope nothing's happened to him," he gasped then grabbed the cub and sprang to his feet. "Excuse me. I need to take a walk." Danny hurried from the room.

Nick and Jerry exchanged looks.

"There's something else you may find interesting," Jerry remarked to his brother. "When Barbie became agitated with me, she seemed to forget the pain in her throat."

"Any marks on her neck?" Nick asked while raising a curious brow.

"None that I could see. Ironic that the murderer decided to strangle Barbie after stabbing everyone else," Jerry scoffed.

When Jerry and Nick reached Barbie's room, Karl was still there. Nick looked out the window while Barbie told Nick about Danny attempting to strangle her. The window ledge was a foot wide, which was wide enough for someone to walk along. To the right of Barbie's room was Danny's and to the left was Bart's. Nick looked at the ground below. There didn't appear to be any fresh footprints in the soft, damp ground. Nick stuck his head out a little further and looked at the nearby windows. None of the windows were open or broken. He pulled his head back inside and looked at Jerry.

"I want you to check the rooms on either side of this one and examine the locks and the connecting doors," Nick informed his brother.

"What are you going to do about Danny?" Barbie demanded to know.

"Nothing for now," Nick replied. "There's not one shred of evidence that suggests Danny tried to kill you."

"I heard him." She bounced on the bed in anger like a spoiled child. "So it's his word against mine, and you're siding with him? Typical man," she scoffed and clucked her tongue.

Nick approached Barbie on the bed and stared at her as he folded his arms across his chest. "Show me the strangle marks."

Barbie stared at him with surprise. "What?"

"You were strangled unconscious with a robe sash," Nick announced. "I'd like to see the marks. After an attack like that, you would have sustained some bruising."

Barbie's mouth opened slightly as she touched her neck then sat up proudly. "There aren't any bruises."

Chapter Twenty-two

Carrie entered the security office behind the front desk a little after ten o'clock that night. She carried a mug of coffee and her cup of tea. Nick looked up as she entered and cast Chester's journal aside.

"Bad day at the office, dear?" she asked sweetly while handing him the coffee.

He accepted the mug, set it on the console, and rested his temple on his knuckles. "Absolutely murder," he teased while watching her. "I appreciate the coffee, but I actually get to sleep tonight. Jerry's relieving me any minute now."

Carrie frowned, revealing her disappointment.

Nick eyed her expression and laughed. "What's that face about?"

She shrugged with little enthusiasm. "I'm not tired, but Jerry and I don't have much to talk about."

"I guess you'll just have to hang out in your room with Kera," he replied as his smile mocked her.

"She's busy reading her book," Carrie informed him while rolling her eyes at the thought. "If I talk while she's reading, she gives me the 'look'."

"Your options are limited," he remarked with little emotion. "You can either hang out with Jerry down here, watch your sister read a book, or talk to me while I sleep."

She glared at him and raised her brow, silently scolding him. "What if I choose secret option number four?"

"What's secret option number four?" he asked while folding his arms across his chest.

"Play pool in the billiard room without your permission," she announced while smiling slyly. "Seems to me you have two options. Leave me alone in the billiard room or hang out with me while I play pool."

"Like it or not; I've accepted responsibility for you and your sister," he informed her. "You're not hanging out in any of the common areas alone. I'm afraid you'll need to choose from the first three options. I'm making up the rules."

She set her teacup down and folded her arms across her chest. "And how do you intend to enforce that rule?"

"I'm twice your size, and I have a pair of handcuffs," he announced casually. "I'll let you figure out the details."

They exchanged silent stares as Jerry entered the security office. He eyed them, appeared ready to question their staring match, and then thought better of it; waving them off.

"Whatever," Jerry muttered.

Carrie groaned and let her arms fall to her sides. She shifted her attention to Jerry. "I made you some coffee for your shift," she informed him then eyed Nick. "You may as well walk me to my room. Save you the trouble of following me."

Nick laughed and stood. He patted Jerry on the back. "Enjoy your evening."

"Thanks," Jerry muttered.

§

*C*arrie and Nick walked up the stairs in silence. She didn't want to admit she was now feeling a little tired herself. As she cast a look at Nick, she couldn't deny it was nice having her very own bodyguard, particularly one as handsome as Nick. She felt somewhat slighted. She was pursued by countless men in the past, but the only one she actually wanted chasing her seemed to have little interest. She was fairly certain he wasn't gay, which meant he just wasn't interested in her. Just her luck. As they entered the hallway, Carrie suddenly stopped and grabbed Nick's wrist. He stopped alongside her and looked in the direction she stared. Kera and Duke stood in the hallway just outside his bedroom door, locked in a passionate embrace. She stared with surprise as her sister practically climbed on top of Duke as he fumbled with his bedroom door. The door opened, and the passionate couple practically fell inside the room.

Carrie couldn't take her eyes off the hallway where they once stood and listened as Duke's bedroom door shut and locked. When Carrie didn't move, Nick casually unclamped her hand from his wrist. She shot a look of surprise at him as her mouth fell open.

"Did I just see that?" she practically gasped.

"Yep," Nick replied and sighed with little interest. "It would seem the Professor and MaryAnn intend to play some bedsheet bingo."

Carrie stared at him with surprise and possible horror to his candor. Nick had to keep from laughing, which only infuriated her further.

"That's not funny."

"No," he replied. "But Duke and your sister getting it on certainly is."

She sneered and smacked his arm, barely causing him to flinch. He laughed at her expense.

"Why are you so bothered?" he asked while practically dragging her down the hallway. "You said so yourself; it's natural for men to seek and conquer."

"Not with my sister," she practically cried out.

"Oh, so you just meant me with you," he teased.

Carrie rolled her eyes then spun to face him. "I think I can make it the rest of the way to my room by myself," she snapped hotly then turned and headed for her bedroom door.

Nick chuckled in his throat then called after her. "If you promise to behave yourself, that offer to talk to me while I sleep is still on the table."

Carrie refused to look back at him then entered her room and slammed her door. Nick chuckled and entered his bedroom just a few doors down.

§

*C*arrie paced her bedroom for nearly an hour while remaining fully dressed. She heard the bedroom door unlock and turned as it opened. Kera slipped into the room then realized Carrie was still awake. She appeared slightly embarrassed and attempted to hide her smile.

"I was afraid I'd wake you," Kera announced timidly. "Couldn't you sleep?"

Carrie folded her arms across her chest while staring at her sister and raised her brows demandingly. "I know you were with Duke in his room."

Kera immediately blushed and fidgeted. "I know what you're thinking, Carrie," she attempted to explain.

She shook her head. "No, I doubt you do," Carrie remarked then drew a deep breath while allowing her arms to fall to her sides. "You're old enough to make your own decisions. Under the circumstances, if you think Duke can be trusted, you'd probably be safer staying with him in his room."

Kera stared at her with surprise. "What?" she practically gasped. "You're actually suggesting I sleep with him?"

"No, I'm suggesting you stay in his room with him," Carrie announced, clarifying her comment. "I'm pretty sure you've already slept with him."

"Who are you?" Kera remarked with astonishment.

"If you want to be with Duke, you should be with Duke," she informed her.

"What about you?" Kera asked. "I wouldn't feel right leaving you in the room all by yourself. It's not safe."

"Don't worry about me," Carrie replied and drew a deep breath. "Nick's already taken responsibility for my safety. He offered to let me talk to him while he sleeps."

Kera gave her a puzzled look.

Carrie laughed and nodded at the door. "Stay with Duke," she insisted. "I'll be fine."

Once Kera left the room, returning to Duke's room, Carrie headed down the hall and paused before Nick's bedroom door. She drew a deep breath, held it a moment, and then gently knocked on the door. There was a brief pause before the door was unlocked and opened. Nick appeared half-asleep while practically collapsing against the doorframe with his semiautomatic in his hand.

"I swear," he muttered. "You just wanted to wait until I fell asleep."

Carrie took in an eyeful of the handsome man wearing a pair of old shorts and nothing else. It was the first time she'd seen him without his shirt, and he didn't disappoint. He wasn't excessively muscular, but his broad shoulders and toned chest were enough to catch her attention. She couldn't deny she was a little turned on by the light coating of chest hair begging her fingers to run through it. Before she could respond, Nick walked away from the door leaving it open as if already guessing the reason for her visit. Carrie entered his dimly lit room and watched him return to his bed where he promptly collapsed onto it. She shut and locked the door behind her then insecurely approached his bed. Despite looking as if he'd returned to sleep, when she didn't climb into the bed, he opened his eyes and turned on his side facing her.

"Something wrong?" he asked. "You know I'm not going to jump on you. You're safe."

Carrie ran her fingers through her slightly mussed hair then frowned and shook her head. "I shouldn't have come here," she announced and sighed. "It was a mistake. I'll be fine in my room by myself."

She turned and headed for the door. Before she even turned the lock, Nick was standing behind her and kept her from unlocking the door. His ability to spring from the bed and sprint to the door so fast startled her. She turned and stared at the serious look on his face.

"What's wrong?" he asked with a puzzled look. "Did something happen? I don't understand what has you upset."

She folded her arms across her chest and stared at him suddenly feeling too tired to have this conversation. "I'm not upset, I'm just disappointed," Carrie informed him. "And you're right; you wouldn't understand."

He seemed a little surprised. "Wait," he suddenly announced. "Are you mad at me? What did I do wrong? I've been a perfect gentleman."

"Yes, you have been a perfect gentleman," she replied simply, "and, no, you haven't done anything wrong." Carrie inhaled deeply, held her breath, and then released it while allowing her arms to fall to her sides. "I just mistakenly thought there was something between us."

Nick remained puzzled while staring at her. "I gave you a gun," he announced bluntly. "In my book that practically makes us engaged." He groaned with defeat. "I'm doing my best to be a gentleman, but I've never been good at figuring out women and relationships. If something's bothering you, you'll need to be a little more blunt with me."

Carrie gave the comment some consideration and realized he was right. He'd spent most of his adult life building a business and a name for himself. He freely admitted he'd never had time for women or relationships.

She drew a deep breath while staring at him. "I don't want a gentleman," she informed him and freely rattled off what was on her mind. "I want a sex-starved bastard willing to throw me down on the bed and ravish me."

Nick stared at her a moment looking stunned by the bluntness of her announcement. "Thanks for clearing that up for me," he replied then moved against her, causing her to hit the door as he covered her mouth with his and kissed her passionately.

Carrie was momentarily surprised by his aggressiveness but couldn't deny it turned her on. She placed her hands against his bare chest she had admired moments ago and returned the kiss with her own building desire. He slipped his arms around her, pulled her against him, and then lifted her up by her buttocks with one arm while pulling her leg to his hip with the other. Her heart pounded with anticipation and a little bit of fear toward his aggressiveness. When he turned to carry her toward the bed, she locked her legs around his hips and sank against him while returning his passionate kiss as he carried her. He practically fell to the bed, pinning her beneath him, and allowed his hands firmly to travel her body while she attempted to keep up with his passionate, aggressive kiss. She feared Karl would hear more sounds of a woman screaming tonight, but she didn't care who heard them.

*C*arrie woke to the faint glow of the distant sunrise through the part in the curtains in Nick's bedroom. She felt Nick's arm securely around her with his hand cupping her breast beneath his shirt she wore as a nightgown. He had slept pressed against her from behind, periodically straining his hips against her buttocks, and allowing her to feel his morning enthusiasm against her bare backside. Nick stirred, caressed the breast he lovingly clung to, and then kissed her warmly on the back of the neck. Carrie turned in his arms and faced him, realizing he was awake this time. He smiled with a look of contentment on his pleasantly weary face.

"Good morning," he announced warmly.

"How did you sleep?" she teased while hiding her smile.

He groaned in response. "One thousand and one erotic dreams," Nick replied and pulled her against him, nuzzling her. "I wouldn't mind acting out a few of them."

She ran her hands along his bare chest and nearly laughed. "I don't have to be at work for another few hours," she teased. "Hit me with your best shot."

Nick tackled her to the bed, causing her to scream playfully. He positioned himself on top of her while pressing his lower body against hers then kissed her warmly but passionately. Carrie's morning was off to a wonderful start.

Chapter Twenty-three

Day eight. Following a night of excessive drinking, Danny and Jerry sat in the lobby holding their aching heads in one hand and a cup of coffee in the other while moaning simultaneously. Jerry half opened his eyes and glared at Danny.

"Nick can't know we were drinking last night in the security office," Jerry announced then clutched his head at the loudness of his own voice.

"In all fairness," Danny remarked. "We didn't drink that much. What the hell was that we drank anyway?"

"Moonshine, I think."

Nick trotted down the steps, with a new, more lively gait. He swung around the banister at the bottom and drifted happily into the lobby. Both men straightened and attempted to act naturally, although unable to succeed.

"Good morning," Nick cheerfully announced while grinning like a schoolboy.

Danny groaned and held his throbbing head. "Who gave you permission to be so happy?"

"I'm going on two hours sleep here, Nick," Jerry moaned while attempting to hide his hungover condition. "Just let me die in peace."

"Serves you right for drinking in the security office," Nick announced as his smile mocked his brother. "Die on your own time."

Danny and Jerry exchanged surprised looks. How could he possibly know they were drinking last night? The front door opened alerting Nick more so than his brother and Danny. Nick turned as Duke and Devlin entered the lobby.

"Nick. Good. You're up," Duke announced.

"It's seven o'clock," Nick remarked while eyeing the man with his wolf sidekick. "Don't you ever sleep?"

"I'll sleep when I'm dead," Duke remarked. "I was out in the old boathouse and found a life raft. It needed some repairs, but it seems watertight now. I'm going to row away from the beach and see if I can flag down a ship."

"Good thinking," Nick said with enthusiasm.

Duke then cleared his throat and adjusted his glasses. "I was also thinking about our current situation with Chester's threat," he remarked while attempting to keep his voice down. "Tomorrow is the ninth day. If it comes down to it, I feel the women should be sent out in the life raft tomorrow morning."

"How many people does the raft hold?" Nick asked.

"Possibly six, but that could be pushing it," Duke replied, appearing defeated.

"That means two of us would have to stay behind," he said aloud then looked at Jerry and took a deep breath. "If that time comes, we'll have to draw straws on who stays."

"If it comes to that," Duke announced proudly and without hesitation, "I'm staying behind. Devlin's my only family. No one's going to miss me."

Nick was about to speak when he suddenly hesitated and looked behind Duke into the lobby entrance. Duke turned and saw Kera standing in the archway with a look of surprise on her face. She'd obviously heard the comment. She turned and left the room without a word. Duke frowned and hurried after her.

§

*L*ater that morning, Kera and Carrie walked along the hallway toward the lobby from the kitchen. Neither spoke for several minutes, as they obviously had a lot on their minds. Carrie finally broke the silence.

"You can't be mad at Duke for giving up his space on the life raft," she remarked. "Besides, we don't even know if Chester's threat is real."

She eyed her sister sharply. "So you won't have a problem if I stay behind with Duke then."

Carrie stopped Kera in the hallway and stared at her with alarm. "I most certainly do have a problem with that."

"I thought you just said--"

Carrie silently seethed and ran her fingers through her hair. "We're not discussing this," she announced then continued down the hallway. "I think we should go to the boathouse and look for life preservers."

"Some brilliant idea Nick has," Kera muttered. "What if a boat never passes the island? Just how long does he think we can float out there before the sharks come to feed?"

"It's still a better plan than staying here with the other alternative," Carrie replied.

"I don't consider being fish bait a better alternative," Kera retorted.

"There's no way in hell you're staying behind with Duke," Carrie suddenly snapped while glaring at her sister. "He made his decision so that the rest of us would be safe."

"Two people will need to stay behind," Kera insisted. "I'm allowed to make that decision."

"Yeah, sure," Carrie replied casually. "You can make that decision, but you're going to have a tough time following through with it, considering I intend to handcuff you to me and drag you on that raft."

Kera eyed her sister and sneered with annoyance. Carrie would do it too. They heard a loud thud from the stairs. Kera and Carrie ran to the steps and found Danny lying on the floor at the bottom of the steps. His body was limp and motionless. The little tiger cub staggered across the floor, looking dazed.

"Danny!" Kera cried out and dropped to her knees alongside him.

Danny groaned lowly and barely moved. "I may need mouth-to-mouth," he said then opened his eyes halfway to look at her while managing a grin.

"Stop joking," Kera scolded and smacked his shoulder. "I'm not amused by your fake falls."

Danny groaned and rolled onto his back. When he removed his hand from his arm, she saw it was covered with blood. "Who was joking?"

Jerry ran from the lobby and nearly tripped over the tiger cub. "What happened?" he asked.

"Barbie stabbed me," Danny groaned and slowly sat up with Kera's assistance. "She's upstairs."

Jerry stared at Danny with a look of surprise and shook his head. "That's impossible," he announced sternly. "I was watching her on the security monitor from the back room. She went into the lounge five minutes ago."

"I'll have to disagree," Danny replied simply. "Or do you think I stabbed myself?"

Jerry removed his gun and ran up the stairs. Kera attended to Danny while Carrie returned his tiger cub to him.

Danny cuddled the cub close to his face. "Are you okay?" he asked then kissed the cub on the head.

"The wound doesn't look too deep," Kera announced as her adrenaline rushed. She then sprang to her feet. "I'll get the first aid kit from the kitchen."

Before Carrie could protest her sister going off on her own, Kera bolted down the hall.

§

Nick walked along the upstairs hallway and stopped to look at the open bedroom door by the stairs. The room appeared dark although someone was heard moving around. Nick removed his gun and approached the bedroom. A floorboard creaked beneath his feet. The bedroom door flung open from the inside. Nick aimed his gun into the doorway while Jerry stood just inside the bedroom with his gun pointed at Nick. Both men stared at each other then groaned and lowered their weapons.

"What the hell are you doing?" Nick demanded. "That's a good way to get shot."

"We have a small problem," Jerry said and replaced his gun to his shoulder holster.

"What sort of small problem?" Nick asked.

Jerry nodded toward the dark bedroom. He entered as Jerry turned on the light and stared at the bed where Bart lay dead. His shirt was soaked with blood from a brutal stabbing. They walked closer and studied the stab wounds in his chest. One of the daggers from the knife case lay on the floor, covered with blood. The tip of the knife was broken in the same fashion as the one used to kill Vicki. The low-quality replicas weren't made as strong as the originals.

"The blood's fresh," Nick muttered and touched Bart's body. "He's still warm. I would say he's been dead no longer than fifteen minutes."

"Danny claimed Barbie tried to kill him about ten minutes ago," Jerry announced. "He has a decent size cut on his arm. Kera and Carrie found him after he fell down the steps."

Nick glared at Jerry and raised his brow suspiciously. "Didn't he say he used to fake falls as part of his comedy act?"

"Yes, he did. He demonstrated a fake fall for us on the ship. It was rather convincing," Jerry replied then frowned before reporting the rest of the news. "I also saw Barbie enter the lounge on one of the security monitors. It would have been impossible for her to stab him while he was on the second floor when she was in the lounge on the first floor."

Nick frowned with disgust and shook his head. "It's possible his wound was self-inflicted to make Barbie look guilty. Go downstairs and watch Danny," he reluctantly announced. "I think we've caught our killer."

Jerry hurried from Bart's room, rounded the corner, and headed down the stairs. Once he reached the bottom, he turned the corner and entered the lobby where Danny now sat on a sofa while Carrie held pressure to his arm with a towel she found behind the front desk. She looked up when Jerry entered and immediately showed her concern.

"Where's Kera?" she practically demanded.

"I haven't seen her," Jerry replied. "I thought she was with you."

Carrie abruptly stood. "I need to find her."

Before Jerry could protest, Carrie ran from the lobby for the kitchen. She entered the kitchen without slowing and saw the first aid kit still on the island counter. Kera was nowhere to be found. She glanced around with a puzzled look then saw the partially open basement door. Had Kera gone into the basement? Why would she do that?

§

*C*arrie walked across the basement and entered the wine cellar. She noticed streaks in the dust along the edge of the rack, indicating someone had been through. Nearly everyone on the island had been in the basement since their arrival. Carrie realized she might have been the only exception. The streaks in the dust were thin enough to be from a woman's fingers. Perhaps they were from Cindy's tragic visit, but maybe they weren't. She searched the area more closely. Carrie approached the rack against the wall and saw a woman's watch around the neck of the only dust-free wine bottle. She grabbed the watch and stared at it with concern. It was Kera's watch! How did Kera's watch get on a wine bottle? A horrifying thought crossed her mind as her eyes widened. Kera put it there for someone to find! Carrie wasted little time popping the lever to open the secret passageway she'd heard so much about. She saw the infamous elevator and immediately took it down to the underground dock.

Once the elevator stopped, the door opened, and Carrie peeked out. She cautiously walked along the dock and paused by the crates near the boat. The boat seemed fairly quiet. Perhaps too quiet. Carrie removed the gun Nick had given her and silently approached the boat, keeping low to the plank as she boarded. She crept along the deck and paused just short of the steps leading down into the lower cabin. She didn't hear any sound coming from anywhere onboard. She slowly walked down the steps and cautiously entered the cabin. Carrie paused with surprise to see Kera tied to a chair and her mouth taped shut with duct tape. She ran to her sister, removed the duct tape from her mouth, and swiftly untied her wrists.

"We have to hurry," Kera gasped.

Carrie untied Kera's ankles and pulled her sister to her feet. She then saw the open, hidden compartment in the floor. As Kera turned toward the steps, she suddenly screamed, alerting Carrie. Carrie turned just in time to see Barbie grab Kera around the neck, using her as a shield while holding a gun to her head.

"Drop it," Barbie snarled, indicating the gun, "or your sister gets it."

Carrie reluctantly tossed her gun aside.

Barbie laughed while giving Carrie a snobby once over. "You're so predictable."

Kera clutched the arm around her neck, attempting to loosen Barbie's grip as panic seemed to sweep over her. Kera suddenly shifted her attention to Carrie, and her eyes turned almost emotionless. Carrie felt concern flooding her body, uncertain what was going through her sister's head. Kera stepped backward into Barbie, yanked on her arm while dropping herself to her knee, and flung her over her shoulder. Carrie gasped with surprise as Barbie crashed to the floor, her gun firing mid-flip.

Carrie was about to dive for the gun, but the bullet ricocheted off a steel sword that hung on the wall near her head. She screamed and ducked, placing her hands on her head. As Barbie reclaimed her gun while jumping to her feet, Carrie grabbed the decorative sword from the wall. Barbie aimed the gun at Kera and was about to squeeze the trigger when Carrie swung the sword for Barbie's back, hitting her with the dull blade. Barbie was thrown forward a step, although barely injured. Carrie was about to swing again when Barbie panicked and ran for the steps without firing the gun. The rich girl couldn't handle the slightest confrontation, leading Carrie to believe she couldn't have killed the others without help.

On deck, Karl had just boarded the yacht and saw Barbie running toward him. He didn't even have time to raise his gun as she plowed into him, catapulting him over the railing and into the water. Carrie ran up the steps from the living quarters of the yacht and looked over the rail. Karl surfaced and gasped for air. She then looked toward her left and saw Barbie running along the dock toward the exit. Carrie ran along the deck, leaped over the railing, and jumped onto the dock below. When she reached the sub-basement elevator, Barbie was already taking it up. Carrie pressed the button, but nothing happened. The elevator didn't return. Barbie must have jammed it somehow. Carrie turned and ran back to the yacht. Karl was already climbing the ladder onto the dock as Kera ran onto the yacht deck.

"She got away and trapped us down here," Carrie informed them.

"There's another way up," Karl announced while panting after his impromptu swim. "There's a staircase that leads to the basement and one to the library. She'll be long gone before we get up there." He shook water from his soaked body while attempting to catch his breath. "We found out why she and her partner were willing to kill anyone who got in their way," he told them then motioned for them to follow him.

They followed Karl along the dock to the crates near the elevator. He opened one of the crates and removed a bag of white powder. Although Carrie had only seen cocaine in the movies, she knew that's what it was.

"She and her partner have been removing the contents of the crates and stashing the drugs in a hidden compartment on the yacht," Karl informed her.

"I saw the open compartment," Carrie informed him.

"How did you discover this?" Kera asked.

"I stumbled upon it a not long ago while looking for the missing boat part," Karl replied then frowned, obviously disappointed with himself. "I was on my way upstairs to tell Nick when Barbie showed up and knocked me out." He shook his head. "For a petite girl, she came at me like a wild animal."

"That's the truth," Kera announced. "I ran into her in the kitchen as she was running down the back steps. I saw blood on her shirt and realized it was Danny's blood."

"We'd better warn the others," Carrie announced.

Chapter Twenty-four

Nick had Jerry gather everyone in the lounge after hearing the news about Barbie. Duke was the only one missing, having still not returned from his rafting mission. Jerry was assigned to watch the remaining people while Nick hunted Barbie. Kera nervously paced the lounge floor while Danny sat against the arm of the sofa and watched her. Kera spun on her heels and faced him.

"Someone should check on Duke," Kera said while rubbing her chilled shoulders. "What if something's happened to him?"

Danny stared at her and shifted positions. "Duke would be the last person something would happen to," he replied. "He's into martial arts; he has a gun and a wolf sidekick. Barbie would be crazy to go after him."

"She's worried about Duke and with good reason," Carrie remarked. "He's been gone several hours."

A faint scratching could be heard at the front door. It was followed by a loud bark. Jerry drew his gun, ran into the foyer, and approached the door. Carrie hurried after him. He pushed her to the side and flung open the door. Devlin stood on the porch, barked repeatedly, and ran to the porch steps. The wolf spun around before the steps and barked again.

Jerry stared at him then looked at Carrie. "Do you get the feeling he wants us to follow him?"

Kera appeared on the porch alongside Jerry. "Something's happened to Duke!" She ran off the porch before anyone could stop her.

Devlin ran through the woods with Kera following. Carrie groaned and ran after her sister.

"I suppose no one cares that this is my ass if Nick finds out!" Jerry called after her.

Carrie ignored Jerry and hurried into the woods after Kera. Once she neared the beach, Carrie removed her gun from the back of her pants and stopped just before the sand. She looked toward the water and saw Devlin jumping through the surf while tugging on the deflated, yellow raft. Kera ran into the water and looked for any sign of Duke. Carrie walked onto the beach and cautiously surveyed the entire area. She didn't see Duke either. Kera turned around and looked at Carrie with fear on her face. Devlin continued to bark without letting up. The wolf splashed in the waves, attempting to swim past the raft. Kera's head turned toward the boathouse, catching Carrie's attention as well. A fire could be seen burning just beyond the window.

Kera stared with horror. "Duke!"

"Kera, no!"

Carrie ran across the beach as Kera ran from the surf for the boathouse. Carrie tackled her sister to the sand just fifty feet from the building. There was a tremendous explosion, vibrating the entire beach. Both women pushed their faces into the sand and covered their heads. Wood and burning debris rained from the sky. Devlin yelped as a large wave carried him away from the dock. Carrie and Kera slowly lifted their heads and looked at what remained of the boathouse. Jerry skidded onto the beach and looked at the inferno then ran across the sand and slid to his knees alongside them. Both women slowly sat up.

"Are you all right?" Jerry asked while kneeling before them.

Carrie nodded. Kera stared at the blaze with a horrified look on her face while her sister clung to her.

"I'm sure he wasn't in there," Carrie whispered.

They moved to their feet and watched the fire swiftly burn out. Devlin swam back to shore and shook the water from his gray coat. Kera stared at the fire without a word while Devlin sat beside her and whimpered. Kera looked at Devlin then lowered herself and sadly hugged the wolf while holding back her tears. He licked her face then whimpered again.

*B*arbie hurried along the path in the woods and veered left, heading away from the hotel. She jogged along the less traveled path, paused within the clearing, and looked around while impatiently glancing at her expensive watch.

"Come on," she groaned. "Where are you?"

She again looked at her watch then heard a strange sound. She uncertainly turned and looked around the clearing. Barbie heard the strange sound again and took a few steps toward it. She peered into the snake pit then cringed while staring at the hundreds of snakes slithering over one another.

"Great," she muttered while making a face. "We could've just met in the lounge like normal people." She heard a twig snap and spun around then sighed with relief. "It's about time. Why did you want to meet here?" she practically demanded.

She barely saw the metal fire poker before it struck her temple. Barbie cried out with surprise and agony while clutching her bleeding head. The fire poker fell to the ground as gloved hands grabbed her arms and shoved her backward. Barbie cried out while fighting the hands on her arms. She was cast backward into the snake pit. Barbie screamed as she fell backward down the ten-foot drop, thankfully having a soft landing. She opened her eyes and looked around. Several snakes bit at her while hundreds slithered over her body as she was engulfed within the massive pool of reptiles. She attempted to scream, but her screams were quickly silenced as she disappeared beneath the mound of slithering creatures.

*C*arrie kept her arms securely around Kera while hurrying her along the path toward the hotel. Kera sobbed while clinging to her sister. Jerry led the way then suddenly stopped and looked into the woods. Carrie stopped with concern and looked in the direction he stared.

"What is it?" Carrie practically gasped.

"I thought I saw someone in the woods," Jerry replied while squinting. "I should check it out."

Devlin barked and ran in the direction of the snake pit. When Jerry removed his gun and veered left onto the small path, Carrie hesitated only a second before forcing Kera to follow him. She certainly wasn't going to wait in the middle of the woods for Jerry to return. There was no telling who was lurking around. They entered the clearing, looked around, and saw Devlin standing over the snake pit while barking into it.   Jerry uncertainly approached the pit alongside the wolf.

"Uh, not a good idea," Carrie informed him.   "That's the snake pit."

Jerry peered into the pit.   His expression dropped when he saw what had caught the wolf's attention.   "Ah, hell--"

"What?" Carrie gasped.

She released Kera and uncertainly approached him.   Carrie peered into the pit and saw Barbie's deathly pale face and the horrified expression frozen on it.   Her dead eyes were open and conveyed the agony of her last minutes.   Her face alone had nearly a dozen bite marks, but it was the cut on her temple that caught their attention.

"She didn't fall in by accident," he informed Carrie.

Carrie turned away while grimacing.   She then saw something glistening on the ground.   She moved closer to the object, lowered herself to the ground, and picked up Barbie's expensive gold watch. Jerry eyed the watch then met Carrie's gaze.

"I'm guessing that didn't just fall off on its own," Jerry muttered.   "She must've fought someone before they knocked her out and tossed her into the pit."

"For her sake, let's hope she was unconscious when she went in," Carrie muttered.

"What is it?" Kera cried out from several yards away.

Carrie and Jerry exchanged looks then hurried for Kera.   Carrie placed her arms around her sister and guided her in the direction of the hotel.

"It's nothing," Jerry told her.   "We should get back to the hotel."

When they reached the hotel, Karl and Danny were no longer in the lounge.   Jerry shook his head in disgust.   Kera collapsed on one of the lounge sofas and sobbed softly.   Devlin placed his nose on her lap and whimpered.   She sniffed and stroked his head.   Carrie sat beside Kera and placed an arm around her, holding her against her. Kera placed her head on Carrie's shoulder and again sobbed.   The three remained alone in the lounge for several hours without signs of the others.   It was already becoming dark outside.   Carrie still sat beside Kera, who had barely spoken since the explosion. She stared over top of Devlin's gray head and stroked his coat repeatedly. Thunder rumbled just outside the hotel. Devlin whimpered and leaned against Kera's leg.

"What's taking them so long?" Carrie asked. "Where's Nick? Shouldn't he have returned by now?"

Jerry tapped on the back wall of the lounge. Carrie finally stood and walked toward him.

"What are you doing?" she asked becoming irritated.

"I saw Barbie come in here right before Bart was killed, yet she wasn't here when Danny fell down the steps," Jerry insisted while studying the wall.

"That's because she was upstairs stabbing Danny," Carrie snapped.

Jerry glared at her. "He could be a killer."

"You don't appear convinced either," she remarked simply while folding her arms across her chest.

"No, actually, I'm not." He felt alongside the fireplace. A panel opened to reveal narrow stairs leading to the second floor. Jerry looked into the passageway.

"What's above the lounge?" Carrie asked.

Jerry looked back at her and frowned. "Bart's room."

Thunder cracked loudly causing the lights to flicker and then go out. Kera gasped with alarm. Devlin whimpered and sat on her feet.

"No one move," Jerry announced in a calm tone. "There should be candles around the room."

"There aren't," Carrie insisted. "Someone took them into the kitchen during the last power failure. I don't remember seeing any others."

"Then I need to go to the kitchen and get them," Jerry firmly insisted.

"We'll come with you," Kera said and sprang to her feet.

Carrie and Kera followed Jerry down the dark hall to the kitchen. Devlin remained by Kera's side as if glued to her leg. Carrie strained to see through the dark hall but couldn't see anything. The thunder continued to rumble as lightning flashed, occasionally lighting the rooms on either side of them. Carrie usually enjoyed thunderstorms but the continuous rumbling muffled sounds in the hotel. Devlin's whimpering filled any lull from the storm. The lightning flashed through the large library window. Carrie saw several shadows moving about in the split second of light. She grabbed Jerry's arm, alarming him.

"What's wrong?" Jerry asked.

"I thought I saw something move in the library," Carrie told him. "But I think it was just the lightning distorting shadows."

"We'll take a look on the way back just to be certain," he replied as they entered the kitchen. "I thought women were supposed to scream when they saw shadows and spiders."

"Show me a spider," Carrie remarked, "and you'll hear me scream."

Jerry laughed then fumbled around the counter, searching for a candle. Kera released Devlin's choker collar and helped locate the candles. Her hand hit the base of the candlestick. She lifted it and held it toward Jerry.

"I have it," she announced.

Jerry took it from her then appeared unusually silent. "Damn it. What did I do with those matches?"

Carrie could hear someone approaching from the basement. Devlin growled lowly, alarming them. "Someone's coming," she whispered.

"Relax," Jerry said. "I'll have the candles lit soon."

A step creaked near the basement door.

"Jerry," Kera whispered with fear.

"I got it," he said and lit a match.

Just as the candlewick burned, the basement door opened. Both Carrie and Kera screamed, Devlin barked, and Jerry raised his gun. Duke jumped backward into the door.

"Duke!" Kera cried out and ran to him

She threw her arms around his neck and hugged him. Duke's arms lightly circled her waist then immediately pulled her away from his wet body. Carrie saw the drained expression on his face. His wet clothes hung on him, his hair was mussed, and he had several scratches on his face.

"What happened?" Kera asked as she looked over him with concern.

"Someone fired shots at me from the boathouse," he remarked while groaning and wearily raked his fingers through his damp hair. "I fired back, but the raft was hit and ruptured. I was thrown into the water. I didn't want to take a chance leaving the water, so I swam for another part of the beach and found the tunnel into the underground dock."

"But the boathouse was on fire," Kera told him.

"It may have started from the shot I fired," Duke informed her then looked at Devlin. The wolf rubbed against his legs. "And you, you damned mutt, where were you when I needed you?"

Devlin whimpered softly.

"Don't yell at him," Kera scolded. "He feels bad enough."

Duke glared at Kera then groaned. "I need to change out of these wet clothes."

"I'll come with you," she insisted.

Carrie looked at Jerry and saw him prepare to object, lifting a finger. Carrie captured his hand, lowered it, and shook her head. He remained silent. Duke found another candle, took Kera's hand, and led her up the back staircase to the second floor. Devlin wagged his tail and followed.

"How do you know she can really trust him?" Jerry asked and raised his eyebrow.

Carrie had to smile when she saw a little of Nick in his expression. "How do I know I can trust you?"

Jerry shook his head. "I bet you're never at a loss with a wise remark."

"Damn right," Carrie replied then insecurely rubbed her arms. "Since it's just the two of us, I suggest we look for Nick."

"I'm supposed to protect you, not parade you about the hallway," Jerry insisted. "If something happens to you, Nick kills me. Does this mean anything at all to you?"

"No," she replied then tilted her head gently. "I'm worried about him, Jerry. He should have returned by now."

"It's a big hotel," Jerry reminded her. "If he doesn't find her, he'll find his way back."

"What if he's hurt?" Carrie asked demandingly. "What then?"

"Nick's been shot, stabbed, poisoned, and thrown from a speeding car," Jerry informed her. "He can handle himself."

Carrie placed her hands on her hips. "I'm going with or without you."

Jerry stared into her eyes then groaned. "Nick can have you. You're more than I can handle."

Carrie smiled lightly and followed him into the hall. The candle, with its flame casting dancing shadows on the walls, provided enough light to see several feet in all directions. They stopped outside the library and cautiously entered. Carrie looked at their shadows on the back wall. The movement was enough to startle her, which was probably what she saw earlier. She then noticed that the bookcase near the bay window was pulled partially away from the wall.

"Jerry," she said and pointed.

He looked where she indicated and walked toward the bookcase with her following. Jerry pulled it away from the wall and held the candle to the narrow passageway. Stone steps led down, possibly to the basement. He stared at the opening for a long moment then looked at Carrie.

"I suppose I should see where they go," he said then fidgeted slightly.

"You don't know what you'll find at the bottom," Carrie remarked with a concerned look.

Jerry looked around the library then found a candle on the desk and lit it for her. "I'm going to check this passageway," he said and handed her the candle. "Stay here until I get back, and whatever you do, don't close the entrance."

"I won't." She touched his arm and offered a tiny, sincere smile. "Be careful, Jerry."

He returned the smile. "I will."

She watched him walk down the steps knowing he was fearful of what might await him. She then looked around the library with a strange realization as horror suddenly crossed her face.

"Wait here?" she gasped. "Is he kidding?"

Chapter Twenty-five

Carrie nervously paced before the library window and listened to the thunder while the rain poured down, beating violently against the glass. Her thoughts strayed to Barbie sticking partway out of the pit filled with snakes. It frightened her to think anyone being capable of so viciously and violently taking another's life. She wondered how Barbie got involved in this entire affair. Was it her love of a man that provoked her? Or was she in it for the money? Barbie seemed like a woman who enjoyed the finer things in life. Danny came to mind more than once. The Parkers suspected he was the killer, but what did he have to offer Barbie? Was he secretly wealthy? Was he really a drug lord? It didn't fit together.

She thought about the murders and tried to put the pieces together. The jewelry Barbie wore suggested wealth. It was established from their first encounter that Barbie was a snob. Carrie removed Barbie's gold watch from her pocket. It was solid gold with a diamond accent at each hour. She couldn't even guess its value. Carrie wondered if it was a gift. It was her opinion that most women didn't buy such a watch for themselves. Did a lover buy it for her? Carrie turned it over, held it close to the light, and read the inscription on the back.

"To Barb, With Love, Kale." Carrie let the information sink in and then frowned. "So that's the connection," she announced. "Barbie was dating the lawyer or whoever was pretending to be the lawyer."

Even for an attorney, the watch seemed a tad expensive. She stuffed the watch back into her pocket. What about the lawyer? They assumed there hadn't been one since Chester wasn't really dead, but the watch inscription suggested otherwise. A thousand thoughts raced through her mind while she stood in darkness and silence waiting for Jerry. She approached the bookcase and held the candle up to read some of the titles. They were in alphabetical order, making it easier. Carrie removed a book on names and flipped through it. She found the name Kale and read the meaning. "Kale; Arabic for Karl." And there was the connection! Her eyes widened in horror as she tossed the book aside and hurried to the passageway.

"Jerry," she called into the darkness.

There was no response. Carrie heard a knock on the front door. Her heart pounded harshly as she spun on her heels. The thunder cracked loudly. She jumped causing the candle to fall from its base and extinguish when it hit the floor.

"Hello?" someone called from the foyer.

Carrie remained immobile a moment. Who was out there? She gathered her courage and felt the floor by her feet. She grabbed the candle and put it back on its base. Unfortunately, she didn't have any matches on her.

"Damn it," she whispered while trembling with fear.

"Anyone home?" the male voice called out.

Carrie cautiously felt her way around the edge of the library until she found the double doors to the hall. She stepped into the hall and flattened herself against the wall. Carrie nervously removed the small pistol from her pants and aimed it into the darkness. Lightning flashed. She saw a male outline in the open doorway as the rain poured beyond him. Carrie felt her entire body tremble. The man stepped into the foyer.

"Is someone there?" the man with a thick English accent asked.

"Who are you?" Carrie asked in a shaken voice.

"Drake Remington," he responded in a confident yet cautious tone. "I'm looking for a friend."

She slowly walked toward him as her heart pounded in her chest while she kept her back to the wall.

"Yes, we've met before," she said and flexed her hand around the gun handle.

"We have? What a relief," he announced cheerfully and chuckled in his throat. "For a moment, I thought you were pointing a gun at me."

"I am," she replied and stopped at the base of the staircase. She nervously looked up the stairs. There was nothing but vast darkness, hiding any immediate danger. She shifted her attention back to the man in the foyer.

"I see," he said simply. "Shall I assume you don't care for my novels?"

"How did you get here?" she asked the most important question at the moment.

"My yacht is anchored just offshore," he replied while attempting to sound calm. "What's happened?"

"Don't ask," she moaned and lowered her gun. "Do you have a match?"

"Yes," he replied and seemed hesitant. "Are you still pointing a gun at me?"

"No." She could see his outline, but apparently, he couldn't see hers. She thrust the candle into his hand. "We ran into some trouble when we arrived on the island."

He lit the candle and held it between them. Despite his soaked condition, Drake Remington was a handsome, distinguished man in his mid-thirties. He had neatly trimmed dark brown hair, high arched brows, thin lips, and a strong jawline. His clothing suggested great wealth. His suit was undoubtedly hand tailored, and his watch glistened with gold.

"What sort of trouble?" he asked.

"It's a long story, and I don't have the time," she replied. "It's important that you go back to your ship. We need to leave this island in a hurry. I'll get everyone together and meet you on the beach."

"Where's Danny?"

She stared into Drake's eyes with some concern. "He's around here somewhere. We were separated when the lights went out," she replied. "You have to trust me, Drake. It's very important we leave right away."

Drake brushed past her and approached the stairs. "Danny!" He hurried up the stairs. "Danny!"

Carrie ran after him. "Don't go after him," she called out. "It's too dangerous. Let him come to you!"

He continued up the stairs without acknowledging her.

"Drake?" came the familiar voice of Danny from the bottom of the steps.

Drake spun around on the stairs and hurried past Carrie, nearly knocking her down. She grabbed onto the railing to keep from falling. Drake reached the bottom of the steps and placed a hand on Danny's shoulder.

"Danny? Are you okay?" he asked with concern. "Why did you come here?"

"A little excitement," Danny remarked. "Damned if I didn't get it. You didn't let them drop you here, did you?"

"No, the yacht's just offshore," Drake replied almost as if knowing better. "What happened?"

Carrie hurried down the steps and paused just behind Drake.

"You won't believe what I've been through this week," Danny muttered.

"Uh, Danny," Carrie remarked with concern. "Don't you think we should get the others and make a hasty exit?"

"Carrie's right," he replied. "Rumor has it the island might blow sometime tomorrow." He thrust the tiger cub into Drake's arms. "Take my kitten back to the ship. Carrie and I will get the others and meet you there."

Drake nodded and set the lit candle on the hall table. "Is there anything I can do?"

"Yeah, hurry," Danny replied then looked at Carrie. "I think the others are in the underground dock."

Drake turned and hurried toward the foyer as the rain continued to pour down beyond the open doorway.

"Kera and Duke were upstairs," Carrie added.

"We should separate to cover more ground," Danny announced. "I'll take the basement. You find Kera and Duke."

Carrie nodded and ran for the stairs in the darkness. There was a loud crack of thunder, causing her to jump. It only took a second for her to realize it wasn't thunder. She looked over the banister and saw Danny clutch his shoulder as he fell against the opposite wall. Drake spun around as Danny slid to the floor. He dropped the cub and ran for Danny. Carrie fired blindly over the railing and into the dark hallway then ran down the steps to help Danny.

"Danny," Drake said and tapped his face. "Danny!"

Carrie kept her gun pointed into the darkness to cover them while Drake looked down the hall as well.

"What's happening?" Drake demanded to know.

"Get him to the ship," Carrie gasped nervously. "We'll be right behind you!"

Drake nodded and placed Danny's arm over his shoulder and practically carried him out on his hip. Danny groaned in agony. Carrie couldn't see anything, but she guessed she startled the shooter when she fired back. She could hear someone running upstairs, suspecting it was Duke and Kera. She cautiously walked down the hallway, keeping her back to the wall. Carrie didn't want to risk them coming downstairs just to be ambushed by Karl.

"Carrie," Kera called from somewhere upstairs.

"Down here," she called out softly.

The gun was snatched from her hand, alarming her. She spun to face Karl in the near darkness.

"I'm disappointed in you, Carrie," Karl snarled. "I didn't think you'd so readily give your position away."

She wanted to alert Kera and Duke, but she couldn't risk any sudden movements. She knew Karl wouldn't think twice about shooting her.

"I need a hostage," Karl said and pushed her down the hallway. "You weren't my first choice, but thanks to Duke, Kera wasn't accessible."

"Hostage?" she asked. "Hostage for what?"

"You're going to get me past those Parkers on my boat," Karl replied. "It's really nothing personal, Carrie. I actually like you. There's just too much at stake to allow personal feelings to get involved."

"If you like me so much, why'd you shoot me?" Carrie demanded to know.

He forced her into the library. "That wasn't me," he announced with disgust in his voice. "That was Barbie. She thought it would be so easy to kill Nick. I would never have condoned such a stupid act. Poor bitch is really better off dead. She was too dangerous to keep around."

"So you killed your own girlfriend, *Kale*?"

"You're smarter than I'd anticipated," Karl remarked. "She was messing around with Troy behind my back. She thought he could offer her something more. If you think I felt bad about killing her, you're sadly mistaken." He shoved her across the library. "We have a lot of work to do if we're going to leave before morning."

Karl forced her into the dark passageway beyond the bookcase. As he stepped into the opening, Carrie grabbed his wrist and kept the gun from her face while body slamming him into the wall. He was only momentarily dazed, but those few seconds were all she needed to close the passageway and wedge a candle beneath the opening. Karl threw his body against the passageway door, rattling the bookcase, but he was unable to open it. Another few shots would undoubtedly move the candle, but he didn't know that. She heard him running down the passageway steps. Carrie ran from the library, knowing it wouldn't take Karl long to reach the basement and work his way back up. She saw movement on the stairs and turned her head only a moment, witnessing Devlin running down the stairs to join her. While focusing her attention on the wolf, Carrie collided with someone in the dimly lit hallway and let out a startled scream.

She stared at Jerry through the dim light, barely taking time to catch her breath.

"It's Karl," she gasped warning him. "I trapped him in a secret passageway. He'll be coming through the basement doorway any minute."

"I'll take care of it," Jerry announced while clutching his gun. "Wait here and don't make a sound."

She watched Jerry run down the nearly dark hallway and only heard him cry out once while running into a hall table. Devlin took off after him, possibly viewing it as a game. As she waited for Jerry to return, she heard a crash coming from the lobby. Carrie grabbed the lit candle on the table and looked around. There was another crash. She carried the candle and approached the lobby archway. When she looked into the lobby, she saw the tiger cub tangled in a cord with a broken lamp on the floor nearby. Carrie groaned while approaching the cub, set her candle down on the floor, and untangled the tiger. She held the cub then retrieved her candle and hurried back to the foyer. She saw Duke and Kera enter the library by the light of a small flashlight.

"I heard something," Duke announced as they disappeared into the library. "Maybe from here."

Carrie was about to call out to them when she heard one of the steps creak and looked up the staircase where she saw Karl. The secret passageway must have offered access to the second floor as well as the basement. Carrie screamed and ran toward the library. The candle fell from her hand and extinguished upon hitting the floor. A gunshot echoed through the hall. Carrie threw her back into the wall just near the study door. Duke and Kera appeared from the library and practically ran into her against the wall.

"It's Karl," Carrie gasped. "He's on the stairs."

Footsteps echoed along the upstairs hallway. Carrie looked up to the ceiling as her heart pounded harshly. They remained completely silent. Was it Karl who ran along the second floor? What happened to Nick? There was a gunshot from upstairs, alarming all three. The lights came on at that moment. Karl stood only five feet from them, startling them. He aimed his gun at Duke and pulled the trigger. Kera screamed and leaped in front of him. Carrie cried out while dropping the cub as she witnessed Kera taking the bullet intended for Duke.

Kera was thrown into Carrie. She attempted to catch her falling sister, but she hit the floor, taking Carrie with her. Duke's gun fired simultaneously. Karl fell backward against the opposite wall as blood exploded from his shoulder, but he didn't go down. His gun fired again, striking Duke, and threw him against the wall near the fallen women. Carrie watched Duke hit the wall then fall to the floor not far from where she clung to Kera. The upstairs hall vibrated with thundering feet. Carrie could do little more than stare at Kera and Duke on the floor. Her heart pounded as she looked back at Karl and the gun now aimed at her.

"You don't know how lucky you are that I need you," Karl snarled. "Get up!" He looked at the stairs while listening to thundering feet and nervously waved his gun toward the library. "Downstairs--now!"

Carrie picked up the tiger cub and clung to it with fright. She backed up several steps as he approached. Karl continued to wave his gun nervously toward the library doorway and passed Duke where he lay motionless with his eyes closed. Carrie then saw Duke's hand grip his gun as his finger tightened on the trigger. She held her breath, uncertain what was about to play out.

"Move!" Karl cried with panic in his voice.

Carrie's eyes locked on Karl as her lips twisted in anger and her eyes narrowed. She suddenly threw the tiger cub at Karl. The cub flailed through the air and attached itself to Karl's face; it's sharp claws tearing into his flesh. Karl cried out and ripped the cub off his face, tossing it to the floor. Carrie threw herself against the wall as she heard someone run down the stairs. Karl spun toward the sound on the stairs and aimed his gun at Nick as he appeared over the railing. Jerry suddenly appeared in the first floor hallway with Devlin by his side.

As Karl's finger tightened on the trigger with Nick in his sights, Duke, Nick, and Jerry simultaneously fired several rounds into Karl. Karl jolted violently as bullets riddled his body before he fell against the wall. The firing ceased and, for a moment, there was silence. Karl's eyes were wide as he stared blankly at nothing before sinking to the hall floor. Duke dropped his gun while gasping to catch his breath as he clutched his bleeding shoulder. Carrie leaped to the floor to check on Duke and her sister. Kera was quick to sit up once the firing had ceased. It would seem Duke had told her to stay down and play dead.

"I'm okay," Kera gasped while Carrie studied her mild arm wound.

Nick sprang over the banister and ran to assist with the injured man and woman. Duke waved his hand while clutching his bleeding shoulder.

"I've had worse," Duke informed Nick with a hint of a humored smile.

The men exchanged strange grins and laughed, although Carrie didn't see anything funny.

"The first aid kit is in the lobby," Jerry announced and ran for the front desk.

"Danny's friend came back," Carrie informed them. "He's waiting for us at the dock."

Once Jerry applied a quick patch job to Kera and Duke's injuries, they helped them toward the foyer and out the front door into the pouring rain. Duke stopped at the base of the porch steps and looked back at the hotel.

"Devlin," Duke called.

Carrie looked toward the hotel. Devlin appeared on the porch with the tiger cub in his mouth, hanging by its scruff.

Carrie ran back to the porch and took the cub from Devlin. "Good boy," she said and patted him on the head.

Devlin barked and ran past her. Duke yelled something Carrie didn't hear. The wolf ran past Duke and down the muddy path. Carrie held the cub to her chest and joined Duke.

Chapter Twenty-six

Day nine. Just after sunrise, Drake's yacht was on course for Hawaii and away from Demon Island. Nick, Jerry, Carrie, Danny, and Kera stood on the deck taking their last look at the island now almost a distant memory. Duke walked toward them and gingerly placed his injured arm around Kera.

"So all this was over drugs?" Kera finally asked.

"Karl killed Vicki because she recognized Barbie," Duke replied. "And, yes, it's been established the motive was cocaine related, but what about Kristy and Cindy?"

"Wrong place at the wrong time. I can only speculate what transpired between Karl and Chester," Nick informed them. "It would seem they were in on the revenge scheme together, but Karl planned to double-cross Chester for the stolen shipment of cocaine."

"That's why Cindy died," Duke said. "She witnessed the murder, right?"

Nick nodded. "That seemed more than obvious by the blood on the downstairs elevator. She'd been in the underground dock when she was stabbed."

"But Karl couldn't have killed Kristy," Danny said. "He was back at the hotel before Jerry saw Kristy fall. I'd swear to it."

"That's where Barbie came in," Jerry said and shifted against the railing. "Kristy was trying to tell me something, and she did. She told me something about nails. Carrie told us Barbie had long fingernails when we arrived on the island, and she cut them short by the second day. She must have broken one when she pushed Kristy. It was possibly the last thing Kristy saw."

"But why was she killed?" Carrie asked.

Nick shrugged. "We may never know."

"I think I have a theory," Danny announced. "Kristy commented on someone leaving the hotel the first night. Karl and Barbie were both there when she mentioned it."

"Vicki's body was moved," Nick said simply. "They may have suspected she saw them from her bedroom window sneaking out in the middle of the night. They certainly couldn't be seen together."

"And Troy knew about Karl's plan?" Danny asked as he gingerly flexed his arm.

"No, I'm convinced Troy didn't know anything about Karl's motives," Nick said. "I don't think he even knew Karl was his uncle's lawyer. But Bart, on the other hand, discovered Karl's secret. Kera told us something Bart said to Karl in the billiard room."

Kera looked puzzled. "But that was nothing," she replied. "Bart was just being a jerk."

"Had I heard the statement sooner," Nick replied. "I may have come to a different conclusion. Bart was actually blackmailing Karl. He must have witnessed something and figured he'd make a little money on the side. We did find cocaine in Bart's room. If he suspected there were drugs involved, he may have wanted a cut."

"Bart wasn't exactly a saint to begin with," Danny retorted and eyed the others. "But I don't understand why Karl didn't just leave. He had the boat and his cocaine. Why stay?"

"First he needed to get Chester out of the way," Nick replied. "After that, there was always someone in the underground dock. He couldn't get to the boat or the crates. He couldn't move them without our knowledge. He removed a boat part right after killing Chester, so we couldn't leave if we managed to find the boat, but he never really counted on us finding it in the first place. A small mishap on Duke and Kera's behalf."

"And Carrie was shot because Karl wanted Nick out of the way," Danny announced while petting the tiger cub.

"Actually," Nick countered, "Karl confessed that it was Barbie's idea."

"I'm just glad we're away from that cursed island," Kera said with a groan.

Nick snickered and shook his head. "It wasn't the island's fault."

"Maybe not," Kera said abruptly and stared at Nick, "but I don't ever intend to return there."

Jerry leaned on the rail, shook his head, and stared at the distant island. "I'm with Kera. I hope, to God, I never see that place again."

There was a loud explosion that rocked the ocean beneath them. The island erupted into debris and dirt as rocks and boulders fell to the water not far from the ship despite their distance from the island. The underwater vibration caused the ship to rock and crash through large waves. A cloud of debris formed over the area Demon Island once occupied. Everyone except Nick dove to the deck.

Nick leaned casually over the railing and showed little reaction. "Crazy old man," he said and shook his head. "Six hours early."

Carrie slowly straightened and glared at him. He eyed her with a humored look, placed his arm around her, and pulled her against him.

Nick chuckled and grinned. "Farewell to Demon Island."

The End

Other books by Holly Copella!
Reviews left on Amazon are appreciated!

"The Battle for Andrea Maria"

A cruise ship attack turns six survivors into overnight celebrities after they take credit for the heroic act of a stowaway who died saving them.

The cruise is just what Jess needed--a bit of harmless fun far from her daily grind. But what begins as a relaxing vacation turns into a desperate fight for her life when terrorists take over the ship and start piling up bodies. Teaming up with a mysterious stowaway, Jess attempts to send out a distress call but knows they cannot wait for help to come. If she or the few remaining passengers have any hope for survival, Jess must act now. The papers dub it "The Battle for *Andrea Maria*," but to Jess it is the moment she fought side-by-side with her enigmatic Romeo, saving the ship--and losing him. She thinks the story ends there, but really, the nightmare is just beginning...

"Insanely Deadly"

When the dead return to life, it's up to an admiral's daughter and a mildly insane, former war hero to save their small town.

Jetta Cross, a Navy Admiral's daughter, is tasked with keeping her father's comrade, a former war hero turned town crazy, grounded in the real world. Capt. John Hunter is still fighting the war in his head, where imaginary dead people are part of his world. When a viral outbreak brings about a zombie uprising, Hunter is left to his own devices. He must resume his role as a one-man commando unit in order to destroy the ravenous undead. With Hunter still fighting his own inner demons as well as the undead, the townspeople fear their zombie neighbors may not be the only threat. Stranded at the island's luxurious resort with a handful of workers, Jetta is forced to live up to her father's reputation and take charge of the deteriorating situation at the hotel. She must wage her own war against the infected before the government declares her hometown a total loss.

"Deadly Institution"

A town recluse suspected of killing his wife teams up with a young woman in order to stop a killer.

After being accused of murdering his wife, Konrad Asher turns his back on the town that once adored him. Ten years later, he still holds his grudge and the title of the most feared man in town. With the reopening of the burned mental institution, where his wife had died, former employees are now murdered one-by-one, throwing suspicion back on Asher. A young local reporter, Jacey, is forced to reveal her long-time friendship with the infamous recluse in order to clear his name not only in the recent murders but to exonerate him in the death of his wife as well. Will Jacey's relationship with Asher invite the killer closer to her? Or is the killer already in her life?

"Screenplays: The Island Collection"
"Jungle Princess", "A.L.F. Resort", "Brighton Island"

Discover how romance and fun in the sun can be downright *chilling*!

"Jungle Princess" is a romantic/thriller that leaves a teenage girl stranded on an island with two male shipmates and a creature of "unknown" origin. She soon discovers the island is home to an abandoned prison with several prisoners roaming free. What really killed over one hundred prisoners? And is it still out there--?

"A.L.F. Resort" is a romantic/thriller set on an island resort with Artificial Life Forms as the main draw. At this resort, all your fantasies come true...until a malfunction removes safety inhibitors on the A.L.F.'s. Zombies, biker gangs, and mobsters run amuck, turning fantasies into nightmares. A young reporter gets more of a story than she anticipates, but will she survive long enough to write the story?

"Brighton Island" is a romantic/thriller set on a private island. When the owner's niece brings her psychic friend to the mansion, his presence awakens the spirits' tortured souls. As the psychic attempts to solve the old murders, the niece is confronted with the possibility that she's next to join the mansion ghosts. Stranded on the island with a crazed killer, her uncle wages his own war to save them. Will his "shock and awe" tactics actually save them or get them killed?

"Death Displacement"

A grief-stricken man travels back in time to seek revenge on the woman who murdered his girlfriend but inadvertently falls in love with her.

Kane is about to marry the woman he loves. His life is perfect. A few weeks before the wedding, a vindictive woman from his girlfriend's past mysteriously arrives and kills her. He learns of a traumatic accident that happened five years earlier, which triggers Riley's hatred for his girlfriend. Distraught over his girlfriend's death, Kane uses an antique time machine to travel into the past in order to find and destroy the woman responsible. When he runs into Riley's younger self, he realizes she's not the monster she later becomes, and he can't bring himself to destroy her. With a little help from his oddball friend from the past, they formulate a plan to prevent the accident that sends Riley down her destructive path. Kane's plan backfires when he falls for the younger Riley. His new tortured existence is further complicated when future Riley, his girlfriend's killer, shows up with her own devious agenda that doesn't include him. Will he be able to stop the time ripple, which ultimately ends with his girlfriend's death? Or will future Riley take him out of the timeline forever--

"Dead Village"

After strange happenings isolate a small resort town from the rest of the world, nearly one hundred residents seek refuge at the closed hotel. Only eight survive the night. And that's just the beginning...

One day after the entire population of Fox Ridge Village disappears, a car wreck forces several unsuspecting crash victims to seek help at the closed summer hotel. Within the hotel, they discover the grisly aftermath of a brutal slaughter. Crash victims Vander and Devon, a reluctant clairvoyant, team up to solve the riddle of the "haunted hotel" and the mass hysteria plaguing the remaining survivors. By the time they discover the hotel's secret, they're already drawn into the hysteria. As the body count continues to climb, it's a race to isolate the source and bring everyone back to reality before they kill one another. Will Devon be able to communicate with the traumatized spirits before their fate becomes her own?

"Misfits, Inc."

A seemingly ordinary, young woman meets four misfits who claim she has given them supernatural powers.

While on a business trip to a remote island paradise, a bored secretary, Hailey, has her world turned upside down when her path collides with a psychic freak, Skyler. He attempts to convince her that they had met in his dreams, and she had chosen him as one of her four mystic warriors. After Skyler foresees a woman's death, they discover an unidentified creature has killed one of the guests. They are joined by a lounge pianist and a rich playboy, who also claim they had met her in their dreams. If Skyler's prophecies are genuine, the evil entity controlling the ravenous creatures needs to destroy Hailey to ensure its survival. Reluctantly accepting her fate, Hailey has to locate the last and most powerful of her chosen warriors, The Guardian. Their fate is in doubt when The Guardian turns out to be a self-absorbed, former cat burglar with a bad attitude. Can Hailey turn her company of misfits into an elite team of mystic warriors? Or will The Guardian's secret agenda destroy them all?

"Basement Dwellers"

A viral outbreak at a hospital leaves a mortician, sheriff, and coroner fighting for their lives against a horde of undead and the CDC.

After a massive car wreck leaves several survivors in critical condition at the local hospital, a surgeon uses experimental drugs on his critical patients and accidentally causes a zombie outbreak. When local mortician, Lexx, receives an infected corpse as her client, she becomes stranded in the hospital basement during CDC quarantine along with the local sheriff and the coroner. The infamous surgeon struggles to find a cure for his infectious blunder by using the other survivors as test subjects. Meanwhile, Lexx and the sheriff attempt to locate his missing sister, who's stranded somewhere in the battle zone that once was the emergency room. It's a race against time and the ravenous undead. Can they survive the undead before CDC sanitizes the hospital of all infection?

"Witness Protection"
Also available in audiobook!

After witnessing an execution, a resourceful young woman attempts to disappear while being pursued by a hitman and a handsome federal agent.

A helicopter pilot, Jackie Remus, reluctantly agrees to go on a date with one of her clients, but her date is unexpectedly cut short when she witnesses a man being murdered. After narrowly escaping with her life, she is placed into protective custody. When the safe house is breached, Jackie makes a daring escape from both the hired killers and the handsome FBI agent, who wants to return her to protective custody. With a little help from her sly and crafty friend, Monroe, Jackie is convinced she can disappear until the trial. While on her journey to meet with her friend, she solicits help from a few shady but lovable characters along the way. Although she manages to stay one-step ahead of the hired killers, the federal agent remains in hot pursuit. Will Jackie reach Monroe before she's captured by the FBI and returned to protective custody? Or will the hired killers silence her first?

"Town Darling"

After surviving a brutal attack that claims the lives of those she loves, a young woman seeks revenge on a corrupt town.

Going back home is never easy, but for Casey, it means returning to her corrupt hometown where she barely survived a brutal attack. Accompanied by two family friends, she seeks justice for the night that destroyed her life. Her physical scars are nothing compared to her emotional ones, forcing the local sheriff to believe that the town darling is back for revenge. As the conspiracy for her revenge appears to be leading up to the coveted town fair, the sheriff is determined to stop her from fulfilling her vengeful scheme...but guilt over his role on that fateful night continues to haunt him. Will his desperate need for Casey's forgiveness be his undoing? Or will Casey's desire for revenge destroy them both?

"Unconditional"

A young woman puts her life on hold to care for an unstable, highly skilled combat soldier, who believes someone is trying to kill him.

A botched military coup leaves a team of elite fighters injured with one clinging to life in a coma. When Harlan wakes from his coma, he's left with no memory of his past life. His commander's daughter, Indy, takes it upon herself to care for the fallen war hero. She's challenged with more than just his physical care as she combats with not only his memory loss but also his newly found desire for her. His infatuation with her becomes the least of her worries when he sinks back into his role of a combat soldier. Believing his life is in danger, his fighting skills surface, turning him into an unpredictable and dangerous man. Will his memory return to him before Indy is forced to commit him? Or will he finally find his nemesis, "the coyote", and possibly claim the life of an innocent person?

"Witness Protection 2"
The Return of Whiskey Tango Foxtrot

Believing she holds the clue to millions in missing laundered money, a young woman is placed into the protective care of a former Navy SEAL team.

Feeling sorry for her recently separated co-worker, Leeann invites Wiley to join her and her friends on their night out. Little does she know that finding her co-worker murdered is just the beginning of her nightmare. Leeann unknowingly holds the key to fifty million dollars in potentially laundered mob money. With hired killers pursuing her, the FBI places her into a different kind of protective custody. Former Navy SEAL team Whiskey Tango Foxtrot reunites to keep Leeann alive at their secret hideaway. What should be an easy assignment takes an unscheduled turn when secrets, lies, and betrayal threaten to derail their mission. Is the team prepared for a war on their own doorstep? Will Leeann's misguided trust endanger the lives of those sent to protect her?

"Deadly Institution 2"

When blackmail turns into murder, a young woman finds herself caught in the killer's crosshairs.

The small town of Stony Ridge is no stranger to scandal and persecution of the innocent. When a brutal killing shakes the town's prestigious country club, Jacey McMurray seeks help from a self-proclaimed vigilante, Konrad Asher. As her professional and personal worlds collide, Jacey fears the stress of the country club killings have finally taken their toll on Asher. Can a stressed out vigilante stop the killer before he strikes again?

"Witness Protection 3"
Alpha Mike Foxtrot

A helicopter pilot risks her life to help a team of retired Navy SEALs rescue two girls from a killer.

When former Navy SEAL team Whiskey Tango Foxtrot asks for a simple favor, Jackie reluctantly offers her air-taxi services. What could go wrong? What begins as a search and rescue for two girls turns into a fight for survival against a heavily armed drug cartel. Wanted by the law with the cartel in hot pursuit and their home base breached, the team is forced to call in a favor from a questionable ally. Unfortunately, their new safe house isn't what it seems. Without knowing who the real enemy is, can Jackie and the team save their young witnesses from the hands of a killer?

"The Pen Pal"

In order to save her friend, she must enter the mind of a serial killer.

When her best friend is abducted, no one believes Jolynn saw it in a psychic vision. With nowhere to turn, Jolynn reluctantly joins Agent Harris Slade and his team on their hunt for a sadistic serial killer known only as "The Pen Pal". Finally confronted with the killer, Jolynn realizes she must enter the mind of the psychopath in order to stop the brutal killings. But when her vision reveals a particularly disturbing death, can Jolynn sacrifice her lover for her friend?

"Awaken the Dead"

A grieving innkeeper struggles to keep her haunted hotel out of foreclosure.

After losing her parents in a suspicious boating accident, Harley Brandon is determined to keep the family hotel out of foreclosure. Unfortunately, the hotel ghosts have other plans. Built with tainted money, the century old Horizon Hotel thrives on a tradition of murder, scandal, and suicide. As the paranormal activity increases to alarming levels, Harley discovers the truth about the hotel and its residents. Can Harley save her friends from the hotel's frightening hidden secrets?

"Already Dead"
Supernatural Collection

From the already dead to the undead. Three supernatural tales of "things that go bump in the night".

"Bloodletting" - A vampire themed resort allows guests to *participate* in their Bloodletting Ritual to celebrate the island's legendary vampires.

"Reaper of Souls" - A young woman must outwit an evil sorcerer in order to save her brother or become one of his minions forever.

"Already Dead" - When Flight 220 crashes, ten passengers make it to an isolated island, but only one man lives to tell the lie.

"Witness Protection 4"
O-Dark-Hundred

A simple assignment turns deadly when a retired Navy SEAL team uncovers a plot to kill a notorious mob boss.

When Whiskey Tango Foxtrot embarks on a simple stalking case, they're not prepared for a trip to a private island paradise owned by an infamous mobster. With one of their own suffering from traumatic head injuries, the team is left scrambling to decide what is real or imagined. The situation escalates even further when they uncover an assassination plot where everyone is a suspect. Now targets themselves, can the team survive their trip to paradise?

"Witness Protection 5"
Outside the Wire

After suffering several casualties on their last assignment, a retired Navy SEAL team discovers their misery is just beginning.

When Whiskey Tango Foxtrot returns home after suffering a devastating loss, they're hit with even more bad news regarding the rest of their team. Their grief is cut short when they discover their names are all on the same hit list. Hunted by relentless assassins, the scattered team must decide whether to remain safely hidden or find the man who put the price on their heads. Against the wishes of her teammates, Jackie strikes out on her own in order to save a friend who wants her dead. In a kill or be killed situation, will Jackie's emotions finally betray her?

Coming Soon!
"Jungle Princess"
Paranormal Collection

"Once Upon a Disaster"

A young homicide detective finds herself at the mercy of a hitman in the aftermath of an earthquake

While investigating the murder of a hitman, Detective Jade Wesson pursues a lead connecting the dead man to a break-in at a computer programming company. She's drawn into the world of nightclub owner and front man for the mob, Cody Riley. Her investigation keeps pointing to Cody's right-hand man and possible hitman, Vahn Lott. Despite her efforts to keep her investigation on track, Vahn has plans of his own for the attractive detective. When an unprecedented earthquake rocks their east coast town, Jade must put her life in Vahn's hands if she wants to survive. Can she trust a man who might be the killer she's hunting?

"The Murder of Emily Fisher"

After finding their favorite teacher murdered, the lives of two teenage girls are forever changed.

Everyone loved Emily Fisher. While walking home one afternoon, two teenage girls, Sidney and Trisha, stumble upon a gruesome murder scene. The brutal murder of Emily Fisher, a young, attractive schoolteacher, shocks the small town of **Marilina**. After graduation, Sidney moves far away from the memories of the small town while Trisha retreats deeper into denial. Eight years after the murder, Sidney receives a desperate call from her childhood friend, forcing her to return home. Trisha believes Emily's killer was falsely accused and she manages to turn the entire town against her while attempting to prove it. When Trisha receives a death threat, Sidney realizes there may be some credibility to her friend's wild accusations. Is Trisha's mental breakdown a result of childhood trauma? Or is the real killer actually attempting to silence her? In order to save her friend, Sidney must answer the eight-year-old question. Who murdered Emily Fisher?

ABOUT THE AUTHOR

Holly Copella has been writing since the age of twelve when her frustration at a book's poor plot drove her to author her own story. Over the last decade, she's written a number of screenplays, some of which she's now adapting into novels. Her fascination with zombies and other darker material lends an edge to her writing, which tends to lean toward horror. As a fan of Agatha Christie, she appreciates the craft of a good plot and the importance of creating significant characters.

Hailing from Pennsylvania, Copella lives in the Endless Mountains on a farm with her rescue horses and other animals. In addition to writing and reading fiction, she enjoys riding horses and traveling to Las Vegas and Disney World.

www.ingramcontent.com/pod-product-compliance
Lightning Source LLC
Chambersburg PA
CBHW060416260626
47161CB00011B/294